STAR WARS

THE LANDO CALRISSIAN ADVENTURES

LANDO CALRISSIAN
AND THE MINDHARP OF SHARU

LANDO CALRISSIAN
AND THE FLAMEWIND OF OSEON

LANDO CALRISSIAN
AND THE STARCAVE OF THONBOKA

L. NEIL SMITH

RANDOM HOUSE WORLDS
NEW YORK

T0053798

2024 Random House Worlds Trade Paperback Edition

Published in the United States by Random House Worlds,
an imprint of Random House, a division of
Penguin Random House LLC, New York.

RANDOM HOUSE is a registered trademark, and
RANDOM HOUSE WORLDS and colophon are trademarks of
Penguin Random House LLC.

This compilation originally published in mass market
paperback by Del Rey, an imprint of Random House, a division of
Penguin Random House LLC, in 1994.

ISBN 978-0-593-72609-9
Ebook ISBN 978-0-307-79549-6

Printed in the United States of America on acid-free paper

randomhousebooks.com

2 4 6 8 9 7 5 3 1

Book design by Edwin A. Vazquez

THE
LANDO CALRISSIAN
ADVENTURES

THE ESSENTIAL
LEGENDS COLLECTION

For more than forty years, novels set in a galaxy far, far away have enriched the *Star Wars* experience for fans seeking to continue the adventure beyond the screen. When he created *Star Wars*, George Lucas built a universe that sparked the imagination and inspired others to create. He opened up that universe to be a creative space for other people to tell their own tales. This became known as the Expanded Universe, or EU, of novels, comics, video games, and more.

To this day, the EU remains an inspiration for *Star Wars* creators and is published under the label Legends. Ideas, characters, story elements, and more from new *Star Wars* entertainment trace their origins back to material from the Expanded Universe. This Essential Legends Collection curates some of the most treasured stories from that expansive legacy.

CONTENTS

A long time ago in a galaxy far, far away. . . .

LANDO CALRISSIAN
AND THE MINDHARP OF SHARU

———

PROLOGUE

"*S*ABACC!"

It was unmercifully hot. Tossing his card-chips on the table, the young gambler halfheartedly collected what they'd earned him, an indifferent addition to his already indifferent profits for the evening. Something on the unspectacular order of five hundred credits.

Perhaps it was the heat. Or just his imagination.

This blasted asteroid, Oseon 2795, while closer to its sun than most, was as carefully life-supported and air-conditioned as any developed rock in the system. Still, one could almost *feel* the relentless solar flux hammering down upon its sere and withered surface, *feel* the radiation soaking through its iron-nickel substance, *feel* the unwanted energy reradiating from the walls in every room.

Especially this one.

Apparently the locals felt it, too. They'd stripped right down to shorts and shortsleeves after the second hand, two hours earlier, and looked fully as fatigued and grimy as the young gambler felt. He took a sip from his glass, the necessity for circumspection regarding what he drank blessedly absent for once. No nonsense here about comradely alcohol consumption. Most of them were having ice water and liking it.

Beads of moisture had condensed into a solid sheet on the container's outer surface and trickled down his wrist into his gold-braided uniform sleeve.

What a way to live! Oseon 2795 was a pocket of penury in a plutocrat's paradise. The drab mining asteroid, thrust cruelly near the furnace of furnaces, orbited through a system of plea-sure resorts and vacation homes for the galaxy's superwealthy, like an itinerant junkman.

The gambler was wishing at the moment that he'd never heard of the place. That's what came of taking advice from spaceport attendants. A trickle of moisture ran down his neck into the up-right collar of his semiformal uniform. Who *said* hard-rock min-ers were always rich?

He shuffled the oversized deck once, twice, three times, twice again in listless ritual succession, passed it briefly for a perfunc-tory cut to the perspiring player on his right, dealt the cards around, two to a customer, and waited impatiently for the ama-teurs to assess their hands. Real or imagined, the heat seemed to slow everybody's mental processes.

Initial bets were added to the ante in the middle of the table. It didn't amount to a great fortune by anybody's standards—except perhaps the poverty-cautious participants in the evening's exercise in the mathematics of probability. To them the gambler was a romantic figure, a professional out-system adventurer with his own private starship and a reputation for outrageous luck. The backroom microcredit plungers were trying desperately to impress him, he realized sadly, and they were succeeding: at the present rate, he'd have to drain the charge from his electric shaver into the ship's energy storage system, just to lift off the Core-forsaken planetoid.

Having your own starship was not so much a matter of being able to buy it in the first place (he'd won his in another *sabacc* game in the last system but one he'd visited) as being able to af-ford to operate it. So far, he'd lost money on the deal.

Looking down, he saw he'd dealt himself a minus nine: Bal-ance, plus the Two of Sabres. Not terribly promising, even at the best of times, but *sabacc* was a game of dramatic reversals, often at the turn of a single card-chip. Or even without turning it—he watched the deuce with a thrill that never staled as the face of the electronic pasteboard blurred and faded, refocused and solidified as the Seven of Staves.

That gave him a minus four: insignificant progress, but progress nevertheless. He saw the current bet, flipping a thirty-credit token into the pot, but declined to raise.

It also meant that the original Seven of Staves, in somebody's hand or in the undealt remainder of the deck, had been transformed into something altogether different. He watched the heat-flushed faces of the players, learning nothing. Each of the seventy-eight card-chips transformed itself at random intervals, unless it lay flat on its back within the shallow interference field of the gaming table. This made for a fast-paced, nerve-wracking game.

The young gambler found it relaxing. Ordinarily.

"I'll take a card, please, Captain Calrissian." Vett Fori, the player in patched and faded denyms on the gambler's left, was the chief supervisor of the asteroid mining operation, a tiny, tough-looking individual of indeterminate age, with a surprisingly gentle smile hidden among the worry lines. She'd been betting heavily—for that impecunious crowd, anyway—and losing steadily, all evening, as if preoccupied by more than the heat. An unlit cigar rested on the table edge beside her elbow.

"Please, call me Lando," the young gambler replied, dealing her a card-chip. "'Captain Calrissian' sounds like the one-eyed commander of a renegade Imperial dreadnought. My *Millennium Falcon*'s only a small converted freighter, and a rather elderly one at that, I'm afraid." He watched her for an indication of the card she'd taken. Nothing.

A nasal chuckle sounded from across the table. Arun Feb, the supervisor's assistant, took a card as well. There was a hole frayed in the paunch of his begrimed singlet, and dark stains under his arms. Like his superior, he was small in stature. All the miners seemed to run that way. Compactness was undoubtedly a virtue among them. He had a dark, thick, closely cropped beard and a shiny pink scalp. Drawing on a cigar of his own, he frowned as he added what he'd been dealt to the pair in his hand.

Suddenly: "Oh, for Edge's sake, I simply can't make up my mind! Can you come back to me, Captain Calrissian?"

Lando groaned inwardly. This was how the entire evening had gone so far: the speaker, *Ottdefa* Osuno Whett, for all his dithering, had been the consistent big winner, perhaps owing to his tactics of continuous annoyance of the others. Fully as much a stranger in the Oseon as the young starship captain, at the moment he was operating on considerably less goodwill.

"I'm sorry, *Ottdefa,* you know I can't. Will you have a card or not?"

Whett assumed an expression of conspicuous concentration that might have been a big success in his university classes. *Ottdefa* was a title, something academic or scientific, Lando gathered, conferred in the Lekua System. It was the equivalent of "Professor."

Its owner was a spindly wraith, ridiculously tall, gray-headed, with a high-pitched whiny voice and a chronically indecisive manner. It had taken him twenty minutes to order a drink at the beginning of the game—and even then he'd changed his order just as the drink arrived.

Lando didn't like him.

"Oh, very well. If you insist, I'll take a card."

"Fine." Lando dealt it. Either the academic had an excellent poker face, or he was too absentminded to notice whether the resulting hand was bad or good. Lando looked to his right. "Constable Phuna?"

The squat, curly-headed tough guy he addressed was T. Lund Phuna, local representative of law and order under the Administrator Senior of the Oseon. It was not, apparently, the happiest of assignments in the field. The uniform tunic hanging soddenly over the back of his chair looked nearly as worn as his companions' work clothes. He lit cigarette after cigarette with nervous, sweaty fingers, filling the cramped, already stifling room with more pollution. He wiped a perspiration-soaked tissue over his jowls.

"I'll stand. Nothing for me."

"Dealer takes a card."

It was the Idiot, worth zero. Given the circumstances, Lando felt it was altogether appropriate. If only he'd headed for the Dela System as he'd planned, instead of the Oseon. He'd seen richer pickings in refugee camps.

Bets were placed again. Vett Fori took another card, her fourth, as did her assistant, Arun Feb, asking for it around the stub of his cigar. *Ottdefa* Whett stood pat. A Master of Sabres brought the value of Lando's hand up to a positive ten, as a final round of wagering commenced.

Arun Feb and Vett Fori both folded with a nine and minus nine respectively. The cop Phuna hung grimly on, his broad features misted with sweat. Lando was about to resign himself, when Whett excitedly cried, *"Sabacc!"* slapping the Mistress of Staves, the Four of Flasks, and the Six of Coins down on the worn felt tabletop.

The *Ottdefa* raked in a meager pot: "Ah . . . not exactly the Imperial Crown jewels, nor even the fabulous Treasure of Rafa, but—"

"Treasure of Rafa?" echoed Vett Fori.

She might as well ask, thought Lando. She isn't doing herself any good playing cards.

"I've heard of the Rafa System," the mine supervisor continued. "Everybody has. It's the closest to our own. But I haven't heard of any treasure."

The academic cleared his throat. It was a silly, goose-honk noise. "The Treasure of Rafa—or of the Sharu, as we are now compelled to call it, not for the Rafa System, my dear, but for the ancient race who once flourished there and subsequently vanished without a trace—is a subject of some interest."

This had been delivered in Whett's best professional tones. Vett Fori's weathered face, impassive enough when it came to playing cards, plainly displayed annoyance at being patronized. She picked up her cigar, stuck it between her teeth, and glared across the table.

"Without a trace?" Arun Feb snorted with disbelief. "I've *been* there, friend, and those ruins of your—what'd you call 'em?—'Sharu,' are the biggest hunks of engineering in the known galaxy. What's more, they cover every body in the system bigger than my thumbnail. They—"

"Are not themselves the Sharu, my dear fellow, of whom no trace remains," Whett insisted, his tone divided between pedantry and insulted reaction. "I certainly ought to know, for, until recently, I was a research anthropologist for the new governor of the Rafa System."

"What's a bureaucrat want with a tame anthropologist?" Feb asked blandly. He blew a final smoke ring, mashed his cigar out on the edge of the vacuum tray, and took a long drink of water. It dribbled down his chin, soaking the collar of his soiled shirt.

"Why, I suppose," sniffed Whett, "to familiarize himself thoroughly with all aspects of his new responsibilities. As you are no doubt aware, there is a native humanoid race in the Rafa; all of their religious practices revolve about the ruins of their legends of the long-lost Sharu. The new governor is a most conscientious fellow, most conscientious indeed."

"Yes," Lando said finally, wondering if the anthropologist was ever going to deal the next hand, "but you were speaking of treasure?"

Whett blinked. "Why, yes, yes I was." A shrewd look came into the academic's eyes. "Have you an interest in treasure, Captain?"

More interest than I've got in this game, Lando thought. I wish I'd steered for the Dela System, no matter how much easier it is to land a spaceship on an asteroid than a full-scale planet. Soon as this farce is over, that's precisely what I'm going to do, win or lose, even if the astrogational calculations take me twenty years.

"Hasn't everybody?" Lando answered neutrally. He extracted a cigarillo from his uniform pocket and lit it. Treasure, eh? Maybe there was something to be learned here, after all.

"Not quite everybody. Speaking for myself," the scientist intoned, beginning at last to shuffle the thick seventy-eight-card deck, "my interest is purely scientific. What use have I for worldly wealth? One for you, one for you, one for you, one for you, and one for me. One for you, one for you, one for you . . ."

"Well, you surely came to the right place, then!" Vett Fori guffawed, picking up her cards. "No worldly wealth to get in your way at all! What *are* you doing here, anyway? We didn't hire any anthropologists."

Lighting another cigarette, Constable Phuna spoke bitterly. "Seeing how the other half lives, that's what! I saw his entry papers. He's studying life among the poor people of a rich system—on a fat Imperial grant, speaking of worldly wealth. We're *specimens*, and he—"

"Please, please, my dear fellow, do not be offended. I aspire only to increase our understanding of the universe. And who knows, perhaps what I learn here can make things better in the future, not just for you, but for others, as—"

Vett Fori, Arun Feb, and T. Lund Phuna spoke almost simultaneously: "Don't do us any favors!"

"Do *me* one," Lando suggested in the embarrassed silence that followed. "Tell me about this treasure business. And kindly deal me a card while you're about it, will you?"

Bets were placed again and additional cards dealt out. Lando, having actually lost interest in the increasingly slim pickings the game afforded, watched absently as the card-chips in his hand transmuted themselves from one suit and value to another. He paid a good deal more attention to what the anthropologist had to say.

"The Toka are primitive natives of the Rafa System. As Assistant Supervisor Feb has so cogently pointed out, they and the present colonial establishment co-exist among the ruins of the ancient Sharu, enormous buildings which very nearly occupy every square kilometer of the habitable planets. I'll see that, and raise a hundred credits."

Arun Feb shook his head, but tossed in a pair of fifty-credit tokens from a dwindling stake. Vett Fori folded, a look of disgust on her face. She placed her still unlighted cigar back on the table's edge.

Phuna raised another fifty. "Yeah, but the really important thing about the Rafa is the life-crystals they grow there." He fingered a tiny jewel suspended in its setting from a slim chain around his sweaty neck.

Whett nodded. "Important to you, perhaps, good Constable. It is true, the life-orchards and the crystals harvested there are the chief export product of the colony, but my interest—and what I was paid to be professionally interested *in*—were the Toka legends, especially those bearing upon the Mindharp."

Glancing at his cards, Lando saw he had a Mistress of Coins, a Three of Staves, and a Four of Sabres. He dropped the requisite number of tokens into the pot just as the Three turned into a Five of Flasks: twenty-three, but it didn't really matter; Fives were wild anyway.

"*Sabacc!*"

He gathered in the largest pot of the evening thus far. "Mindharp?" the gambler asked. "What in the name of the Core is that?"

Ottdefa Whett wrinkled his nose, passing the rest of the deck to Lando. "Oh, just a ridiculous native superstition. There is supposed to be a lost magical artifact designed to call the Sharu—with whom the Toka identify in some strange fashion—to call the Sharu back when the Toka need them. Silly, as the Toka could not possibly ever have been contemporary with a civilization millions of years in the past, any more than human beings and dinosaurs—"

"I've seen dinosaurs," Arun Feb interrupted. "On Trammis III." The gigantic reptiloids of Trammis III were famous the galaxy over, and a chuckle circulated around the table.

"I take it, however," Lando said as he shuffled and dealt the cards, then watched the bets pile up again, "that you have your own theories." Somehow the talk of treasure seemed to have loosened up the purse strings a bit, except perhaps for Vett Fori and her assistant. The gambler took a puff of his cigarillo. "Would you mind talking about them?"

The anthropologist looked as if he wouldn't mind at all, even if requested to discourse standing barefoot on a large cake of ice while his ample gray hair were set on fire.

"Well, sir, the ruins, for all that they are ubiquitous, are impenetrable, closed completely on all sides without a sign of entryway. I daresay that all the collected treasures of a million years of advanced alien culture await the first adventurer to gain admittance. I don't mind confessing to you all that I attempted it myself on several occasions. But the ruins are not only impenetrable, they are absolutely obdurate. No known tool or energy yields so much as a smudge upon their surfaces. I'll see that, and raise five hundred. Constable?"

Grudgingly, the policeman threw in five hundred credits' worth of tokens. Lando saw the bet with mild amazement and raised it a hundred credits himself.

"*Sabacc!*"

Hmmm. Things were looking up a little. He was now ahead two thousand credits. He dealt the cards a third time, wondering what prospects for a gambler might be met in the Rafa. The idea was tempting: only a handful of straight-line light-years to navigate across, and, if he recalled correctly, a major spaceport with good technical facilities—which to him meant landing assistance from Ground Control. The *Millennium Falcon* was completely new to him. He'd be playing cards in the Dela System this very moment if he weren't such an abysmally amateurish astrogator and ship-handler. He'd balked at the long, complicated voyage and reputedly tricky approach to a mountaintop landing field, despite well-founded rumors of rich pickings in an atmosphere friendly to his profession.

But the Rafa . . .

He won the third hand and a fourth; was now ahead some fifty-five hundred credits. The prospects of action seemed to be encouraging him, and he wasn't noticing the heat as much anymore.

"Oh, I say, Captain Calrissian . . ." It was Whett again. As the stakes mounted, the anthropologist seemed the only one whose interest in desultory conversation hadn't lagged.

"Yes?" Lando answered, shuffling and dealing the cards. "Well, sir, I . . . that is, I find myself somewhat embarrassed financially at this moment. You see, I have exceeded the amount of cash I allowed myself for the evening's entertainment, and I—"

Lando sat back disappointed, drew on his cigarillo. It was too much, he reflected, to have expected to get rich off this emaciated college professor. "I move around too much to extend credit, *Ottdefa*."

"I appreciate that fully, sir, and wish to . . . well, how much would you consider allowing on a Class Two multi-phasic robot, if one may ask?"

"One may indeed ask," the gambler replied evenly. "Thirty-seven microcredits and a used shuttle pass. I'm not in the hardware business, my dear *Ottdefa*." There was an idea, however: he could rent a pilot droid to get the ship from here to the Rafa— or wherever else he decided to go. He reconsidered. A Class Two was worth a good deal, perhaps half again the value of his spaceship. In these circumstances . . .

"All right, then, a kilocred—not a micro more. Take it or leave it."

The Professor looked displeased, opened his mouth to bargain Lando up, examined the determined expression on the gambler's face, and nodded. "A kilo, then. I haven't any use for the thing in any event. It was attempting to help me break into the Sharu ruins, and I—"

"Will you have a card, Supervisor Fori?" Lando interrupted.

"I'm out; this game's gotten too rich for me, and I'm on shift in fifteen minutes." Much the same was true for Arun Feb. They sat through the hand, enjoying watching somebody else lose for once.

Osuno Whett, however, bet heavily with his borrowed thousand, perhaps in an attempt to tap the gambler out. He was assisted in this by Constable Phuna. The money on the table grew and grew as Lando met their every raise, increasing the stakes himself. He wanted the game over with, one way or the other.

He'd dealt himself a Two of Sabres and a Four of Coins, taking an additional card after his two opponents had accepted them. Abruptly, the Four became a Three of Flasks, and his extra, which had been a Nine of Staves, transformed itself into the Idiot.

"*Sabacc!*" Lando cried in double triumph. To judge from the money on the table before him, and the lack of it in front of Whett and Phuna, that was the game. "Where can I pick up that droid, *Ottdefa*? I'm going to put it to work immediately as a naviga—"

"On Rafa IV, Captain. I left it in the custody of a storage-locker company, intending to sell it there or send for it—now, please don't get angry! I have here the title and an official tax assessment indicating its true value. You may take these with you, or use them to get a fair price for the robot here!"

Lando had risen, violence flitting briefly—very briefly—through his mind. That he had been gulled like any amateur was his first coherent thought. That he had a small but powerful pistol secreted beneath his decorative cummerbund was his second. That he could wind up dead, or in jail, on this sweltering fistful of slag was his third.

There wasn't time for a fourth.

"Hold on there, son!" the Constable said, seizing Lando's

arm. "No need for any uproar. We're all friends here." He pointed with his free hand to the papers Whett had proffered. "The *Ottdefa* here can post bond to you in the full amount of—say, what's *this*?"

Lando felt something small, round, and cool thrust up beneath his embroidered sleeve. He glanced down just as Phuna was pretending to remove it, and groaned. It was a flat, smooth-cornered disk a centimeter thick, perhaps four centimeters in diameter. He knew precisely what it was, although he'd never owned one in his life.

"A cheater!" the indignant Constable exclaimed. "He had a cheater all the time! He could change the faces of the cards to suit him any time he wanted! No wonder—"

With a feral snarl, Osuna Whett took advantage of the asteroid's minimal gravity, launching himself across the table at Lando. Just as his skinny frame was halfway to its target, a dirty denim jacket flopped over his head, followed by a knobbly set of knuckles belonging to Arun Feb's right hand. There was a dull thump of contact and a muffled squeak from the anthropologist.

"Get out of here, kid!" Feb shouted. "I saw Phuna plant the cheater on you!"

The lawman whirled on Feb, fist upraised. Apparently Vett Fori trusted her assistant's judgment—and knew how to maneuver in the absence of gravitic pull. She snatched up the nearest solid object—which happened to be the anthropologist's already battered head—and dashed it sideways against the startled cranium of the police officer. Eyes crossed, he collapsed, drifting slowly to the floor. Still holding Whett by the occipital region, Fori pried the wad of official-looking papers from the unconscious scientist's fingers.

"Take these and get your ship out of the Oseon, Lando. I'll talk sense with Phuna when he comes around. He's crooked, but he isn't crazy. Besides, in theory, he works for me."

It wasn't the first rapid exit Lando had made in his brief but eventful career. However, it was passing rare for those whose

money he had taken to assist him at it. With a pang of gratitude—
and the feeling he'd regret it later—he made to toss his winnings
back on the table beside the insensate *Ottdefa*.

"Don't you dare!" Vett Fori growled. "You want us to think
you didn't win it fair and square?" Behind her, Arun Feb tapped
Phuna on the pate again with a stainless steel water carafe, *thunk!*
He looked up from the pleasant occupation and nodded confirmation.

Lando grinned, waved a wordless farewell on his way out the
door. Twenty minutes later, he was aboard the *Millennium Falcon,* bolting down a very hastily rented pilot droid. Ten minutes
after that, he was above the plane of the ecliptic, blasting out of
the Oseon System and headed for the Rafa. It was the last place
Whett would look for him, he told himself.

GOLD-BRAIDED FLIGHT cap carefully adjusted to a rakish angle, a freshly suave and debonair Captain Lando Calrissian bounded down the boarding ramp of the ultralightspeed freighter *Millennium Falcon*—and cracked his forehead painfully on the hatch coaming.

"Ouch! By the Eternal!" Staggered, he glanced discreetly around, making sure no one had seen him, and sighed. Now what the deuce *was* it Ground Control had wanted him to look at?

They'd put it rather ungenteelly . . .

"What's that garbage on your thrust-intermix cowling, Em Falcon? *Over."*

Well, it *had* been something they could say without insulting references to the amateurish way he'd skidded, setting her down on the Teguta Lusat tarmac. Atmospheric entry hadn't been anything to brag about, either. Gambler he may have been, scoundrel perhaps, and what he *preferred* thinking of as "con *artiste.*"

But ship-handler he was definitely not.

He frowned, reminded of that rental pilot droid he'd wasted a substantial deposit on, back in the Oseon. Let 'em try to collect the rest of *that* bill!

Stepping—gingerly this time—around the hydraulic ramp lifter, he backed away from under the smallish cargo vessel (which invariably reminded him of a bloated horseshoe magnet), shading his eyes with one hand.

Intermix cowling . . . intermix cowling . . . now where in the name of Chaos would you find—

"Yeek!"

The noise had come from Lando, not the hideous leathery excrescence that had attached itself to his ship. It merely flapped and fluttered grotesquely, glaring down at him with malevolent yellow eyes as it scrabbled feebly at the hull, unaccustomed to the gravity of Rafa IV.

Two hideous leathery excrescences!

Four!

Lando pelted back up the ramp, slamming the Emergency Close lever and continuing to the cockpit. The right-hand seat was temporarily missing, in its place bolted the glittering and useless Class Five pilot droid, its monitor lights blinking idiotically.

"Good evening, ladies and gentlemen," the robot smirked, despite the daylight pouring through the vision screens from outside, "and welcome aboard the pleasure yacht *Arleen,* now in interstellar transit from Antipose IX to—"

The young gambler snarled with frustration, slapped the pilot's OFF switch, and threw himself into the left acceleration couch, just as one of the disgusting alien parasites began suckering its way across the windscreen, fang corrosives clouding the transparency.

"Ground Control? I say, Ground Control! What the devil *are* these things?" A long, empty pause. Then Lando remembered: "Oh, yes . . . *over!*"

"*They're* mynocks, *you simpering groundlubber! You're supposed to shake them off in orbit! Now you've violated planetary quarantine, and you'll have to take care of it yourself: nobody's gonna dirty his—*"

With a growl of his own, Lando punched the squelch button. If they weren't going to help him, he could do without their advice. Mynocks . . . ah, yes: tough, omnivorous creatures, capable of withstanding the rigors of hard vacuum and Absolute temperatures. They were the rats of space, attaching themselves to unwary ships, usually in some asteroid belt.

The Oseon System was nothing *but* asteroids!

Hitching a ride from sun to sun, planet to planet, mynocks typically—

Good grief! He jumped up, banging his head again, this time on the overhead throttle board—*stupid place to put it!*—and made quick, if clumsy progress aft to the engine area. He'd just remembered something else he'd read or heard about mynocks: subjected to planet-sized gravity, they collapsed, dying rapidly . . .

After reproducing.

In a locker, he found a vacuum-tight worksuit, also scrounged up a steamhose and couplings. Shucking into the greasy plastic outfit—a pang of regret: he was ruining his mauve velvoid semiformals!—he ratcheted the steamline to a reactor let-off, cranked open the topside airlock, and, trailing hose, clambered out onto the hull.

A mynock waited greedily for him, alerted by the unavoidable rumble of the hatch cover, its spore sacs shiny and distended. It was ugly, perhaps a meter across, winged like a bat, tailed (if that was the proper word for it) like a stingray, poison-toothed like a—

"Yeek!" The mynock, this time.

It floundered toward him, dragging itself along by a ventral sucker-disk. The only thing uglier than mynocks, Lando thought, were the larvae they spawned on planet surfaces. He leaped as it flicked a clawed wingtip at him, his awkwardness aboard ship bred more of unfamiliarity in a new environment than any native lack of agility. He twisted the hose nozzle, spraying the monster with superheated vapor from the *Falcon*'s thermal-exchange system.

It screamed and writhed, flesh melting away to expose the cartilage it used instead of bones. This, too, reduced quickly, washed down the curved surface of the ship, leaving nothing but gelatinous slime steaming on the spaceport asphalt.

A noise behind him.

Side vision impaired by the suit, Lando whirled just in time to ram the nozzle into a second mynock's gaping maw. It swelled and burst. Fastidiously, he played steam over himself to remove the dissolving organic detritus, then stalked grimly forward, finally destroying seven of the sickening things in all.

"*Good going, Ace!*" Teguta Lusat Ground Control sneered through his helmet receiver as he wiggled back through the upper airlock hatchway. "*Didn't you get an instruction booklet when you sent your box-tops in for that pile of junk you're flying? Over.*"

Pile of junk?

The only pile of junk in the neighborhood, thought Lando, sweating in his bulky armor as he cranked the hatch back down and stowed the steamlines, was that brainless rent-a-bot up forward. Hmmm. That gave him an idea.

"Hello, Ground Control," he warbled pleasantly from the cockpit only seconds after worming back out of the plastic vac-suit. "I'll have you know that this stout little vessel's often made the run to your overrated mudball in record-breaking time."

Once *upon* a time. At least that's what her former owner claimed, trying to bid up the battered freighter's pot value in a *sabacc* game he was losing badly. Lando's rented droid had failed miserably to coax anything near the advertised velocities out of the ship.

Probably some trick to it.

"By the way," Lando continued, "I seem to have the knack of handling this baby now. Would anyone care to purchase a practically new pilot droid? Over?"

"*We've heard that one before, Millennium Eff. That rental outfit in the Oseon may not maintain offices here, but they've got treaty rights. You'll have to send it back fast-freight. Expensive. Over and out.*"

IT WASN'T QUITE as bad as he'd expected.

Lando shipped the droid back slow-freight, balancing the extra rental time against the transportation costs. Evening had begun to fall before he'd taken care of that, *plus* all of the complicated official paperwork attendant upon grounding an interstellar spacecraft anywhere the word "civilized" is considered complimentary.

Tonight, he'd relax.

He needed it, after traveling with that confounded robot. Get a feel for the territory—by which he meant identifying potential marks, locating those social gatherings that others foolishly regarded as games of chance.

Tomorrow, he'd take care of business.

The Rafa System was famous for three things: its "life-crystals"; the peculiar orchards from which they were harvested; and what might have been called "ruins" if the colossal monuments left by the Sharu hadn't remained in such excellent repair.

The crystals were nothing special—as long as you regarded quadrupling human life expectancy "nothing special." Varying from pinhead to fist-sized, their mere presence near the body was said to enhance intelligence (or stave off senility) and to have some odd effect on dreaming.

They could be cultivated only on the eleven planets, assorted moons, and any other rocks that offered sufficient atmosphere and warmth, of the Rafa System.

The life-orchards themselves were nearly as famous—after the manner of guillotines, disintegration chambers, nerve racks, and electric chairs. It was not the sort of agriculture amenable to automation—the crystals were harvestable only under the most debilitating and menial of conditions. However, the operation was attractive financially because it came with its own built-in sources of cheap labor, two, to be exact: the subhuman natives of the Rafa, plus the criminal and political refuse of a million other systems.

The Rafa was, among its other distinctive features, a penal colony where a life sentence meant certain death.

That much was known by every schoolchild in civilized space—at least that minority with an unhealthily precocious bent for unwholesome trivia, Lando reflected as he secured the *Falcon* for the night. He strolled across the still-warm asphalt to the fence-field surrounding the spaceport, intending to catch public transport into Teguta Lusat, capital settlement of the system-wide colony.

An old, old man dressed only in what appeared to be a tattered loincloth, hunched over a push broom at the margin of the tarmac. He looked up dully for a moment as Lando strode by, then back at the ground, and resumed pushing dead leaves and bits of gravel around to no apparent purpose.

Slanting sunset caught odd angles of the multicolored alien architecture that constituted foreground, background, and horizon everywhere one cared to look on this planet. Pyramids, cubes, cylinders, spheres, ovoids, each surface was a different brilliant hue. The least of the monumental structures was vastly larger than the greatest built by living beings anywhere in the known galaxy. What passed for a town lay wedged uncomfortably into the narrow spaces between them.

Under a scattering of stars, Lando stepped lightly aboard the open-sided hoverbus, arrayed in his second-best blue satyn uniform trousers, bloused over bantha-hide knee boots. He wore a soft white broad-sleeved tunic, dark velvoid vest. Tucked into his stylish cummerbund was enough universal credit to get him into a semihealthy table game—and the tiny five-charge stingbeam that was all the weapon he ordinarily allowed himself. Those who carried bigger guns tended, in Lando's brief but highly observant experience, to think with *them* instead of their brains.

Alone aboard the transport, he leaned back on the outward-facing bench, unsure whether he enjoyed the unique scenery or not. Traffic was a modest trickle of wheels, hovercraft, repulsor-lifted speeders. Not a few pedestrians clumped along the quaint and phony boardwalks that fronted the human buildings, and among them Lando spotted many more like the old man at the port. Perhaps they were old prisoners who had served out their sentences. The bus wheezed into the center of Teguta Lusat. Lando paid the droid at the tiller, dismounted, and stretched his legs.

The colony was an anthill built on soil scrapings in the cracks between ancient, artificial mountains. Whatever effort had been invested decorating the place (and it didn't amount to much), it remained drab by comparison with the polychrome towers surrounding it. Streets were narrow, angling oddly. Human-scale homes, offices, and storefronts merely fringed the feet of titanic nonhuman walls.

Lando walked into the least scruffy-looking bar. The usual crowd was there.

"Looking for a cargo, Captain?"

The mechanical innkeeper of the Spaceman's Rest polished a glass. Bottles and other containers from a hundred cultures gleamed softly in the subdued lighting. A smattering of patrons— not very many: it was the dinner hour and Rafa IV was mostly a family planet—filled the unpretentious establishment with an equally subdued burble of unintelligibility.

Lando shook his head.

"Too bad, Captain. What else can I do for you?"

"Anything that burns," Lando said, childishly pleased to be recognizable as a spaceman. He was puzzled, however, over the robot's commercial pessimism. This was a healthy, thriving colony, with enormous and growing export statistics. "*Retsa*, if you've got it."

In one dark corner, what might have been the same underclothed old man leaned on the same old push broom.

"Coming up, Captain." Deft maneuvering with glassware followed.

Lando turned his back, put elbows on the bar, inquired over his shoulder: "Where could a fellow find some action around here?" He put it in a colonial accent—when in hick city, act hickier than the hicks. Civilized polish scares money away. "I just got in from the Oseon; my evening's free."

"How free?" The machine's optic regarded Lando appraisingly. "There's Rosie's Joint, down the street. Has a real nice revue. Just turn left at the big red neon—"

Lando shook his head. "Later, maybe. Perhaps a game—*sabacc*? Folks back home used to say I was pretty good."

Cynicism in its voice, if not upon its unyielding features, the automaton put on a show of thinking deeply. "Well, sir, I don't know . . ."

Lando offered twice the going price for *retsa*.

"I *might* know of a game—my memory stacks just aren't what they used to be, though, and . . ."

Lando placed another bill on the bar top. "Will this cover having them recharged?"

The bill seemed to evaporate.

"Don't go away, Captain. Make yourself comfortable. I'll be right back."

The 'tender vanished almost as impressively as had Lando's money.

THE FLEDGLING STARSHIP owner/operator had scarcely picked up his drink, selected a dark, heavy, quasi-wood table, and seated himself, carefully adjusting the creases in his trousers, when another figure appeared, a tall, cadaverous, nearly human individual wearing something loose, with polka dots.

They clashed badly with his mottled orange complexion.

"Allow me to introduce myself, sir: I am the proprietor of this establishment." The creature stroked its moustaches—two separate levels filling the inhumanly broad space between nose and upper lip—took a chair to the gambler's left, and lit a long green cigarette. The young gambler noticed with amusement that the fellow hadn't really introduced himself at all.

"I understand," said the alien, "that you have expressed an interest in the scientific theories regarding the phenomenon of probability."

Lando had wondered how the subject would be broached.

He settled back with a grin, assuming the facade, once again, of an overconfident colonial, put his feet up on the chair opposite, and winked knowingly.

"*Purely* scientific, friend. I'm a spacer by profession, an astrogator, so my interest's only natural. I'm especially intrigued by permutations and combinations of the number seventy-eight, taken two at a time. Fives are wild."

"Ah . . . *sabacc*." The owner took a long drag of orange smoke, exhaled softly. "I believe you could be inducted into the, er, research foundation practically instantaneously." He paused, as if embarrassed. "But first, Captain . . . well, a small formality: your ship name if you please, sir, strictly for identification purposes. There are certain regressive, antiscientific enemies of free inquiry—"

"Who carry badges and blasters?" He laughed. "*Millennium Falcon,* berth seventeen. I'm Calrissian, Lando Calrissian."

The proprietor consulted a datalink display on his oddly jointed wrist. "A pleasure, Captain Calrissian. And your credit, I observe, is more than sufficient to support this, er, research program of ours. If you will follow me."

IT'S THE SAME the galaxy over, Lando thought. A small back room, emerald-color dramskin tabletop, low-hanging lamp, smoke-filled atmosphere. In an honest game, there was a modest house percentage, and the cops were all paid off—that routine of the tavern owner's had merely been a chance to check Lando's credit rating. Only the particular mingling of smoke odors varied from system to system, and that not as much as might be expected. He might be out of his depth at the controls of a starship. For that matter, he didn't know very much about asteroid mining or needlepoint. But here—wherever "here" happened to be—he was at home.

He took his place at the table.

There were three other players, and a tiny handful of spectators currently more interested in their drinks and breathing down each other's necks than the game. He placed a few creds on the firm green surface. Card-chips were dealt around. He received the Ace of Sabres, the Four of Flasks, and Endurance—which counted as a minus eight.

That made eleven.

"One," said Lando neutrally. He drew a Seven of Staves, which promptly flickered and became the Commander of Coins.

Twenty-three.

"*Sabacc!* Dear me, beginner's luck?" He allowed excitement

to tinge his voice as he raked in the small pile of money, accepting the deck and dealing.

He carefully lost the next three hands.

It wasn't easy. He'd had to dump two perfect twenty-threes and might have drawn to a third if he hadn't stood pat with a fourteen-point hand, praying that the card-chips would keep the faces they'd begun with.

The local talent thought they had a live one.

In a manner of speaking, they were right—but not in any manner of speaking they'd find pleasant or profitable. It was one of those evenings when the young gambler felt *made* of luck, filled to the brim with spinning electrons and subnuclear fire. He ran the pot up gradually, so as not to frighten the others, conspicuously losing on the low bets, making steady, quiet gains.

Drinks flowed freely, compliments of the polka-dotted proprietor. This may have been a spaceman's bar, but at least two of the players were townies, likely splitting with the boss what they skinned from visiting sailors. The same glass of *retsa* Lando had begun with, diluted now with ice he kept having added, stood sweating on the plastic table-edging near his elbow.

"*Sabacc*," breathed Lando, flipping the trio of card-chips face upward. It was a classic: the Idiot's Array, lead-card worth the zero printed on it, plus a Two of Staves and a Three of Sabres— an automatic twenty-three.

"That cleans out my tubes," grunted the player opposite Lando, a dough-faced anonymous little entity with slightly purplish skin. Like the gambler, he wore the uniform of a starship officer. Despite the coolness of the evening, there was a fine sheen of perspiration across his forehead. "Unless I can interest you in a small cargo of life-crystals."

Lando shook his head, adjusted an embroidered cuff. First a beat-up freighter, then a robot he hadn't even had time to inspect, now a holdful of trouble with the local authorities.

"Sorry, old fellow, but it's cash on the tabletop or nothing. Business is business—and *sabacc* is *sabacc*."

Born of fatigue, this partial transformation from rough-edged (if preternaturally fortunate) amateur into no-nonsense professional startled at least one of Lando's opponents, a stalky, asymmetrical vegetable sentient from a system whose name the young gambler couldn't quite recall. It placed three broad leaflike hands on the table—Lando thought the contrasting shades of green looked perfectly terrible together—and garbled through an electronic synthesizer fastened to its knobbly stem.

"Awrr, Captainshipness, being a sports!" It turned a petal-fringed face toward the small technician. *"Negatordly give these person ill considerations. Cargo of value, inarguability."*

The third player, a hard-bitten bleached blonde with a thumb-sized oval life-crystal dangling from a chain around her wattled neck, hooted agreement.

"Sure, Phyll," Lando replied, ignoring the woman. "Is that how you obtained that marvelous translator you're wearing—in lieu of credits in a *sabacc* game?"

The plant-being shivered with surprise. *"How thou understanding these?"*

"With considerable difficulty."

He paused, thinking it over, however. To a gambler, particularly one who was both reasonably honest and consistently successful, good will represented an important stock in trade.

"Oh, very well, Chaos take me! But only this once, understood?"

The amorphous-featured fellow nodded enthusiastically; he lasted only two more hands. On his way out the door, he reached into a pocket of his coveralls, presented Lando with a bill of lading and a few associated documents.

"You'll find the shipment at the port. Thanks for the game. You're a real sport, Cap'n Calrissian, honest to Entropy, you are."

Lando, now some seventeen thousand credits ahead, and ready to bow out of the game as gracefully as he could—or as firmly as he must—scarcely heard the little nonentity. He had blessedly near the price of the *Millennium Falcon,* right there on the table before him. A *plague* on interstellar freight-hauling! Let somebody *else* worry over landing permits and cargo manifests. He was a *gambler*!

It sure beat scraping mynocks off a starship hull!

SHORTLY AFTER MIDNIGHT, strolling the few boardwalked blocks toward the modest luxury of Teguta Lusat's "finest hotel"—the droid bartender's recommendation—Lando kept one hand on the credits in his pocket, the other on his little gun. It didn't seem to be *that* kind of town, but still, there were *that* kind of people everywhere you went.

Beside him shambled the weirdest apparition of the mechanical subspecies he had ever seen—or even wanted to.

"Vuffi Raa, Master, Class Two Multiphasic Robot, at your service!"

The transport station with its dozens of storage lockers had been on Lando's way to the hotel. Desiring an early start on the morning's business, the gambler had thought it a good idea to pick up the droid he'd won immediately. Now he wasn't sure.

Some things are better faced in daylight.

It stood perhaps a meter tall, about level with Lando's hip pocket—hard to judge, as it could prop its five tentacles at various angles, achieving various heights. It was the shape of an attenuated starfish with sinuous manipulators—which served both as arms and legs—seamed to a dinner-plate-size pentagonal torso decorated with a single, softly glowing many-faceted deep red eye. The whole assemblage was done up in jointed, glittering, highly polished chromium.

Utterly tasteless, Lando thought.

"Most people," he had observed, watching the thing unfold itself from the rental locker, "have forgotten that 'droid' is short for 'android,' meaning *manlike*." It stretched its long, metallically striated limbs almost like a living being, and carefully examined the tips of its delicately tapered tentacles. "And what kind of name is that for a robot, anyway: 'Vuffi Raa'? Aren't you supposed to have a number?"

It regarded him obliquely as they squeezed past a geriatric janitor and left the terminal through automatic glass doors, headed up the boardwalk.

"It *is* a number, Master, in the system where I was manufactured—in the precise image of my creators.

"I wish I could recall exactly where that is: you see, I was prematurely activated in my shipping carton in a freight hold during a deep-space pirate attack. This seems to have had a bad effect on certain of my programmed memories."

Wonderful, thought Lando, keying open his hotel room. A ship he couldn't fly, and now a robot with amnesia. What had he done to deserve this kind of—never mind, he didn't want to know!

The Hotel Sharu wasn't much, but it was regarded locally as the best, and he had certain standards to uphold with what he thought of as his public. He mused: in this age of wide-ranging exploration, it was entirely possible for a commodity such as Vuffi Raa to change hands many times, be bought, sold, resold, won, or lost, winding up half a galaxy away in a culture totally unknown where the product had originated.

Or vice versa, as seemed to be the case here. He couldn't recall any sapient species shaped even remotely like Vuffi Raa. Somehow, he hoped he'd *never* run across them. In any event, he thought, that'll make *two* white elephants for sale in the morning.

He'd already come to a decision about the *Millennium Falcon*.

Table talk during the *sabacc* game had been understandably sparse, but one thing was obvious even before he'd accepted those crystals for cash. The life-orchards operated on a combination of unskilled labor supplied mostly by the near-mindless natives of the Rafa—he wondered if he'd see any of the creatures while he was there, but came to the same decision about that that he had concerning Vuffi Raa's manufacturers—and supervision by offworld prisoners. The whole enterprise was a monopoly of the colonial government.

As nearly as Lando could determine, consignments of life-crystals traveled only via the Brother-In-Law Shipping Company (whatever its local equivalent was actually called), and freelance haulers were simply out of luck. There would be no cargo for the dashing Captain Lando to *write* manifests on.

Well, that suited him. He'd trade off the cargo tomorrow.

Door-field humming securely, and the bed turning itself down with cybernetic hospitality, Lando undressed, carefully supervising the closet's handling of his clothing. Vuffi Raa offered its services as a valet, the appropriate skills being well within the capacities of its Class Two architecture, which supposedly approached human levels of intellectual and emotional response.

But Lando declined.

"I haven't had servants for a very, very long time indeed, my fine feathered droid, and I don't intend starting again with you. I'm afraid you're to change hands once more, first thing in the morning. Nothing personal, but get used to it."

The robot bobbed silent acknowledgment, found an unoccupied corner of the room, and lapsed into the semiactivation that in automata simulates sleep, its scarlet eye-glow growing fainter but not altogether dimming out.

Lando stretched on the bed, thoughts of ancient treasure dancing through his head. Of course, he considered, life-crystals weren't the only possible cargo he could take away from this place. The ancient ruins were supposedly impenetrable, but whatever race had built them, it hadn't stinted on strewing the system with more portable artifacts. Museums might be interested—and possibly in the crude statuettes and hand tools fashioned by the savage natives, as well. High technology past and primitive present: quite a fascinating contrast.

But the treasure . . .

Come to think of it, there were also a few colonial manufactured goods. But that meant he'd have to chase all over the Rafa just to line up a single decent holdful—with a messy, embarrassing, and possibly dangerous takeoff and landing at each stop along the way, he reminded himself.

Of course, there was always the treasure . . .

No. Better stick to the original plan: find a buyer for the *Falcon*. It had been fun for a short while, but he was no real space captain, and she was far too expensive to maintain as a private yacht, even if he'd wanted one. Find somebody to give him a fair price for Vuffi Raa, as well. Perhaps the same suck—*customer*. Then ship out, tens of thousands of credits richer, on the very next commercial starliner.

He whistled the lights out, then had an afterthought. "Vuffi Raa?"

The faintest whine of servos coming back to full power. "Yes, Master?" Its eye shone in the darkness like a giant cigarette coal.

"Don't call me master—gives me the creeps. Can you, by any chance, pilot a starship? Say, a small converted freighter?"

"Such as your *Millennium Falcon*?" A pause as the droid examined its programming. "Why, yes, er . . . how *should* I call you, sir?"

Lando turned over, the smug look on his face invisible in the darkened room. "Not too loudly, Vuffi Raa, and no later than nine hundred in the morning. Good night."

"Good night, Master."

CRAAASH!

The door-field overloaded, arced, and spat as the panel itself split and hinges groaned, separating from the frame.

Lando awoke with a start, one foot on the floor, one hand reaching for the stingbeam on the nightstand before he was consciously aware of it.

Four uniformed figures, their torsos covered with flexible back-and-breast armor, helmet visors stopped down to total anonymity, stomped over the smoking remains of the door as the room lights came up of their own accord. Their body armor failed to conceal the sigil of colonial peacekeepers. They carried ugly, oversized military blasters, unholstered and pointing directly at Lando's unprotected midsection.

He removed his hand from the night table, hastily, but without sudden, misinterpretable movement.

"Lando Calrissian?" one of the helmeted figures demanded.

He eyed the wreckage of the door.

"Wouldn't it be embarrassing if I weren—um, on second thought, let me revise that: yes, gentlebeings, I am Captain Lando Calrissian, in the flesh and hopeful of remaining that way. Always happy to cooperate, fully and cheerfully, with the authorities. What can I do for you fellows?"

The bulbous muzzle of its weapon unwavering, the imposing armored figure stepped closer to the bed, its companions immediately filling up the space behind it.

"Master of the freighter *Millennium Falcon,* berth seventeen, Teguta Lusat Interstellar—"

"The very same. I—"

"Shut up. You are under arrest."

"That's fine, officer. Just let me get my pants—or not, if it's inconvenient. I'll be happy to answer whatever questions His Honor may wish to ask. That's my policy: the truth, the whole truth, and nothing but the truth. Support your local—*umph!*"

The big cop hit Lando in the stomach with his blaster, followed it with the empty hand, balled into a mailed fist. A second figure went to work on the hapless gambler's legs. The other two swung crisply around the bed, started in on him from the other side.

"*Ow!* I said I'd go peaceably—*ghaa!* I—*unhh!* Vuffi Raa, *help me!*"

The robot cowered in its corner, manipulators trembling. Abruptly, it collapsed, curled up into a ball. Its light went out.

So did Lando's.

III

S QUAT.

Squat and ugly.

Squat and ugly and *powerful*—at least locally, Lando reminded himself with an inward groan as two of the helmeted officers dragged him into the presence of Duttes Mer, colonial governor of the Rafa.

Lando hadn't had time yet—nor the inclination—to inventory the indignities inflicted on him by the Colonial Constabulary. He seemed to be one solid, puffy bruise from neck to ankles. Avoid trouble with the cops in one system, get it in the next when you least expect it.

It hurt, rather a lot.

Yet nothing really serious had been done to him, he realized, nothing broken, nothing that would show if they ever gave him back his clothes. A thorough, workmanlike, professional beating, it had been, and, for all that it had seemed to go on and on forever, apparently a purely educational one, a few well-placed contusions meant to underline the fact that he was totally at their mercy.

He'd bloodied his own nose, stumbling against the jamb as they'd frog-marched him over the broken door of his hotel room. In hopes of not acquiring any further damage, he wished they'd put a plastic sheet under him now, to keep him from getting blood all over the governor's fancy imported carpet, the only extravagance apparent in an otherwise spare and utilitarian office.

There was a useful clue there, if only Lando's head would begin working well enough to ferret it out.

The governor blinked. "Lando Calrissian?"

At least everybody seemed to know his name. It was a startlingly high-pitched, feeble voice, considering the ponderous bulk it issued from—and perhaps a touch more nervous, Lando thought, than current circumstances seemed to warrant. Gamblers make much more careful studies of such nuances than psychologists. They have to.

Thickly muscled, improbably broad, resembling more than anything else a deeply weathered tree stump crowned in fine, almost feathery hair, the governor looked like the kind to play his cards close to the chest, never to take wild chances, to be a merciless, implacable player.

Turn the tables and he'd holler like a baby. Lando knew the type well.

In the present context, he felt the information wasn't terribly helpful. He glanced uncomfortably at the armored visor-wearers on either side of him, then back at the governor. It doesn't matter a whit if a bully's a coward at heart—as long as he has all the guns.

The governor blinked, lifted a blocky arm, repeating the salutation—or, more likely, the accusation: "Lando Calrissian?"

"Flatten the first A a bit," Lando answered, more bravely than he felt. "A little more accent on the second syllable of the last name. Keep trying, you'll get it right."

He ran a tongue across his lips, tasted blood. His head hurt. So did everything else. Egg-sized eyes under the silly head-thatching regarded him coldly from behind a small, uncluttered, impossibly delicate-looking desk of transparent plastic.

"Lando Calrissian, we have here a list of very serious charges against you that have been brought to our attention. Very serious charges indeed. What, if anything, have you to say for yourself?"

The governor blinked again as he finished, this time as if the very sight of Lando was painful to him. The young gambler bit back a second snappy reply. He wasn't aware of anything illegal he had done. Lately, anyway. He hadn't any qualms, particularly, about breaking the law: there were a lot of silly little planets with a lot of silly little laws. It was just that he'd rather—as an aesthetic point, mostly—be caught when he'd actually *done* something.

He decided, more or less experimentally, to add truth to the courteous obsequiousness that had failed with the cops. One never knew, the combination might work on this fat tub of—

"Sir—Your Excellency—I know nothing about any charges. To the best of my knowledge, I haven't done anything to be charged with."

He left it at that; a complaint would be carrying things too far.

The governor blinked.

Lando opened his mouth to speak. A loop of fabric from his tattered pajamas chose that moment to slip embarrassingly from his shoulder and swing. He sniffed, lifted it with whatever dignity the occasion afforded, attempted to smooth it back in place.

The governor blinked.

It was not a large room they were in. There was a wide door— but then, it was a wide governor—on either side of the desk. Like the door facing the desk, through which Lando had been escorted, both were framed in plain undecorative alumabronze, the spare motif echoed in wainscotting, baseboards, and a border around the high, somehow intimidating ceiling. The place was tinted a bilious yellow to match the governor's eyes. Instead of draperies, the windows displayed recorded scenes Lando recognized from other systems: greenish gravelly beaches, deep orange skies, scarlet vegetation. Entire *worlds* done up in bad taste.

The governor, apparently deciding Lando had been sufficiently intimidated by the longish silence, lifted a thick arm from his desk, regarded the troopers half holding the much-abused starship captain erect.

"You are advised," Duttes Mer squeaked menacingly, "to *improve* the best of your knowledge, then, young miscreant."

Miscreant? Lando thought. Did people really say *miscreant?*

The governor perused a printout laying on his desk, raising his downy eyebrows.

"Quite a record! Reckless landing procedures. Illegal importation of dangerous animals. Mynocks, Captain—really? Unauthorized berthing of an interstellar—"

"But, Governor!" Lando forgot himself momentarily, struggled free of the policeman on his left—then remembered where he was and clamped the astonished man's armored hand back around his elbow with a short-lived sheepish grin.

He'd realized, with a sudden, stifled gasp, that the transparent desk the governor occupied was composed entirely of gigantic, priceless life-crystals—enough to extend the life spans of hundreds of individuals. Power, then, was the key. It explained the barren office. Money and display wouldn't impress the malevolent lump of wasted hydrocarbons sitting before him; he would be motivated only by the prospect of controlling and disposing of the lives of others.

"Sir, I had all the clearances and permits. I—"

"Truly, Captain? Where? Produce them and the charges against you may be reduced some small but measurable fraction."

Lando looked down, seeing his own frame—the thought whisked by that this might be an unfortunate choice of words—draped in pocketless pajamas much the worse for their recent intimate acquaintance with Teguta Lusat law-enforcement procedures. He looked back up at the governor. "I don't suppose you'd let me go back to my hotel . . . no, I didn't think so. Well, better yet, check with the Port Authority. They should be able—"

"Captain," the governor sighed with affected weariness, "the Port Authority have no record whatever of any permits being granted to either a Lando Calrissian, or a . . ." He checked the list again. ". . . a *Millennium Falcon*. Of this I assure you, sir. In fact, you might say I ascertained the data in the matter *personally*."

"Oh," Lando answered in a small voice, beginning to understand the situation.

"There is also," the governor continued, satisfied now that he had a properly attentive audience, "conspiracy to evade regulations of trade. You see, we know of your attempts to obtain an unlicensed cargo. Carrying a concealed weapon—my, my, Captain, but you *are* a bad boy. Finally, assaulting a duly authorized police officer in an attempt to resist arrest."

The governor got a thoughtful look on his face, looked down at the list again, picked up a stylus and made a note. "*And* failure to settle your hotel bill as you departed those premises.

"*Now* what have you to say?" The governor blinked, licked fat lips in anticipation.

"I see," Lando said, barely concealing his glee. His spirits had begun to lift considerably in spite—or because—of the list of charges against him. The governor was someone he could deal with, after all.

Ante: "My gun was on the night table, it wasn't concealed. And if 'assault' consists of willfully striking a constable in the fist with my stomach, then I'd say you've got me, fair and square. Governor. Sir."

Raise: "Very well, Captain. Or ought I to make that '*Mister* Calrissian'—you will not likely be doing very much more captaining from now on. What have you to say to the probability of finishing your days doing stoop-labor in the life-orchards amidst other criminals, malcontents, and morons like yourself?"

Lando saw that and raised with a grin: "In all truth, sir, I wouldn't like that very much. I've heard that the life-orchards tend to take it out of you."

The governor nodded, not exactly an easy feat for someone without a discernible neck. "If you had it to begin with, Captain— if you had it to begin with."

Call: "I'd also say you're about to offer me some less-unpleasant alternative. That is, unless you make a custom of trumping up silly charges against every independent skipper who makes your port. And I guess I'd have heard about that long before I got here."

The governor resembled a frowning tree stump covered in feathers. "Don't anticipate me, Captain. It takes all the fun out of occasions such as this."

He blinked, then pressed a button on his desk.

LANDO REPLACED THE CUP on its saucer, leaned back in the large soft chair a servant had been ordered to bring him, and drew deeply on one of the governor's imported cigars. Yes, indeed, all of life was one big *sabacc* game, and he was coming out ahead, just as he had done the night before.

The servant—one of the Rafa System's "natives"—offered to pour more tea. *That* had come as a surprise (the native, not the tea). It stood there with a look of worshipful expectancy on its seamed, vacant, elderly gray-hued face. Lando shook his head. One more cup and they could *float* him out of there.

Another puff. "You were saying, my dear governor?"

"I was saying, my boy—by the way, are you finding that dressing gown adequate? Your baggage should be here from the hotel by now. But I'd rather we didn't interrupt ourselves at this point in the conversation. I was saying that, among the intelligent species of the galaxy, we humans are a most prolific, preternaturally protean people."

"And alliterative as all get-out, too, apparently." Lando flicked two centimeters of fine gray ash into the vacuum tray on the governor's desk.

Mer ignored the jibe, indicated the stooped and withered servant as it quietly shambled through the main office door behind Lando. "Consider, for example, the Toka—known locally as 'the Broken People.' Entirely devoid of intellect, passion, or will. Subhumanoid in intelligence. Every one of them bears what would be the signs of advanced age among our own kind—white hair, sallow, wrinkled faces, a bent, discouraged gait. Yet these are but superficialities of appearance—or are they?—they carry each of these dubious attributes from birth.

"Domestic animals, really, nothing more. Useful as household servants, they're too unintelligent to be anything but discreet. And in harvesting the life-orchards. But nothing else."

Lando stirred uncomfortably in his chair, adjusting the front of his borrowed bathrobe to conceal his discomfiture. The fabric was velvoid, a revolting shade of purple, sporting bright green-and-yellow trim. If everyone took to using the fabric—and with such egregious taste—he'd have to reassess his entire wardrobe. He wondered precisely what all the palaver was leading up to. He'd heard slavery justified a thousand different ways in a thousand different systems, yet it did seem to him that the Toka lacked some spark, some hint of the aggressive intelligence that made people *people*.

"You said 'for example': 'Consider, for example, the Toka'—don't you mean 'by contrast'?"

The governor signaled for yet another cup of tea. "Not at all, my dear boy, not at all. With offworld prisoners as overseers, a few droids for technical tasks, the Toka are content to eat food intended for animals, and will quite willingly work themselves to death if it's demanded of them."

Lando allowed himself a small, cynical snort. He'd heard that working in the orchards had some kind of *drainage* effect. Most human prisoners had purely supervisory positions, as the governor had suggested. Ditto for nonhuman sapients that had gotten themselves into trouble. Those unfortunate few "special" prisoners of both classifications, condemned to menial labor, wound up sub-idiots within a year or two. Apparently it didn't affect the Toka that way.

They were already sub-idiots.

"All that must be highly convenient," he said, "for the owners of the orchards."

Mer looked at Lando closely. "The government owns the orchards, my boy. I thought you understood that. The point is, the Toka are quite as human as ourselves."

Lando's jaw dropped. He scrutinized the servant as it poured the governor's tea, oblivious to the highly insulting things being said about it. How could this acquiescent, wizened, hunched, gray-faced nonentity, with its tattered homespun loincloth and thinning white hair, be human?

The governor blinked, managing to look smugly proprietary in spite of it. He opened his mouth to speak . . .

WHAAAM!

The air was split by an explosion that rocked the office. There was a blinding flash; a column of blue-black smoke boiled into existence, floor-to-ceiling, at the right of the governor's desk.

Oh, brother, Lando thought, what now?

IV

"ENOUGH OF THIS!" the blue-black smoke column shrieked, evaporating into tiny orange sparks that winked and disappeared.

A Sorcerer of Tund, Lando thought, groaning inwardly, how quaint. Members of an allegedly ancient and rather boringly mysterious order from the remote Tund System, they were *all* given to flashy entrances. The rest of the column condensed into a vaguely humanoid figure about Lando's height and general build. The old boy had probably tossed his flash-bomb into the office, then stepped through the door quite casually into the center of the smoke.

Nobody was quite sure what species the Tund wizards were, or even if they were all members of the same species. Swathed entirely in the deep gray of his order, the newcomer wore heavy robes that brushed the carpet, totally concealing the form beneath. A turban-like headdress ended in bands of opaque cloth across the face.

Only the eyes were visible. To his surprise, Lando found himself wishing fervently that they were not. Despite the absurdity of the sorcerer's melodramatic actions, the eyes told a different, more sobering story: twin whirling pools of—what? Insane hunger of some sort, the gambler decided with a shiver. Those ravenous depths regarded him for a moment as if he were an insect about to be crushed, then turned their malevolent power on the governor, Duttes Mer, who blinked and blinked, and blinked.

"You prolong these preliminaries unnecessarily!" a chilling voice hissed through the charcoal-colored wrappings. Lando couldn't quite determine whether it was a natural utterance or one produced by a vocal synthesizer. "Tell the creature what it needs to know in order to serve us, then dismiss it!"

The governor's composure disintegrated completely. He swiveled his enormous bulk in his chair, short stubby arms half lifted in unconscious and futile defense, his large yellow eyes rolling with abject terror. His walnut-shaded skin had paled to the color of maple. Even his feathery hair seemed to stir and writhe.

"B-But, Your Puisssance, I—"

"Tell the tale, you idiot," the sorcerer demanded, "and be done!"

Lando spat out a bit of ceiling plaster jolted loose by the intruder's showy appearance.

With a terrible effort, the frightened governor turned partially toward Lando, never quite daring to take his eyes altogether off the sorcerer.

"C-Captain Land-do Calrissian, p-permit me t-to introduce Rokur Gepta, my . . . my . . ."

"*Colleague,*" the sorcerer supplied with an impatient hiss that sent goose bumps up the starship captain's spine. It didn't seem to do the governor much good, either. He nodded vaguely, opened his mouth, then slumped in his chair, unable, apparently, to utter another word.

"I see," the sorcerer hissed, taking a step forward, "that *I* shall have to finish this."

Another step forward. Lando fought the urge to retreat through the back of his own chair. "Captain Calrissian, our friend the governor, in his slow, bumbling way, has informed you of the failings of the Toka. They are manifold, I shall warrant, and conspicuous. What this oaf has *not* seen fit to mention thus far—and the very heart and soul of the matter before us—is their most interesting and singularly redeeming feature.

"For you see, despite their humble estate, they observe and

practice an ancient system of beliefs which, if taken literally, not only explains the present unenviable condition of the Toka, but promises more for the properly prepared and sufficiently daring.

"Much, much more."

The inhuman voice died with a hiss, as if its owner expected some question or remark from the gambler seated before him. Instead, Lando simply looked at the odd figure, forcing himself, despite an inner cringing, to gaze calmly into the lunatic eyes of the sorcerer.

Meanwhile, the governor had managed to recover enough to press a button on his desk, order the Toka servant it summoned to obtain another chair for his "colleague." But the elderly creature could not be induced by kind words (of which the governor uttered but few) or threats (of which he had many in supply) to come near the threatening gray-swathed figure.

In the end, after an embarrassing impasse, Mer himself was forced to rise from his oversized office swiveler, bring the chair in from the next room, and place it for the robed magician. To Lando's amusement, the fat executive had nearly as much difficulty as the Toka forcing himself to come near Rokur Gepta.

Lando himself attempted to relax, settled back, and regarded his cigar, which had long since expired from inattention. Again, seemingly from nowhere, the Toka servant materialized to light it, then, still cowering under the baleful gaze of the sorcerer, vanished once again with a shuffle of bare feet on plush carpet.

"Promises precisely *what*?" Lando asked after a long time, somehow managing to sound casual. Half a hundred wild speculations formed in his mind as he said it, but he repressed them savagely, waiting Gepta out.

"Among other things," the sorcerer whispered, "the Ultimate Instrument of Music."

Great, thought Lando, his fantasies collapsing. It could have been diamonds, platinum, or flame gems; it could have been immortality or Absolute Power; it could have been a good five-microcredit cigar. The guy wants zithers and trombones.

———

"THE MINDHARP OF SHARU," Gepta explained as he seated himself, "has been an article of the simple faith among the Toka for centuries uncounted.

"As you are no doubt aware, the current human population of Rafa—not to mention numerous representatives of many other associated species—dates from the early days of the late, unlamented Republic. What is not generally appreciated by historians is that, in the chaotic, erratically recorded era preceding, a respectable amount of exploration and settlement was also carried out, albeit haphazardly. Thus, when Republican colonists arrived in the Rafa for the first time, they discovered it already occupied by human life.

"The Toka.

"I must explain that, for some decades, I have employed others—anthropologists, ethnologists, and the like, many of them incarcerees of the penal colony here and thus anxious to reduce the burden of their sentences—to observe, record, and analyze the ritual behavior of the Toka, believing that, in the long run, such an effort might produce some particle of interest or profit. I have made many such investments of time and wealth throughout civilized space.

"The Toka, savages that they be, have little or nothing in the way of social organization. Infrequently, however, and at unpredictable intervals, they gather together in small bands for the purpose of ritual chanting, to all appearances the passing-on of a purely verbal heritage.

"Their legends acknowledge that they came, originally, from elsewhere in the galaxy—would-be pioneers and explorers, employing a technology which they subsequently somehow discarded or lost. They, too, found the Rafa already occupied. Their tradition speaks of the Sharu, a superhumanoid race perhaps billions of years advanced in evolution, too terrible to look upon directly or contemplate at any length.

"The Sharu were, of course, responsible for the monumental construction which characterizes this system, a style of architecture betraying a bent of mind so alien that, for the most part, even the purpose of the structures cannot be guessed. It is unclear whether mere contact with the Sharu 'broke' the Broken People, or whether it was the Sharu's later hasty departure.

"For depart they did. Legends maintain that their flight was in the face of something even more terrible than they, something they feared greatly, although whether another species, some disease, or some unimaginable something else, we cannot so much as conjecture. They left their massive buildings, they left, apparently, the life-orchards whose original function is as obscure as everything else regarding the Sharu, and they left the Toka, crushed and enfeebled by some aspect of their experience with the Sharu."

LANDO REFLECTED ON Gepta's words while he let himself be offered another cigar.

It seemed to him that the question of what broke the Broken People was of considerably less pragmatic interest than whatever put such a scare into their superhuman masters. He hated to think of something like that still hanging around the galaxy. A starship captain's life (he knew better from vicarious experience than from any of his own) carried him through many a long, lonely parsec in the darkness. And many a ship has disappeared without so much as a trail of neutrinos to mark its passing.

The Toka servant, skirting Gepta, lit Lando's cigar.

The latter said, finally, "What's all this got to do with me?"

From within the voluminous folds of his ash-colored robes, Gepta extracted an object about the size of a human hand, constructed of some lightweight, bright untarnished golden metal.

It was Lando's turn to blink.

Viewed from one perspective, the device seemed to be a large three-tined fork—until the gambler looked again. Two tines or four? Or maybe three again? The thing just wouldn't settle down in his field of vision, giving him, instead, the beginnings of a headache when he stared at it too closely or for more than a few seconds.

Gepta placed the object carefully on Duttes Mer's crystalline desk, where it seemed to writhe and pulse without actually moving. The governor gazed down at it with an uninterpretable expression on his face—somewhere between dismay and greed.

"We have reason to believe," Rokur Gepta hissed, "that this object is a Key—perhaps it is a miniature of the Mindharp itself, although that is only surmise. It was . . . shall we say, *obtained* in an altogether different system, from a small, shabby museum. But it came originally from the Rafa System and is a Sharu artifact. Of that there is not the slightest doubt."

Somehow, without being told, Lando knew that there were volumes of adventure, betrayal, and deceit behind the sketchy explanation Gepta had just given. He had no doubt it was a story best left untold.

"A key," he repeated. "What the blazes does it unlock, if one may ask?"

"One may ask," the sorcerer replied in a threatening whisper, "but with a great deal more deference and respect in the future than is your customary practice!"

"A thousand pardons!" Lando tried to keep the sarcasm he felt out of his voice, with only partial success. "Pray what does it unlock, noble magician?"

Gepta paused as if trying to gauge Lando's sincerity, then shrugged it off as of no practical consequence. "There is evidence to indicate it provides access to the Mindharp of Sharu. The Mindharp is the focus of a thousand Toka rituals. The fools believe it produced music so sweetly compelling—isn't that just precious!—that it was capable of swaying the most unfeeling of hearts, even across vast distances of space."

The Rafa *was* a multiplanet system, but, given the millions of miles of hard vacuum between planets, Lando reserved judgment. He'd seen legends come to nothing before.

Gepta mentioned that some versions of the legends had the Mindharp as the principal means of communication between the mighty Sharu and their human "pets." What the Mindharp looked like and precisely where it might be found, these questions remained unanswered.

It was up to Lando to answer them.

Or else.

For his part, Lando wondered what the value of such an instrument might be to a system governor or a Sorcerer of Tund. And he wondered again about the terrible unnamed agency that had caused the presumably powerful Sharu to flee their home system like so many panicky mice.

"Okay," he answered finally, "what's in it for me if I find the Mindharp for you?"

The sorcerer turned slightly in his chair, gave Lando the full benefit of his terrifying gaze. "How about your continued liberty?"

For the first time since fetching the sorcerer a chair, Duttes Mer found the wherewithal to speak for himself. "There is also your ship to consider."

"And your life!" Gepta finished in a tone that made Lando's tailbone quiver uneasily.

He ignored it, pretending a nonchalance he didn't feel. "Well," he said, "two out of three isn't bad. I was planning to sell the ship. It's of no use to—"

"That you shall not do, foolish mortal!" Gepta seemed suddenly to swell in size and power. "This entire system is covered with Sharu ruins. We have no idea, as yet, in which of them the Mindharp lies awaiting us. You may very well need the vessel to—"

"Okay, okay. I get your point." Secretly, Lando congratulated himself on having been able to interrupt the sorcerer. He hated being intimidated by anyone and made a practice of *dis*intimidating himself as quickly as he could. "I get a ship I don't want, my life and liberty—which I already had before I stumbled into this rustic metropolis of yours. I don't want to appear unappreciative of your boundless generosity, my dear fellow-beings, but let's negotiate a bonus. A little something for the overhead?"

Mer leaned forward over his desk, not a particularly easy feat considering his treelike torso and the neck nature had seen fit not to endow him with. A threatening look darkened his face as he opened his mouth to speak, but he was stopped short by a hiss from Gepta.

"Incentives, my dear governor, incentives. Do not seal down the intakes of the droids who refine the fuel. We shall indeed offer our brave captain a little something as recompense. Captain Calrissian, would a full cargo of life-crystals from the orchards be acceptable?"

The sorcerer's tone implied it had damn well better be. Mer looked sharply at Gepta. He might be afraid of the gray-robed figure, but it was his bread and butter they were negotiating away. He opened his mouth again, saw that Gepta was serious, and closed it to stifle a groan.

Lando grinned. "I imagine that it will take rather a deal of fancy paperwork to cover up the shortage."

"Which is precisely, my dear Captain"—the sorcerer turned contemptuously toward Mer, and the governor shrank from his gaze—"what bureaucrats are for."

"Okay, Gepta, so far, so good. But what's to keep you two from seizing my ship and returning me to the tender mercies of the constabulary once I get the Mindharp for you? The most extravagant offer in the universe is a cheap price to pay if you don't intend—"

"Peace!" A long pause for consideration, then: "We shall deliver the cargo to your possession before you begin your search for the Mindharp—*silence, Governor*! However, we shall also have our menials at the port of Teguta Lusat render your *Millen-*

nium Falcon incapable of leaving the system—in case you decide to play us falsely yourself—while leaving it perfectly suitable for travel from planet to planet *within* the system. Once you have secured that which we all seek so ardently, your vessel will be repaired and you will be free to go. Is this agreeable?"

Lando thought. It still wasn't much of a guarantee. In fact, it was the same lousy deal as before, with his ship—or at least its ultralight capacities—as bait instead of the life-crystals. Still, it was all, he was sure, they were going to offer him.

It was a great deal more than he'd expected after Mer's thugs had worked him over.

"All right," he said through a weary sigh that was at least half genuine. "It beats sitting around in jail."

Or having one's mind sucked away by the life-orchards, he thought grimly to himself.

V

"I HAVEN'T THE FOGGIEST NOTION! Anyway, what possible business is it of yours?"

Lando stalked moodily along the narrow streetside toward a transit stop. His gaudy shipsuit had at least been restored to him, even his diminutive stingbeam. This last decorative touch, he reasoned bitterly, was yet another educational message from Rokur Gepta and Duttes Mer, underlining ironically what they imagined was his utter helplessness. Well, they'd learn better.

Trouble was, Lando couldn't think of how to accomplish that at the moment.

Vuffi Raa clattered beside him, carrying the rest of his luggage, which had been somewhat battered during the assault in the hotel room.

"But Master, I mean, Captain—"

"Call me Lando!"

"Er, Lando, how am I to help you if you won't tell me what's required of us? I know nothing about what's going on. I spent the entire night in the Confiscated Properties Room at Constabulary headquarters, sandwiched between bales of illicit smoking vegetables and wire baskets overflowing with vibroknives, murder hatchets, and the like."

At the thought, the little droid suffered an involuntary mechanical shudder, which originated at its torso seams and rippled along all five tentacles to their slim-fingered extremities.

Lando's bags bobbed up and down until the seizure passed.

"Did you know," the robot offered in a subdued, conciliatory voice, "that most of the spouse killings in this system are accomplished with cast-titanium skillets?"

Lando stopped suddenly, stared back at Vuffi Raa in anger. "With a sharp blow to the cranium, or simply bad cooking? Look, my mechanical albatross, there's nothing personal in this. It's simply that I haven't the faintest clue where or how to begin the idiot quest they've blackmailed me into, and I stand a far better chance if I *don't* have to spend my time stumbling over a useless—"

"Master, I do not wish to oppose your will in this matter. In fact, such would violate my most fundamental programming to the point of incapacitating me. However—"

"I don't give a damn *what* happens to your capacitors!"

"—however, before you sell me again, I am determined to prove to you that I am, indeed, far from useless. Perhaps even slightly indispensable."

Lando stopped again in the middle of the boardwalk, looking down with contempt at the little suitcase-laden automaton. He took a deep breath.

"*That,* my esteemed collection of clockwork cowardice, would be something to see. What precisely have you in mind?"

Vuffi Raa paused. A lengthy silence followed, and hovercars and repulsor vehicles were suddenly audible swishing by in the narrow, twisted avenue.

Without warning the droid suddenly spoke once more.

"So that is the difficulty; I believe I understand at last. The hotel room. The Constabulary. Your cries to me for help. Your preference, as I understand it, is that I should have been somewhat more, er . . . physically demonstrative. Even, perhaps, at the risk of worsening the charges against you?"

Lando turned on a booted heel, wordlessly resumed his march down the street. A bus went by, bearing half a dozen gawking tourists being lectured by the driver droid on what little was known of the Sharu.

"*Master!*" the droid cried behind him, scurrying to catch up.

"There was nothing I could do! I am specifically enjoined by my programming never to—"

"*Stow it!*" Lando snorted, taking some visceral satisfaction in the terse, blue-collar monosyllables. He'd kept his back to Vuffi Raa this time, hadn't even slackened his pace. The robot, with a sudden burst of speed made awkward by his master's bags, slipped around Lando and stopped, blocking the young gambler's further bad-tempered progress.

"Sir, I am not programmed for violence. I cannot harm a sentient being, organic or mechanical, any more than you could flap your arms and fly from this planet."

"Which only goes to show," Lando asserted, startled at the droid's sudden insistent solemnity, "that I was right in the first place." He stepped around the robot and started walking again. "You're useless."

"You are saying, then," the robot's voice inquired, very small, at the captain's rapidly receding back, "that violence is the only solution to this problem, the only capability that is useful or desirable to you in a friend or companion?"

Lando froze, one foot still in the air, stopped dead by the icy disgust he heard in Vuffi Raa's voice. He set the foot down, turned slowly to face the machine. Not only was he arguing with an artifact—he was losing!

Of course the little droid was right. Why else did he, Lando himself, insist on carrying nothing more than the minimal and minuscule weapon tucked away in his sash? Men of whatever species or construction acted with their minds, survived by their wits. Only a stupid brute would automatically limit himself to the resource of his fists or those of a friend.

That stopped Lando a second time: just exactly when had he begun to consider Vuffi Raa his friend?

"WELL, MASTER," Vuffi Raa mused, "as I understand the situation, you're to search for whatever lock the Key may fit. Yet you haven't any idea whether the lock—and it may be a more meta-phorical than material entity—is even on this planet. Correct?"

Lando nodded resignedly. He'd let three regular hoverbuses to the spaceport whistle past the stop while he carefully explained things to the droid.

"You've got it, exactly as I just told it to you. So far, old lube-guzzler, you've proved your usefulness as a suitcase caddy and an audio recorder. Any more talents you haven't revealed?"

He shifted on the transit-stop bench so that his back was to the little robot. He wasn't so much annoyed with Vuffi Raa for being useless, as for the fact that the automaton had forced him to confront some of his own failings.

"I beg your pardon, Master, all of my internally lubricated subassemblies are permanently sealed and require no further—"

Lando turned back suddenly. "All right, cut out that robotic literalness. You're a smarter machine than that, and we both know it. What I mean is, do *you* have any ideas? I'm fresh out, myself."

Something resembling a humorous twinkle lived in Vuffi Raa's single red optic for a fleeting moment. "Yes, Master, I have. If I had something ancient and historic, and valuable to look for, I know precisely where I'd look for information. I'd—"

Lando frowned, brightened, and leaped up off the bench. "By the Eternal, of course! Why didn't you say so before? Why didn't *I* think of it? It's certainly worth a try! You may have some use, after all." Lando paced hurriedly down the block just a few yards, turned in to the nearest bar, then poked his head back out through the swinging doors.

"Wait for me out here!" he shouted, pointing to a sign in the window of the drinking establishment:

NO SHOES, NO SHIRT, NO EXTEE HELMET FILTERS
NO SERVICE
NO DROIDS ALLOWED

"But Master," the little robot protested to the empty swinging doors, "I was referring to the public library!"

HAVING SHAKEN HIS unwelcomely helpful companion, Lando gratefully entered the cool quiet of the Poly Pyramid, one of Teguta Lusat's many inebriation emporia. There was nothing special about the place, appearancewise or otherwise; he'd merely availed himself of the first, nearest ethanol joint on the boardwalk.

He sat down at a table.

What he'd really needed all along, he'd known the minute he left the governor's office, was some kind of Toka gathering of the clans. Unfortunately, life rarely provides what one really needs. To judge from what Gepta had told him, the only people who truly knew what was what where the Sharu were concerned were much too primitive to *hold* conventions—or much of anything else. They had no villages, no tribes, not even any real nuclear families.

Every now and again, at unpredictable intervals, the Toka simply collected in small bunches to bay at the moon like wild canines. Rafa IV didn't *have* a moon, but, Lando thought, it was the principle that counted.

All right, the young gambler reasoned, one place he'd noticed the reliable presence of Toka—even before he'd known who and what they were—was in saloons, usually swamping the floors and polishing spittoons, the kind of occupation reserved in other systems for lower-classification droids. Here, the innkeepers could afford to entertain their prejudices and those of their clientele against the mechanical minority; Toka semislaves were handier and far cheaper.

Lando looked around. He'd selected a table in the approximate center of the room, halfway toward the back, and halfway between the bar that ran down the left side of the place, and the booth-lined wall opposite. Ordinarily, he'd prefer a position where he could see everything that went on and not have to turn his back to the door, perhaps something toward the rear.

Now the important thing was to *be* seen.

The Poly Pyramid was a working-being's establishment. On the walls, lurid paintings alternated with sporting scenes from a dozen systems. On a less cosmopolitan planet, racy shots of unclad females would predominate, but, in places where one being's nude was another's nightmare, sensuality had given way before such items as incompetently taxidermized galactic fauna, which were nailed to the walls or suspended on wires from the ceiling: fur-bearing trout from Paulking XIV, for example, and a jackelope from Douglas III.

As bars go, it was brightly lit and noisy, especially considering the small number of patrons so early in the afternoon. On both sides of the traditional louvered doors the inner, full-length doors were propped open with a pair of giant laser drillbits, souvenirs of the deep-bore mining of Rafa III, whose vacationing practitioners habituated the place.

In the back, the ubiquitous native was emptying ashtrays over a waste can.

The bartender, a scrawny specimen of indeterminate middle age, approached Lando, wringing his knobbly hands in a dark green apron. What little hair he still possessed was restricted to the back and sides of his otherwise highly reflective pate, and cut short. He had a nose friends might have called substantial, others spectacular. Tattooed permanently beneath it, a mild sneer, punctuated by a small mole on his chin.

"Spacers' bars're all downtown about three blocks, Mac," he said in a peculiar drawl. "This here's a hard-rock miners' joint."

Lando raised an eyebrow.

"Ain't sayin' y'can't drink here. Just likely y'won't want to— once the off-shift R and R crew starts t'fillin' the place up."

It seemed a long speech for the wiry little man. He stood there, balanced on the balls of his feet, relaxed but ready, looking down at Lando from under half-closed eyelids, a foul-smelling cigar butt dangling from his mouth. A large, dangerous-looking lumpiness was apparent beneath one side of his apron bib.

Lando nodded slightly. "Thanks for the advice; I'm meeting somebody here. Have you a pot of coffeine to hand?" Until he'd sat down, he'd almost forgotten the night's sleep he'd lost. Now it was catching up to him.

"Some of m'best friends drink it," the barkeep replied. "One mug comin' up."

He began to walk away, then paused and turned back to Lando. "Remember what I said, Mac. Splints an' bandages'll cost ya extra."

Lando nodded again, extracted one of the governor's cigars from a breast pocket, and settled back. Then, casually, he pulled the Key from an inside pocket. An optometrist's nightmare, it wouldn't hold still visually, even locked firmly in his hands. First it seemed to have three branches, then two, depending on your viewpoint. If you didn't shift the angle you were watching it from, it would oblige by shifting it for you. Lando averted his eyes.

He sat like that for forty-five minutes without any seeming reaction from anyone. Having long since finished his coffeine and tired of the cigar, at last he rose, left a small tip on the table, nodded amiably at the gnarled little bartender, and stepped outside on the boardwalk.

"Master?"

"Don't call me master! Let's find another bar."

VI

T HE NEXT PLACE sported a small bronze plaque beside the door
that stated: "FACILITIES ARE NOT PROVIDED FOR MECHANO-
SAPIENTS."

It meant "No droids allowed."

And it wasn't even true, not in its original rendering. Vuffi Raa
had a sort of waiting room to park himself in, nicely furnished,
quiet, with recharging receptacles. Only bigotry of the very nic-
est, highest-class sort was practiced there. Lando left the robot
with a couple others of its kind watching a domestic stereo serial.

Inside, three Toka swampers were distributing dirty water
evenly all over the floor. That they and their employers probably
thought they were washing only demonstrated that pretensions
and sanitation don't necessarily go together.

It was not quite dark, so the real drinking crowd hadn't arrived there yet, either. It didn't matter; Lando wasn't interested in
them.

Nearly an hour went by this time, Lando sipping a hot stimu-
lant and toying discreetly with the Key. The thing was as evasive
to the tactile senses as it was visually, he discovered, closing his
eyes and examining it by touch. "Perverse" might be a better
word, and even more nauseating, somehow. He opened his eyes
with something resembling relief.

On several occasions, he could have sworn that one or another of the natives was staring at him intently when he wasn't
looking in their direction.

Which was also precisely what he'd expected. He began to allow himself a feeble hope.

Another hour, and two more saloons, brought him back to the Spaceman's Rest, the first such establishment he'd visited in Teguta Lusat, the day before. It seemed like a thousand years ago. The double-moustached alien proprietor was nowhere to be seen so early in the evening, but the droid behind the bar seemed to have had his memory banks attended to. He recognized Lando with a cordial mechanical nod.

By then, the gambler was thoroughly coffeened out. He leaned against the bar, ordered a real drink, then took it back to a table and sat, unobtrusively displaying the weird, eye-straining Key as before, for everyone to see.

One thing *was* different about the place: its multispecies clientele and robot bartender encouraged Lando not to leave Vuffi Raa outside in the street. After all, the little fellow was an item of valuable property (to somebody, someday, Lando hoped), and probably wouldn't like being stolen, either.

That small mechanical worthy presently bellied—figuratively speaking—up to the bar, cutting up electronic touches while the 'tender polished glasses. Lando had always wondered what robots talked about among themselves, but never enough to eavesdrop.

Despite the tolerant atmosphere of the Spaceman's Rest, the usual Toka flunky was there, an elderly wretch distributing synthetic plastic sawdust on the floor from a bucket. Lando grew hopeful as the shavings around his table deepened to two or three times the thickness of those covering the rest of the barroom floor.

The Toka kept circling, reluctant yet fascinated, rather like an insect around a bright light. He stared at the Key, tossed a worried glance toward the bar, then turned back to the Key again, drawn irresistibly. If he was concerned about the bartender's reaction, he needn't have bothered; the droid didn't even seem to notice, wrapped up as he was in his work and in conversation

with Vuffi Raa. Maybe native productivity wasn't his department.

On an odd impulse to see what would happen, Lando tucked
the Key back into his pocket.

Abruptly, the Toka dropped his pail with a crash and bolted
out through the back of the room, leaving a fabric door-drape
swinging behind him and a few gaping mouths among the sparse
scattering of customers. Ordinarily nothing would induce the le-
thargic and prematurely senile natives to do *anything* in a hurry.

Lando held his breath: could his lucky break have come so
soon?

He signaled the 'tender for another drink. Vuffi Raa obliged
by bringing it over to the gambler.

"I still think we'd make better progress in the library, Master." He set the glass on the dark polished wood of the tabletop.
Lando was having a *talmog* that evening, one part spiced ethanol
to one part Lyme's rose juice, popular in a unique sunless, center-
less system many hundreds of light-years away. It burned. Lando
hated the things, which made them another drink he could nurse
and re-ice all night if he had to.

"Listen, little friend, let me do the detecting. For your information, I think I've got a bite already."

"A bite, Master?" The robot reached a free tentacle to the
floor, scooped up a pinch of sawdust, and held it closely to his
large red eye. "I would have thought the place to be cleaner kept
than that. Perhaps the Board of Sanitation—"

"Vuffi Raa, how would you like to be reprocessed into sardine
cans?"

For the second time that afternoon, there was mirth in the
robot's eye. "*Master—*"

"Don't call me—" Lando stopped. The sawdust-spreader who
had observed the gambler so closely was holding back the hanging for a veritable grandfather-of-grandfathers among the grand-
fatherly natives—a wizened, shriveled super-ancient nearly
doubled over with the burden of his long life.

The bartender had stopped his glass cleaning, stood silent as he watched the geriatric native hobble toward the gambler. The old man's straight white hair hung in matted tangles to his shoulders.

"Lord," the ancient Toka wheezed almost inaudibly, bowing until his forehead touched the tabletop. "It is as it was told. Thou art the Bearer and the Emissary. That which thou concealest is indeed the Fabled Key lost long ago."

The other Toka was suddenly nowhere to be seen. Somehow the spell was broken. The barkeep gave a metal-jointed shrug, resumed his work.

"I, er . . ."

Now that Lando had made his contact, he realized he didn't quite know what to do with it. The ancient glanced at Vuffi Raa. Lando gave the little droid a scowl, which failed to rid him of the machine at what could be a delicate point in the proceedings. Vuffi Raa remained standing by the table, all attention focused on the old Toka.

"Lord," the worthy repeated. "I am Mohs, High Singer of the Toka. Knowest thou what thou holdest on thy person?" The elderly character straightened—as much as he was ever going to again in this life—and Lando noticed a tattoo on his forehead, a crude line drawing of the Key itself.

"An unaccountably odd artifact," he answered, unconsciously patting the irregular lumpiness of it in his inside jacket pocket. "Some kind of three-dimensional practical joke. But, please—sit down. Would you like something to drink?"

The ancient glanced around, a furtive expression tucked deeply into the wrinkles in his face. The tattoo puckered on his forehead.

"Such is not permitted, Lord. I—"

"Master," the droid interrupted again.

"Shut up, Vuffi Raa! Well, old fellow," he said turning to Mohs, "wilt—*will* you at least tell me something more about the Key?" He took it out, held it in his hand.

Mohs had to wheeze a little while before he could get the words out. "Thou wishest to test thy servant, then? So mote it be, Lord. Thy wish is my command."

The Toka launched into a long, whining gargle in a language that was vaguely familiar to Lando. Perhaps it was an obscure dialect from some system he'd visited.

The effect on the dozen or so other patrons wasn't exactly salutory: they watched and listened, but Lando couldn't persuade himself to believe the expressions on their faces were friendly. He found himself wishing he'd sat a little nearer the door.

The Toka's monolog went on and on, one of Mohs' bony hands indicating the Key occasionally, the rest of the time his weathered face turned upward toward the ceiling. Finally, the chanting ceased.

"Have I recited rightly, Lord?"

Lando scratched his smoothly shaven chin. "Sure. Perfectly. And—just as another test, mind you—let's have an abbreviated version in the vernacular." He indicated the rest of the room. "Might win a few converts among the heathen. Think you're up to it?"

"Lord?"

The old man reached out shakily toward the Key, apparently thought better of it, withdrew the gnarled hand with obvious reluctance, then began. "This is the Key of the Overpeople, Lord Bearer, the Opener of Mysteries. It is the Illuminator of Darkness, the Shower of the Way. It is the Means to the End. It is—"

"Hold it, Mohs, just tell me what it does."

"Why, Lord, as thou knowest perfectly well . . ."

Mohs tapered off. Was that a hint of sudden skepticism in the ancient High Singer's eye? He began again, in a very slightly different tone of voice.

"It releaseth the Mindharp of the Sharu, which in turn—"

"Bull's Eye! Look, Mohs. As official Bearer of the Key, I have personally selected you to lead—in a purely ceremonial sense, of course—to lead a pilgrimage. We're going to use the Key. What do you think of that?"

The thought that everything was happening too easily began to seep into the back of Lando's mind, but he repressed it savagely. He was stuck with his task and welcomed any lead that would get it over with.

"Why, whatever else would we do, Lord? It must be as it has been told, else it would not have been told to begin with."

"I'm sure there's a hole in your logic somewhere, but I'm too tired right now to go poking for it. How soon can you start, then?"

The old man raised his snowy eyebrows, and the crude representation of the Key on his forehead squashed itself from top to bottom like an accordion.

"This very instant, Lord, if that be thy desire. Nothing supercedeth Their holy plan."

He cast a pious eye toward the ceiling fixtures again.

"Good," the gambler answered, once the native's gaze returned from its rafter rapture, "but I think we'll—"

"Master!" The little droid's tone was urgent.

"What is it, Vuffi Raa?"

"Master, I hear trouble coming!"

"Just what we needed." Lando groaned.

Suddenly, a man with a gun in his hand burst through the door.

"All right, spaceboy," he growled, pointing his massive weapon at the gambler, "get ready to die!"

VII

"M<small>R.</small> *J<small>ANDLER</small>!*" the barkeep shouted, a panicky harmonic apparent in its electronic voice, "I'm terribly sorry, sir, but my employer has permanently restricted you from entering this—"

"Shut up, machine! Now where in blazes was I? Oh, yeah—you there! Yeah, I'm talkin' to you! It's just like Bernie down to the Pyramid told me! And not only with a snivelin', job-stealin' droid at the table, but a dirty Toka, too! What are you, sailor, some kinda pervert?"

The few patrons in the establishment instantly cleared a broad aisle between Lando and the intruder.

"I don't know," Lando replied evenly. "It wasn't my turn to watch. Now just who in the galaxy are *you*?"

The man was good-sized, maybe eighty-five kilos, perhaps a shade under two meters tall. Over the powder-blue jumpsuit that draped his broad frame, he wore a dark blue tunic and neckcloth. He was neat, clean, shaved, and surprisingly sober for a thug, Lando thought. And with surprisingly good taste, as well.

The man walked closer; the muzzle of his pistol didn't waver.

The robot bartender hurried to Lando's table, placing himself between the two men. "He's the former owner of the Spaceman's Rest, Captain Calrissian, that was before I worked here. When the place changed hands, he tried to get a clause put in the agreement, never to allow—"

"What do you mean 'tried,' you miserable junk heap? A contract is a contract! People got a right to make any contract they want!"

Apparently undecided whether to shoot the young gambler or the bartender, Jandler was waving his gun around in a manner that tied knots in Lando's stomach. If it came to a choice, Lando hoped he'd choose the bartender as less messy—the bigot did seem to have some aesthetic sensitivities. The robot stood its ground.

"Not when there's a system-wide ordinance against discrimination, sir, and especially not when you lost the place in a table game to a being who doesn't believe in discrimination."

The man swiveled on the machine—Lando thought about jumping him just then, but it remained a thought—and brought the weapon down hard on its plexisteel dome-top with a sickening crunch!

"That for your ordinance," he hollered, "and *that—OUCH!*"

"You should never kick a droid, sir," Vuffi Raa advised sympathetically as the man hopped around on one foot, cursing. Somehow Jandler found the concentration to peer menacingly at the starfish-shaped robot.

"Quite right," Lando offered, diverting Jandler's attention even further. "He might have another droid. *Sic 'im, Vuffi Raa!*"

Jandler whirled on Vuffi Raa again. The five-tentacled 'bot stared at his master in bewilderment, but the distraction worked. The stranger took an ugly step toward Vuffi Raa, on his guard against the totally harmless little droid, and the bartender, despite its severely dented cranium, walloped the fellow on the back of the neck with a chair Lando toed over toward it.

Jandler went down like a sack of mynock guano.

A cheer rose from the dozen or so patrons in the room. They began gathering about Lando's table—somewhat unjustly ignoring the injured and heroic 'tender—lining up to shake the gambler's hand and pat him on the back.

"I'm gratified," Lando observed with a highly necessary shout—he hadn't so much as risen from his chair during the excitement and was taking a far worse beating now from his new admirers—"I'm gratified to see that not all robots are programmed categorically against violence." More specifically to the crowd he said, "Thanks, it was nothing, honestly, thank you very much."

"He's only programmed against *starting* it, sir," the bartender answered. "I'll just haul this fellow out in the street now, if you don't mind. By way of restitution for the disturbance, will you have a drink on the house?"

"I'd rather have it on the table in front of me. And bring one for my friend, here. Mohs?"

Lando jumped up. Mohs was gone.

So was the Key.

TURNING QUICKLY, Lando glimpsed the raveled tail of a gray-rag garment whisking through the door-drape at the back of the room. He was through the little crowd and across the room with a speed that startled even the robots.

He grabbed—

And received a collection of knobbly knuckles in the teeth!

Spitting blood, Lando seized the wrist attached to the knuckles, bit down hard in the meaty edge of the palm. Mohs let out a yelp and brained his erstwhile Lord left-handed with the Key. Releasing the old man's arm, a dazed, surprised, and angry Lando went for the throat with both hands, catching Mohs' knee, instead, right between the legs.

Lando groaned and sank down to his knees, fighting the urge to vomit.

This, however, put him in a position of advantage. As the elderly native—Lando couldn't make himself stop thinking of the savage in this manner—came in for another shot with the Sharu Key, Lando grabbed the nearest naked, dirty ankle that came to hand. Mohs went down on his back, with Lando on top, the old man biting and scratching.

By this time, Vuffi Raa had made it to his master's side, where he hopped up and down, shouting advice that Lando couldn't hear and probably wouldn't have followed. It was scarcely a fair fight. As much as he would have liked to, Lando couldn't punch the "helpless" old fellow into submission. He simply attempted to hold on and ride the furious storm to its conclusion.

They rolled across the storeroom, crashing into crates and cartons, and at one point fetching up against the lower extremities of the bartender, who had joined Vuffi Raa in supervising and kibitzing. For a brief crystalline moment, Lando looked up.

"You're being a lot of help," he said to the bartender.

The mixerbot remained motionless. "Beating up old men is a little out of my line, Captain. Besides, you look like you could use the practice."

Abruptly, Lando was sucked back into the fight. Mohs bashed him on the head again, but a bit more weakly. Lando grabbed the Key, then managed to lever himself into a sitting position astride the Toka Singer, grab a forelock of shaggy white mane, and bounce the elderly head once, gently but firmly, on the floor.

Mohs struggled for another moment, then relapsed into passivity.

"Naughty, naughty, Mohs," Lando said, gasping for breath as he looked down at the ancient. "No fair doing Holy Things without the duly constituted Key Bearer's help."

Mohs concealed his face in his long, emaciated hands. "Thou mayest kill me now, Lord. I have sinned greatly."

With considerable effort, Lando cranked himself back into a standing position, reached a hand down to the native, and helped him up.

"By the Emptiness, that's the first sign of spirit I've seen from any of you people."

He sat down, panting, on a stack of plastic cartons in the dingy rear hall. "But, from now on, just keep in mind who's the sacred emissary here, will you?" He held up the Key. "I'm in charge of this eyeball-bender for the duration. Keep that in mind, and we'll get along fine. Vuffi Raa?"

The robot trundled up beside him, his tentacles a tangle of nervous excitement. "Yes, Master? Sorry I couldn't help you back there, but—"

"I know, I know. In your estimation, how long will it take for Gepta's crew to sabotage the *Falcon* the way they said they were going to?"

The droid considered. "Not more than an hour, Master. It's merely a matter of unshipping the toroidal dis—"

"Spare me the technical details." Lando turned to the old man, who seemed to be recovering more quickly than he was. "Mohs, we're headed for the spaceport to begin our little excursion. Are you ready to come along and behave?"

The old man nodded humbly, bowing. "Yes, Lord, I am."

"Then let's get moving—and don't call me Lord."

Mohs stole a glance at Vuffi Raa, nodded again. "Yes, Master."

"Mohs"—Lando scrutinized the wrinkled figure carefully— "are you trying to be funny?"

"What is 'funny,' Lord?"

Lando sighed, beginning to be resigned to permanent exasperation. "Something about this whole confounded setup. Here I neatly avoid a messy conflict with that character out in the bar, and then you go and try to set yourself up in the Key Bearer business. And I don't see why Gepta and his pocket-piece governor need me to do their dirty work in the first place. They had the Key, why not just . . . Come on, Vuffi Raa, we're getting out of here. I need a chance to think. We'll doss down aboard the *Falcon* tonight and get a fresh start in the morning."

He paused, then added, "And I want you to help me rig up a few booby traps in case anybody else wants to try grabbing the Key."

"Master, I'm not sure my programming will allow that!"

The bartender stood, impassive, then turned and went back into the bar. "Good luck, sir. I think you're going to need it."

Keeping a suspicious eye glued to Mohs, Lando said to Vuffi Raa, "Very well, then, whether we can overcome your cybernetic scruples or not, we're *still* spending the night aboard the *Falcon*. Get out front and find us some transport—a bus, a vegetable gravlifter, anything." He shrugged uncomfortably, trying to unwind a painfully twisted muscle in his shoulder. "Do you think they might have any taxis on this misbegotten mudball?"

The robot knew a rhetorical question when he heard one.

Lando watched him go, rubbed at his bruised shoulder, stood up and stretched.

"Stay a moment, Lord." It was the old Toka. "It is not meet that thy servant mount the same conveyance as thyself."

Lando snorted. "What do you propose as an alternative?"

Mohs shook his snowy head. "Worry not, Lord, neither trouble thyself over the minor travails of thy servant, but go thou, instead, thine own way, even as thy servant shall go his."

"Catchily put. Does that mean you'll meet us at the spaceport?"

The old man looked puzzled. "Is that not what I just said?"

"Somewhere in there, I suppose; it got lost in the transubstantiation. Very well, old disciple, have it your own way." Blast, there was a snag in his tailored uniform trousers. They simply weren't intended for brawling. "We'll leave a light burning in the starboard viewport."

He left by the front door to join Vuffi Raa. Mohs presumably exited through the back. A hoverbus swooshed along almost immediately. Lando and the robot were whisked the ten kilometers to the landing field in as many minutes.

They were not unanticipated.

"What in the name of the Core is that?" Lando asked the equally astonished droid.

Outside the chain-link gate that filled a gap between the force field pole-pieces around the port, a considerable and highly unusual crowd had gathered. Absently, Lando paid the driver droid, turned to stare at the hundreds of stooped gray figures standing in their loincloths in the moonless dark, chanting to the cold unanswering stars.

As the gambler and his companion approached them, the primitives stepped back en masse, forming a broad, open corridor. To one side, a spaceport security officer was visible through the transparency of his guard booth, gesticulating at the visicom.

Lando and Vuffi Raa, the former growing more reluctant by the minute to surround himself in an unpredictable mob—especially after his recent wrestling match with one of the natives—made slow, involuntarily stately progress as the crowd folded itself back before them, the rhythmic chanting never missing a beat.

At the end of the living aisle, they encountered Mohs.

VIII

I T HAD BEEN a couple of very long sleepless days. Lando didn't even want to think about how an ancient savage on foot had beaten a fusion-powered hovercraft across ten kilometers of twisted, ruin-strewn thoroughfare to the spaceport.

Let the robot figure it out, he told himself groggily. That's what Class Two droids are for.

Mohs, High Singer of the Toka, had, of course, been leading the high-pitched, disharmonious chant. Now the old man signaled the others to provide a more subdued background music as he addressed the gambler:

"Hail, Lord Key Bearer"—he turned to Vuffi Raa—"and Emissary. It is, indeed, as it has been told. Long have we awaited thee. Vouchsafe now unto thy servants what it is that shall next come to pass."

"We shall climb aboard yon *Millennium Falcon*." Lando pointed to the crab-like vessel sitting on the asphalt a hundred meters away, and yawned. "Tuck ourselves into our little beddy-byes, and get some—*yipe!*"

He stopped short. Across the tarmac, half a dozen repulsor trucks, overhead lights blazing like novas, surrounded the small starship. Along with what appeared to be at least two squads of heavily armed constabulary.

"Good grief," the gambler said to the robot. "Your ethical virtue will remain unscathed tonight, at least. *Everybody* seems to have beaten us to the spaceport. So much for the wonders of public transportation. What do you suppose we've done now?"

" 'We,' Master?"

"Very funny, my loyal and trusty droid. Your support underwhelms me."

Approaching the lowered boarding ramp, Lando, the robot, and the Toka Singer—who had detached himself from his departing congregation—were met by armored, dark-visored cops, blasters drawn and at the ready.

"Okay, officer, I'll pay the two credits." Lando was tired and angry. He didn't even want to know how they'd gotten in past the locking-up he'd done the previous night. But he kept his tone good-natured. With those fellows, it paid to.

"Good evening, Captain," came an equally good-humored reply from beneath a helmet with two decorative bars across its highly reflective forehead. "We're here to guard your cargo while it's being loaded."

"Really?" Lando marveled. He was always suspicious of favors from policemen. The trooper pointed an armored finger toward the trucks, from which a steady stream of packages ran up automated conveyors into the *Falcon*'s open cargo hatches.

"That's right," the guardsman answered, then added in a more subdued and, Lando thought, somehow civilian tone, "I sure hope your bruises are healing up okay. We were pretty careful. Nothing personal, you understand, sir. A guy has orders to follow."

And plenty of morally evasive clichés to fall back on, Lando thought as he peered into the anonymous helmet visor. He gave it up. "Think nothing of it, my dear fellow. I understand completely. I'll try and do as much for you, someday."

The cop chuckled, snapped to attention, clicked booted heels, and brought his heavy handweapon to port arms. Lando suppressed an unmilitary snigger of his own at the display, and climbed aboard the *Falcon* with Vuffi Raa and Mohs behind him.

The interior of the *Millennium Falcon*, Lando thought for the hundredth time, was more like the innards of some great living beast than the inanimate human construction that it was. Starliners and other vessels he was familiar with were as rectilinear and orderly as the hotel where he'd spent an uncomfortable night in Teguta Lusat. But aboard his ship were no separate compartmentalized cabins of any sort, nor any clear demarcation between cargo and living space, simply lots of unspecialized volume, currently being rapidly and compactly filled with cartons and crates of highly valuable life-crystals.

Lando watched the port's longshorebots work. It appeared Gepta was more than keeping his part of the bargain—Lando made a note to have the crystals assayed as soon as possible. There was nothing about the sorcerer, or his governmental flunky, that inspired trust, even had Lando been the trusting type.

Parking Mohs at a convenient bulkhead frame, Lando and Vuffi Raa stopped off beside the ultralightspeed section of the ship's drive area. There had been some changes made. And not for the better, Lando thought.

"Oh, Master!" the dismayed Class Two robot wailed. "Just see what they have done to her!" He rushed to the faster-than-light drive panels and stood, wringing his metallic tentacles and making the kind of high-pitched squeal humans call tinnitis and see physicians about.

All along the wall, access panels had been left rudely hanging open. Frayed wires and broken cables dangled from the overhead. Small bits and pieces of machinery, mechanical detritus such as nuts and washers and scraps of insulation littered the decking. The faint foul stench of soldering and scorched plastic defied the ventilating system's best efforts.

"It's quite a mess, all right, old home appliance. But don't fret, she's only a machine, after all, and they've promised to make full and complete repairs, once we—"

"*Only a machine?*" The robot's voice was disbelieving, scandalized, and almost hysterical. "Master, I, too, am 'only a machine'! This is horrible, unbearable, cruel, evil. It's—"

"Oh, come now, Vuffi Raa, don't exhaust your vocabulary. You're a *sapient* machine. The *Falcon*'s big and smart, but she's way, way beneath you on the scale of things. Otherwise I shouldn't have had to rent that confounded, idiotic—"

"Master," the droid interrupted, more gently this time, "how does it make you feel to see somebody's furry pet run over by the roadside? Do you dismiss it, say it's only an animal, beneath you on the scale of things? Or do you feel like . . . well, the way I feel now?"

Lando shook his head, too tired to argue further. The point, within limits, was certainly well taken. And he hated to think that the little automaton was a more humane being than he himself.

"I'm going forward," he said abruptly. "There's no telling what trouble somebody like Mohs can find to get into with all those dials and pretty buttons going unsupervised."

"Very well, Master. With your permission, I'll remain here a little while to comfort her as best I can and tidy up this . . . this butchery."

"As you will." Lando paused in the bight of curving corridor, turned back to see the droid collecting washers and sheared rivets from the decking. "Er, uh, sorry I didn't understand your feeling at first, old cybernet. It's just that I . . ." His voice trickled off.

There was a long silence between the two, then: "That's all right, Lando. At least you understood after I explained it. That's more than most organic beings could do, I think."

The gambler cleared his throat self-consciously. "Yes, well, er, ah . . . see you forward in a little while, then—and don't call me Lando."

IN THE TUBULAR cockpit forward, Lando took an inexpert look at the indicator lights on various control boards, then thumbed through the *Falcon*'s dog-eared flight manual to see what they meant.

Mostly, the unfamiliar lights he saw were warnings of open hatch covers where the loading was being carried out. Clunks and thumps and groans below confirmed the telltales. The entire section of instrumentation given over to the ultralight drive had only solid reds and yellows glaring balefully.

Behind Lando, in the high-backed jumpseat where the gambler had placed him firmly, Mohs seemed to have lapsed back into senile passivity. Lando couldn't blame him: he almost wished he could do the same. It had been a long, hard day for the poor old savage. The Toka sat, eyes wide open, staring down at the decking plates, knobbed hands lying palms up in loinclothed lap.

"Mohs?" Lando asked gently.

The old man started, as if he'd been thoroughly asleep despite the open eyes and hadn't seen Lando turn around to speak to him. He blinked, rubbed a slow and shaky hand over his stubbly chin.

"Yes, Lord?"

"Mohs, what was it that you and your people were chanting out there by the fence?"

The old man breathed deeply, resettled himself in the heavily padded jumpseat. He'd never placed his scrawny fundament in so luxurious a resting place before. He patted the arms a little, almost in disbelief.

"It was the Song of the Emissary, Lord, in honor of the advent of you and—"

"I see."

A long, thoughtful few moments followed. The old man's breathing was almost loud in the control cabin. Lando hadn't really thought very much about this Emissary business. There hadn't been time. It was beginning to dawn on him that there might be more to all the chanting and Key-Bearing stuff than Gepta had seen fit to tell him.

"Well, old fellow," Lando said, not unkindly, "if you're not too played out after all the excitement, why don't you tell me—"

With a clank at the doorsill betraying whatever weary clumsiness robots happen to experience, Vuffi Raa chose that moment to return from the drive area aft, clambered into the right-hand seat, which Lando had replaced after sending the pilot droid back to the Oseon. The little automaton was uncharacteristically subdued.

"Everything shipshape and tidy to your liking, then?" Lando asked conversationally. "Good. Did you happen, by the way, to overhear that guard-captain out there? He more or less directly identified himself as the unreconstituted son of a—"

"Yes, Master," the robot responded somewhat dully. "I must say, it was something of a surprise."

Lando mused. "I don't know about that. I don't suppose it's all that great a coincidence. In the first place, they can't have an endless supply of uniformed thugs to call upon in Teguta Lusat to do their dirty work. And in the second place, assigning that particular one to greet us would be Duttes Mer's idea of a joke. Actually, I thought it rather sporting of the fellow to apologize and ask after my health and all that sort of thing."

Once more imitating human beings, Vuffi Raa did a double take, turning to "face" Lando. "And especially considering the effective way in which you got even, afterward, Master."

It was Lando's turn to blink surprise. "Got even? What in the name of the Galactic Drift do you mean?"

"Why, Master, I thought we were talking about the *same* so-called coincidence. Aren't you aware of who that—"

"Certainly: the paramilitary bully from the hotel, last night."

"And more recently, Master, a civilian 'Mr. Jandler' from the Spaceman's Rest. I thought you recognized his voice, as I did—and the painful stiffness with which he moved his neck."

"You don't say!"

Perhaps there is some justice in the universe, after all, Lando thought with satisfaction. Then he screwed his face up sourly: another blasted mystery! What had that charade in the saloon been all about, then? He'd taken it for a bit of bigoted random stupidity on a highly bigoted and randomly stupid planet. And what did it all imply about the robot bartender (or its owner), who seemed—

A previous idea demanded Lando's attention quite suddenly: "Tell us about the Emissary, Mohs, old fellow—no, *don't* sing it! Make it short, intelligible, and to the point."

The Toka ancient stirred. "Legend foretelleth of a dark adventurer, an intrepid star-sailor with preternatural luck at games of chance, who shall come with a weird inhuman companion in silvery armor arrayed. They shall possess the Key with which to liberate the Mindharp, which in turn shall liberate the—"

Lando slammed a palm on the armrest of his chair. "Well, I'll be doubled-dyed, hornswoggled, and trussed up like a holiday fowl! We were set up, Vuffi Raa! Gepta must have had his convict spies watching the port for months—possibly years—to find a sucker with the right qualifications: gambler, spaceship captain, with an unenameled droid and a weak mind. That's why neither a creepy old Tund magician nor that ugly neckless governor of his could play this hand themselves: they don't fit the Toka legend!"

"And we do, Master?"

"Ask Mohs, here; he's the local Keeper of the Flame."

"Master?"

"Never mind, a figure of speech. Let's go back aft and get some shut-eye. We've got some heroing to do in the morning—and don't forget to polish your armor, old can-opener!"

IX

Came the dawn, with a full night's rest under his stylish if somewhat wrinkled satyn semiformal cummerbund, Lando was in a worse mood than ever. He loathed the idea that he might have been taken by one of the marks, and the nasty suspicion was growing within him that he'd only begun to discover the extent to which he'd been outmaneuvered by Rokur Gepta.

The takeoff of the *Millennium Falcon*, shortly after sunrise, had proceeded as smoothly as clockwork, as fluidly graceful as a textbook exercise. Even the Teguta Lusat control tower had complimented Lando on it. This failed to cheer him. He passed the compliments along to Vuffi Raa, who had been at the controls.

The troopers and freight-handlers had departed sometime the previous evening under the cover of the moonless sky, sealing the *Falcon*'s hatches tightly behind them until the control boards displayed a solid, unbroken tapestry of green pilot lamps. Mohs had curled up on a lounger, snoring like some impossible archaic internal combustion engine. Vuffi Raa had tidied up and tinkered through the night.

Sapient robots do need sleep—the brighter they are the greater the need—but Lando never had been able to discern a pattern in their nightly habits. He himself had tossed and turned, sweating into the fancy and expensive synsilk bedroll he'd spread under the common-room gaming table, and finally achieving an unrestful semiconsciousness from which the robot had awakened him, stiff and groggy. Several large containers of hot, black coffeine had only deepened his already gruesome mood.

"All right," he snarled unnecessarily at the old Toka shaman. They were forward in the cockpit once again, Mohs perched on the jumpseat, Vuffi Raa occupying the right-hand copilot's couch as a token concession to the human captain, but very much in control of the ship. Someday, thought Lando, when it all was over, he'd sell both blasted machines, Vuffi Raa and the *Millennium Falcon,* to someone fully capable of appreciating them.

"So where do we go from here?"

They were lying in a close orbit around Rafa IV. From there they could reach any point on the planet's surface within minutes or strike out freely across space for any other body in the system. Mohs closed his eyes, mouthed the rote-memorized words of an ancient ritual to himself, and finally pointed a dessicated finger out the viewport.

"Lord, the Mindharp lieth in that direction."

Perfect, Lando thought sourly to himself, I've got a mechanical kid's toy for a pilot, and an elderly witch doctor for a navigator! A sadistic little voice inside him insisted on adding that he also had a *sabacc*-playing conman for a captain. Even all around, then. He gave it up and peered through the faceted transparency.

How in the devil do you discuss the details of navigational astronomy with an utter savage? "You mean that bright light in the heavens, there, Mohs?"

"Of a certainty, Lord: the fifth planet of the Rafa System; it possesseth two natural satellites, a breathable atmosphere, and approximately nine-tenths of a standard gravity, not unlike Rafa IV beneath us, whence we came—except in the matter of the moons. Is it not pleasing in thy—"

"Forget it!" The gambler peered suspiciously at the old man. "How is it that you know so blasted much about astronomy, all of a sudden?" And who's really the utter savage here? he asked himself quietly; he'd never have been able to pick out the next planet from the local sun against the starry sky, not without the ship's computer as a crutch.

The ancient Singer shrugged, gave Lando a saggy, toothless grin. "It is all there, Lord, in the Song of the Reflective Telescope, which detaileth all things in this system. Should it not be so?"

There was a long, long silence, during which the only thing accomplished was Vuffi Raa's computer-guided confirmation that Lando's "bright light in the heavens" was, indeed, Rafa V. "How many of these bloody chants do you know, anyway?"

The savage considered: "Many beyond counting, Lord. More than the fingers and toes of all my great-great ancestors and children. I would say approximately seven point six two three times ten to the fourth. Does this please thee, Lord?"

For a humble worshipper, the old boy was getting pretty sarcastic, Lando thought. "I suppose that last comes from the Song of Scientific Notation." He shook his head. He understood fully now why Gepta and Mer hadn't gone on this wild *falumba* chase themselves. It had nothing to do with conforming to ancient Toka legends. They simply wanted to stay sane.

The question now was, why did Vuffi Raa and Mohs need him?

"What now, Master? Do you want to go to Rafa V?"

"DON'T CALL ME MASTER!"

THE RELATIVELY SHORT jump of a few dozen million kilometers was blessedly uneventful for the captain and "crew" of the *Millennium Falcon*.

They hadn't started it at once. Vuffi Raa and Lando quizzed the elderly Mohs, had made him repeat and translate the appropriate stanzas of the appropriate Songs until they, too, were as certain as they could be, under the circumstances, that Rafa V was the place to find the Mindharp.

That is, if you were willing to place much confidence in an

intermittently senile shaman mouthing rhymed and metered legends of an indeterminate age.

Lando spent the few hours of transit catching up on his sleep, while Mohs and Vuffi Raa carried on whatever passed for conversational small talk between them. The pilot's acceleration couch was infinitely more comfortable than the sleeping bag, and by the time Vuffi Raa woke him again, he felt halfway human. Downright cheerful, in fact. Or at least as cheerful as he ever—

SPANG!

Something struck the roof of the control cabin, hard.

"What in the eternal blue blazes was that?" Lando shouted. Behind him, the old man cringed, began gibbering to himself in a high-pitched, hysterical voice. Something about the wrath of—

SPENG!

This time, it was somewhere aft, near the engines. A yellow light winked on the control board. Vuffi Raa stabbed console buttons, his tentacles blurring with speed into near invisibility. "One moment, Master, while I—"

SPING! SPONG!

Red lights flickered now. There was the faint but definite whistle indicating loss of atmosphere. Lando swallowed hard. His ears popped as the pressure equalized, although that hadn't been his intention.

Something was striking the *Millennium Falcon* repeatedly and with great force. For some odd reason, the image of Constable Jandler (if that was really his name) flashed through Lando's mind. They were in close orbit over Rafa V, preparing to use the old Toka chants as a guide to selecting a landing site.

Vuffi Raa heeled the *Falcon* over so she could take whatever was hitting her on her better-armored underside, but they had already received at least minor damage.

SPUNG!

"In the name of the Galactic Center, what's *that*?" Lando hollered.

An unlikely object had wedged itself into the space between the cockpit transparency and a small communications antenna. It resembled nothing more than a fancy cut-glass plumber's helper, complete with handle and suction cup, but rendered in some crystalline substance reminiscent of Rafa orchard produce.

"I don't know, Master!"

Was that hysteria in the robot's voice? Wonderful, thought Lando.

The ship rolled, stabilized, and they were traveling in orbit on her side. The bombardment seemed to slacken off. The droid turned to Lando.

"It's an artifact of some kind, Master. Archaeoastronomers believe that Rafa V was the original home of the Sharu, the planet they evolved on. Mohs' Songs seem to agree with that. I suspect, Master, that we're seeing—and suffering—the remnants of their first attempts at spaceflight, objects launched by primitive rockets, others expelled by small spacecraft as they prepared to re-enter atmosphere."

It made sense. Planetary orbits were always the richest fields in which to discover the leavings of primitive technology. There were probably cameras out there, used spacesuits, free-fall table scraps, all of them practically as good as the day they had been jettisoned—barring a little micrometeorite and radiation damage.

A thought came to him.

"Vuffi Raa, why didn't you just power the *Falcon*'s shields up when we started taking hits? There's nothing out there the deflectors couldn't have handled, especially given our relative speeds in orbit."

Reading through the flight manual over and over again seemed to be doing him some good, Lando thought. Maybe if he watched the robot fly this machine long enough, he'd pick up the knack himself.

On the other hand, right now he could be aboard a luxury passenger liner, sipping a tall cool drink and shearing two-legged sheep.

"Why, I don't know, Master," came the reply. "I simply acted as quickly as I could. Brace yourself, everybody, we're going in!" The droid began punching console buttons again.

RAFA V—BIRTHPLACE of the fabled Sharu or not—was not the favored planet for human colonization. There was atmosphere, the usual thick scattering of titanic multicolored buildings, and, most importantly, the ubiquitous life-orchards. But the place was just a trifle too cold, a trifle too dry, and Rafa IV, the planet they'd just come from, was moist and shirtsleeve comfortable over a wide range of latitudes.

Here and there, according to their orbital survey and maps programmed into the *Falcon* at Teguta Lusat, lay small settlements, orchard-stations where a combination of Toka (native to the planet, as they were to all bodies in the system with sufficient resources), convicts, and government horticulturists harvested life-crystals, although on nowhere near the scale of Rafa IV.

No doubt in another hundred years or so, there would be towns, eventually cities other than those the Sharu had abandoned. But for now, there were a paltry few hundred individuals sprinkled over an entire planetary surface.

The colossal pyramid Mohs pointed them toward was at least a thousand kilometers from any contemporary outpost of civilization.

Vuffi Raa brought the *Falcon* to a gentle leaflike landing in a space between several ancient constructs at the foot of the pyramid that dwarfed even them. There were no convenient words to describe the building that now loomed over them. At least seven kilometers of it protruded above ground level. The *Falcon*'s various scanners had disclosed that it kept on going beneath the surface, but the depths exceeded the capabilities of her instruments. It was a literal mountain of smooth impervious plastic that served no discernible function.

The pyramid had five facets (not counting the bottom—

wherever *that* was), the angles between each of them not particularly uniform, giving the gigantic construct an eerie, dangerous, lopsided look. Each face was a different brilliant color: magenta, apricot, mustard, aquamarine, turquoise, lavender.

Execrable taste, Lando thought, well deserving of cultural extinction.

There was no finishing ornament at the top; the sides simply came together in a peak sharp enough to give anyone who reached it a nasty puncture wound.

Not for the first time, Lando wondered who or what it was that had scared off creatures capable of creating such an edifice. He rummaged through the ship's chests and his own wardrobe looking for suitable clothing, settled finally on a light electrically heated parka, heavy trousers, micro-insulated gloves, and rugged boots with tough, synthetic soles. It was a measure of his uneasiness about the place that he broke long precedent, slinging a short, weighty two-handed blaster over his shoulder and filling his pockets with extra power modules.

The weapon hung at his waist, muzzle swinging with his body when he moved.

Mohs flatly turned down the offer of additional warm clothing, joined the gambler and Vuffi Raa at the boarding ramp. Lando wondered if the old fellow wanted to add frostbite to the rest of his infirmities. If nothing else, they already made an impressive collection.

"Now, you're absolutely certain this is the place?"

Mohs nodded vigorously as the ramp lowered them and itself to ground level, unaffected by the cold as the angle beneath their feet steepened and a deep chill entered the belly of the ship. Air puffed out in visible vaporous clouds. They tramped down onto the dry-frozen soil.

"Master," Vuffi Raa admonished, "I trust you're carrying sufficient water. The humidity in this region does not quite reach two percent."

Lando slapped the gurgling plastic flasks tucked into the pockets of his parka. "Yes. And I brought a deck of card-chips, as well." He looked out over the barren surface of the planet. Fine reddish sand lapped like a frozen sea around the bases of the abandoned buildings. "Chances are we'll die of boredom before thirst gets to us."

Mohs turned, an odd look on his face as he watched Lando open a small panel at eye level on one of the *Falcon*'s landing legs. The gambler pushed a sequence of buttons that started the boarding ramp groaning upward again into its recess under the ship's belly.

"Hast thou also the Key, Lord, the Key which—"

"What is this? Are you two seeing me off to summer camp or something?"

He led them out from beneath the ship, took a deep invigorating breath—and promptly froze the hairs in his nostrils. "Well, I can see why nobody much has staked a claim on this forsaken stretch of—"

"Master," Vuffi Raa clattered up beside him and tugged at the hem of his jacket. "Master, I don't like this. There's something—"

"I know, old junkyard, I can feel it, too."

The sky, a light greenish color, was cloudless. Nevertheless, somehow it impressed them all as gray, bleak, and overcast. And it was *cold*. The whine of Vuffi Raa's servos was clearly audible, a sign that perhaps his internal lubrication was thickening. Lando replaced the glove on the hand he'd used to retract the ramp, thrust it deeply into a warm pocket where the blaster swung.

"*Master!*"

Something went *zing!* and a short, stubby, wicked-looking arrow suddenly protruded from the seam between the robot's leg and body. In the next instant, a hailstorm of the primitive projectiles whistled toward them, bouncing off the *Falcon*'s hull, burying themselves in the sand at their feet. Vuffi Raa went down, looking like a five-legged pincushion. He didn't utter a word.

Curiously, not a single arrow struck either Lando or Mohs. The former swung his weapon up on its strap, panned it along the low dunes a few yards away. He felt a *slap!* and turned the blaster, staring at the muzzle orifice with disbelief.

An arrow had found its way straight down the bore, turning the gun into a potential bomb, should Lando touch the trigger. He tossed the dangerous thing away, began struggling with the fastenings of his coat to find the stingbeam. It wasn't much, but it was all—

"Stand where you are, '*Lord*'!" Mohs exclaimed. "If you resist, you will die before you draw another breath!"

The old man raised a hand. From behind the sand dunes, half a hundred Toka emerged, dressed as he was in nothing more than loincloths.

In his hands, each held a powerful crossbow, pointed directly at Lando.

X

S O THIS WAS a genuine life-orchard.

The trees were a little odd, but nothing spectacular. In the wild grove perhaps five hundred of the things grew, in no particular pattern, yet each was of an identical size and spaced several meters from its nearest neighbor. The trunk was relatively ordinary, too—until one examined it closely and discovered that what appeared to be bark-covered wood was in fact a fibrous, glassy, pigmented stem approximately half a meter through and a couple of meters tall under the spreading branches.

The first oddity one noticed, however, was the root system. Each tree seemed to rest on a base, an irregular disk two meters across, like a toy tree in a model monorail set. Composed of the same substance as the trunk, the disk spread from the tree, forming a platform that curved abruptly downward at the edge and buried itself in the ground. The entire undersurface was covered with hair-fine glassy roots reaching downward perhaps a kilometer but spreading laterally only as far as the longest of the branches.

The branches, in some ways, reminded one of a cactus. At about average head height, they began to sprout from the trunk, departing at a right angle for a little distance (the lower the branch, the longer the distance, none exceeded the span of the root system), then turning straight upward. Outer branches— lower ones—had shorter vertical components. Inner ones had longer, so that the entire tree was somewhat conical in shape.

At the slender, tapering tip of each branch, a single, faceted, brilliant crystal grew, varying from fist-sized, on the outer branches, to tiny gems no bigger than pinheads. Each tree bore perhaps a thousand crystals. In the center, along the line of the trunk, one very tall, slender branch reached skyward like a communications antenna, unadorned by a crystal.

These trees were a little shorter, a little stockier than Lando had been led to believe was normal. Perhaps the milder climate of Rafa IV had something to do with that. It was hard to understand how anything could grow on Rafa V.

For grow they did, those trees—despite the fact that they were some odd cross between organic life and solid-state electronics. From some unknown spread of seeds, each orchard grew, every tree at the same rate. Remove a crystal from its branch tip—something that had to be done with a laser—and another would replace it within a year's time. Elsewhere in the Rafa System, Lando knew there were groves of trees no more than a hand's-width tall, others in which no tree stood less than ten or twelve meters. All bore crystals proportionate to the tree size. Some life-crystals, useless for commercial purposes, were microscopic. Others were the size of Vuffi Raa's body.

The thought of Vuffi Raa caused Lando to stop thinking about trees and reflect, instead, on how he'd gotten into this predicament.

BACK AT THE SHIP, he'd turned in dismay to look at the little robot. Its red-lit eye was out; arrows stuck from nearly every chink and crevice of its body. A light clear fluid ran from many of the wounds, darkening the reddish soil around it.

Mohs strode up to him, no longer bent and stooped. He thrust out a hand, palm up.

"Give me the Key, *imposter*!"

Lando set his jaw. He didn't have much to lose, and he was

mad—more at himself than anything else. He folded his arms across his chest, planted his feet in the sand, and grunted.

"The Key! It is not yours, it is ours! Give it to me!"

"Don't be silly, old fellow!"

Quite inexplicably, a look of dismay spread over Mohs' face. He dropped his hand to his side, turned to the other natives surrounding the pair in a heavily armed and dangerous-looking ring, and shrugged. He turned again to Lando.

"I say once more, you fake, you fraud, you, you . . ."

"If you do," said Lando, not understanding what was happening, but willing now to hope, "I'll just say something insulting. In fact, I think I will, anyway: your mother sang off key." He nodded for emphasis.

Mohs took a step backward, aghast—whether at the magnitude of the insult or in surprise at the general turn of events, Lando couldn't tell.

Mohs turned once again to his people—and there's another problem, Lando thought idly: Mohs was from another planet. How was it that the locals seemed to know him and acknowledge his leadership?

Come to think of it, how had the ambush been set up in the first place?

The savages conferred for a while in their own language. A decision appeared to have been made.

"You will come with us, imposter!" Mohs ordered. He started to walk off on a course paralleling the nearest face of the giant pyramid. Lando stood where he was.

"I will when the Core freezes over! *Ouch!*" This last was due more to surprise than injury. A crossbow bolt had whistled past Lando's head, skinning an ear already made painful by the cold, striking the hull of the *Falcon,* and catching him on the rebound in the seat of his insulated pants. A pattern seemed to be emerging: they didn't want to kill Lando; they couldn't take the Key away without his consent (although Mohs had tried that back on

Four, he reminded himself), but they could threaten and coerce him in other ways.

They seemed to be pretty good at that.

He reached for his discarded blaster, intending to pull out the arrow and create a little mayhem before they shot him down. He hadn't moved a meter when another flight of arrows virtually buried the weapon, pinned it to the ground by its sling, trigger guard, and other apertures in the stock and fore-end. So much for that idea.

As one, the fifty or so natives swung their weapons back on Lando.

"Okay, okay, I'm coming! Anybody think to call a cab?"

Two hours later, Lando wished it hadn't been a joke. They'd marched him for mile after endless mile, climbing over random angular ruins, sloshing through deep-drifted sand, scrabbling through scrubby brush. His feet hurt and his legs ached and, no matter how high he turned his suit controls, he was still cold.

At last he stopped.

"All right, everybody, I've been a nice guy so far, but this is as far as I go. If you want the Key, you'll have to take it off my dead body. I'm not going another meter."

The silent natives who surrounded him looked to Mohs. The old man nodded. They loosed a flight of arrows that plucked at his clothing, kicked sand up in his face, whistled mere angstrom units over his head. These fellows were impressive markspersons, Lando found himself thinking, I hope none of them gets the hiccups. He stood his ground again until they started shooting between his legs.

It wasn't worth the risk. He waited until they paused to reload, then began marching again.

What he had thought were crossbows had turned out to be something entirely different, some kind of spring-loaded contraption with hinged arms—which he'd mistaken for the limbs of a bow—that flailed forward, hurling the stubby arrows out through the front of the weapon. They didn't seem to need reloading every time they were fired. He guessed there were perhaps half a dozen projectiles stashed in a magazine hidden within the mechanism. The weapons weren't very powerful, as projectile throwers went, but the speed and accuracy with which they could be used made him realize he could die from a thousand pinpricks as easily as from a single blaster shot.

And a great deal more painfully.

They marched.

Another couple of hours went by. Lando wasn't sure exactly— he didn't want to look at his watch, because he didn't want to remind the natives that he had several items concealed beneath his winter clothes, notably his five-shot stingbeam. It would take a lot of figuring to get any good out of it in this situation, but it was something to fall back on, and it gave him a bit of hope.

Step after endless step. The country didn't vary much: something between desert and tundra, most of the space taken up with giant Sharu buildings. Sand, sand, and more sand. Occasional weeds. The clear, yet somehow foreboding sky. He worried about Vuffi Raa, hoped that robots die a swift and merciful death.

All during the long, pauseless ordeal, the Toka around him chanted, sometimes slowly, sometimes more rapidly. And to his continuous annoyance, *never* in rhythm with the marching. This caused him to stumble awkwardly every now and again. He didn't know how the Toka mind worked, but he knew he didn't like it. They sang low-pitched Songs, they sang high-pitched Songs. They sang in harmony, disharmony, and counterpoint. They would be great to record—they had an endless repertoire.

At long last, the marching ended at a grove of life-crystal trees. Mohs approached him.

"Imposter, hear me: we are forbidden to remove the holy Key from the Key Bearer, even should the Bearer be a false one. You have somehow guessed this. Nor may we kill him who bears the Key, although we *have* killed the false Emissary, which makes us glad."

So *that* was it! Somehow Lando had gotten the idea that the Key Bearer and the Emissary were the same fellow, namely himself. Had he betrayed that belief to Mohs, setting up the debacle? He tried to recall what he'd said to Mohs on the subject, then realized it didn't make a bit of difference anyway—and besides, the old man was still talking.

"—let them do it themselves. Come with me!"

Lando followed him to a tree. Several of the other Toka handed their weapons to comrades, joined Mohs and Lando, and, between them, produced a loincloth.

By the time Lando decided to resist, it was too late. They forced him into a sitting position, bound him to the tree trunk by the waist, and used the same length of cloth to tie his hands behind him. They pushed back his hood, unfastened his jacket, and tore it rudely from him.

"Hey! Do you know what my tailor charged me for—now hold on a minute, that's going too far!"

Mohs had pulled off one of Lando's boots, bent to seize the other. When this was accomplished, the boots tossed aside near his discarded parka, they tore his tunic off, and the light shirt beneath it.

Then Mohs produced a knife.

"Now wait a blasted minute, here! You can't do that!" He kicked at the old man until a pair of natives held his ankles. He'd never believed in strong, silent heroes, and since the only thing he had left to do was yell, he yelled.

He yelled the entire time it took Mohs to slit his trouser legs, exposing bare skin to the chilling air.

"Now," said the ancient Singer, when he was satisfied with Lando's disheveled condition. "All will notice that the Key remains with the Bearer."

This was true. They'd taken it from his tunic and tucked it

into the dirty gray cloth about his waist. That had been a scary moment—he'd held deathly still so they wouldn't clank it against the tiny beamer hidden beneath both loincloth and cummerbund.

"Now we shall wait. In Their own time, They will take his life, either in the cold or through the tree. We shall then return and claim the Key which is our rightful heritage. We go."

They went.

As the sun sank behind the highly unnatural skyline, shadows crept inexorably toward the helpless gambler, and as they did, his heart sank at approximately the same rate as the sun. He watched as small plants curled themselves into little protective balls for the night. He watched as frost formed on his toes. He watched as moisture in the ground forced up the top layer of the soil on frozen ice columns.

Mostly, he watched his nice warm parka, tunic, boots, and socks gather frost of their own, not three meters beyond his bound and helpless reach.

He began cursing, first through genuine anger at himself and Mohs and Gepta and Mer, then simply in order to keep warm. He cursed in his native tongue and in the dozen and a half others he'd learned during a long and checkered career. He cursed in three computer languages and the warbling *cheep* of a race of musical birds he'd once played cards with—until it reminded him of the Toka.

He cursed the Toka all over again. And again. And again.

He woke up with a start!

And began cursing for no other reason than to stay awake. If he didn't, he would freeze to death.

XI

D EATHLY SILENCE.

Beneath a looming, monstrous crustacean form resting on stilted legs, the twin pale moons of Rafa V picked out metallic reflections in the night-blackened sand. Shadows overlaid at different angles with slightly differing shades: the enormous double shadow of the *Millennium Falcon,* hundreds of tiny double shadows of stubby wooden projectiles buried in a fragile metal carapace and nearby soil.

Deathly silence and deadly cold.

Everywhere within sight of the *Falcon,* small ground-hugging plants had rolled themselves into compact olive-colored balls in order to survive the frigid darkness. The air was dry, even drier than the daytime atmosphere. The subtlest sparkling of frost showed here and there, on half-frozen plant life, on the crest of miniature dunes, on the rims of a thousand footprints that surrounded the ship, even on the tortured, tangled mess of chromium cables lying in a heap just outside the *Falcon*'s shadow.

Fluid still stained the sand for a short distance around the pitiable heap, slow and thick and gummy now, in the frozen quiet. Yet, a few inches beneath the grainy surface, there was movement. Pseudo-organisms, shiny and metallic, mote-like, hovering at the edge of human visibility, stirred within the thickened fluid, migrated a millimeter at a time back toward the larger pseudo-organism they had tumbled from before dark.

Microscopic flagella beat languidly, laboriously. Yet, centimeter by centimeter, millions of the tiny objects swam what was to them enormous distances, back to where they belonged. In their wake, the fluid became thinner, more liquid, and withdrew after them, carrying minerals and trace metals from the soil with it.

THE SAME TWO MOONS cast double shadows several kilometers away. Beneath a spread of glassy boughs, a figure huddled, trying to stay alive in the cold. Lando Calrissian was dying. As Vuffi Raa's life had run out into the sand, so he could feel his own life running out through his exposed skin into the frigid air, into the hungry sinister plant he was bound to.

Around him, if he'd cared to look, he might have seen the same small plants rolled up into the same small, heat-conserving spheres. He might have wished that he could do the same. But he was past all that, by now. From time to time he shivered, convulsions wracking his body, seeming to tighten the painful fibers around his waist, around his wrists, cutting off the circulation even further.

It was getting hard to think, and Lando didn't know whether the cold was causing that or the tree. It seemed important to figure it out. What had he heard about trees like this? That there was nothing free in the universe—that what the crystals gave to those who wore them, they had first taken from someone else. Were they taking from him now?

Most of all, it hurt. His naked feet felt as if they were on fire. Even in the parched air, frost was forming on their tips, on the nails. How cold does tissue have to be before frost will form on it? Cold enough for gangrene?

Well, they weren't going to get him *that* easily! He nodded confirmation to himself, and only then noticed the tears that had run down his cheeks and frozen there. If he could still feel his feet—he wished he couldn't because the agony was as distracting as the coid itself—he ought to be able to feel his fingers. They were cold, too, but shielded from the air by his body, the little clothing they'd left him, and the tree.

The tree.

Its glassy trunk was like a block of ice at his back. Overhead, its strangely precise limbs showed a bit of transparency—or was it translucency?—where they crossed the moons.

He shook his head, and a pattern stopped. Dully, he tried to figure out what was missing. Had his heart stopped beating? He didn't think so. He was still breathing—only now that he was conscious of it, it became an effort, an added burden to keep on doing so. He wished he could forget about it, begin breathing automatically again.

That was it! Unconsciously, he'd been doing something with his hands, his fingers. Why did the tips of his fingers hurt? Were they frozen, like his toes? They shouldn't be—but "shouldn't" was a funny word: he *shouldn't* be there, trussed up to a tree that was eating his mind. He should be . . . should be . . . what should he be doing? Something about long corridors and beautiful women and . . . and . . . *card-chips*! What would he do with card-chips?

Trying to figure that one out, he didn't notice that his fingers had gone back to picking the fabric at his wrists, stripping the aged cloth one shredded fiber at a time.

BEGIN WITH A METAL PENTAGON, approximately thirty centimeters across its longest dimension, seven or eight centimeters thick at the edges, perhaps twice that in the rounded center.

In the center, a lens, deep red, the size of a man's palm. And dark. Dark where it should be glowing softly, warmly. Dark as death itself.

Back at the edges, seams. On the other side of each seam, a tubular extension, joined every centimeter or so, tapering gracefully, each joint a little closer, a little finer than the one that preceded it. Sinuous, serpentine, and very, very highly polished, reflecting a curve-distorted picture of the frozen moons and cruel stars. Tangled now, heaped up and disheveled.

And at nearly every joint, at nearly every seam, a crude stubby brown pencil, rough and splintered, hundreds of them, jutting out at every conceivable angle. Where each arrow pierced the thin, fragile metal, a tiny pool of thick, transparent fluid welled. Some of it dripped off curved shining surfaces to the sand a few centimeters below.

Travel down the graceful, violated sinuosity, tapering, tapering, slimming impossibly. Approximately a meter from the torso seam, the tentacles branch again, into five delicate tapering fingers. Usually, these are held together so the tentacle seems to have a single, well-proportioned tip, concealing a tiny red optic in each "palm," replicas of the larger eye in the torso. Now they are splayed, whether in haphazard array or in the agonies of death, only the mechanically sentient can tell, and they are a taciturn, unsentimental lot, for the most part, and will not say what it feels like for a machine to die.

Perhaps, exactly like their creators, they don't know, will never know until they experience it themselves and can't relay the sensations to others. Perhaps it's just as large a mystery to them as it is to everybody else. Perhaps.

Each slender, dainty finger is divided into joints, precisely like the tentacles—fine, impossibly tiny joints, such as a watchmaker would create, looking through his loupe, trying to still the microscopic trembling of his hands. After a few centimeters, the fingers branch yet again—something absolutely *no one* ever notices. The joints continue marching, tapering, growing smaller and finer until they vanish from unaided vision—and continue.

Those subfingers, at their ends, are hair-fine, wire-slender . . . alloy strong. Their inner composition is just as sophisticated, just as complex as any other portion of the creature they belong to. Yet, unlike the pentagonal metal torso, unlike the sinuous jointed tentacles, unlike even the slender adroit fingers, they are too small to be seen, too fine to be hit with an arrow.

One of them stirs. It waves back and forth languidly a moment, living a life of its own. It coils and uncoils, testing itself. It stretches minutely, contracts minutely. It doubles back, wraps itself around the base of an intruding wooden object that had pierced the body above it.

It pulls.

There is a gentle, sucking noise. Slowly the arrow surrenders, sliding out, grating through tortured metal. The hair-fine subfinger plucks it out, casts it away. Elsewhere, other wirelike extensions perform similar tasks. And on the inside, where torn and dented metal protrudes in sharp triangular, ragged, toothlike edges, nearly microscopic flagellated motes begin pushing, thrusting, hammering the metal skin back into place, almost a molecule at a time.

"THE BANTHA IS a shaggy beast, although it has no hair. . . . Its feathers are unique, at least, because they aren't there. . . . Hee, hee, hee, hee, hee!"

Lando began coughing uncontrollably, choking on his genius as a poet. He was disappointed. No one would ever get to hear his cleverness—although he couldn't quite remember why at the moment. Whatever it was, it made him sad, and he lapsed directly from laughter into sobs.

His fingers, highly trained and skillful at manipulating cardchips, coins, the entrances to other people's pockets, went right on thinking for themselves, picking at the rough-woven cloth that bound the wrists above them, threatening to cut off their circulation before they had quite finished their self-assigned task.

"The governor of Rafa IV is fat as he can be. . . . With fuzzy crown and stubby limbs, he looks just like a . . . bee? Fee? Me? Thee? *Thee!* He looks just lika thee, old man, he looks just lika thee!"

Behind Lando, between his body and the pseudoplant, a final fiber gave way. With something akin to shock, Lando jolted back to reality, momentarily, surprised that he could move his wrist, almost sorry as warmth crawled back into his right hand and the pins and needles began.

VUFFI RAA HAD problems larger than pins and needles. His own fingers were free, now, where the primitive arrows had pinned them to the ground and punctured them. His joints would be stiff and uncooperative for some while to come—shoot a bullet through a hinge sometime and learn why—but he was already plucking the projectiles from his tentacles.

The congealed fluid in each wound was hardened, not by cold, this time, but deliberately, by design, protecting his incredibly delicate inner mechanisms. He was through reclaiming fluid from the sand. The traces of raw materials he'd picked up that way wouldn't serve him long: he'd require refueling—something he'd only done once before in his long, long memory—perhaps even an unprecedented lubrication.

But he was alive.

Moreover, he was conscious, having the spare power, at last, to divert into consciousness. He had taken over the programmed simple-minded self-repair mechanisms, and the work was going at quadruple speed. He was beginning to feel good again, knowing that what he could do for others of his kind he could also do for himself.

The frozen desert saw the first faint glow of ruddy amber from the lens set in his pentagonal torso, a luminescence vastly dimmer and less conspicuous than the moons above—another conscious decision.

His body stirred the sand around it, continued plucking arrows out and healing.

LANDO CALRISSIAN PONDERED one of the deep philosophical problems of all time. His right arm was completely free, but he didn't know why that was important. What had he intended to do with that arm?

Something about being cold.

Well, that was silly: he wasn't cold at all. He was nice and warm. Nice and rosy warm. The warmth spread from his toasty feet, up through his legs, into his body, out through his shoulders. His ears were warmest of all. They were practically on fire.

Fire!

He looked around him. It was smoky enough for a fire. The grove where he sat so warmly comfortable seemed to be full of haze. Someone hadn't opened the damper on the fireplace, evidently. Well, he'd just have to get up in a few minutes and do it himself. Couldn't trust anybody these days, ever, with so simple a task as tending a—

Fire!

Something about a gun! Now what in the blazes would he do with a gun if he had one? There was nothing to shoot here, nothing to fight, nothing to eat, even if he'd been the wild-game type, which he wasn't. Besides, they'd plugged his gun up with an arrow. Devilishly good shots, those . . . those . . .

Now *who* had been that good a shot, shooting?

Shooting?

What did *that* have to do with anything? He'd been going to tend the fire, hadn't he? Well, no time like the—he tried to sit up. Great Galactic Core, he thought, I'm paralyzed from the waist down! No—I was simply careless putting on my pants and looped the belt around this . . . this . . .

With sudden, momentary clarity, he reached into his cummerbund, extracted his five-shot stingbeam pistol, flipped off the thumb-safety, and *fired*. The rough cloth fell from his waist. Almost in panic, he rolled away from the life-tree, and had to restrain himself from wasting his remaining four shots on the thing that had been sucking his brains away.

It cost him. Every bone, every muscle in his body, every square inch of his skin was in agony. Each movement threatened to shatter him or tear him. All he really wanted to do was go back to sleep. All he really wanted to do was rest. That was it: he knew he had other things to do, but he could rest up, first. Get warm again—not really sleep, just close his eyes and—

Nearly shrieking defiance—at what he was never afterward able to say—he rolled, crawled, pushed himself along the ground, inflicting new pains with every centimeter of progress. At last he reached the heap of clothing Mohs and his bravos had stripped from him, nearly dived into the parka, and turned the thermo-knob to Emergency Full.

And the agony *really* began.

There wasn't much he could do about his pants. They'd been sliced open from cuff to crotch—Lando remembered the knife, seemingly made from a life-crystal. The abandoned loincloth still clung to his waist. With stiff fingers, he spread it out, tore it into strips, wrapped the strips around his legs, and tied them at strategic points to hold his trousers together.

Bundled up in the parka, he put the gloves on next. The sting-beam was small enough to conceal inside the right glove so that he could shoot it in a hurry if he needed to. The little weapon was blessedly warm from the one shot he'd expended.

Time to think about standing up. Should he take the parka off, replace his undershirt and tunic? It would be in better taste, but somehow that didn't seem to matter right now. Oh, yes! He'd almost forgotten about his boots and socks.

When he got around to examining his feet, he almost wished he hadn't. He was going to miss those toes, and regeneration was a long, fairly painful process. Oh, well, to paraphrase an old, old saying, it beat the hell out of having to regenerate new feet. With great tenderness, he pulled his socks on—being careful to dump as much sand out of them as possible—and, over those, his boots.

How the dickens was he going to stand up? He didn't dare approach one of the deadly trees close enough to lean against. He rolled over on his side, pulled his knees up, rolled up onto them. It felt as though someone had clamped his feet in a vise and was tightening it. He told himself that at least he was alive enough to feel pain. Somehow that didn't cheer him much. He told himself that at least he had his mind back, could think, wasn't going to be a drooling vegetable.

He clambered to his feet, forced himself to walk around.

So this was a genuine life-orchard. It had bloody well nearly been a death orchard, he thought. Wouldn't Mohs be surprised, come morning, to find his victim gone, and along with him—

The Key!

He felt beneath his cummerbund. Even through both gloves and coat, he couldn't mistake the lumpy weirdness of the artifact. Well, *that* was going to upset the old man. Lando chuckled to himself.

The thought came to him that perhaps he was being watched. Well, *let* them watch! The stingbeam didn't have an orifice like a blaster; its muzzle was a pole-piece, more like a thick, stubby, rounded antenna than anything else. He was alive, intelligent, on his feet—he was going back to the *Falcon* for a hot cup of—

Vuffi Raa!

It had been one monster of a day! He'd nearly been killed, certainly been hijacked, and lost his best friend. No, he wasn't ashamed to say it: the little droid had been a better, more loyal friend to him than any he'd ever had before. He was going to miss the little guy.

Now, which way was the *Falcon*? Simple: just follow the tracks, which, with the double portion of moonlight and the dry, still atmosphere, were still plainly visible in the sand.

He took a step.

"LANDO CALRISSIAN!"

Before he realized it, the glove was off his right hand, the stingbeam pointed aloft. Overhead, a repulsor vehicle hovered, bright with running lights, a searchbeam shining down on him and illuminating the entire grove.

It settled to the ground.

"Drop your weapon," a familiar voice said over the loud-hailer, *"and put your hands over your head!"* Lando didn't move.

Nor did he move when four constabulary troopers, their armor glinting in the moonlight, jogged up beside him, took his gun away, and held their own weapons leveled at his chest.

Captain Jandler—if that was his name—had rendered his own visor transparent, this time. He strutted over from the hovercar.

"Well, Captain Calrissian, we meet again. As soon as we've taken care of you, we'll recover your vessel and get that cargo back to its rightful owners. If you thought you were in trouble before . . . By the way, you have something else we want. Where is it?"

"Where is what?" said Lando between gritted teeth.

"The Sharu artifact. The Key the governor gave you. Where is it?"

"Come and get it, thug!"

"All right, men, we're going to do it the hard way. Search him. Strip that clothing off and search him!"

XII

THUNDER BOOMED OVERHEAD!

Bathed in a glorious dawn that hadn't yet reached the ground beneath it, the *Millennium Falcon* roared down upon a constabulary detachment frozen with confusion and surprise, and stood hovering a dozen meters over their heads.

Lando seized Guard-Captain Jandler's weapon muzzle, swung it aside, and kicked the hapless policeman. Jandler sank with a moan to his knees, eyes crossed beneath his helmet visor, and, with a preoccupied gurgle, collapsed onto his face. Lando resisted the urge to kick him again, someplace more breakable.

Two things happened at the same time: one of the other police officers leveled his blaster at the gambler, a finger whitening inside his gauntlet on the trigger. Roiled dirt and fire spurted up into a wall ahead of him as a turret on the *Falcon* spat energy down at him. He dropped his gun and raised his hands unbidden, as did two of his comrades. They were out of the game.

The fourth wasn't giving up so easily. He seized the opportunity to dash for the repulsor cruiser where a heavy beamer was mounted on the transom. Before he'd taken three hurried steps, the starship's turret pivoted, a second energy bolt lashed down from above, and the police cruiser heaved upward from the ground, fell back in flaming wreckage. Smoke poured from the ruined vehicle into the rapidly lightening sky.

Keeping a wary eye on Jandler, Lando sat down heavily himself, wondering where all his vim and vigor had come from all of a sudden. And where it had gone just as abruptly. The *Falcon* settled, its active turret still aimed at the policemen. Lando noticed the guard-captain's heavy blaster lying in the sand a few inches from his rag-wrapped knee, picked it up, and rested it in his lap.

The *Falcon*'s long, broad boarding ramp creaked down slowly. After a while there was a flash and twinkle at the dark, inner end of the passage. Vuffi Raa came slither-marching down to the ground, his posture and movements conveying somehow that he was rather pleased with himself—although he looked a bit worse for the previous evening's wear.

"Master! I'm gratified to see you're still alive. I feared I wouldn't get here in time, but I see you've taken care of nearly everything yourself already."

The gambler grinned wearily, accepted the proffered tentacle. "I'm gratified myself, considering some of the alternatives. But you look like you've been out in a meteor shower! Or is that the latest robot fashion you're wearing?"

From eye lens to manipulator tips, the little droid was covered with small, rounded dents. Where they overlapped his joints—which was practically everywhere—his movements were a little stiff and uncertain, and he sounded, when he replied, just the slightest bit self-conscious.

"Yes, well, these arrow wounds are healing, Master. In not too many days I'll be quite myself again. But you have suffered damage which will not be repaired so quickly. We must get you into the ship, where I can administer—"

"Hold it." Grunting, Lando hauled on Vuffi Raa's tentacle, pulled himself onto his knees, and, placing a palm firmly in the middle of the little robot's lens, pressed himself upward, to his feet. He swayed a little, but he was vertical—and still had the blaster pointed straight at the constabulary contingent.

Meanwhile, Captain Jandler was beginning to do some grunting of his own. He rolled over, tears welling from his eyes and dripping on the inside of his visor, shook his head from side to side, and lay there, still doubled up.

"We'll administer to me later, old pencil-sharpener. First we're going to 'administer' to our military friend, here. He seems to be among the living, again, although how long . . ."

Lando offered the blaster to the droid, glancing significantly at the four undamaged troopers. "While I'm attending to Jandler, I don't suppose you could . . ."

"Hold them at bay? I'm afraid not, Master. I cannot threaten a living being with bodily harm. Sorry."

"Well, I'm not complaining, not anymore. I'll just have to keep an eye on them myself. But I am curious: how was it that, ten minutes ago, you could—"

"Use the *Millennium Falcon*'s armament to keep them from attacking you?"

"And to do that demolition job on the police cruiser. Neat, but a little outside your specialties, wouldn't you say?"

Lando approached the semiconscious guard-captain, toed him not too roughly in the armored ribs. "All right, time to rise and shine! We've got a little talking to do!"

Vuffi Raa shambled up beside the gambler. "Master, I can watch the troopers for you, and they needn't know I can't initiate force against them." The little robot continued in a louder voice, intended for a broader audience, "If one of them so much as twitches an earlobe, we'll burn him off at the kneecaps!"

Lando chuckled. "Yeah, right up to the armpits! Just be sure"—he whispered to Vuffi Raa—"that you don't compromise yourself into a nervous breakdown." Then he added, more loudly, "I said get up, you!"

Jandler stirred, did some more groaning, rolled over, and sat up painfully. Wincing, he took off his helmet and wiped sweat from his face.

"Calrissian, you just plain don't fight fair, do you?"

Lando aimed the confiscated blaster at its former owner's nose. "I don't like to fight at all. When I have to, I try to get it over with as quickly and neatly as possible. Now, *WHAT IN THE BLAZES IS THIS ALL ABOUT?*"

Jandler, his troopers, even Vuffi Raa jumped a little at this outburst. The police leader blinked, considered, then shook his head and sighed.

"Okay, Calrissian—I wish to perdition I knew! I've been sent on more crazy errands in the last couple of days than in my whole career, up until now: your hotel room, the Spaceman's Rest, the spaceport, and now this. It puts a man in mind of retiring early, pension or not. What do *you* know about it?"

Lando squatted down on his haunches, keeping the blaster centered on Jandler. "I hate the devil to steal your line, Captain, but *I'm* asking the questions here. Tell me, exactly where— rather, from whom—did you receive your orders, if one may ask?"

Jandler glanced quickly at his men, then back to Lando, and licked his lips. "Where do you think? From that fat son of a—"

"Captain!" shouted one of the cops. "You can't—"

"The Entropy I can't! Do you think that overstuffed chair-warmer gives a nit in a nova what happens to any of us? All he cares about is that Sharu doohicky, and if we come back without it, we might as well not come back! Well, I—"

"You mean this?" Lando drew the Key from his waistband. It gleamed in the early morning sunlight and, if anything, seemed more disorienting than before.

Lando could see the guard-captain calculating whether it was worth the risk jumping for it. He looked from the Key to his former blaster muzzle, across to Lando, up at Vuffi Raa, then back to the Key again. Finally, he shrugged.

"Let him get it for himself!" Jandler decided out loud. "Is there any way my men and I can get out of this alive, Captain Calrissian? I won't give you those hull-scrapings about 'just following orders' again—only, well, I'm not too fond of the idea of dying, just now. Especially since I seem destined to taste the fruits of civilian life for a while."

Lando turned, winked at Vuffi Raa, and looked back at Jandler.

"Well, old Constable, you people do seem to present us with a problem. I'm impressed with your change of heart, but insufficiently so to be too happy about your breathing down my neck while I'm on this planet. Giving you all the Big Push would seem to be the answer—"

He held up a hand.

"—But I am highly disinclined in that direction, believe me. As you know, I am a gambler by profession, certainly no killer. I live by my wits, not by the gun, however useful the things may prove to be at times. If we can think of a way to let things work out for everybody, I'll certainly cooperate."

Jandler grinned, scratched his head. His men, a few yards away, seemed to relax a few notches as well.

"Now, Captain Jandler," said Lando, "this is what I think we'll do . . ."

THE IDEA WORKED out better than Lando had expected.

Aboard the *Millennium Falcon,* there were several tough, inflatable life-bubbles that could be jettisoned, with air and other short-term supplies. A man could live inside one for several days in moderate discomfort. They weren't much use if something went wrong in interstellar space, but, in the neighborhood of a solar system—where most accidents happen anyway—they could keep one alive until assistance, summoned by an automatic radio beacon, arrived.

Lando's original plan was to haul the constabulary contingent out a few astronomical units and abandon them in space. They'd be out of his and Vuffi Raa's figurative hair for a few days, and yet live to tell their grandchildren about the experience. Happy ending all around.

The little droid made it happier.

"Well, Master, that takes care of that. I believe the gentlemen can go aboard now." He was exiting a hatch in the side of a powered interplanetary cargo barge, large, dark, and rusty, in which the police team had originally traveled to Rafa V. The humble vessel's presence had helped Vuffi Raa to locate Lando in the nick of time.

Lando transferred the blaster to his left hand, extended his right to the constabulary boss. "I suppose this is farewell, then, old bluecoat. I trust you and your comrades will enjoy the trip."

Jandler grinned. "It beats a beam in the eye from a hot laser, Captain Calrissian—"

"Call me Lando, nobody else seems to be able to do it."

"Lando, then. And when we get there, none of us will be in any particular hurry to report, *will we, guys?*" This last had a bit of an edge to it. The other four policemen quickly assumed a "what? who, me?" expression, and Lando trusted Jandler to keep them all in line. Not that it mattered. The plan was perfect.

The officers trooped aboard. Lando waved, then watched Vuffi Raa weld the hatch shut behind them.

"Thirty seconds, Master."

"Very well, let's get back out of the way."

Slowly, gently, with impossible grace, the ungainly tub of a spaceship lifted from the sand, guided by a program Vuffi Raa had punched into its minuscule electronic mind. Lando glimpsed the fused and blackened end of a communications antenna, one of three the little droid had ruined. For the duration of its trip, the barge would be out of contact with the rest of the Rafa System. It would take the vessel a week to reach Rafa XI, last and least planet of the colony, a bleak ball of slush circling in the dark.

A considerable research installation had been built there, and a fairly impressive helium refinery.

"You didn't forget the torches, did you?"

"*Please,* Master, it was difficult making myself do it. Don't rub it in."

"Oh, very well. But sabotaging the ship's controls was *your* idea, I'll remind you. The cops can't alter the taped course, and they can't communicate with anyone until they're close enough to do it with flashlights out the viewports. You did send along that Oseon brandy, I trust?"

"Yes, Master, and those . . . those . . ."

"Holocassettes? Absolutely imperative, old gumball machine. The scenery where they're going is remarkably boring." He gave a final salute as the barge lifted through a rack of rare high cirrus clouds and disappeared.

Vuffi Raa said nothing. In truth, he was rather proud of his master for sparing the men's lives, and especially for parting with them under somewhat cordial circumstances. Perhaps humans—this one in particular, at least—weren't such a bad lot, after all.

"All right," Lando said, breaking into the robot's reverie, "let's get moving ourselves. We've got to find the Toka. I'm going to kill that buzzard-necked Mohs if it's the last thing I ever do!"

THE FIRST THING they had done, after sending off the constabulary contingent, was to attend to Lando's wounds. Frostbite—of which he had been plentifully supplied by the previous evening's adventure—is no minor matter, can be as serious as a blastershot under some circumstances, and, even with all the facilities of modern medicine, can lead to gangrene in a matter of hours.

The *Millennium Falcon* did not provide all the facilities of modern medicine. In a locker, Vuffi Raa discovered a portable gel-bath, miniature version of the large full-body devices used to heal serious wounds. It would fit Lando's feet nicely. He unfolded it in the common room and slid it under the gametable where Lando was considering a problem in Moebius chess.

Or appeared to be.

"Dash it all, Vuffi Raa, where would *you* be, on this planet, if you were an ancient savage with an angry outworlder after you?"

"I couldn't say, Master, the inscrutabilities of the organic mind—"

"Nonsense, old android. Your mind is every bit as organic as—"

"*Please*, Master, I have done nothing to deserve insult. If you truly wish, I will consider the problem you have just posed." Silence, then: "Why do you suppose he had us land the *Falcon* near that giant pyramid, Master?"

Lando gave up on the game, slapped the OFF switch, and watched the weird serpentine playing board fade and vanish from the tabletop.

"I've been wondering about that, myself. It's much the largest building on the planet—perhaps in the system, which would make it the largest in the entire galaxy, I'm sure. On the other hand, the Sharu—now *there* are some inscrutable minds for you—the Sharu may have used it to store potatoes."

"Or the Mindharp."

"Yes, although I'd venture that if the Mindharp were simply a device to tell the Toka to run and fetch their masters' pipe and slippers, it wouldn't deserve quite so august a resting place. However, one thing is certain: it *is* where that scoundrel Mohs met up with his savage cohorts. As such—"

"As such," Vuffi Raa ventured, "it may be a wonderful place to get ambushed—again. Hold still, please, Master, while I tape your ears."

"Leave my ears out of this, you mechanical menace. They were fine before."

"Master, please! I am programmed to—"

"All right, all right! Then limber up your piloting appendages. We're headed for that pyramid again. Only this time, I'm carrying *two* heavy blasters—and an umbrella to keep arrows out of the muzzles."

MOHS WASN'T HARD to find. When the *Millennium Falcon* arrived, he was sitting on a sand dune in the shadow of the pyramid, smoking a lizard.

XIII

"TWICE HAVE I doubted thee, O Lord, yea, even as twice hast thou proved me in error! Kill now thy miserable excuse for a servant, that he may disgrace thee no further!"

The fire, built of twigs and leaves in a scooped-out hollow in the ubiquitous reddish sand of Rafa V, was no larger than a teacup. It failed to warm Lando although he sat cross-legged not more than two feet away, trying to avoid noxious fumes rising from a branch that sported a small, disgusting reptile skewered neatly from end to end.

An ugly way to die, the gambler thought, even for a lizard. And it made an even uglier lunch.

"Look, Mohs, see me about that sometime when I'm not so tired. I may surprise you and take you up on the offer. In the meantime, are you still interested in trying to use the Key?"

"Of a certainty, Lord! Too long have my people, the wretched Toka, suffered under the tyrannical thumb of the—"

"Save it for the union meeting, Singer. All I want to know is where to put this thing. If somebody—your people, for instance—benefits, and somebody else loses as a result, well, that's no paint off my hull, I can assure you."

Secretly, the amateur star-captain was thoroughly enjoying the chance to use what he imagined was tough-sounding space-faring jargon. Now that he'd had a hot meal, plenty of coffeine, and was wearing a fresh change of clean, undamaged clothes, he felt downright jaunty, even considering the miserable night he'd spent in the life-orchard.

"I don't give a hiccup out the airlock, even if *Gepta* benefits, as long as I get out of this confounded system with a full cargo and a whole skin—not necessarily in that order, mind you."

Mohs had started a little at the mention of the sorcerer's name. Now he positively reeled, managing to wring his bony hands at the same time. "O Lord, they servant knoweth full well that thou sayest these cynical things only as a test of my faith, fortitude, and other virtues—"

"Which are too microscopic to mention."

"—which are too microscopic to mention, as thou sayest, Lord. Yet, wouldst thou mind very much not making such vile, blasphemous, and mercenary utterances in the mortal presence of thy humble servant? It causeth unease."

"Oh it doth, doth it?"

Lando glanced back over his shoulder. He was pretty sure that at least half of the old man's "unease" derived from the imposing presence of the *Millennium Falcon* about fifty meters away across a clear expanse of sand, her full batteries trained in a protective circle to prevent a reenactment of the earlier ambush. In an inner pocket of his parka, her captain carried a transponder that kept the *Falcon*'s guns from sweeping within a couple of degrees of whoever wore it. This was a necessary precaution because Vuffi Raa was not at Battle Stations, inside.

He was programmed against it.

Somewhere back along the line, Lando had ceased resenting the little robot's programmed pacifism, and simply begun planning around it. In the right-hand outside slash pocket of his parka, he carried a second device with which he could trigger every weapon aboard his ship. Vuffi Raa could handle opening the boarding ramp as Lando ran for it, if anything went wrong. It wasn't against his built-in ethics to *save* a life. In fact, the droid had proved himself quite useful in that department already.

But to the problem at hand.

"Okay, old theologue, we'll change the subject: How did you know we had survived this morning, and why did you wait for us here, when you knew how sore I'd be about last night?"

Lando wanted to move back from the fire. About a thousand meters would do nicely. The cooking reptile, presently hovering somewhere between second-degree blistering and third-degree charring, smelled exactly like . . . like . . . well, he'd smelled more appetizing things attached to starship hulls while he was melting them off with live steam. Nonetheless, even the idea of the fire was warming; he hadn't felt really comfortable since he'd landed on that stupid clot of sand, not even aboard ship.

The elderly Singer opened his mouth. "Lord—"

"MASTER, HUMAN FORMS ARE MOVING BEHIND THOSE DUNES OVER THERE."

Mohs *jumped* at least a meter. The little droid's voice had come amplified through the ship's external loudhailers.

"Thanks, old cogwheel." Lando answered in a normal tone. *Millennium Falcon* had excellent hearing, and so did Vuffi Raa. He chuckled as the antique shaman regained his dignity.

"THEY APPEAR TO BE CARRYING THOSE CROSSBOW THINGS, MASTER."

"Mohs," the gambler said evenly, "I'm going to give you just thirty seconds to send your people away, and if they're not gone by then, you're going to swap places with that poor uncomfortable creature you're cooking. I ought to turn you in to the ISPCA—or at least the Epicures Club."

The Singer slowly cranked himself into a standing position, rattled off a few discordant stanzas—probably the Song of Strategic Withdrawal, Lando thought—then he sat again, turned the lizard on its stick, and addressed Lando.

"I have told them to depart, Lord. They came only for your protection. Now, if thy servant may have a few moments in which to fortify himself and attend to bodily needs, then we shall go to a place I know . . . where the Key may be used."

He seized the lizard by its head, pulled backward in a peeling motion, and tore it off the stick.

"Good heavens," Lando cried, gulping to control his upper gastrointestinal tract, "are you going to eat that thing?"

FIFTEEN MINUTES LATER, they were standing at the base of the pyramid. Even tilted backward as the wall before them was, it seemed to loom over them like some fantastic, infinitely high cliff, threatening to topple and bury them at any instant.

Vuffi Raa, having locked the spaceship up securely, joined them. The Toka Singer cast around, seeming to look for something recognizable on what appeared to be a featureless magenta wall. Finally, he stopped and pointed.

"*There,*" he said with finality, "about a meter downward, Lord." He folded his arms.

Lando rolled his eyes in exasperation. "Well, don't look at me. I'm the Key Bearer. *You're* the peon. You want a shovel, or will you perform this ceremony by hand?"

The old Toka was aghast. "*Me,* Lord? I am Singer of the—"

"One moment, gentlebeings," the robot said. "I can have it done before the two of you are finished arguing about it."

With that, his tentacles became a blur of motion. He resembled a shiny circular saw blade with a glowing red center. Sand poured upward in a wake behind him like an absurd dry fountain, and he was, as he had promised, soon finished.

"Escargot and Entropy!" Lando swore, struck by what he saw where Vuffi Raa had dug. Mohs was startled into silence, fell to his knees, and began chanting in a low, whimpery tone.

It shouldn't have been possible. Draw a line around your hand and rout out the material within the outline to a depth of approximately a centimeter. It can be done, and easily.

Now try it with the blade of an eggbeater. The human hand is, in its simplest representation, a two-dimensional form. Something requiring three dimensions can't be represented in the same way, not including its essential element—its three-dimensionality. Not unless that object is a Sharu artifact, and the people doing the bas relief are the Sharu themselves.

In some ways, it was rather as if the wall were transparent— which it was not—and the molded impression of the Key were buried yet visible inside it. But that wasn't truly the case. In another way, it was like seeing the Key itself, inside out, glued to the side of the pyramid—except that the "image" (or whatever it was) neither protruded from the surface nor was inset into it. The whole thing looked just as preposterous, just as impossible, as the Key itself, only more so.

And it hurt the eyes in just the same way.

Lando stepped back, blinked, and shook his head to uncross his eyes.

"All right, Mohs, suppose you tell us exactly what you know— what your Songs have to say, if anything—about what we're seeing and what happens if we use the Key in it."

The old man hummed a little to himself, at first as if to get the right pitch, then as if he knew the data only by rote and had to find the right place before he could start properly.

"This is the Great Lock, Lord. For generations uncounted, no Toka—no, nor any interloping stranger from the stars—has entered into the least of the many sacred shrines They left behind."

"Marvelous. We already knew that."

"Ah, yes, Lord, but now it is as it has been told: we shall enter, *without entering*. We shall walk the hallowed halls and yet they shall not echo to our feet. We shall travel to their farthest corners without going anywhere. We shall dream, therein, without sleeping, and know without learning. And, in due course and in Their time, we shall discover the Harp of the Mind; setting free the Harp, we shall set free the—"

"All right, all right. Politics again. Let me think this over a minute." He kicked experimentally against the bottom edge of the pyramid where it showed above the ground. There was no sound, no sensation of impact. It was like kicking at water or fine dust. "Vuffi Raa?"

"Yes, Master?"

"Don't call me master. What do *you* think about all this inter-loping business?" He took the Key from his pocket, turned it over in his hand, and thrust it back in his pocket.

"I think I'm long overdue for a lube job, Master, and would just as soon go home and—"

"I thought your lubricated areas were permanently sealed."

Was that a sheepish look in the droid's single eye? "Yes, Master, although I *did* get rather badly punctured and lost a good deal of . . . oh, I *can't* see any alternative to using the Key as Mohs suggests, Master. Much as I would like to."

Lando laughed. "I don't much like this enter-without-entering, sleep-without-dreaming stuff myself, truth to tell. Look here, Mohs, what else have you got for us—in plain language."

For the first time, the old man appeared to be uncomfortable on Rafa V. He had goosebumps all over him and was shivering with the cold—or something else.

"That is all that is known to the Toka, O Lord. It is all that the Song hath to tell. Thy humble and obedient servant confesseth, in his unworthy manner, that, were I thee, I would consider depart-ing this place without using the Key. All those numberless gen-erations, waiting, waiting . . . Why me, Lord? Why in my time?"

"Congratulations, Mohs, you've just joined the ranks of some great historical figures. That's what *they* wanted to know, and usually in about the same miserable, desperate tone of voice."

Again, Lando extracted the Key, looked it over grimly. "Well, there's no time like the present. Keep your eye open, Vuffi Raa. Mohs, what do your Songs say about using this thing?" He sup-pressed a shudder.

The old man gave a highly articulate shrug.

"That's what I like," Lando said, "help when I really need it. Here goes nothing!"

Which is precisely what happened. Lando pressed the Key against the lock in a position and at an angle that seemed most likely. It was a little like putting a ship in a bottle—at least it seemed that way at first. Then, in a manner that defied the eye and turned the stomach, the Key was in the lock.

The sun shone. The wind blew. The sand lay on the ground.

Lando looked at Mohs, who still had some of his shrug left. He used it. The gambler looked at Vuffi Raa. Vuffi Raa looked back at him. The robot and the elderly shaman exchanged glances. They both looked at Lando.

"Well, Mohs, I realize you've had breakfast, or whatever you call it, but I could use another bite. This seems to be a bust. What say we repair to the ship and—Vuffi Raa?"

As he had spoken to the old man, he'd turned to look at the robot.

Vuffi Raa had vanished.

"Mohs, did you see that—Mohs?"

The instant Mohs was out of Lando's field of view, *he* had disappeared, exactly like the droid, without a sound, without a movement.

The sun shone. The wind blew. The sand lay on the ground.

XIV

LANDO CALRISSIAN WAS NOT, ordinarily, a physically demonstrative young man. His livelihood and well-being depended on dexterity and control, the subtle, quick manipulation of delicate objects, the employment of fine and shaded judgment.

He smashed a fist into the pyramid wall.

And reeled with surprise. Where, before, contact with the building had been much like ducking one's head into a stiff wind—elusive but unquestionably real—now the experience had taken on the aspect of fantasy.

His hand passed into the wall and disappeared as if the structure were a hologram. He withdrew the hand, looked it over, flexed it. He inspected the wall without touching it: the material itself was featureless, seemingly impervious to time, weather, the puny scratching and chipping of man. Yet there was a fine patina of dust, a film of oil or grease that seemed to coat everything within the planet's atmosphere. Lando could plainly see a single fine hair, neither his own nor one of Mohs'—perhaps that of some animal that had wandered by or one that had been borne on the wind until it stuck here.

He thrust his hand into the solid-looking wall again. Again it disappeared up to the wrist. He stepped forward until he lost sight of his elbow, shuddered, backed away. And, again, his hand, his arm, were intact, unharmed.

Lando Calrissian was nothing if not a cautious individual. Someone else might have plunged through the wall in pursuit of

Vuffi Raa and Mohs, for it was clearly where they'd gone. But to what fate? If your best friend zipped from sight into a trapdoor in the floor, would you follow him onto the steel spikes below?

Lando pushed his hand into the wall again, meeting no more resistance than before. It was as if the wall weren't there—except as far as the eyes were concerned. He closed his own, and felt around. There wasn't enough breeze outside that he could tell about the wall's effect on air currents. The temperature felt the same. He was free to wiggle his fingers, clench and unclench his fist. He snapped his fingers, felt the snap—but couldn't hear it outside the wall.

Thrusting in a second hand, he felt the first. Both felt quite normal. He clapped them, feeling the sensation, missing the usually resultant noise. Odd. He placed his right hand around his left wrist, slid the hand slowly up the arm until it reappeared, much like a hand and arm emerging from water—except that this surface was vertical. He stooped, picked up a handful of sand, reinserted his arms, poured sand from one hand to the other.

He pulled his arms out, threw the sand away . . .

. . . and stepped through the wall.

Sometimes you have to take a gamble.

HE HADN'T THOUGHT of that before.

Old man Mohs, ancient and revered High Singer of the Rafa Toka, had been leaning against the pyramid wall when the Key Bearer inserted the Key. Suddenly, it had been as if the wall weren't there, and, in the short fall into darkness that resulted, his garment had nearly been lost.

All his long, long life, Mohs had put up with the chilly draft that found its way beneath the simple wraparound. Now, even in the darkness, even in this terrifying, holy place, it had occurred to him that he could take a long free end of the cloth, tuck it up between his legs, and eliminate the draft.

Why hadn't he thought of that before? Why hadn't anybody

else among his people? He found himself thinking cynically that
this little piece of information alone was worth a hundred silly
Songs about—no! That's blasphemy! He cringed, trying to peer
into the utter darkness around him, fearful of . . . of . . . what?

He thought about that.

He seemed to be doing a *lot* of thinking in the past few minutes.

Finally, he decided—in what may have been the first real decision he'd ever made for himself—to wait until his eyes adjusted.
He sat—on some firm, resilient surface—enjoying his newfound
warmth.

And the newfound working of his mind.

It had been hours!

Four hours, twenty-three minutes, fifty-five seconds, to be precise, by Vuffi Raa's built-in chronometer. He never had to see the
time, he simply knew. The trouble with built-in faculties, he reflected, such as being able to pilot a starship, for example, is that
they denied or dulled the urge to acquire new ones for oneself.
Better to be like a human being, he thought, without innate programming, with the ability and necessity—

A human being? What was he thinking?

He'd been approximately—no, exactly—seventeen centimeters from touching it with his nearest tentacle, and yet, when
Lando had activated the Key, suddenly, he, Vuffi Raa, was here
(wherever here was) on the other side of the wall.

Five hours, twenty-nine minutes, thirty-one seconds.

Exactly *what* here was, Vuffi Raa thought rather ungrammat-
ically, was a good question in itself. He'd felt strangely isolated,
lonely for quite a while, and, oddly, that feeling had preoccupied
him so thoroughly that he'd failed to examine his surroundings
with much enthusiasm. The feeling hadn't gone away. It had gotten worse, much worse. Now, it was necessary to investigate, if
only to take his badly shaken mind off his emotions.

Of the presumed-to-exist inside wall of the pyramid, he could see no evidence. He stood in a brightly lit corridor, seemingly kilometers between him and the ceiling. His doppler radar, not his strongest sense, couldn't reach quite as far as the roof, although he got some tantalizing echoes from it.

The area he occupied was a longish rectangle, five meters by perhaps fifty. Behind him was a semitransparent wall through which he could see what appeared to be a vast circular drum, several stories high, much like a fuel storage tank, yet made of the same plastic-appearing material as everything else here. In front of him, a smaller circular subchamber filled the corridor from wall to wall, yet he could see beyond it with several of his senses, knew it divided his chamber precisely in half.

To the right and left were similar, exactly parallel corridors, "visible" through walls much as the one behind him, and identical to the corridor he occupied except that they lacked the smaller circular "storage tank."

He turned left.

As far as he went along the wall, there was no exit. The available space grew smaller and narrower as he approached the circularity. Finally, he stopped, retraced his steps, and took the right-hand direction. This time, near the angle of the wall and the tank, he found a permeable area. He stepped through into the next corridor. The predominating light was blue, as it had been in the chamber he had left, but here it was slightly brighter. He crossed the corridor, found another "soft" spot in the wall, went through into a third chamber, identical to the second.

The fourth chamber was shaped differently—five-sided, but not regularly so. The only permeability was in the far right-hand wall, a very short one, forcing him to take a right turn. The next chamber was the mirror image of the last, then a series of rectangular chambers began again.

He kept walking, lonely, and, for the first time in his life, really afraid.

Seven hours, sixteen minutes, forty-four seconds.

FROM THE INSIDE, the pyramid was transparent.

That was the first thing Lando noticed. Outside, he could see the sun shining, the reddish color of the sand, a few scrappy shrubs, and, comfortingly close (although farther away than he would have liked), the *Millennium Falcon* sat patiently awaiting his return.

He hoped she wouldn't have to wait very long.

It was difficult to judge the thickness of the wall. It was not quite perfectly transparent, but shaded a very pale bluish tint. Behind him was an empty chamber—and he realized that there was a good chance his eyes were being tricked somehow. Not a hundred meters away, he could see one of the farther walls of the five-sided building, more sandy desert beyond. The walls came to a point perhaps two hundred meters overhead.

The trouble with all that was that the building was several kilometers in any dimension you chose to measure.

The walls, then, were sophisticated viewing devices, conveying the illusion that the building was much smaller—human-scaled, in fact—than it really was.

He called out: *"Vuffi Raa! Where are you? Mohs? Answer me!"*

There wasn't even a decent echo. He—

What was *that*? Embedded in the wall he'd come through, stuck like a fly in amber, was the Key. He reached for it—and barked his fingers badly. The wall could have been made of solid glass, and the Key was at least a meter beyond his reach. It had been his way—and Vuffi Raa's, apparently, and Mohs'—inside the pyramid.

He looked around the featureless chamber he occupied. From wall to wall, a smooth reflective floor stretched, devoid of furniture or fixtures. It was rather like being in a large, deserted warehouse. Through the walls, the sky was a slightly more brilliant blue than it had really been.

The desert was a trifle darker: red and blue make purple. The transparency had another odd effect: it made everything outside seem very far away, subtly shrunken by perspective and refraction. Perhaps the walls were curved minutely. The *Falcon* almost looked like a model, a child's toy.

Perhaps he'd better find another way out.

There had better be another way out.

GROWN CONSIDERABLY MORE DESPERATE, Vuffi Raa stopped to rest.

He was internally powered; a microfusion pile that was practically inexhaustible burned within him at all times, requiring only a minimal amount of mass to keep itself (and Vuffi Raa) going.

But the little droid was tired.

In a lifetime vastly longer than his current master would have found comfortable to contemplate, the robot could not recall ever feeling lonelier or more isolated. There, in that endless series of empty chambers, it was like being a piece in a huge meaningless game, shuffled from one spot to the next by vast, uncaring, uncommunicative fingers.

The little droid was afraid.

He'd come a considerable distance. Six featureless rectilinear rooms, after the one he'd first appeared in, with its almost transparent circular tank in the middle. Then another tankroom. The four empties, the last of which had forced him into a sharp left-hand turn. The next room had had a circularity, although there had been a narrow space to get by it. Then another empty room, another left-hand turn, three more flat blue chambers, and another tank.

The pattern had repeated itself, again and again, the robot growing more disconsolate with every fruitless turn and passage. This didn't even seem like the same planet—the same reality—let alone the same building he'd somehow accidentally entered.

He wandered onward.

Thirteen hours, forty-five minutes, twenty-eight seconds had passed.

Another right-hand turn (the first since the initial one), two more lefts, and another right. Two more lefts. And always the same stark, empty, blue-tinted rooms, the occasional empty circular columns in their centers, more left turns, fewer rights. How long could this go on?

Nineteen hours, eleven minutes, four seconds.

LOST IN THOUGHT, Mohs didn't notice that he couldn't see. It didn't matter much to him. He didn't have anyplace to go at the moment. There wasn't any hurry. He'd only been here for a minute or two, and before another minute or two went by, the Bearer and the Emissary would come and get him.

Or not.

It wasn't very important, really. He'd just realized, thinking about his loincloth once again, that if he took the long, rectangular strip of cloth, pulled it around end to end, but twisted it a half turn before joining the ends together, he'd get a very odd result: an object with only one side and one edge. How that could be, when everything had at least two sides, *had* to have, he wasn't sure. There must be some important secret to this cloth shape, he reasoned, some hint at the fundamental nature of the universe. But the secret kept eluding him, there in the dark, seemed just barely out of reach. It was annoying.

He pondered the question, picked at it, unraveled it like the homespun fabric his single garment had been made from. It wasn't easy going, but the more he thought, the simpler things seemed to become.

Presently, they became very simple, indeed.

Mohs laughed.

———

Lando heard somebody laugh.

He turned, and there was Mohs—where he had not been a moment before—squatting on his heels, one arm across his naked lap, the other braced between chin and knee. Forgotten on the floor before him lay three or so meters of gray, aged loincloth, laid out in a circle and twisted into a giant, floppy Möbius cylinder. The old man's back was toward Lando.

"Mohs!" Lando cried. "Where did you disappear to?"

The old man chuckled without turning. "Apparently the same place that you did, Captain. What time is it?"

An odd question from a naked savage, thought Lando. He glanced at his watch. "I'd say it's been perhaps twenty minutes since you vanished through the wall. What have you been doing all this time, just sitting?"

"What would you suggest I do, Captain?" The old man rose, pivoted on a heel to face Lando. "I thought it better than getting lost. You can't see your hand in front of your face in here."

"Good heavens, man! What's happened to your eyes?"

The old man blinked, lids wiped down over eyeballs that might as well have been opaque white glass.

"My eyes? There's nothing wrong with my eyes, Captain." The ancient Singer smiled. "What's wrong with yours, can't you see the darkness?"

Vuffi Raa wasn't lost; he simply didn't know where he was.

Since he'd first popped through the pyramid wall, he'd wandered through this strange, blue-lit maze for what seemed like days, taking pathways that offered no alternative. The only choice he'd had was to stay where he was or go where he could, and he'd always preferred action to inaction.

He'd taken four right turns (each carrying him through two of the oddly shaped rooms), and six left turns, not necessarily in that order. Before very long, he'd wind up exactly where he'd begun, no closer to any meaningful destination, no wiser con-

cerning what this rat-run was intended and constructed for, and
no likelier to find his friends.

Just a machine, Lando had said once. Vuffi Raa wondered if
his master knew how lonely a machine could get. Vuffi Raa hadn't
known, not until the last few hours. Twenty-seven of them, to be
precise, plus thirty-six minutes, eleven seconds. He was three
rooms past one of those with the small circular subchambers.
That meant he ought to be entering a fourth, which would force
him to take a left turn. After that, one more left, four more rooms,
and he'd be back to where he'd started from.

And a lot more discouraged, in the bargain.

He found the soft spot in the wall, slithered through. Sure
enough, none of the walls within this place—including the one
he'd just passed through—would let him pass except the left-
hand one. He took it, the light dimmed a little as it always did in
rooms with circular tanks, and he walked automatically the
length of the room, past the tank, and to the end wall.

And banged right into it. It wouldn't let him pass.

Well, here was something new. Oddly enough, it failed to
hearten him, or even relieve the tedium that had become his only
companion. Had he been a mammal, he'd have stood there,
scratched his head, folded his arms in exasperation, and sworn.

He stood there, raised a tentacle to his chromium carapace,
scratched at it absently while folding two more tentacles in disgust.

"Glitch!" he said, and meant it.

Exploring the unprecedented chamber, he traveled along the
left wall, squeezed back through the narrow opening past the
circular tank. The short wall through which he'd come was totally impermeable. He began feeling his way along the half of the
other long wall he could reach before he had to make a circuit of
the tank again—and made another discovery.

Up until now, the rounded sides of the features he chose to call
tanks were just as solid and impassable as any of the other walls.
This one was different. He could stick a tentacle through it. For

lack of any better course, he followed the tentacle into the circular area, where, on one spot along the curved inner side, there was a deep purplish glow. As he expected, the "tank" wouldn't let him back out, so he felt the glowing section carefully. Yes, it, too, was permeable.

He stepped through into a rectilinear room, exactly like the tankless blue ones he'd spent the last day wandering through.

Only these were a brilliant scarlet color.

One, two, three, four. He should be between two of the blue tankrooms, now, but there wasn't any tank in here. Five, six, seven—something odd. The far wall seemed to tug at him, and the red glow was a little fainter here. He backed up and thought.

Thirty-two hours, fifteen minutes, forty-two seconds had passed since he'd gotten into this mess. He didn't much care, now, how he got out of it.

He let the wall pull him toward itself and stepped through . . .

LANDO SAT BY the transparent pyramid wall, his head in his hands. The last half hour had had its shocks, but this was the worst of all. Where the old Singer's eyes had been, there were now a pair of deep ugly wounds—healing rapidly, it was true, and showing no signs of infection, just as the old man showed no signs of pain. But he was blind, horribly, hideously blind.

And happy about it.

"Captain," said Mohs, "please do not be distressed. There is nothing free in this life. I seem to have exchanged my eyes for a certain understanding. I now know what I was: a retarded savage who could see but did not know what it was he saw. Now I am an intelligent, civilized man, who happens to be blind. Do you not think it a fair trade?"

Lando grunted, poked a finger idly at a tiny line of dust gathered in the corner between wall and floor. Something tiny sparkled there, like a speck of metal, a fleck of mirror silvering. Curious, Lando brushed the dust away from it. It was better than answering Mohs, either truthfully or insincerely. *Nothing* could make up for blindness.

"Further, Captain. My newfound reasoning capacities seem to serve me in the stead of eyes to some extent. I can tell that you are sitting to my left, turned mostly to the wall, poking with a finger in the corner. I believe I know this by deducing from the sounds you make, what I know of your personality and habits—it's quite as if I could see you."

"I'm happy for you, Mohs," Lando mumbled irritably. Suddenly, the minute sparkly bit grew larger, and Lando drew his hand back abruptly. "Son of a—look at this!"

Not noticing what he'd said to a blind man, Lando watched the corner. There was a spider there, a tiny one, very shiny, very fast. It skittered about frantically, trying to escape Lando. It couldn't have been much more than three millimeters in diameter.

Lando reached down, unafraid, let the spider race up his thumb, turned the thumb down into the palm of his other hand . . .

And watched a nearly microscopic Vuffi Raa, accelerated to sixty times normal speed, trip over his lifeline and go sprawling.

XV

No one had ever accused Vuffi Raa of being stupid.

Of course he'd recognized the hundred-meter giant looming over him, the instant he'd popped out of the final red-lit chamber and through the inside wall of the pyramid. It was his master, and what surprised him was the feeling that, whatever their current predicament, he was home.

Apparently, Lando grasped the weird situation, too. He'd held his thumb down on the floor in front of Vuffi Raa, keeping it amazingly still for the full minute the little—very little—droid required to climb its length.

For his part, Vuffi Raa was very careful: the thumbnail at this scale was rough and full of convenient handholds, but the flesh seemed soft and spongy. He went gently, using all five tentacles and spreading them, outward and flat, to distribute his mass. One misstep would cruelly pierce his master's flesh like a needle and, perhaps, precipitate the robot into disaster.

Not that that wasn't the situation now.

With incredible slow steadiness, Lando had raised the robot up to his eye level, then across his mountainous chest, over to the other hand. Vuffi Raa tumbled down into the waiting palm, righted himself, and looked up into the giant eye that peered down at him.

"Master! What a mess! What are we going to do?"

"EEEVVVUUUFFFEEE EEEUUURRRAAAHHH," responded

Lando, taking at least twenty seconds to do it, his voice low and thunderous. A human being in Vuffi Raa's position might not have been able to hear what Lando said—the little droid's range of hearing was impressive—but he'd certainly have felt it.

Now the robot understood his master's unnatural rock-steadiness. There seemed to be some difference in their perception of time, correlative to the difference in their sizes. Lando was living at a vastly slower rate than Vuffi Raa. He considered the problem for what would have seemed a millisecond to his master, then gave forth a series of loud chirps, spaced evenly over about a minute's time, each burst carefully shaped and calculated to blur with the ones before and after into something the giant could follow:

"*Can't understand you, Master,*" Lando heard a tiny voice say. "*Can you hear me?*"

Lando wasn't stupid, either. He could see how quickly, jerkily, Vuffi Raa was moving about in his hand, and figured out that time—or at least metabolism—was flowing differently for each of them. He even had a good idea how Vuffi Raa was managing to communicate with him, although none whatsoever as to how he could communicate back.

He decided on short words: "Yes."

Vuffi Raa received this as "EEEYYYEEEAAASSSSS," but the part of him that was a high-powered computer quickly squashed it all together (as it had eventually learned to do when Lando called him by name) and formulated a brief reply—although it would take a much longer time to transmit:

"*Ask Mohs about this.*"

"OOOGGGAAAIIIEEE!"

Giant-to-giant: "I say, Mohs old fellow, what does your new-found cogitational capacity tell you about *this* distressing turn of events? I believe I've got the galaxy's smallest droid here, but I don't think he's appreciating the distinction very much."

Wrapping the loincloth back around his middle by feel, the

old shaman shuffled up beside the gambler, cocked an ear over the tiny robot in lieu of peering down at him with ruined eyes, and thought his answer over for a moment.

"I do not know of any Song which speaks of such a thing as this. He can hear us, can he not?"

"*Yes,*" came the small, clear reply, almost as quickly as Mohs has asked the question, and long before Lando could respond. This method of communication seemed to work satisfactorily for the organic giants, Lando realized, but it must be agonizing unto tears for the tiny speeded-up droid, each word requiring many seconds to assemble, then the even more annoying molasses-like wait for the humans, with their slower reaction time, to answer.

"Captain," the old man said, seemingly unwilling to address a spider-sized machine directly, "I can see—in a manner of speaking—no intelligent alternative but to go on with our search for the Harp. We can do nothing for your friend here. Perhaps some solution lies ahead of us."

"*Agreed,*" Vuffi Raa said before Lando had a chance to think about it. Meanwhile, the miniature automaton had also had time to think to become thoroughly fascinated with the examination of his giant master's hand. The epidermis was shingled like a shale field, and the fine ridges were like furrows made by a plow. Lando's pulse was a quiet, steady earthquake every few minutes. Open pores lay scattered about like gopher holes.

Finally, long after Vuffi Raa had tired of his explorations:

"AAAIII EEEGGGIIIEEESSS EEEIIIYYYOOOUUURRR EEERRRAAAIIITTT."

Eventually, Vuffi Raa managed to convey a question about travel arrangements. He was willing to make his exploration of the building on foot, as the humans intended to do, but his own far greater rate of operation would be more than offset by his size and the (to him) roughness of the terrain. Accordingly, he suggested that he ride, somehow, and asked diffidently how and where.

"I've always rather fancied an earring," Lando told the surprised robot. "D'you think you could manage it without tearing off my earlobe?" That would make communications a bit easier, and there would be little chance of Vuffi Raa's getting injured or dropped, since Lando would be inclined to be careful about injuring his own head.

"Captain," Mohs asked, once that had been settled, "there is supposed to be a way out of this chamber, somewhere near the center. Can you see it?"

For the relatively short time they'd been there, Lando's attention had been directed outward, through the transparent walls. Then it had all gone to Mohs and the pitiable condition of his eyes, and finally to Vuffi Raa. Now he took a good hard look around. It wasn't easy: the floor was glossy, as if it were transparent glass over some darker base. He guided the old Singer toward the center of the room, approximately fifty meters away, the little droid clinging with all five tentacles to his ear.

Before them lay a downward-slanting ramp set neatly into the floor, flush, without guardrails or other embellishment. Lando thought they hadn't noticed it before because of this, and the fact they'd been looking straight across its foreshortened length to the reflective surface on the other side.

It was strangely dim in the middle of the room, beneath the pyramid's peak. The brightly shining sun outside lent an eerie contrast, which got on Lando's nerves.

"Well, friends, shall we?" Lando asked no one in particular.

No one replied.

He shrugged, took a step—remembering, once it was too late, that this sort of thing was what had gotten him into . . . well, this sort of thing in the first place. As soon as it rested on the gently downward-slanting surface, his foot began to slide forward of its own accord. He gave a hop, his other foot joined the first, and he found himself moving without walking—just as Mohs' prophetic Song had had it—on a sort of glassy, featureless elevator.

He looked behind him. Mohs was in the rear, expression a bit unsettled—apparently not very happy to realize his Songs had come true.

Well, Lando thought, are any of us ever, really?

The place that they had entered was broad, perhaps ten meters wide, and as they settled down through the floor and the tunnel seemed to level off, they saw that the roof overhead was about the same distance—ten meters—from the moving floor. The walls went straight up, tipped over into an arch overhead.

At first the walls were featureless, the same impression as above of transparency over darkness. The floor showed no signs of mechanical moving parts; an object placed upon it simply flowed along at the same rate Lando, Mohs, and Vuffi Raa were traveling. Whether the floor itself traveled with them, they were unable to determine.

"EEEIIIUUU OOOGGGAAAIII, EEEVVVUUUHHHVVVIII EEERRRAAAHHH?"

Vuffi Raa clung to Lando's ear, watching, measuring, trying to do his part—since someone else was carrying his minuscule weight. Yet most of his mind was on the matter of his size. Assuming it was he who had diminished—never mind how or that the disparity was supposed to violate several laws of physics—he certainly didn't want to spend the rest of his life that way. Droids live a long, long time.

On the other tentacle, suppose Lando and their native companion had somehow *grown*, violating different laws. Vuffi Raa didn't think he'd have to ask them how they'd feel about that.

His contemplations were interrupted by the part of him that was watching. He gave an internal, mechanical sigh as he prepared himself for another of the tedious attempts at communication:

"Master, the corridor's beginning to curve."

"Not so loud, Vuffi Raa! Curve?" Lando glanced around. He couldn't see it; it must be very gradual. A thought occurred to him: "What's the rate? At some point, it's got to bend back on itself, and we should see the junction—for whatever good *that* does us."

"*I don't think so. . . . It never fully leveled out. . . . Starting a gradual downward spiral.*"

"So? At what rate?" Lando repeated. The old Toka Singer listened to this exchange as it went on, a strange look on his blinded face. "What's the apparent diameter of the spiral?"

"*Whose scale?*"

Lando chuckled. "A good question. Make it mine, if you don't mind. I've got to figure it out, haven't I?"

Vuffi Raa refrained from saying that Lando hadn't been much good so far at figuring out anything—and only partly because communications were such a chore. Instead, he simply divided everything his sensors told him by approximately sixty.

"*Ten klicks at current rate. Drops a hundred meters every thirty kilometers.*"

"Can you tell how fast this thing is carrying us?"

"*About twenty kph. One full spiral every one-twenty-third of a planetary revolution.*"

The journey went on and on. Hours passed.

It was Vuffi Raa who first noticed the changes in the walls.

"*Master. Please observe that something is visible.*"

"I see it." Lando peered through the transparency. Where before there had been inky blackness, now some form and structure could be seen, like a highway cut through a mountain pass. "We're out of the pyramid! Below it!"

XVI

THEY TRAVELED THROUGH the heart of the planet.

This was not precisely true, as Vuffi Raa was already pointing out, but it was a metaphor that suited Lando.

The geological strata they were seeing dated, according to the little droid, from the beginnings of life on Rafa V. Beds of stone formed by tiny microscopic creatures living in seas that no longer existed on the ancient, dried-up sphere alternated with slabs of solidified lava from volcanic eruptions. Vuffi Raa's fine vision—and perhaps the fact that he was so small—enabled him to see and describe the smallest details through the transparent glass.

"And here we see . . . Master . . . the evidence of the first cellular colonies . . . the precursors of multicelled animals."

"Don't call me master, especially when you're lecturing me. Do you want a bite of this, Mohs?"

Lando had delved into the pockets of his survival parka for water and condensed rations. Vuffi Raa hadn't any need of them, but the old man surprised Lando by accepting only a small portion from the plastic canteen.

Otherwise, the ancient High Singer had been strangely quiet for hours, watching the walls, peering ahead into a gloom that was something other than darkness, listening to Vuffi Raa. How much the old man understood of the droid's paleontological dissertations, he had no way of guessing.

"But if we're seeing the slow, steady progress of microscopic life," Lando asked Vuffi Raa, "doesn't that mean we must be gaining altitude again?"

"On the contrary . . . Master . . . the corridor leveled out some time ago . . . and straightened. . . . We're traveling in a diagonal upthrust formation."

For some reason, this bothered Lando. He wished the robot had kept him informed on the shape and direction of their travel. More, this was almost as if . . . as if . . .

"They chose this route deliberately, didn't they? So we'd see what we're seeing!"

"They, Captain?" Mohs spoke up, surprising Lando. The old man had long since discovered that he could travel on a moving sidewalk just as easily by sitting down as standing. Lando had joined him, and they were sitting a few feet apart now. Lando had been thinking about taking a nap before the walls grew transparent and the geology lectures began. He was still thinking about it.

"You know perfectly well who I mean. There's some purpose to all this, isn't there?"

"If so, Captain, the Songs do not—"

"I'll bet they don't! Mohs, the primary purpose of those Songs of yours was to make sure somebody, someday, wound up sitting precisely where you are."

"So I, too, had surmised."

Lando searched through his pockets, found a cigarette. He didn't smoke much at all, and when he did, he preferred cigars. Whoever had packed this parka—an Imperial surplus model— had left very little missing. Lando lit a dried-up cigarette with a tiny electric coil built into one sleeve of the jacket.

"The question, then, is *why*. What's so flaming important about your seeing all these rocks and suchlike?"

The old man lifted his sightless head. "There must be a better word than 'seeing,' Captain."

"Great heavens, man, I'd almost—" He *had* almost forgotten about Mohs' eyes. At least the hideous wounds were healing.

Yet Mohs had not been moving like a newly blinded man, had not been stumbling and groping. He had peered at the walls, down the tunnel, listened to Vuffi Raa as if he could—

"What do you mean, 'a *better* word,' Mohs? Is there some sense better than seeing?"

The Toka Singer swiveled himself where he sat on the floor and faced Lando. He drew in a deep breath, then let it out.

"It would appear so, Captain. You are carrying the Emissary on your right ear. You have a container of water in your left hand, the remains of a food-stick in your right. Your coat is unfastened; the shirt beneath has a missing fastener, second from the top. You hold a burning weed-stick in the same hand which holds the canteen. It is approximately one-third consumed."

Lando was as impressed as he ever was by anything. "What color are my eyes?"

"They are the color of deceit, the color of avarice, the color of—"

"Enough, enough! Don't go getting poetic on us. Somehow you are 'seeing' all these things. Any idea how: clairvoyance, telepathy, psychometry . . ."

"I do not know the meaning of these words, Captain. I can hear the water gurgling, the weed-stick crackling, the tones within your voice and that of the Emissary. I smell things and feel vibrations in the floor. Here it is warm, there it is cold. Pictures form themselves in my mind. My remaining senses assemble information which tells me everything my eyes once did."

"Pretty good trick. How many fingers am I—*ow!* Take it easy, Vuffi Raa, that's my earlobe you're destroying!"

"Apologies . . . Master. . . . Observe the walls. . . . There are the first large creatures to appear on this world."

Vuffi Raa's method of communication was far from perfect, but it didn't fail to convey his excitement. Lando wondered what was so terrific about the fossils of old marine animals. Why, they looked like ordinary urchins, starfish, and the like. Perhaps that was what had moved the little robot. These things weren't unlike him in their rough anatomy: five-sided, five-limbed.

That didn't account for Mohs' excitement: "Behold! Look upon the very ancestors of Those whose name it is not wise to speak in this place!"

"You mean the Sharu?" Lando said defiantly. He hated mumbo jumbo, even in a good cause, and this wasn't.

"Yes, Captain," the old man sighed resignedly. "I mean the Sharu."

They were nothing more than a bunch of formerly slimy starfish, no matter *whose* ancestors they were.

THE HOURS WORE ON, Vuffi Raa and Mohs alternating in rapture over what they observed embedded in the walls. Lando yawned, slid over onto the moving floor surface, arranged the hood of his parka comfortably, and did a little sliding of his own, in the direction of sleep.

The floor was solid, but resilient, and it was warm.

Even in his sleep, the science lectures wouldn't leave him alone. He recapitulated the slow, steady progress—boring every step of the way—from the tiny, disgusting single-celled inhabitants of the planet's soupy primeval waters, through the first colony organisms, up into multicelled animals, and from there to things with backbones and legs that eventually crawled out on the land.

Oddly, the further these imaginary entities got, climbing the tree of evolution, the vaguer and more nebulous they grew in Lando's mind. Queer, shadowy shapes beat at one another with broken tree limbs. Even more intangible figures took those tree limbs, scratched the dirt with them, and planted the first seeds. By the time the ancestors of the Sharu were building tiny, crude cities, it was almost as if the cities built themselves and were inhabited by invisible citizens.

Continents were explored, migrations carried out. Wars were won and lost, with rapidly increasing technology. Discoveries were made, more wars fought. The pre-Sharu touched the boundaries of space in primitive explosive-powered machines, depositing the first installment of the junk the *Millennium Falcon* had had to fly through, getting to Rafa V.

All the while, Lando experienced a growing sense of unease, some vague pain or nagging that made his sleep less restful than it might have been. He'd had no idea, all day, where they were going. There wasn't any choice in the matter for him: he had to find the Mindharp, and then figure out how to get out of the tunnel, away from the ruins, off the stinking planet, and, ultimately, clear of the Rafa once and for all.

They'd never catch *him* bringing mynocks into the Rafa System again!

Or anything else.

The sense of unease grew, gradually metamorphosing into something resembling real pain. Lando tossed and turned in his sleep, but kept on dreaming.

The ancestors of the Sharu had built roads and buildings that wouldn't be unfamiliar to any civilized inhabitant of the galaxy. They had traveled in powered vehicles, eventually spread themselves to other planets of the system. At first they endured the harsh conditions on some of these globes, living in domes or underground. Finally, they had begun transforming them into replicas of their own home planet.

It hadn't always been a desert. There had been oceans and trees and lakes and snow-covered mountains. There had been moisture in the air, and weather. How long ago all that had been, the part of Lando that did the dreaming wasn't prepared to guess. How long does it take for the seas to go away?

Gradually, however, as their technology surpassed that which was currently available in Lando's civilization, the shapes of buildings changed, the roads disappeared. The unseen entities who were becoming the Sharu fought no more wars, but struggled, instead, with the environment. No rock, whirling in its independent orbit around the Rafa sun, was too insignificant to be altered into a garden. To what precise purpose became increasingly unclear. Cities ceased to resemble anything that made sense. The first of the gigantic plastic structures appeared—on Rafa V. Then they appeared on the other planets, as well.

Taken altogether, they were nightmarish things. Lando squirmed in his sleep, flailed his arms, and sweated. Every surface and angle was somehow *wrong,* things were added that seemed without function, passageways tapered out into tiny pipelines, hair-fine fractures became vast thoroughfares, in no logical order. The seas began to vanish, red sand replacing landscape everywhere. Had something gone wrong with the Sharu environment, or did they like it better the new way, plan it?

Lando sank deeper into a dreamless, pain-filled sleep. His last thought was a question: would this passage funnel down until the inexorably moving floor ground them into tiny pieces?

LANDO WOKE UP.

Somewhere, for a fraction of a second, he had the feeling that everything made sense after all. Then the feeling went away and left him with a terrible lingering headache.

"Vuffi Raa, are you awake? You're going to have to find another perch for a while. My whole head hurts!" He rolled over on his back from the curled-up position he'd taken in the night.

"Masteryou'reawakeatlasthowdoyoufeel?"

He sat up—a sudden blast of pain hit him and he settled back again for a moment. "Take it a little slower, will you?" He lifted a hand to his ear. "Hop down a minute while I get rid of this headache."

He felt a feather touch his palm. The pain subsided. Bringing his hand down, he looked at Vuffi Raa. Something was funny, but he couldn't place it in his present groggy state.

The walls rolled by, this time showing discarded metal and

plastic containers, parts of machinery and electronics frozen into the geological matrix. How long does a civilization have to last before its radios and televisions become fossils?

"Now, what was it you were saying, little fellow?"

"Merely . . . greeted . . . you. . . . Asked . . . how . . . you . . . feel."

"Lousy, but thanks for asking. Anything interesting happen in the night?" He scrounged around for a cigarette, started thinking about which of the ration bars to eat for breakfast.

"It . . . is . . . nighttime . . . now . . . outside . . . Master. . . . You . . . slept . . . through . . . the . . . day."

"I don't see that it makes all that much difference, down here. Where's Mohs?" Lando had glanced around, up and down the tunnel, and hadn't seen the old man. Perhaps he'd—

"What . . . Master?"

"We seem to be having some difficulty understanding one another this—er, afternoon. I said, where's Mohs, did he wander off somewhere?"

"Master . . . there is something I must tell you."

Lando felt a vague alarm. "What's that, old watch-movement?"

"I believe . . . from measurements . . . that you're shrinking."

"What?"

"Everything is shrinking. . . . The tunnel grows narrower by the kilometer. . . . You have shrunk just enough that my weight upon you causes pain. . . . The previous rate at which I communicated is too fast. . . . We are nearing each other's size and time-passage."

"Which could mean just as well that you're growing, did you ever think of that?" Lando examined the tiny robot in his hand. Let's see, he'd estimated Vuffi Raa's previous size at perhaps three millimeters. Yes, no question of it, he was very nearly twice that size now and his minuscule weight was actually perceptible in Lando's hand.

"Yes. . . . I considered it. . . . I think you are shrinking."

"Well, I think you're growing. What about Mohs?"

"Who . . . Master. . . . Who is Mohs?"

"Vuffi Raa, don't do this to me! Mohs—the High Singer of the Toka—the old guy who *led* us here! *Mohs!*"

There was a long, long pause. It must have been vastly longer to the speeded-up droid. Finally:

"Master . . . I recall no Mohs. . . . Are you certain you feel all right?"

XVII

A S THE TUNNEL carried them along, they argued.

"Who was it that we met in the bar, who sang the Songs that pointed the way to Rafa V?"

"Why, Master, something that Rokur Gepta said must have given you the clue, and you guessed. Very good guessing, Master, highly commendable."

"Well, then, damnit, what about that crowd at the port. Who had been leading the singing?"

"Why, no one, Master. It was simply community chanting, spontaneous on the part of the natives."

"Arghhh! Okay, why did we land at the pyramid—never mind, I know: it was the biggest building on the planet. Tell me this: if there wasn't any Mohs, who ambushed us, shot you full of holes, and carried me off to the life-orchard to die?"

"The natives, of course, Master. But there wasn't any chief or head witch doctor or whatever. The Toka don't have enough social structure for that."

"Or to build crossbows? Look, Vuffi Raa, I *couldn't* have made up that part about eating a lizard, I just *couldn't*."

"What do you expect me to say, Master?"

"I expect you to say that this is all an elaborate practical joke, and that you're sorry and will be a good little droid from now on." Lando shook the plastic package. There weren't any cigarettes left. "Life is just full of annoyances these days."

Vuffi Raa stood on the floor by Lando's knee. He was five or six centimeters tall, by then, looking very much like one of those tropical spiders that eat birds.

"I wish I could do that," he squeaked, no longer coding his messages in pulses. He had to make a conscious effort to slow them down for his still-gigantic master. "What reason would I have to lie, Master?"

Lando crushed the pack, started to throw it away, then, looking around him at the clean, uncluttered tunnel, thought better of it and put it in his pocket. "I'm not saying you're lying, Vuffi Raa. One of us is wrong, that's all. By the Eternal Core, I can describe the old man to you in the finest detail, from the tattoo on his wrinkled forehead to the dirt on his wrinkled feet!"

Vuffi Raa said nothing to that. He simply sat there growing—or watching his master shrink. That was something else they hadn't been able to agree about, but they'd tired of arguing about it.

They were also tired of asking one another when the journey would be over. Lando extracted the deck of *sabacc* cards he carried with him, began to shuffle them. Vuffi Raa looked on with interest.

"Did you know, old pentapod, that these things were once used for telling fortunes?" He shuffled the deck again, cut it, and began laying the cards out on the floor.

"Highly irrational and unscientific, Master."

"Don't call me master. I know what you mean, though—except that sometimes they can help you solve a problem, simply by getting you to look at it in a way you hadn't thought to before."

"I've heard that said, Master, but so can a sudden blow to the head, if you're looking for random stimuli."

That's right, Lando thought, what I really need now is a fresh machine to banter with. The first card to fall was the Commander of Staves, one that Lando had often associated with himself. It was the apparently chance appearance of the right card—as happened so often—that made him wonder if his "scientific" analysis was all there was to the things.

"That's me," he explained to the robot, "a messenger on a fool's errand. Let's see what stands in the way." He dealt a second card, laid it across the first. "Great Gadfry!" he exclaimed.

"What is it, Master?"

"Not what, *who*. It's Himself—the Evil One. I'd guess that to be Rokur Gepta. Hold on, now, it's changing."

As *sabacc* card-chips are prone to do now and again, the second card transformed itself into the Legate of Coins—but the image was upside down.

"Duttes Mer!" Lando laughed. "A being corrupt and evil if ever there was one! Well, that makes sense, even though it tells us nothing new. Let's see what else."

The third card he placed above the others. The Five of Sabres, Lando explained, represented his own conscious motivations, in this case, the desire to relieve the weak and unwary of the burden of their excess cash. He chuckled, dealt a card below the others, indicating his deeper, possibly subconscious motives. He groaned.

"The Legate of Staves. Don't tell me I'm a do-gooder at heart!"

"Master, this is simply a random distribution of images. Don't take it seriously."

Lando looked at the little robot cautiously. "I think I've just been insulted. Well, the next card should tell us something. It represents the past, things coming to an end."

It was the Six of Sabres. Lando placed it to the left.

"Oh-ho! This usually denotes a journey, but its position indicates the journey is nearly at an end. What do you think of that?"

"I think, Master, that journeys can end in many ways, not all of them pleasant or productive."

"That's what I keep you around for, to bring me down whenever I feel too good, to remind me that every silver lining has a cloud. Say, you know, you're getting bigger—eight, maybe nine centimeters. And your voice is changing, too."

The little robot didn't reply, but simply watched Lando lay the next card down to the right of the center pair.

"Flame and famine! You spoiled the run, Vuffi Raa—it's the Destroyed Starship!"

"Does that mean harm will come to the *Falcon*, Master?"

"Don't call me master. I thought you didn't believe in any of this."

"I don't. But what does it mean?"

"Cataclysmic changes in the near future, death and destruction. It may be the worst card in the whole deck. Maybe. One thing I've learned from all this: there's always a worse card. This next will tell us what will happen to us and how we'll react to it."

"*We*, Master?"

"There you go again—*great*: the Satellite. It means a lot of fairly nasty things, things that you find under rocks. Mostly it means deception, deceit, betrayal." He looked closely at the robot again. "Are you getting ready to double-cross me, my mechanical minion?"

"There, Master, is the greatest danger in such mystical pursuits. You trusted me before you started playing with those cardchips, didn't you?"

"I still do, Vuffi Raa. The next card, up above the Satellite, here, is supposed to tell us where we'll find ourselves next. Hmmm. I wonder what that means?"

The Wheel sat shimmering on the card-chip, an image denoting luck, both good and bad, the beginning and the ending of things, random chance, final outcome—it gave Lando no information whatsoever.

The third card in that part of the array, placed in line above the Satellite and the Wheel, represented future obstacles. Lando cringed when he saw what had appeared.

"Gepta again! Well, I suppose that's only logical. Want to see the final outcome, old clockwork? Well, you're going to, anyway. Here we go. Well, that's not too bad, after all. It's the Universe. It means we'll have a shot at everything we want to do. Join the human race and see the world. Something like that."

"Master."

"Yes, Vuffi Raa, what is it?"

"Master, that Six of Sabres: that's a journey over with?"

"That's what I said although it can mean other things, in other—"

"Master, our journey's over with."

And, indeed, so it appeared to be. The floor slowed as they came upon the towering doorway of a chamber large enough to park a fleet of spaceships in. A long, long distance away, something resembling a giant altar was raised, all the lights in the cavernous room focused upon it.

Even from several hundred meters off, Lando could tell it was the Mindharp of Sharu. It hurt his eyes to look at it.

XVIII

I T WASN'T AS easy as all that.

There were other things inside the hall besides the podium or altar where the Mindharp stood, and a giant replica of the Key Lando had carried until the wall of the pyramid had taken it.

"What do you make of that, Vuffi Raa?"

The robot, standing now as high as Lando's knee, peered into the same odd well-lighted gloom that had filled the tunnel behind them. The light was a brownish amber and seemed to emanate from the floor. The room, a vast auditorium of a place, was lined with something between sculpture and painting—a pageant that seemed, to the gambler, to recapitulate his dreams of the night before.

Here, at the entrance, shaggy forms, barely erect, shambled along the walls in a frozen march, growing straighter, taller, beginning to carry things in their hands, to lose their furry coverings, to wear clothing.

Lando and Vuffi Raa followed the right wall, which curved gently into the vast circularity that was the chamber of the Mindharp. By the time the figures on the wall were playing with internal combustion engines and rocketry, the pair had only walked a few dozen meters. Uncounted thousands of centuries of history lay ahead of them.

The robot hadn't spoken. Lando looked down at him. His eye was glowing peculiarly—or perhaps the peculiarity was in the lighting of the chamber.

"Vuffi Raa, did you hear me?"

"Why yes, Lando," the droid said, seeming to be waking from a sort of walking dream. "What do I make of this? The same that you do—that this is somehow the center of Sharu culture. What they left behind of it, anyway. That the Harp is somehow even more important than we thought it was."

Lando hadn't been thinking that at all. He'd been thinking that the chamber was a place of worship, that the figures on the wall were human—Toka—that the bas-relief murals would convey to them the story of how they arose on some far-off planet and came to the Rafa System. That somewhere along the wall the story would be told of how they met the Sharu and discovered their masters.

He didn't want to wait. "I'm going on across the room—enough of this historical nonsense. Coming with me?"

Vuffi Raa turned, followed Lando without a word.

It was a long, long trip. The Sharu had discovered the same secret that many human cultures had: that if you make the floors of a public building slick enough, keep them polished and slippery, they'll force the people who have to walk there into little mincing steps that magnify the distances and humble the spirit—just as high ceilings tend to do.

Lando wasn't having any. He took a few running steps and slid along the floor.

"Wheee! This is fun! Come on, old tinhorn, try it!"

"Master!" said the robot in a scandalized voice. "Have you no respect?"

Lando stopped, gave the robot a sober look. "Not a grain of it—not when it's being imposed on me by the architecture."

He took another running start, slid several meters this time. The robot had to hurry to catch up. By the time he had, he was very nearly his original height.

"Lando," he said, "speaking of architecture, there's something very odd about this place."

Lando had to stop to catch his breath. He sat down on the floor.

"That would be consistent with everything else around here. What is it this time?"

"Well, from the entrance, the room looked circular, with a high domed ceiling, and perhaps a thousand meters across the floor to the altar."

Lando looked around. "Still seems that way to me."

"And to my vision, too. But, checking with radar and a number of extra senses, the room is ovoid—shaped like an egg with a big end and a small end. The big end was the entrance. The roof keeps getting closer to the floor."

Lando had another flash of his dreams. Something Vuffi Raa said earlier had triggered the first, something about the idea that it wasn't he, the robot who was growing, but Lando who was shrinking. Yet if that were true—the tunnel had seemed to stay the same size the duration of the two-day trip—then the moving passageway had to have been shrinking. Lando had appeared to Vuffi Raa to be a hundred and ten or twenty meters tall in the beginning. Now he was back to being a little shy of two. The corridors had to have been shrinking accordingly.

At that rate, when they reached the Mindharp, Vuffi Raa would tower over Lando, and they'd both have to travel on hands and knees to reach the artifact.

"HALT!" said a voice.

"*What?*" Vuffi Raa and Lando cried simultaneously.

"IT IS NOT PERMITTED TO CROSS THE HALL."

"What happens if we do?" inquired Lando.

The voice paused, seemed confused. "WELL, I'M NOT SURE I KNOW. NO ONE EVER ASKED ME. BUT IT IS NOT PERMITTED."

Lando opened his mouth—

"Just who in the Hall are you, anyway?" Vuffi Raa said. Lando looked at the robot sharply. He hated having his good lines stolen. It was exactly what he'd been planning to say himself.

"WHY, I AM THE HALL, OF COURSE. YOU'RE SUPPOSED TO LOOK AT THE EXHIBIT AS YOU APPROACH THE SACRED OBJECT."

"And it's your job," Lando suggested, "to make sure we do? Well, let's get a few things straight here, Hall: I've been tugged along by everything that's happened so far. I'm not going to let an empty room tell me what to do. Now answer me truthfully: does anything bad or dangerous happen to someone if they *don't* skulk along the wall like vermin?"

"NO, I DON'T SUPPOSE IT DOES."

"Then I guess we'll go on. You don't happen to have a cigarette, do you?"

"I'M AFRAID I DON'T KNOW WHAT YOU MEAN."

"I thought you were going to say that. Come on, Vuffi Raa."

They continued across the broad expanse of the Hall, Lando sliding occasionally just to demonstrate his spirit. Vuffi Raa's legs twinkled in the weird lighting. Lando had a thought:

"Hey, Hall?"

"YES, HAVE YOU DECIDED TO GO BACK TO THE WALL?"

"No. I was just wondering: how much do you know about this place?"

"ABOUT MYSELF?"

"No, about the pyramid and the moving tunnel we were in before we got here."

The Hall considered. "A GREAT DEAL. WHAT, SPECIFICALLY, WOULD YOU LIKE TO KNOW?"

"Well, just to begin, what size am I?"

A very long pause this time. "IN WHAT UNITS OF MEASUREMENT?"

"Skip it, then. What I really want to know is, was I gigantic a few kilometers back, or was my friend, here, very tiny?"

"DOES IT MATTER?"

"Of *course* it matters. Would I ask, otherwise?"

"Organic entities seem to take considerable delight in doing things to no good purpose," Vuffi Raa offered. "But in this case, Hall, I'd be interested in knowing, too."

"Right," Lando said under his breath, "so the two of us can compare notes on the frailties of humankind. Play your cards right, Vuffi Raa, cozy up to this Hall and they may make you a telephone booth or something."

"VERY WELL. THE CHANGES IN THE DIMENSION WERE WROUGHT ON THE ORGANIC LIFE-FORMS HERE. IT IS A NECESSARY PART OF THE PROCESS WHICH CULMINATES, PROPERLY, IN TRAVELING AROUND THE CIRCUMFERENCE OF THE HALL AS YOU ARE INTEN—"

"Skip the commercial, Hall," said Lando, "and get on with the explanation."

"VERY WELL. THIS INSTRUMENTALITY IS CAPABLE OF ALTER-ING THE PROPORTIONS OF INANIMATE MATTER AS WELL, BUT IT MUST BE IN THE PROXIMITY OF ORGANIC LIFE. OTHERWISE, IT IS ABSORBED BY THE MAINTENANCE SYSTEMS."

Vuffi Raa described his journey through the blue and red maze. "Can you tell me what all that was about?"

"CERTAINLY. YOU WERE MISTAKEN BY THE WALL FOR A SMALL HOUSEKEEPING DEVICE AND ROUTED THERE FOR REPROGRAM-MING AND REPAIR. HAVE YOU BEEN REPAIRED?"

"Not that I know of."

Lando laughed. "Any secret urges to sweep up or take out the garbage?"

"Lando, this is serious. I want to know what happened!"

"Touchy! Okay, I concede, I grew, I shrank—but I've got you on another one: Mohs. The Hall said organic life-forms, plural."

"QUITE CORRECT, SIR. YOUR INTESTINAL FLORA, OTHER SYM-BIOTIC ORGANISMS, ALL WERE GREATLY ALTERED IN SIZE, THEN BROUGHT BACK TO NORMAL MAGNITUDE AS PART OF—"

"What about Mohs. Was there *another* human being with us when we entered, and what happened to him?"

The Hall was silent—a guilty silence if ever there was one. Lando realized suddenly that relations between mechanical intel-ligences weren't all that different from those between organic ones.

"Well?"

More silence.

Lando looked at Vuffi Raa. "That thing mistook you for a maintenance bug and bummed up your memory trying to 'repair' you. *That's* why you don't remember Mohs. Now it feels ashamed."

Vuffi Raa looked at Lando. "I certainly hope so, Master, I certainly hope so. What are we going to do, once we reach the Harp?"

"Shhhh! The walls have ears. We're going to use it in whatever manner was intended—rather, take it to somebody who knows how to and let him do it."

"You mean the governor?"

"That fat ape? No, I mean Gepta. He's the one who really says when we get to leave this lousy system."

They shuffled onward, trying, occasionally, to get the Hall's attention again. Since it obviously hadn't gone away, it must have been ignoring them. Finally they reached the base of the raised platform on which the Mindharp stood. It wasn't as bad as Lando had predicted: the ceiling *was* much lower—Vuffi Raa was now his old familiar size again—and the room felt smaller, but it was still huge and awe-imposing. As was the altar.

A dozen meters high, it was cut from a single perfectly transparent slab of what appeared to be life-crystal. It was hexagonal in cross section, with corners one could practically cut himself on. Otherwise, it was smooth and featureless.

It would be a long, difficult climb.

Lando sat down to consider the problem. His survival kit included no rope, suction cups, antigravs. Its designers had anticipated he would be among others—fellow soldiers—and had shared out supplies in a package that was sold originally to an entire squad. They had not anticipated that survival would necessitate committing a burglary.

"Any ideas, Vuffi Raa?"

"No, Master. If I were small again . . ."

"You never were small, remember? We argued about that and you won."

"Oh, that's right. You argued so persuasively that I forgot for a moment."

"Vuffi Raa, I think that's the first nice thing you've ever said to me."

"You're welcome, Master."

"Don't call me master." He thought some more, then: "Hey, Hall?"

"MAY I BE OF ASSISTANCE?"

"I hope so. How come you didn't answer us back there?"

"I'M SORRY, I WAS THINKING ABOUT SOMETHING. MAY I HELP YOU NOW?"

"Sure. Does this pylon sink into the floor or anything?"

"NO, I'M AFRAID THAT IT DOES NOT."

"You don't happen to have a ladder handy, do you?"

"NO, SIR, I AM NOT SO EQUIPPED."

Lando mused for a long time. Despite his long sleep, he was tired and hungry—jacket rations aren't everything their manufacturers claim for them. In fact, they aren't *anything* their manufacturers claim, except that they'll keep you alive.

"Say! Can you make me big again?"

"CONGRATULATIONS, SIR, YOU HAVE PASSED THE TEST. YES, I CAN ENLARGE YOUR SIZE. DO YOU WISH ME TO BEGIN NOW?"

"Can you make me normal again, afterward? The size I am now—provided that's the size I started out before we entered the pyramid?"

"IMMEDIATELY UPON YOUR REQUEST, SIR."

He looked at Vuffi Raa. "Well, here we go again."

"'We,' Master?"

"Now don't start that! Okay, Hall, let's do it!"

This time it was perceptible. Lando watched the room and everything in it shrink around him: Vuffi Raa grew smaller, the altar shorter. It only took a few moments. "How the devil does this work, anyway, Hall? I thought it was supposed to be impossible—cube–square relationships and my bones not supporting my weight above a certain size and everything. That's why I figured Vuffi Raa had shrunk—plenty of problems there, but fewer, I think."

"OH, NO PROBLEMS AT ALL, SIR," the Hall began. Lando noticed that its voice wasn't disturbed at all by the change in scales. Good engineers, those Sharu. "WHAT ARE YOU, NO OFFENSE, SIR, BUT ORGANIZED INFORMATION? WHAT DOES IT MATTER HOW DENSELY THAT INFORMATION IS COMPRESSED? AN OLD-FASHIONED BOOK MAY BE PRINTED UPON THICK PAPER, WITH THE LINES DOUBLE-SPACED. STILL, IT IS THE SAME INFORMATION, IS IT NOT?"

"You trying to tell me I've been sort of spread out, like? I'm not sure I like that thought. Well, here we are. Vuffi Raa? That's all right, you don't have to talk back. Just help me with this thing once I get it down—it's going to be *big*."

At present, the Mindharp rested on the flat upper surface of the pylon. It was a precise replica of the Key, except for size, and, in his present condition, it felt the same to Lando as the Key had. He reached down to take it, and it came away without resistance. He started to put it in his pocket—

"Master . . . don't . . . do . . . that."

"Right! It'd mess up my jacket a bit when I shrank back down, wouldn't it? Okay, Hall, let's lower me back where I belong."

Silence.

"Hall? Hey, you're supposed to shrink me again! Get with it!"

There was no reply.

"Look, Hall, if you don't listen, I'm going to take this obscene artifact and—"

"OH, I'M VERY SORRY, SIR. WOOLGATHERING AGAIN. I HAVE AN INCREASING TENDENCY TO THAT, AS THE MILLENNIA ROLL ON. I TAKE IT YOU WISH TO BE REDUCED AGAIN."

"You take it right."

With that, Lando began to shrink once more, the Mindharp

growing perceptibly in his hands as he did so. He stooped gently, set it on the floor beside Vuffi Raa, straightened, and folded his arms over his chest.

The Mindharp was an armful when Lando had been restored to his natural size. Perhaps a meter in its greatest extent, it was even more visually distressing than the tiny model he had played with in the beginning.

"Vuffi Raa, take one end of this. Hall, how do we get out of here?"

"BEHIND THE PILLAR, SIR, AND GOOD LUCK."

"Well, good luck to you, too. Maybe someday they'll hold concerts here."

"I CERTAINLY HOPE NOT, SIR. I RATHER LIKE THE PEACE AND QUIET."

Behind the pylon was a wall.

Embedded in the wall was a Key.

Perhaps it was the same Key, Lando thought—this building seemed to like little jokes like that. The question was, how did you use it? It protruded somehow from the wall. He let one hand go from the Mindharp, reached out to touch its smaller counterpart.

There was a *flash!* and a hole began opening in the wall, like the iris of an ancient camera. Lando and Vuffi Raa stepped through.

Into the busy daytime streets of Teguta Lusat.

XIX

"OFFICER," VUFFI RAA demanded, summoning the first constabulary cop he saw on the street. The robot pointed a tentacle at Lando. "Arrest this man immediately. Orders of the governor."

Lando stopped, stunned. They hadn't taken three steps away from the side of the Sharu ruin they'd emerged from. He looked back—the aperture they'd walked through was gone. He held the Mindharp to his chest, walked back a step, another, until his back was against the wall.

"Why, you little—"

"That'll be enough of that," the cop ordered. "I can't arrest a man on the word of a machine. I'll have to check it out with H.Q." He touched the side of his helmet, communed momentarily with the radio inside it, then waved off with one hand the small crowd that was beginning to gather.

Lando took a small, quiet step sideways. No one seemed to notice. He took another, and another. Only a few more steps to a corner where he just might be able to—

"Officer!" Vuffi Raa shouted. "He's trying to get away!"

"Thanks a lot, you atom-powered fink!"

The policeman drew his blaster, held it steady on Lando's chest. "Well—first time I've ever heard of a droid with a security clearance like that, but—hold still, you! We'll have some transportation in a minute, then we'll all take a nice little ride."

———

THE GOVERNOR'S OFFICE looked much the same as it had before, even to the absence of Rokur Gepta, the Sorcerer of Tund. With the Mindharp laying across the crystalline desk, Lando wondered why the wizard wasn't present to claim the prize he'd sought so avidly.

He didn't wonder very long.

"Good afternoon," Duttes Mer said, entering from the right and easing himself into his chair. "I see you have the object. Very good. You could tell me one little thing, though, if you would be so kind."

Lando was standing between two of Teguta Lusat's finest once again. This time Vuffi Raa was present, standing beside the governor's desk.

"Anything you want to know," Lando said, trying hard for cheerfulness and not quite making it.

"*EXACTLY WHERE HAVE YOU BEEN THESE LAST FOUR MONTHS?*" The governor calmed himself down, straightened his neckcloth, blinked.

"Four months?" Lando asked, reeling from one astonishing development after—so *that* was it! The time differential. What had seemed like a couple of days to him had actually been sixty times that long. "Governor, you wouldn't believe me if I told you. Ask your treacherous friend here. He'll tell you—unless he's a congenital liar."

"Don't be too hard on the droid, Captain. He did what he was programmed to do: play the Emissary's part so that the natives would help you find the Harp. Also, to report to me the instant the Harp was in your possession. It would seem I've had a stroke of luck in that respect, however. How is it that you flew to Rafa V and returned here without being picked up on planetary defense sensors? We really have a nice, modern system, you know."

"*You* tell him, Vuffi Raa, since you're such a blabbermouth anyway."

"Sir," the robot said, "the Sharu appear to have some method of matter transport. I'm not certain when the transition occurred, and I am told that you lost track of my telemetry the instant we entered the pyramid on Rafa V. The shift could have been any time afterward, from the inside wall of the pyramid to the aperture through which we stepped into the street here in Teguta Lusat."

The governor patted his stumpy fingers together. "Well, well. A technological bonus, if we can unravel its secret. In the meantime, as I said, a stroke of unexpected luck. You see, Captain, my, er, colleague is orbiting Rafa V this very minute, waiting for your emergence there.

"Haw, haw. *I* am *here*. And *I* have the Mindharp. It would appear that I am something of a lucky gambler, too, wouldn't you say?"

Lando shrugged indifferently. This wasn't going to turn out good, no matter what he did, and there wasn't any point in giving the fat slob any satisfaction.

"Come now, Captain, consider: Rokur Gepta hired an anthropologist—a *real* one, mind you, with genuine credentials—to investigate the system. The poor fellow thought he was working for me, which gave us the opportunity to appropriate his paycheck from Imperial funds, and yielded Gepta the enjoyment of misdirection he seems to treasure so much for its own sake.

"Meanwhile, we set a little trap. In return for the offer of a new job, once his investigations here were finished, the anthropologist went to Oseon 2795 in search of, well, shall we say a suitably gullible individual to do our work for us."

Interested despite himself, and aware that Mer's desire—for, what, approval?—might show him a way out of the mess, Lando asked, "Why didn't you just hire yourself another sucker—or let your tame scientist get the Mindharp for you? Why me, and why maneuver me into it, rather than simply coming out and—"

The governor laughed. "You know the legends. It had to be a wandering adventurer from the stars, a stranger to the Toka, someone they hadn't seen snooping around, recording their chants and so forth. And the truth. Why, Captain, if you had known the truth about the Mindharp, *you* would be about to assume absolute power over the minds of everyone in the system, rather than myself. That is another mistake my esteemed colleague made. Thus we looked for a freighter captain down on his luck—and on Oseon 2795 everybody's down on his luck—in a place where we had the, er, cooperation of local law-enforcement personnel. We let you think you'd won the robot, and put you in a position where you had to flee—"

"Oh?" the gambler asked beneath raised eyebrows. "Well, suppose I'd fled to the Dela System, as I'd intended, or simply—"

"There was the 'treasure' as an inducement, plus the fact that you had a valuable asset to claim in the droid here. And, of course, if you hadn't come, our *Ottdefa* Osuno Whett would simply have found a new prospect. You were our first—I'm rather proud of the *Ottdefa*."

Lando shook his head resignedly. "I get it. That's why Vuffi Raa was left here: if you'd missed your chance with me, and I'd had him in my possession in the Oseon, you would have lost a valuable 'bot, whereas any poor jerk who took your bait—"

"Precisely. I'm gratified that you appreciate the subtlety of the scheme. That will be all. Officers, take him away."

Lando didn't even have time to protest. The police hauled him from the office, along the corridor, and down a flight of stairs to a waiting hovercruiser. They whisked through the streets to the edge of town, where they entered a force-fence around a series of corrugated-plastic buildings.

"Give him the usual processing," one of the anonymous visored officers told a fat man in a dirty tunic. "You'll have the paperwork in the morning."

"Very well." The fat man beamed. He was short and greasy looking, but the neuronic whip in one hand and the military

blaster in the other added something to his personality. The
cruiser roared away.

"Welcome to the penal colony of Rafa IV." The fat man grinned.

Midnight.

Listening to the chanting of the Toka, Lando lay on a steel-
slatted cot in a barred cell. Offworld prisoners occupied cells on
one side of the corridor; the Toka shared an unlocked kennel-like
affair on the other side. Lando was unusual in that the other three
bunks in his own cell were unoccupied.

He figured that the governor didn't want him talking to anyone until he was "processed"—whatever that meant.

To say he found the native chanting annoying would have
been a calamitous understatement. It was unpleasant enough in
itself, but it further served to remind him of Mohs—the little man
who wasn't there. If he had been. The question bothered the gambler almost as much as his present predicament did.

More, perhaps, because he'd been in jail before.

Less, perhaps, because he'd never faced a sentence in the life-
orchards.

And, unlike the other freshly arrived convicts in the cells
around him, he knew what that meant, had had a taste of his
mind's being sucked away by the trees from which the crystals
were harvested.

And his memories of Mohs were clear; the chanting across the
hallway was in no way inconsistent with them. The language was
distressingly familiar. He could almost imagine he understood it.
Not for the first time, he reasoned that it was a corrupted version
of some tongue spoken in a place he'd been once. If only he could
remember . . .

"ALL RIGHT, RISE AND SHINE!"

The fat man had friends, at least five of them, also armed with blasters and whips. They paced up and down in front of the barred cells, shouting to wake up the offworld prisoners. The Toka were already gone, sometime in the night.

Lando groaned, turned over. Before they'd placed him in the cell, they'd taken his clothes, replacing them with rough-woven pajamas of unbleached cloth. Now he was being ordered to remove even that minimal dress.

He quickly found out why. Two of the guards placed their weapons to one side, manhandled a huge fire hose into place before the cells, and turned it on. Lando was dashed to the back of the cell, where he fetched up against the rough plaster wall and slid to the floor, shielding his eyes against the blast of water. The stream passed on to the next cell. He rose stiffly, put his shirt back on—he hadn't time to undress all the way before the water hit him—and wondered what came next.

He didn't have to wait long.

"All right, prisoners," the fat man shouted, "we will open the cells in a moment, and you will step outside, stand at attention, until told otherwise. Then you will turn left face and march, single file and silently, into the waiting bus. Step out of line, utter so much as a single word, and you are dead where you stand."

Luckily, Lando didn't have a snappy comeback ready anyway.

The door slid open with a clank. He stepped out and stood stiffly, shivering in the early morning breeze. He had his first look at the compound and, having looked around, decided he didn't want to make a habit of it. Boxed into the corner between two plastic Sharu buildings hundreds of meters tall and unsealable, the yard was fenced on the other two sides. Bare earth, a handful of small one-story cellblocks, and an administration building. Home sweet home for the rest of his life.

Like hell, Lando swore to himself. He would be free. He had debts to settle.

The command was given. He turned left smartly, walked behind half a dozen other prisoners to the bus, an old one, driven by another convict. Its skirts were stained and tattered. It would be a rough ride this morning. It—

The ground began to shake.

Across the compound, the earth billowed up like waves on the ocean, heaved at the cellblocks, smashing them to bits, ripped the administration building apart, toppled the hoverbus. The man inside it screamed.

Several convicts ran to help the trapped driver. They were shouted at by the guards. One of the uniformed men opened fire, sending a prisoner up in flames that were mirrored by those that suddenly burst from a leaking fuel line in a building on the far side of the yard.

Lando stood where he was, then decided to fall down, since the quake threatened to do it to him anyway, and there was less chance of getting shot. Suddenly, a figure in the town-cop uniform, mirrored helmet visor and all, staggered up to the warden or whatever he was. Lando could hear him over the rumble, roar, and screaming.

"That man is to be turned over for further interrogation!" The armored finger pointed at Lando. The warden and the cop leaned on each other to stay erect.

"I have no authorization! He's mine! Can't this wait?"

"The governor wants him immediately!" There was sudden menace in the big policeman's voice. "Something about a load of cops he tried to maroon on Rafa XI four months ago."

"Then by all means take him. I—" That was all the fat man had to say. He swayed and fell. The cop ducked back, came for Lando.

"Let's go!"

Grabbing Lando by the pajamaed scruff, the cop bore him along toward a waiting cruiser that had been left aground beside the cell block. "Get in!"

They roared away through the gate, which hung open on one hinge. It wouldn't have mattered: the force-fence was down, even its auxiliary power system apparently destroyed in the quake.

The car rocked and swayed, turned right, and sped down the road.

"Say, old flatfoot, this isn't the way to Teguta Lusat!" Lando shouted. He cringed as they rounded a corner and dashed toward the country.

"What's it to you? Shut up and mind your own business!"

"Would this make it my business?"

The cop looked down to see what was pressing at his side. It was his own blaster. He raised a visored head to the young gambler.

"Very good. I guess you didn't need rescuing that badly, after all. Want to go back and have all the glory to yourself?"

"What are you talking about?" Lando demanded. "Stop this car and take that helmet off. I want to see who I'm talking to!"

The cruiser slowed as per specification. They halted in the middle of the road and waited out an aftershock. Lando leveled the blaster at the policeman's face. "Okay, take it off."

The gloved hands rose, took the helmet and lifted. In place of a head sticking up through the collar, there was—a *snake*! A chromium-plated snake.

"Can I get out of this uniform, Master? It's very uncomfortable."

"Vuffi Raa! You little—but what's going on here? Why are you rescuing me?"

Shucking the rest of the guardsman's uniform—he'd been walking on two tentacles, using two for arms, and the fifth as an ersatz head—Vuffi Raa assumed a more normal position behind the driver tiller.

"Master, I was programmed to betray you from the beginning, and not to tell you about it. But you're my *Master*, Lando, and, as soon as that program had run out, so did I. And here I am. We've got to get off this planet, out of the system, and fast."

"I know."

"You know? How?"

"The dreams, the chanting I heard last night. It's Old High

Trammic—the language of the Toka. I was on Trammis III a couple of years ago. I still can't understand the language very well, but my subconscious apparently made something of it. I woke up this morning knowing the truth about the Mindharp, and I know we've got to get out of this place *now*."

"Why is that, Master?"

"Don't call me master. Because once somebody starts the music up, this system's never going to be the same again."

"Then we must go now, Master. Duttes Mer is using the Harp. That's what the earthquake's all about."

XX

U NLIKE A FICTIONAL VILLAIN, Duttes Mer hadn't gloated or
divulged his plans to the beaten Lando Calrissian. He'd
simply had him disposed of, as quickly and neatly as possible.

Where he'd made his mistake—his first one, anyway—was in
his attitude toward menials. Toka servants were virtually invisible to him—drinks and cigars simply appeared near his elbow,
and that, he thought, was as it should be. He was the governor,
after all. Droids were even more invisible.

So Vuffi Raa had stood in plain sight in the governor's office
as Mer made a transspace call to Rokur Gepta.

"Ahhh, it is you, my esteemed sorcerer. I have some news."

"What is it, Mer? It had better be good!"

"Are you enjoying your stay in orbit around a dried-up desert
planet?"

"My ship is far more comfortable than that heap of bricks you
call a city. Get on with it, Governor. You're beginning to anger
me!"

The governor reached for the pickup on his communicator,
pulled it out on a retracting cable, and pointed it at the top of his
desk. "See anything you recognize, Gepta?"

In the screen, the sorcerer's eyes were filled, by turn, with
wonder, greed, and rage. "The Mindharp! How did you—"

The governor chuckled. "It only matters that I *did*, Gepta, and
that you're millions of kilometers from here. You see, that story
you told Calrissian—that the Harp is the 'Ultimate Instrument of

Music'—may have been good enough for him, but the story you told *me* about its being a master control over all the Toka never washed. Such a thing would be commercially useful, but this"— he indicated the Harp—"is much, much more than that."

"What do you mean, Mer?"

"I am capable of hiring investigators, too, my dear former partner, and I took the wisest course: hiring *yours*. Recall that I have the power to commute sentences, order pardons. I know the truth: that the Mindharp of Sharu is an instrument capable of controlling every mind within the system—possibly beyond it. And the instrument is *mine*!"

"Don't try it, Mer. You don't know what you're doing!" Panic was evident in the sorcerer's voice.

"On the contrary, my dear—"

"*NO!* You don't understand! The Mindharp will—"

The governor smiled benignly. "It will give me absolute power, even over you. I suggest that, if you don't want to feel that power, you turn your ship out of orbit and leave my system. That may buy you a few years, at least."

"Mer, I'll warn you once more: you don't have the knowledge to safely—"

Click.

WHEN THE OPPORTUNITY AROSE—which wasn't until the middle of the night—Vuffi Raa crept from the governor's offices, stole a uniform from the guard laundries, jump-wired a police cruiser in the maintenance yard, and went off to rescue Lando.

"Well, I appreciate it, Vuffi Raa, old criminal, but I trust you'll understand the residue of skepticism that remains within me."

They were whisking back into town at a moderate, legal, and inconspicuous velocity. They had felt several more tremors, but nothing like that first quake.

"I understand," Vuffi Raa acknowledged, "and I suppose tell-ing you I was programmed to betray you is much the same as a human being's saying he couldn't help himself. Well, I came to rescue you by way of restitution."

Lando thought about that. "Very well, and just to show you my good faith, you might as well know that Rokur Gepta and Duttes Mer are *both* wrong about the Mindharp."

Vuffi Raa brought the car to a screeching halt as they neared the outskirts of Teguta Lusat. "What?"

"That's correct. And we've got to get out to the port, steal something that will get us out of the system, but fast."

"Master, I agree about getting out. You don't want your mind controlled, especially by a being like the governor—believe me, I know. But if they're wrong . . ."

"It will be worse, Vuffi Raa. My only regret is leaving the *Falcon* on Rafa V."

"Master, four months have passed. Mer had the *Falcon* brought back. Its cargo of life-crystals hasn't even been unloaded, because until we reappeared in Teguta Lusat, Gepta and Mer didn't know if they might have to bargain more with you."

"What? Why didn't you tell me? He didn't think to have her drives repaired, did he?"

After a long pause, the droid replied, "No, Master, *I* did that, the first thing on the way to Rafa V."

Lando didn't say anything. If he'd realized the extent of the droid's housekeeping back then, they might have taken off and skipped the last four months inside the Sharu ruins. "Well," he said irritably, "let's get out to the port!"

"Yes, Master."

ABOARD THE DECOMMISSIONED cruiser *Wennis,* leaving orbit from Rafa V, a decision had been made. Rokur Gepta lay in a special acceleration couch, being strapped up for the voyage ahead of him. The vessel in the lifeboat bay was not a lifeboat, but an elderly Imperial fighter, refitted as a scout. It could make the trip to Rafa IV in a third the time of its parent vessel.

If the occupant could stand the g-forces involved.

The safety precautions were primarily for the benefit of the crew, Gepta reflected. He didn't need them, but it was dangerous for them to know that. As the last strap and bit of tape were in place and the port clamped down, he relaxed, waited for the tick, and didn't stir a hair when thrust that might have seriously injured a mere human being passed harmlessly through his body.

He'd be in Teguta Lusat within an hour.

DUTTES MER LOOKED down at the Mindharp on his desk, afraid to try again, but desperate to master the weird thing before Gepta could return and take it from him. He had no illusions. If he couldn't control *that* mind, along with millions of others, he was doomed. He placed his short, square hand on the central shaft of the Harp again, suppressed a wave of fear, and tried to concentrate.

"MASTER!"

Vuffi Raa clung to the steering tiller as the road tried to shake them off its back like a wet dog. Lando grabbed the ends of a seat belt, tried to fasten them together as the police car pitched and swayed.

"This is no good!" he shouted, finally giving up the effort. "Look, let's make a run for it!"

The spaceport gates were only a few hundred meters away, and they were traveling twice that distance weaving back and forth across the road. Lando slammed the door open, rolled out, got to his feet, and ran toward the gate. Vuffi Raa, right behind him, took no time at all to catch up.

A guard, well away from his swaying guard post, was standing in the gateway. He aimed a blaster at Lando.

"Halt! Looters will be shot!"

"I'm not a looter," Lando hollered as he approached the

guard. Both were pretty busily occupied just staying on their feet. "I'm the captain of that ship over there, the *Millennium Falcon*, and I've got to get her off before she breaks up with everything else on this planet!"

The blaster came up to Lando's eye level. "That ship's under the governor's seal. You can't—"

Lando stepped closer. The guard fired but, swaying as he was, succeeded only in burning a shrub across the road. By that time, Lando was close enough to seize the weapon, push it upward, punch the other man in the solar plexus with his fist.

Flexible armor is for bullets and energy beams. It's no protection at all against an unarmed man. The guard folded. Lando took his gun away, added it to the weapon he'd taken at the labor camp.

"Let's go!"

They ran toward the *Falcon*, and, as they approached it, the boarding ramp swung downward slowly, as if in welcome. Cautiously, Lando and Vuffi Raa walked up the inclined plane.

At the top, still aged and wrinkled, but sporting a stylish haircut and expensive business suit, stood Mohs, High Singer of the Toka. Where his ruined eyes had been now glittered a pair of faceted multicolored optics like those of a giant psychedelic spider.

DUTTES MER GLARED resentfully at the alien object on his desk. Twice now, following the mental procedure conveyed to him by Gepta's captive sociologists, he had tried to gain control of the Mindharp, and thus—

He slammed his hand down on the desk, making the object jump. He didn't want to try again; all it seemed to do was cause quakes that threatened to tear his administration building apart. Why that should be, he didn't know, but he knew one thing: Rokur Gepta was coming.

The spaceport radar people had confirmed it, just before the communications lines had gone dead. A small, extremely fast craft was no more than twenty minutes from landfall. Mer suspected that Gepta didn't need the port facilities; there was a wide flat space atop the administration building. It would do nicely for—

He hit the annunciator button. "Give me the Captain of the Guard!"

At first there was no answer. Then a terrified secretary told him, "Sir, the guard contingent has left the building because of the tremors. I was about to go myself. I—"

"If you leave, I'll have you shot. Summon those four men who went to Rafa XI. They're under house arrest here in the building. Tell them to get up on the roof and—never mind, I'll tell them myself!"

Once more, he looked upon the Mindharp. It had better work this time.

Rokur Gepta was coming.

"YOU WILL PARDON my dramatic appearance, Captain Calrissian," Mohs said as he ushered them around the curving corridor toward the *Falcon*'s cockpit, "but things are beginning to happen, and I am too busy to be anything *but* dramatic."

"I know," Lando said, throwing himself into the left-hand seat. He flipped a couple of switches and helped Vuffi Raa through the preflight checklist. It was a long list, much too long for comfort. "I know everything—but I'm in something of a hurry myself right now."

Mohs looked puzzled, then relaxed and grinned. "Ah, yes. You put the pieces together. All my life I was the instrument of my ancestors, given orders—the Voices of the Gods—whisked hither and yon at Their bidding. It was terrifying to the savage that I was, for example, to brush near an ancient wall, as I did that night in Teguta Lusat, and appear an instant later, leagues away, amidst a gathering of my people. I apologize also for vanishing from the tunnel; its purpose was elementary education, you see, and I matriculated and went on to higher things." He absently ran a fingertip over his bizarre eyes. "The decision was made *for* me, and I—"

"Had no choice about it?" Lando asked. He looked at Vuffi Raa. "There's a lot of that going around. What in heaven's name is that red light on the life-support panel! Here, let's override—"

"You are in no danger." Mohs smiled. "The two of you helped me, and now I shall help you. We mean you no harm."

"Swell. Can you fend off the governor and his friend the sorcerer?"

"I can tell you that the governor is alone, trying to use the Mindharp, while Gepta is on his way from Rafa V. He ought to be down any minute, but he won't be coming to the spaceport."

Lando turned to look at the old man, no longer bent and wizened. He was still old, but it lent him dignity and authority now.

The tattoo of the Key—the Mindharp, Lando realized—was darker now, stood out more sharply on the old man's forehead. It practically glowed.

"Are there any more like you?" Lando asked.

"No, Captain, I am the only one. I am all there ever was, of *my* generation. The burden was to be passed on next year, but here I am."

"Master, what are you talking about?"

"Quiet, Vuffi Raa. Watch the temperature in that reactor!"

"I assure you, Captain, everything is under control. You'd realize that, if you truly know our secrets."

"I *know* your secrets, Mohs, believe me. There never were any pre-Republican colonists here, right?"

"That is correct, Captain."

"But what are you saying, Master? If—"

"Nor were there really any Toka. Or would that be telling?"

"Master—"

"*Quiet!* You people *are* the Sharu. It's written all over your walls inside the pyramid. You're humanoid and very, very advanced. I don't know what scared you into this masquerade— and I'm willing to bet you don't either!"

"Master, will you please explain—"

"All right, all right. Mohs will correct me over the rough spots. I hardly understand contemporary Trammic, let alone an ancient—and thoroughly synthetic—version. But this is the gist: something pretty scary threatened the Sharu. Something that liked to eat hyperadvanced cultures but that wouldn't bother with savages.

"So, a vast computer system was created. That's all the so-called ruins in the system. The Sharu, before the threat, lived in cities not terribly different from our own, and they're probably concealed beneath the monumental architecture too—along with the *intelligence* of the Sharu. Hand me that checklist a moment."

"Very good, Captain, very good."

"You bet it's good. The life-orchards weren't created to increase intelligence or longevity. They were created to suck it away from the population. I'll bet three-quarters of everybody's mind on the planet is stored inside that pyramid and other buildings like it. That's so succeeding generations would be disguised as savages, too. But, when the crystals were separated from the trees by the colonists, the things absorbed small amounts of intelligence and life-force from the ambient environment, then fed them back to whoever wore the crystal—an accidental and unlooked-for effect."

The old man nodded. "The colonists' harvesting did no harm. What was of real value was stored in the buildings."

"The buildings," Lando continued, "may be the biggest computer system ever created. When this colony was founded, the computer searched our records, came up with a missing pre-Republican colony ship, and decided to use that as a cover story. The Sharu—reduced to mere Tokahood—were poor savage brutes, 'broken' by their experience with the mighty Sharu.

"I just couldn't swallow it. What were the Sharu afraid of? How could they be so mighty, and yet—"

"I still don't know the answer to that, Captain. It was expunged from the records, out of sheer terror, I think. It worries me."

"It ought to. Ready, Vuffi Raa?"

"I think so, Master. Yes, we're ready."

Another tremor rocked the ship.

"Mer's trying to use the Harp again. Boy, will he be disappointed. It's a trap, isn't it, Mohs?"

"I'm afraid so," the old man admitted gravely. "The legends were spread among my people in order to entice members of another intelligence species into finding and using the Harp. That way, we'd know that it was safe to come out of hiding."

"Your giant computer system will regurgitate all those smarts it's been storing for thousands of years, the covers will be stripped off your cities—there's going to be a good deal of earthmoving around here, isn't there?"

"All over the system."

"And when the dust clears, the Sharu will be back in control. Well, considering the governor and the nature of the colony here, it can't happen too soon for me. We're leaving. Better jump off, Mohs. I'd say it's been nice to know you, but I hate being used, by governors, sorcerers, or representatives of semilost civilizations."

ROKUR GEPTA SWEPT down upon the governor's office building. As he'd expected, guards were posted all over the miniature landing field.

He cleared them away with a burst of the craft's blasters and set down lightly amid the smoking remains. The ground trembled again, and this time it didn't stop. Gepta hurried down to the penthouse office.

He thrust the doors aside and walked into a burst of radiance.

Gepta was thrown against the corridor wall as energy streamed out all around him. He squinted his eyes, employed certain other protections, and gazed briefly at the governor's desk.

The Mindharp of Sharu shone far too brightly to be looked upon, even by the sorcerer. Behind it, his fat hands wrapped around the base, stood the governor, his mouth and eyes opened wide, frozen, paralyzed.

And doomed.

Even as Gepta watched, both governor and Harp began to melt, to fuse, showering the room and hall with deadly radiation. He regained his feet and ran back up as the earth tremors redoubled.

It was a scene from hell. All around, as far as the horizon, the giant forms left by the Sharu were shifting, fusing, melting like the Harp or, occasionally, detonating rather spectacularly. Something else was rising from the rubble, something Gepta didn't want to see.

He leaped into his scoutship but neatly tumbled it off the roof before he got it properly airborne. Ahead, toward the spaceport, an ungainly crustacean-shaped object lifted from the runway.

Gepta cursed.

He heeled the fighter around, then aimed it straight for the *Millennium Falcon.* Closing, closing, he laid a thumb on the firing stud, his crosshairs on the unsuspecting freighter.

Two things happened.

Aboard the *Falcon,* another thumb rode another stud. Energy streaked toward the fighter Vuffi Raa had noticed landing on the roof. The *Falcon*'s radar was good, and they'd both been alert against flying debris.

I may not be much of a pilot yet, but I can shoot, Lando thought.

Almost simultaneously, a small obelisk of Sharu manufacture exploded beneath Gepta's fighter, driving fragments into the small craft. The explosion staggered the scout, disabling it but throwing it from the path of Lando's beam.

Seconds later, Rokur Gepta clambered from the wreckage as the *Millennium Falcon* soared away, safe, and with a precious load: the last life-crystals ever to be harvested in the Rafa System. Lando would be very, very rich.

Gepta shook a fist at the departing ship.

Someday . . .

LANDO CALRISSIAN
AND THE FLAMEWIND OF OSEON

———

H<small>E WAS SLIGHTLY</small> over a meter tall, from the faceted wide-angle lens glowing redly atop his highly polished pentagonal body to the fine feathery tips of his chromium-plated tentacles.

Of these, there were five, which he felt was as it should be. After all, hadn't he been created in the image of his manufacturers?

He thought of himself as *Vuffi Raa,* an unsentimental designation from a different numbering system and a different language, half a galaxy ago. It served well enough as a name.

At the moment, he was in a hurry.

The tree-lined Esplanade of Oseon 6845 was a broad, jungly, cobblestoned thoroughfare built exclusively for pedestrian traffic, no matter what the individual sentient's personal means of locomotion. It was equipped with an artificial gravity field three meters deep to accommodate the most attenuated of species. It was lined on both sides with elegantly restrained shops to accommodate the very richest.

It has been said that the commercial footage along the domed Esplanade of Oseon 6845 is the most expensive in the known universe. And that the patrons strolling its landscaped and sculptured kilometers are the wealthiest. Vuffi Raa didn't know about that—a rare failing of information on his part. In the first place, he hadn't the appropriate statistics ready to hand (in a manner of speaking). And if compelled to base his opinion on an *n* of one— the single case with which he was intimately familiar—he'd have had to hold the opposite was true. Not everybody there was rich. Not everybody there had come of what had been, until recently, an embarrassingly lengthy list of thoroughly dissatisfied customers.

Freeble-reeep!

From the heavily planted median on the Esplanade, an entity that might have been a songbird warbled noisily in what may have been a bush, momentarily distracting the little robot. You could never tell. In the plush, cosmopolitan resort, the creature doing the singing might well be a photosynthetic vegetable attempting to attract pollen carriers, and the foliage it perched in, a soil-rooted animal. The entire Oseon System was like that, a rich-man's playground, cleverly intended by those who had ordained its construction to be full of surprises.

But then, so was life itself. Their very presence in this overstuffed watering hole, his and his master's, was ample testimony to that.

Vuffi Raa forced his jumbled thoughts back into relevant channels. He was a Class Two droid, with intellectual and emotional capacities roughly equaling those of organic sapients. And an uncorrected tendency in his programming to let his mind wander and to mix his metaphors on occasion. It was a price he paid for being one of the rare machines abroad with an imagination.

At the moment, it was a luxury he couldn't afford. He held the blackened evidence before his eye again as a reminder. It was a fist-sized chunk of scorched metal and fused silicon. A few hours ago, it had been a neutrino hybridizer, a delicate and critical component in the sub-lightspeed drive of a certain class and vintage of starship.

Now it looked like a microcredit's worth of asteroid mine-tailings.

Unconscious of a gesture he had acquired from long association with human beings, Vuffi Raa raised his free tentacle to scratch at the upper portion of his five-sided torso—the closest thing he had to a head. The little droid was pentadextrous, having no preference as to which of his five sinuous limbs he used for getting around on, which he used for holding, carrying, or manipulating objects. Such as treacherous lumps of recently molten quartz and platinum.

A well-rounded, versatile, and radially symmetrical fellow was Vuffi Raa.

And a very worried one.

His brisk but absentminded pace carried him past a leaf-shaded decorative pond where something between a green mammal and a small many-jointed insect dabbled a line—actually an extension of its right front leg—into half a meter of water. There was a modest ripple, a splash, then a *snap!* The creature reeled in a tiny, colorful fish, devouring it on the spot and spitting the bones back into the water.

Vuffi Raa never even noticed.

At long last he reached the expensively decorated surface entrance of the exclusive Hotel Drofo. With a brotherly salute, Vuffi Raa strode past the door-being, a robot painted in the garish gold and purple livery of the establishment, and went directly to one of the eight down-shafts leading into the hotel proper.

On an asteroid, even one like Oseon 6845, and even where a first-rate hotel is concerned, surface area comes dear. Volume is cheap.

Selecting LOBBY on the miniature display beside the entrance to the down-shaft, he waited for the elevator to take his measure, then fell—"drifted" might be a better word—at a fraction of the augmented surface acceleration of the asteroid gently downward several dozen meters, coming at last to a cushioned rest at the bottom of the shaft. He stepped out into the whispery bustle of the underground hotel.

Plenty of other droids were in evidence, mingling freely with the humans, humanoids, and nonhumans present. Most of the automata here were in service of one sort or another; they were unusually conspicuous in their number and visibility.

The galaxy over, robots were the object of harsh and persistent prejudice. The Oseon was different, however. Cynics pointed out that neither its current inhabitants nor their ancestors were ever likely to have worried much about losing a job. The place was filled with exiled and vacationing nobility. Captains of industry, active and retired, gravitated here, along with majors, colonels, and generals. Mercantile—and literal—pirates who had purchased themselves a little class, sometimes from that selfsame deposed aristocracy, rubbed shoulders and less human body parts with media stars from a million different systems.

The little droid knew the man he was seeking would be in one of the small, comfortably furnished gaming salons just off the Grand Lobby, here on the first, or bottom, floor. Finding the room wouldn't be any problem, but getting in might be. Gamblers tended to be jealous of their privacy. He "shouldered" his way through the richly dressed crowd, thinking about the news he had for his master—and how very reluctant he was to deliver it.

A human being can only stand so much bad news.

It had begun with an adventure. His master had won a starship—a small converted freighter, actually, called the *Millennium Falcon*—in yet another card game, and had whimsically decided to add "captain" to his other professional titles: gambler, rogue, and scoundrel. He was proud of every one of them, though he preferred "con *artiste*" to what the authorities usually had upon the tips of their sharp and unforgiving tongues.

He'd been a perfectly terrible pilot in the beginning. Vuffi Raa, an accomplished ship-handler by virtue of inbuilt programming, was gradually taking care of that in two ways: piloting the *Falcon* when the need arose; teaching his master to do it for himself whenever they had time.

He'd won Vuffi Raa in a card game, as well. That had triggered a series of events that culminated with their leaving the Rafa System with the very last full cargo of the fabulous life-crystals ever harvested there. The only load ever removed from the system legally by a private cargo vessel.

And they were rich. Temporarily.

Yet his master hadn't seemed very happy, filling out landing-permit forms, going over bills of lading, figuring overhead and profit margin. Even with Vuffi Raa along to make the workload lighter . . . It was too much like going straight. The gambler yearned to practice his original profession once again.

Thus, when the invitation had suddenly arrived out of nowhere to come and play *sabacc* in the Oseon, where the pickings were the richest in the galaxy, the pair's freelance cargo days had come to an abrupt and highly welcome end. They'd blazed across a hundred parsecs to be here on time. The *Falcon*'s speed, in competent tentacles, was legendary. And here they were.

Trouble was, someone had attempted to assure that they be not only here, but also back in the Rafa, out on the Edge, down at the Core, and everyplace else tiny little pieces of their respectively organic and mechanical existences could be scattered.

That someone, it would appear, didn't like them very much.

Vuffi Raa approached the heavy antiqued wooden double doors. Standing before these was an enormous humanoid in an elegantly tailored groundsuit at least four sizes too large for any other two men in the hotel. Beneath the hulking fellow's stylish armpits the robot could make out the twin bulges of a pair of Imperial-issue blasters.

"Excuse me, gentlebeing," offered the little droid, "I have a message for one of the players inside." He produced a card his master had given him for use in just such a circumstance.

To Vuffi Raa's overwhelming relief, the bouncer/bodyguard looked at the holocard as the letters of instruction danced across its surface, nodded politely, and stepped aside. The doors parted slightly; Vuffi Raa squeezed past them.

The air inside the small, luxurious chamber was full of smoke, at least a dozen different, mingling odors, despite the best efforts of its starship-class life-support systems. In the center, seated at a table ringed with players and kibitzers, lounged his master, resplendent in tasteful and expensive velvoid semiformal ship-clothes.

The robot approached, waiting until the hand was finished—his master raked in a substantial pile of credit tokens—then tugged gently at the hem of his short cloak.

"Master?"

The figure turned, looked down. White teeth in a dark face, irresistible smile, intelligent and mischievous eyes.

"What is it, Vuffi Raa—and how many times have I asked you not to call me master?"

They were both whispering against a noisy background.

The droid held up the oddly shaped clump of debris for his master's inspection. "There wasn't any spontaneous breakdown in the phase-shift controls aboard the *Falcon*, Master. I'm afraid you were right, that this makes two such incidents."

His master nodded grimly. "So it was a bomb."

"Yes, Master, someone is trying to murder you."

II

Lando Calrissian shook his head ironically and grinned.

He had good reason. His first evening in the Oseon, his first *sabacc* game, and already he was ahead some twenty-three thousand credits.

The dashing young gambler stood, dressed impeccably at an hour when most people were rumpled and tired, before a full-length mirror, stroking the brand-new mustache he'd begun only a few weeks ago, when things looked so much bleaker. Yes, by the Core, it did give him a certain panache, a certain elan, a certain . . .

And without filling out so much as a single form in triplicate (if that was logically possible)—his mind was drifting back again to the money tucked into the pockets of his velvoid semiformals—without acquiring a permit, easement, license, variance, or Certificate of Mother-May-I.

Here was one fat bankroll that wasn't going to evaporate when he wasn't watching it!

What added amusement to triumph was that *sabacc* was a game considerably more complex and infinitely riskier than the entrepreneurship he'd been attempting since he'd acquired the *Millennium Falcon*. It called for quicker judgment, greater courage, and a more sophisticated understanding of human (in a broadly tolerant manner of speaking) nature.

So why was he so casually accomplished at the former and so miserably rotten at the latter?

He shrugged to himself, crossed the hotel room from the door he'd closed and locked securely not very many moments before.

Let's see—just the most recent example. He'd won the *Falcon* and Vuffi Raa, then proceeded to earn a handsome fee (work he'd been coerced into doing) that, by all rights, ought to have set him up for life. Orchard crystals from the Rafa System had never been cheap to begin with. Humanoids who wore them found their life spans extended, their intelligence somewhat enhanced. They were both valuable and rare. They grew in only one place in the universe.

Lando had known, when he and the bot had quit the Rafa, that there would be no more life-crystals, at least for a while. The colonial government there had been overthrown by insurgent natives. Thus, he'd held out for the highest possible prices. Yet, somehow, the money—several millions—had seemed to disappear before his very eyes, eaten up in spacecraft maintenance, docking charges, taxes, surtaxes, sursurtaxes, and bribes. Every time he closed a deal, no matter what margin he'd built in at the beginning, he wound up losing. It didn't seem sensible: the more money he earned, the poorer he became.

If he got any richer, he'd be broke.

Perhaps he simply hadn't been playing in the right league. One of the rules of this new game (new to Lando, anyway) was that they didn't tell you the rules until it was too late. His figurative hat was off to anyone who could *survive* in the world of business, let alone prosper.

A small noise in the next room alerted him. He peeked in: Vuffi Raa was laying out tomorrow's wardrobe for him. He'd told the little fellow a hundred times that it wasn't necessary. He needed no valet, and long ago had begun thinking of the robot as a friend more than anything else. But exactly like a good friend (or consummate servant), the droid understood the gambler's need for some time alone without conversation, while he unwound from the evening's tense preoccupations. Lando suspected that Vuffi Raa actually wanted to discuss the bomb he'd discovered—the second since their last planetfall. Well, morning was time enough for that. He closed the connecting door softly and returned to his private thoughts.

A second irony struck him as he watched the bed turn itself down. He shucked out of his dressy bantha-hide knee boots and reclined, one foot dangling over the edge of the bed to the floor.

The very individuals who had prospered most, either at legitimate businesses like freight hauling, or shadier ones such as smuggling (the avocation, in fact, for which the *Falcon* had originally been constructed), those who had made their way to the top, lived here in the Oseon, where one Lando Calrissian, a dismal failure by their standards, experienced little difficulty at all separating them from their hard-won money.

It was their own fault. They'd invited him . . .

FIRE STREAKED FROM the starboard weapons turret of the *Millennium Falcon*.

In desperate haste, Lando swung the quad-guns down and to the left as the drone squadron whooshed by, their own energy-guns coloring the misted space around the freighter.

"*Missed!* Vuffi Raa, hold her a little steadier!"

The ship ducked and swooped, narrowly avoiding being skewered in a cross fire as the drone fighters split up, attacking from both sides.

"*Master, there are too many of—good* shooting, *sir!*"

The little droid's voice issued from an intercom beside Lando's ear. The gambler made an imaginary chalk mark on a purely mental scoreboard, manhandling the guns around for another shot. The drone he'd splattered was an incandescent and expanding ball of dust and gas, augmenting an already dirty region of space.

Anyone else might have *whooped!* victoriously.

Lando fumed in the transparent gun-bubble.

All right, so it *had* been his idea to shortcut through this small nebulosity on the way to the next port. Blast it all, he was carrying valuable, somewhat perishable cargo. Crates of wintenberry jelly. Stacks of mountain bollem hides. Expensive tinklewood fishing rods. In short, the produce of a frontier planet. His corner-cutting could save them precious days, compared to routes preferred by scheduled cargo haulers.

The shields pulsed with coruscating brilliance. They were taking hits again!

He slewed the quad-guns hard, pressed the double triggers. Bolts of ravening energy rammed directly into a pair of tiny unmanned fighters screaming toward the ship. One exploded, the other, severely damaged, corkscrewed crazily out of Lando's line of vision.

Vuffi Raa rolled the ship, skated into a wild, stomach-wrenching yaw, adroitly avoiding a direct hit. They were a good team together, Lando thought.

Besides, it wasn't much as nebulosities go. Even deep inside the scruffy patch of gas, a few molecules every cubic meter produced very little visible clouding. They did slow a ship down, however, making it dangerous to use the faster-than-light drive. That's probably why the regular lines avoided the place. But Lando, calculating distance over time, had figured that, even at a substantial reduction from lightspeed, they'd still gain time and profit thereby.

He'd been wrong.

Six more meter-diameter drones bore directly for his turret. The enemy seemed to have an endless supply. Lando caught a glance of their mother vessel, a pirate lying off and directing the attack in relative safety. She was approximately four times the displacement of the *Falcon,* clumsily built, a large sphere attached to a slightly smaller cylinder, the whole awkward assembly patched and mottled by hard use and long neglect.

He could imagine half a hundred crew-beings, hunched over their drone panels in a dimly lit control center. They were probably as broke and desperate as he was.

Waiting until the last possible moment, he let loose all four barrels on maximum power and dispersal. Lights dimmed aboard the *Falcon.* Two saucer-shaped drones blossomed into fireballs, the third was holed severely. The fourth, fifth, and sixth zoomed over his head in ragged formation, past the gun-blister, and out of his visual range before he could tell what he'd done to them. He released the triggers.

Full illumination sprang forth again.

Nebulosities *were* good for hiding spaceships. The gas, dust, and ions, the magnetic and static fields made a hash of long-range sensor instrumentation. That's how they'd wound up in this confounded—

"Vuffi Raa!" Lando shouted suddenly. "Close on the pirate herself! I've had enough of this. Give me a pass at her reaction-drive system!"

"Very well, Master."

There was doubt in the robot's doubly electronic voice—not concerning Lando's combat abilities. Quite the contrary. It was simply that the droid's most fundamental programming forbade him to take the life of a mechanical or organic sapient being. He was straining his cybernetic ethics severely even now, conning a fighting ship. Yet strain them he did.

In a long, graceful arc with a little flip on the end, the *Falcon* soared toward the pirate, taking her by surprise. A few guns warmed up feebly—too late—as their startled operators switched attention from remote-control panels to fire-control systems. The tiny flying weapons might be adequate against an unarmed freighter or a pleasure yacht that stumbled into the cloud, but they hadn't been conceived or built for mortal engagement with a vessel like the *Falcon,* half pirate ship herself and bristling with more guns than her crew could handle all at once.

Trusting his ship's shields, Lando bore down upon the quad-gun, drilling its quadruple high-power beams at the reaction-drive outlet at the far end of the pirate's spherical section. Once again the *Falcon*'s interior lights dimmed, and for the first time, it occurred to Lando that his heavy trigger finger was costing something. However, the enemy's thrust tubes were beginning to glow. First red, they quickly became orange-yellow. They'd been molded to withstand heat and pressure right enough, but not from the outside in.

Suddenly, a starburst appeared in space between him and the pirate.

"*Good shooting, Master. You got another one!*"

"Nonsense, I didn't even—*great merciful heavens!*"

All around them, balls of fiery gas stood out against the starry background. The drone fleet was destroying itself! The pirate swiveled on her center of gravity, glowed savagely from her own internal fires, and streaked away.

At the extreme end of her flight line, toward the edge of the nebulosity, Lando could make out the flash as she shifted into faster-than-light. It was a deadly risk even so; they must be frightened badly.

"Well, well! Stand down from Battle Stations," he informed his mechanical partner. "I'll be up to the cockpit in a minute. Put some coffeine on, will you? And by the way, Vuffi Raa . . ."

He unstrapped himself from the gun-chair webbing, turning his captain's hat—the one with all the golden braid—around the right way, and zipped his shipsuit up a couple of inches.

"*Yes, Master?*"

"Don't call me master!"

Stepping into the broadly curving main corridor, Lando passed the sublight-drive area of the *Millennium Falcon*. As if sprouting from the floor, there stood a tapered chromium snake-like entity, about a meter long, tending the control panel. At its slenderest end, it branched into five slim, delicate "fingers" that twisted knobs and adjusted slide-switches. In the center of the "palm," Lando knew, was a small glassy red eyespot.

Farther along, where a cluster of instruments comprised the radar and other detection devices, another metallic serpent stood watch. There were three more like it elsewhere in the ship, giving attention to sensitive areas that could not be handled from the cockpit monitors.

Up front, Lando flopped into the left-hand seat, a pride-preserving concession tacitly made between himself and the real pilot of the vessel. *It* lay in the other seat, a pentagon-shaped slab of bright silvery-colored metal and electronics. A large lens pulsed redly at the top. The object was strapped down firmly to the seat. One of the "snakes" hovered over an instrument panel, half a meter away.

"Vuffi Raa, you've got to pull yourself together." Lando chuckled, fumbling under the panel. He brought out a slim cigar and lit it, eyeing the armless, legless contraption next to him and waiting for a reaction. Outside, the fog began to disperse as their own reaction drives brought them to the margin of the nebulosity. Was he imagining things, or was the plastic window transparency slightly pitted? More dust in the region than he'd calculated—and another expensive repair.

The snake floated downward, attached itself to one flat side of the pentagon, and waggled at the gambler. "Master, that wasn't funny the *first* hundred times you said it." Vuffi Raa began unstrapping his torso from the copilot's seat, one-tentacled.

From the passageway outside, another snake drifted in, settled in the chair, and linked itself, becoming the second of Vuffi Raa's limbs to rejoin his body. Lando looked over the ship's instrumentation, and his glow of combative satisfaction evaporated completely.

"By the Edge! Look at those power-consumption gauges! Those quad-guns are expensive to shoot! We would have used less power going the long way around!"

It was a hell of a note, Lando thought, when even defeating a band of pirates had to be calculated on the balance sheet. And at a loss.

"We'll be lucky to break even on this load, do you realize that?"

Regaining yet a third tentacle, the robot refrained diplomatically from pointing out that he'd opposed the shortcut in the first place. He hadn't known exactly why. The big, regularly scheduled companies avoided the route although it took parsecs and whole days off the run, exactly as Lando had insisted. On the other hand, big, regularly scheduled companies seldom attempted anything new or daring—which was what always made the future so bright for newer, smaller companies.

Now, between the star-fog and the pirates it concealed, both of the partners knew what was wrong with the nebulosity.

Fourth and fifth manipulators in place, Vuffi Raa cautiously punched up the interstellar drive. The stars stretched into attenuated blurs and vanished.

Yet none of that explained what was wrong with Dilonexa XXIII.

III

"FISHING POLES?"

The customs agent was a small man with wiry arms and legs, knobbly knuckles. He was dressed, like everybody else on that self-consciously agrarian planet, in bib overalls. In his case, they were made of a deep green satyn, heavily creased. His shiny pink scalp shone through a field of close-cropped gray stubble.

"You gotta be kidding, Mac! In the first place, there ain't a body of water on the planet bigger'n a bathtub; we don't like to spare the land. In the second place, nobody here has any time for fishing. An' in the third place, the native fish taste *terrible*—lacka trace metals or something."

The sun of the Dilonexa System (a catalog number Lando didn't remember and hadn't bothered asking Vuffi Raa about as they'd made their approach) was a gigantic blue-white furnace. The twenty-two planets nearest it were great places to get a suntan. In a couple of microseconds.

The outer seventeen were iceboxes.

But the planet in the middle, at least in the view of its early colonists, made it all worthwhile. It was large, nearly twenty-five thousand kilometers in diameter, composed mostly of the lighter elements, which gave it a surface gravity not too unreasonable. Nearly everything of metal had to be shipped in.

But Dilonexa XXIII was rich, an agricultural world whose fields stretched unimaginable distances around its surface, providing foodstuffs, plastics, combustible fuels—everything with an organic base. Its inhabitants, fat farmers and their fatter families, had acquired a taste for some of the finer things in life.

Which was why Lando had brought his valuable, somewhat perishable cargo there.

He shook his head ruefully as he watched the Dilonexan ground crew put fuel elements into the *Falcon* where it rested on the ferrocrete apron—and gaping wounds in his credit account.

"Well, then, how about the jelly and the hides? Surely—"

"Had a second cousin once named Shirley," the little man explained, scratching a mole under his chin and squinting up at the cloudless sky as if in aid to memory. "Tried that wintenberry stuff you're haulin'. Broke down with the gallopin' gosharooties. Too many trace minerals for a fourth-generation colonist. We gotta watch what we eat, us Dilonexicans, that's a fact."

Lando shook his head again; it was getting to be a habit. "But look here, Inspector, I—"

"Call me Bernie. You wouldn't happen t'have a cigar on you?"

The gambler visualized the big chest of cigars in his safe aboard the *Falcon*. "Even if I did, they'd be from Rafa IV, a place just *lousy* with heavy metals. Probably kill you. What about the leather, then? I have a hold full of beautifully fur-tanned hides, and—"

The wizened customs officer interrupted Lando again, this time with an upraised hand. He pointed toward the prairie that surrounded them. Lando knew that virtually the entire globe was plains just like the scenery he saw now. He also knew that city-sized tornados swept, unimpeded, around the planet's circumference—that is, they had until gigantic weather-control satellites had been installed. Their potent, tornado-destroying energy-weaponry also made it impossible to smuggle on or off the planet—or to get away with unpaid bills.

"Whaddya see out there, Mac? A zillion acres of grain crop, that's what. We can't eat it, but the native bovines can, an' we can eat them. Lookie here! When's the last time you saw a genuine leather awning? You got it—over on that building right there. We got leather comin' out our ears. There's a sixty-five percent im-port duty on hides, seventy-five percent on fishin' poles an' other recreational goodies, a hundred an' five on poisonous substances like that jelly you're pushin'."

Lando groaned. First the expensive battle with the pirates, now this—plus he was out his landing fees, permits, and refueling costs.

"But say, you're Cap'n Calrissian, ain't ya, from the *Millen-nium Falcon*? Gotta message for you somewhere here." He fum-bled in his overall pockets until he pulled out a chip with a keyboard displayed on its face, punched numbers and letters into it.

"Right! From the Oseon, it says. That's quite a ways away, ain't it? You want it now?"

"Oh, very well," Lando answered despondently. He didn't really care. All he really wanted was a nice quiet place to lie down for a century or two.

"Okay, that'll be thirteen-fifty, Mac."

Lando blinked. So it wasn't a paid message. Odd, and thirteen and a half credits seemed a little cheap for interstellar communi-cation, but . . . He pulled a few bills out of his pocket.

"You don't unnerstand, Mac. There's an import fee on inter-stellar messages here. We figure a fella oughta be content with what's on just one planet, an' not go sashayin' off. . . . Anyway, that'll be thirteen *hundred* an' fifty credits."

"Forget it, then," said Lando in disgust. "It's probably just an—"

The little man grinned up at him. "There's a two-thousand-credit penalty for *not* pickin' up interstellar messages. Ain't neat t'leave 'em lyin' around."

IN THE COMPARATIVE quiet and sanity of what passed for a lounge aboard the *Millennium Falcon*, Lando inserted the coded chip

into a playback machine. An overstuffed, cheerful face materialized above the instrument.

"To Captain Lando Calrissian of the Millennium Falcon:
greetings and salutations! I am Lob Doluff, Administrator Senior
of the Oseon System. You haven't heard of me, I'll wager, but, my
dear boy, I have heard of you!"

The recording continued: "Your reputation as a player of sabacc is perhaps wider spread and more salubrious than you know.
My associates and I, a small group of fanciers of the game, would
like to invite you here at your convenience, to play with us. If you
are interested, please name the time and stakes. Every courtesy
will be extended to you during your stay with us. My very warmest and anticipatory regards to you. Lob Doluff, signing off."

A grin began to spread itself across Lando's face. In that context, he could cut his losses. All he needed was a small stake when
he got to the Oseon. He thumbed a communicator switch.

"Vuffi Raa?"

The robot was below, out on the concrete, supervising the last
of the fueling operation. "Yes, Master?" came his voice.

"Don't call me master." He'd sell the fishing rods to
somebody—there wouldn't be a scheduled import duty if there
wasn't some market, no matter how small. Too bad no one
needed tinklewood radio antennas. Not surprisingly, he'd learned
the agricultural planet would pay top credit for the contents of
his ship's waste-cycling system. "Get up here and give me a hand,
will you? We've got a thousand hides to chop up and several
hundred crates of jelly to put down the disposal."

HE'D USED HIS own communications equipment, once they were
out of the atmosphere of Dilonexa XXIII, saving several hundred
credits in the process. Doluff was delighted that Lando was on
the way, and promised a high-stakes game in the most luxurious
of surroundings. Lando shaved and showered, dressed himself in
civilian clothing, though they were still several days' transit from

the Oseon. He simply wanted to get the feeling back of doing what he was properly cut out to do. As Vuffi Raa droided the controls, Lando sat in the lounge practicing with the cards.

There were seventy-eight of these, in five suits: Sabres, Staves, Flasks, and Coins, plus the special suit of face cards with negative values. The object was to build a two- or three-card hand adding up to twenty-three, no more. What made it especially difficult was that the cards were "smart"—each was, in fact, a sophisticated electronic chip capable of changing randomly to another value, while the card it replaced changed to something else. This made for a fast-paced, nerve-wracking game combining elements of skill and fortune.

Lando thought of it as relaxing.

He held up a card, watched it blur and shift and refocus, from Commander of Staves to Three of Coins. In the surface field of a gaming table, the cards would retain their identities. This was necessary for scoring: imagine tossing down a perfect twenty-three, only to have it transmute itself into a losing hand.

Another card, the Seven of Sabres. It stayed its old familiar self for rather a longish time, finally changed into Endurance, one of the negative cards. Lando shuffled it back into the deck.

The Oseon, he thought, I should know a great deal more about it and its people. Principally, what the traffic will bear. He turned from the cards to a datalink, punched a few buttons. There it was: oh, yes! While it might be remarkable for its rich inhabitants, it was downright famous for its seasonally spectacular scenery.

Oseon was the home of the Flamewind.

Many stellar systems have asteroid belts, where whole planets have come unglued or never quite managed to coalesce. Circular zones occupied by rocks rather than worlds, their constituents could range in size from sand grains to objects hundreds—even thousands—of kilometers in extent. Some few systems had more than one such belt.

The Oseon had nothing else.

In the Oseon there were no planets at all in the proper sense of the word. Not even the Core knew what disaster had taken place there, perhaps billions of years before the advent of humankind. Maybe a rogue star had passed too close, its gravity well disrupting the planet-forming process. Maybe some unique element in the makeup of the system had caused the planets to blow themselves up.

Perhaps there had been an ancient, alien war.

Whatever the cause, the Oseon sun was now surrounded by seven broad bands of floating debris, billions upon billions of subplanetary bodies. The largest of these worldlets, Oseon 6845, was an artificially honeycombed mountain seven hundred kilometers in diameter, filled with luxury hotels, nightspots, and palatial residences. Other rocks in other belts had been converted into estates for the rich and superrich. There was plenty of room.

All of this, while quite extraordinary, was not in itself sufficient to turn the place into a five-star tourist attraction. But once a year (by what reckoning Lando forgot even as he read it), the Oseon System's sun flared in a peculiar manner (giving rise to the theory about a unique element blowing up the planets). As the flares tore streamers of excited vapor from the nearest of the asteroids, the entire system fluoresced, pulsed, resonated, generating enormous bands of shifting color, fairy brilliance, millions of kilometers long and wide, like the spokes of an enormous wheel. Colors ranged across the humanly visible spectrum, exceeding it broadly at both ends.

There was, very possibly, nothing else quite so impressively beautiful in the known universe as the Flamewind of Oseon.

Lando did a rapid calculation: yes, if his luck ran well for long enough, he and Vuffi Raa would be there at the right time. Perhaps that had been intended by Lob Doluff as an incentive of sorts. How nice: a kind of bonus they could both—

KABOOMMMMMM!

The *Millennium Falcon* pitched end over end with sudden violence.

Through the ports, stars whirled crazily about them in a meaningless pattern. Alarms went off, filling the cabin with an ear-splitting wail. Smoke began seeping into the room as random bits and pieces—Lando's cards, his cigars, an old pair of socks—clung in odd, unpredictable places, responding to the primitive artificial gravity imposed on the ship by its wild head-over-heels spin.

"Vuffi Raa!"

Grasping the nearest bolted-down furniture, Lando shouted at the intercom. "What in the name of the Eternal was that?"

There was no response.

Pulling himself hand over hand against the nonsensically vectored drag, Lando made slow, unsteady progress to the bridge. Klaxons beat upon his head, their noise a tangible thing. The final turn of corridor was like crawling up a vertical sewer pipe, each rung of the emergency ladder coming with greater difficulty as he climbed above the ship's new center of gravity.

Once in the cockpit, he climbed exhaustedly into his seat and strapped himself in, trying without much success to catch his breath.

Rendered virtually invisible by their speed, Vuffi Raa's tentacles were flying over the controls. It must be some emergency, thought Lando, if even the multitalented robot was too busy now to talk. To the continued tune of shrilling alarms, Lando began assisting him, newly acquired knowledge coming sure and true to his fingertips. First, they stabilized the ship's insane changes of attitude. Up became up once again, down, down.

Next, they located the source of the explosion. It was in the bottommost level of the *Falcon*, seemingly just under the belly skin. They triggered cannisters of firefoam, then jettisoned the resultant mess into open space. Temperature indicators relaxed, a few red lights winked to green. The alarms shut off; a deafening silence reigned.

Finally, Vuffi Raa laid the proper course back in, and they were on their way to the Oseon once again, although at something less than normal interstellar cruising speed.

"How bad is the damage?" Lando was already unstrapping himself. He wiped a shaking hand over his dampened forehead.

Vuffi Raa looked over the control panel, several sections of which were still ablaze with red and yellow lights. "It would appear, Master, to be superficial. The difficulty began when I shifted into faster-than-light drive. We shall have to inspect it close up, however. I don't trust the remote sensors."

"Very well," the gambler answered, "let's get below. I'll put on a pressure suit and—"

"Master, it is standard procedure in such instances for one crew member to remain at the controls, while the other—"

"All right, then," Lando said, a trifle irritated, "*you* stay here. I'll suit up and—"

"Master, I can operate perfectly well in a hard vacuum without a suit. Explosive decompression doesn't bother me. And I know how to weld. Do you?"

The little droid, of course, showed no expression, but Lando felt as if there were a pair of human arms somewhere inside its shiny chassis, folded across an imaginary chest, beneath an unbearably smug grimace.

"Have it your own way, then! I'll *still* suit up. It seems a sensible safety precaution, just in case you open the wrong door somewhere. Keep me informed, will you—*and don't call me master!*"

Vuffi Raa unstrapped himself from the copilot's seat, rose, and strode to the back of the control area. "I'll do better than keep you informed, Master. Observe that monitor nearest your left elbow."

Swiveling his neck, Lando was suddenly seeing himself, quite plainly if somewhat distortedly, as if by a wide-angle lens held too close to its subject. The colors seemed a bit off, and the gambler realized he was seeing a translation of infrared and ultraviolet information in addition to the usual spectrum.

"I get it: I see what you see. You know, this could come in very handy: like, say, the next time I'm in a game, and—"

"But, Master, that would be unethical!"

"Wouldn't it just? All right, we'll talk about it later. Meanwhile, let's get to work on the damage."

They both shuffled out of the cockpit, headed toward separate destinations.

Ten minutes later, Lando was again seated in his pilot's recliner, watching the monitor through the transparent faceplate of a spacesuit helmet. He thought about opening the visor to smoke a cigar, remembered the magic words "explosive decompression," and desisted. After all, they didn't know yet how badly hurt the *Falcon* was. A footfall, no matter how light, in the wrong place might blow a hull panel, which—

On the screen, Vuffi Raa had made it to the site of the explosion. His viewpoint approached a heavily damaged piece of machinery.

"Why, that's just one of the hydraulic jacks for the boarding ramp," Lando exclaimed, almost indignantly. "There's nothing flammable or explosive in that section—and what does it have to do at all with the ultralightspeed drive?"

The camera angle tilted downward. A tentacle reached for something wedged between two heavy springs. The object had to be sawed and twisted out of its place, then the tentacle lifted it nearer the robot's eye.

"What the devil is *that*?" Lando asked the intercom.

The thing looked like a spring itself, a section of thick-gauge wire coiled and then twisted around into an evasively familiar shape, rather like a doughnut, but with an extra turn, pretzel-wise.

"It's a Möbius coil of some kind, Master," Vuffi Raa answered at last. "They're used as tuners and—my word, it's an *antenna*. Master, someone placed a device here to detect the shift into ultralightspeed. You see, there's a hyperware generated by the—"

"Yes, yes," Lando interrupted impatiently. "But what's the point of all that?"

"There would be a considerable point, Master, if the antenna was connected to a controller that, in turn, was connected to a bomb."

The gambler pondered that. "You mean, someone just walked up and attached it back on Dilonexa, while we were refueling, and when we buttoned up for takeoff, we effectively brought it inside the ship ourselves?"

"Something like that, Master."

"A bomb. Do you suppose they found out about the winten-berry jelly?"

IV

D EEP SPACE.
The officially decommissioned Imperial Cruiser *Wennis*
bored through the blackness like a thing alive, a hungry thing, a
thing with the need to kill. It had been built for that, nearly three-
quarters of a century ago. Now it was an obsolete machine, dis-
placed by more efficient killers.

Still, it served its purpose.

On the bridge, a uniformed crew quietly attended to their duties. They were a mixed lot, officially—again, *officially*—civilians.
Many were the worst of the worst, the scum and misfits of a
million-system civilization. Others were the best that could be
had, the cream of the elite.

Like the *Wennis,* this, too, served a purpose.

All were military personnel, now indefinitely detached to serve
aboard the decommissioned cruiser. In this, they served their Emperor (although not without an occasional—extremely discreet—
grumble) and hoped for early promotion and other rewards.

In practicality, all served an entity who, although somewhat
less elevated than His Imperial Majesty, was nevertheless quite as
frighteningly impressive. This figure stalked the bridge as well,
draped from crown to heel in the heavy dark swathings people
had come to associate with the mysterious and sinister Sorcerers
of Tund.

Rokur Gepta, all features save his burning eyes concealed be-

hind the final windings of his turban-like headgear, barely suppressed a scream.

"*Do you have the temerity to tell me you have failed again?*"

The officer he addressed was not happy with his present assignment. In the first place, his uniform had been stripped of all
rank and unit markings. It made him feel naked. In the second
place, he could not understand why a battle-ready cruiser and its
full crew were pursuing a single tiny tramp freighter.

The officer gulped. "I only mean to say, sir, that the device our
agent planted seems to have gone off prematurely. It was supposed to explode, on your orders, just before atmospheric entry
at their next port of call."

"*So you have failed twice!* You idiot, they're en route to the
Oseon—there will *be* no atmospheric entry! I have had enough of
this!"

The sorcerer made a gesture with his gloved fist. The officer
groaned, sweat sprang out on his forehead, and he sank to his
knees.

"You see how much more effective it is than mere pain, don't
you? Everyone has memories, little items from their past best left
buried: humiliations, embarrassments, mistakes . . . sometimes
fatal ones. All the ways we have failed those we have loved, the
ways they have failed us!"

Gepta made another gesture.

"No, you can think of nothing else! The ignobility races round
and round your mind, amplified, feeding on itself!"

The officer's face went gray, he swayed on his knees, his back
bowed, his clenched fists began dripping blood where the fingernails cut into the palms. A little froth appeared at one corner of
his mouth, followed by more blood as he gnashed at his lips and
tongue. Finally, he lost all control, collapsed in a heap, and lay
there, twitching, moaning.

Gepta released him.

A pair of orderlies appeared, dragged the broken man from
the bridge. Oddly enough, he was far from destroyed. Gepta had

noticed, in the past, a certain increase in efficiency, perhaps even slightly enhanced intelligence after one of these crises. So why not make a good tool better? The tool was not in any position to complain of the stresses involved. Did it hurt a knife to grind it to razor sharpness? Who cared?

Slightly invigorated himself, the sorcerer turned, strode back to the control chair he usually occupied on the bridge. He was not captain on the *Wennis,* but he liked to stay on top of things.

He sat. Beside the chair was a pair of cages, each perhaps half a meter cubed. In the first, he kept his pet.

It was scarcely visible in its bed of gray-green muck, simply three stalky black legs thrusting upward crookedly, curving inward with a certain hungry, greedy energy perhaps only Gepta could see and sympathize with. The legs were sparsely hairy.

In the second cage, Gepta kept another type of creature. There were half a dozen of the things; soon he'd need a new supply. They were about the size of mice, very like mice, in fact, but with curly golden pelts and impossibly large blue eyes. Each creature was sleek and clean, seemed to radiate warmth. Each had a bushy tail, rather like that of a miniature squirrel.

Suppressing a shudder, Gepta reached into the cage of the furry creatures. Using a large pair of plastic tongs, he seized one—it squeaked with surprise and pain—and transferred it from its cage. He opened the top of the other cage, dropped it into the center of the upraised hairy legs.

There was a *squelch!,* another terrified squeak, which was cut off sharply, then a *crunch!* Gepta let the lid drop, a warm glow inside him as his pet preened itself, one dark, many-jointed leg grooming another until all three were clean of the blood and fur of its meal.

It did him good to imagine that the small, furry, helpless creature he had just destroyed was Lando Calrissian. It did him a great deal of good. Others had attempted to interfere with Gepta's plans before. Only one had managed to survive. Why, of all people, this insignificant vagabond, this itinerant gambler and charlatan should so frequently come between the sorcerer and his plans was a mystery. Yet it had happened.

Very few individuals understood how much—and how little— the Sorcerers of Tund believed in magic. Even fewer were those who lived to pass the knowledge on to others. Calling up the *Wennis*'s captain's ugly memories, for example, amplifying them, driving out everything else—there was nothing to it, nothing that couldn't be done by anyone, given the proper electronics.

Yet those of Tund had their own beliefs about things that transcended science, and Rokur Gepta was a superstitious soul. He believed that some perverse kind of luck, some fate, karma, kismet, or destiny kept throwing Calrissian in his face. Sometimes it appeared the young gambler wasn't even aware that it was happening.

Now the sorcerer would have an end to it.

He pressed a button set in the arm of his chair. An officer materialized, one a little younger than the captain.

"You are the second in command?" Gepta hissed.

The officer saluted uncertainly. He'd seen his superior dragged from the bridge. "Y-Yes . . . yes, sir, I am. I, er . . . shall we maintain our course for the Oseon, sir?"

Rokur Gepta waited a while to reply, knowing that the prolonged silence would further ravel the young officer's nerves. In a military hierarchy there was *always* something to feel guilty about. It was designed that way, so that an individual couldn't go through a single day without having to stretch, bend, or break a rule. This, of course, worked to the advantage of those at the top of the pyramid.

Just as it was working now.

When a fine sweat sprinkled the officer's brow, Gepta finally spoke.

"No, no. We shall digress for a short time. I'll give you the heading. Your captain will be indisposed for several hours, and I want to be well on my way by the time of his . . . recovery."

———

MANY PARSECS AWAY, in space equally as deep as that which enveloped the cruiser *Wennis,* a strange apparition manifested itself.

At its center lay the naked core of a dreadnaught-class ultralightspeed drive engine, pulsing, glowing, seeming to writhe with unholy energies as it twisted space around itself to deny the basic laws of reality. A closer examination would have disclosed that it was old, very old, patched and welded together out of many such drive engines, long past obsolescence, verging on dangerous fatigue.

Surrounding it were at least two dozen equally weary and obsolete fighters of nearly as many separate pedigrees, some constructed by inhuman races and sloppily converted. They were connected to the drive core with gleaming cables that glowed and sparked and writhed in time to its fundamental frequency. The fighters appeared to be towing the engine. In fact, the reverse was true. These small craft were incapable of making the translation to faster-than-light velocities themselves. They let the core field do it for them.

Militia Leader Klyn Shanga sat before the controls of his aged spacecraft, his eyes unseeing, his mind turned inward. It had been thus for over eleven days—this was the most excruciatingly dull voyage he had ever endured. Yet it was necessary: honor demanded it.

Though alive with lights, his controls were, for practical purposes, inert, locked into the controls of all the other fighters, each of them in turn slaved to a cobbled-together navigational computer on the drive engine.

There was nothing to do, and all the time in the universe to do it.

He had long since stopped thinking of his home, a little-known backwater planet, settled long generations before the present wave of Imperial colonization—settled even before the Old Republic had sent its own explorers outward. He had long since ceased thinking about his family. There was little point: it was highly unlikely he would ever see them again.

He had devoted even less time to thinking about his present task, the mission of this motley group of militiamen, retired policemen, adventurers, and professional soldiers as ancient and obsolete as the craft they flew. They were their culture's expendables. The task was simple and straightforward: find someone and kill him. It didn't matter that their target, their enemy, had damaged their civilization severely, exposed it to a galaxy-wide culture more potent and wealthy, stripping away its hidden safety. It mattered less that the life they sought to take was the very embodiment of evil. Evil or not, it would pass out of existence if they did their work right.

If they didn't, their fates were academic. Evil abounded in the universe, and one life more or less wouldn't make much difference. The damage was done; this was for revenge, pure and simple—and perhaps to protect other helpless, defenseless worlds.

Klyn Shanga glanced through the canopy of his fighter at the rest of the group clustered around the battleship engine. All together, they looked laughable—the same way, no doubt, their world had looked to the intruder. They resembled nothing more than a grotesque, desiccated plant, an interstellar tumbleweed being blown wherever the fates would have it. Shanga tried to take comfort in the notion that nothing could be further from the truth, that they were a spare and deadly force who would take their adversary completely by surprise.

At that moment, his communications console sprang into life.

There were no greetings, no salutations. The beam was tight, intended only for the cluster of fighters. It boomed and faded with the galactic drift.

On the screen, a young military figure was visible, his gray uniform unadorned by rank or unit markings. Shanga knew him to be the second officer of the decommissioned Imperial Cruiser *Wennis.*

The figure did not speak, but only nodded.

Keying his transmitter, Shanga asked, "He is on his way, then?"

The figure nodded again, but hatred and fear burned in his eyes, just as it burned in the heart of Klyn Shanga and all his men.

"He will be there when we arrive?" asked Shanga.

For the first time, the officer spoke. "There is the possibility of some delay—of a detour, apparently—but I believe the original course will be resumed in a short time."

Klyn Shanga rubbed his calloused hands together. In the many decades since his world's last war, he had been a farmer, living peaceably and contentedly among animals and plants and children. Now that could be no more, because of the person they were discussing. He knew his men were listening to the confirmation that the prey was at last near to hand. They had come a long, long way to hear that news.

"You take considerable risk," Shanga said, some sympathy seeping into his weathered expression.

"It is unnecessary to discuss that. It is well worth it. I must signal off; the chance of detection grows by the second."

Shanga nodded. "Be well, then, and good luck."

"The same to you."

MANY PARSECS AWAY, an impatient Rokur Gepta closed a switch and sat back, to ponder. His first, most immediate inclination was to choke the life—better yet, the sanity—from the young pup who was betraying him. Not for the first time was he grateful to himself for having installed the secondary system of surveillance devices in the personal quarters of his underlings. The second officer had easily fooled the official bugs.

Well, Gepta would have his revenge at the appropriate time.

Now it was important to let this complication resolve itself. He did not recognize the individual with whom the officer had spoken, but then Gepta was very old, so old that the truth would have frightened most ordinary beings. He had seen and done a lot in the many centuries he had lived. He had made many enemies, most of them now long dead.

So should it always be.

One thing he could do: hasten the process. He shelved his earlier plans; they had had a certain hesitancy to them anyway. He keyed a switch on the table beside the bed in his living quarters.

"Bridge? Gepta. Cancel previous orders. Reinstate the course I previously gave you. We will proceed directly to the Oseon."

V

LOB DOLUFF WAS a pear-shaped man who looked larger on the televisor than he was in fact. He had what Lando found himself thinking of as a skin-tight dark beard and a naked scalp that looked as though it had been waxed and polished.

His manner was ingratiating. He was an enthusiastic *sabacc* player, and a good loser. This was something of a necessity, it appeared, since enthusiasm and skill do not always go together.

Sitting across the table from Lando, Doluff managed to hold his cards up while resting his elbows on his protuberant stomach. Fate had presented him with a Six of Flasks and a Mistress of Staves on the initial deal, yielding a value of nineteen. Courage and enthusiasm do not always go together, either. He stood pat, somehow failing to take into account the fact that the longer he held the cards, the likelier it was they would alter themselves before his very eyes.

Lando, with a Seven of Coins and the negative card, Demise, needed something better than minus six to win this hand. He dealt himself an Ace of Sabres, bringing the score to nine—still insufficient. The next player also took a card; the Administrator Senior had already decided to refuse; the player to his left took a card; the one to Lando's right stood pat.

Lando dealt himself another card, the betting proceeding with each turn around the table. They had anted at a thousand credits that night, Lando's fourth in the Oseon, and after three rounds of betting, an impressive amount of money lay on the table.

Mistress of Coins. Lando was one point short of a pure *sa-bacc*. He held his peace. The cards seemed slow tonight, reluctant to perform their transmutations. He could feel his luck glowing warm within him. He was relaxed.

The player to his left took a card. The Administrator Senior still stood pat. The next player took a card—and immediately slammed her hand down on the table.

"Zero!" she grumbled in disgust. There were three ways of going out in the game: exceeding twenty-three, falling below minus twenty-three, or hitting zero. The player to Lando's right stood pat.

A flicker of movement in his hand caught Lando's eye. One of the cards was changing.

"*Sabacc!*" he said with satisfaction. Demise had made itself into Moderation. The odds against such consecutivity were high, and so was the value of the pot the young gambler raked in.

The others tossed their cards on the table. The deal would stay with Lando for another hand.

Shuffling the cards, he considered those playing with him. There was, of course, Lob Doluff, too conservative a player to make any real gains—no threat, but a reliable source of income. He should stick with managing a bureaucracy. He wasn't cut out to be a gambler.

That night they were at Doluff's estate. The game shifted to a new place each night it was played. A few kilometers outside what passed for a city, it was a rather large dome on the surface, filled with moist air and tropical plants. The cold stars rose clearer and sharper than they had any natural right to do above the thick jungle that surrounded the players.

The table had been placed on a broad, tiled walkway in the very center of the giant decorative greenhouse. A fountain burbled agreeably nearby. It was practically the only noise: the Administrator Senior had not seen fit to populate his garden with animals. From time to time, a mechanical servant would emerge from between the heavy plantings to offer the players a drink. Lando stuck with *snillik,* a thick liqueur from somewhere near the Galactic Center, one he actively detested and therefore drank slowly and judiciously.

Having shuffled the deck a fifth and final time, he offered it to the player on his right for a cut. That worthy accepted, divided the deck into three stacks, and reassembled it in a different order. Lando kept an eye on him; he had the look of yet another professional, although he'd claimed to be a retired businessman. Perhaps he was both.

Approximately of middle age, Del Cycer was extraordinarily tall for a human being, well over two meters. He was also extraordinarily thin. He was dressed in a bright green caftan and wore a great many rings on his fingers.

"You have been recently to the Rafa, I heard it said, Captain Calrissian. Is it true they've found the legendary lost civilization that was supposed to be there?" Cycer's tone was conversational, friendly, interested.

Lando reclaimed the cards, dealt them around the table in a practiced, leisurely manner.

"It might be more accurate to say the lost civilization found *us.* I was there when it happened. The ancient Sharu are back and setting up in business."

"How dweadfuw!" the creature to Lando's left responded. It was something nasty looking, with a small trunk dangling beneath its bloodshot eyes. Even more unfortunate, its blood was green. The veins clashed with the deep blue of the irises. "Does that mean theah won't be any mowe wife-cwystals?"

The creature had a large Rafa orchard-crystal pendant on a chain around its thick, wrinkled neck. It wasn't the only one here to sport the expensive gems. Lando had learned that they collected a sort of ambient life force given off by all living things, collected and refocused it on the wearer. He shunned them himself; they made him feel like a vampire.

"No," he answered, handing the creature its second card. "I think the new management will eventually start shipping them again. Probably at substantially higher prices."

Lob Doluff took his second card without comment. It was obvious to Lando that he had a winning hand—and that he'd managed to lose the advantage somehow before the play was over with.

The player to the Administrator Senior's left was a female human being, younger than Lando, blond and not unattractive. She had been introduced to him as Bassi Vobah, and some vague reference made to her being an administrative officer. The young gambler wondered where she got her money. He was unimpressed with her playing so far, and more than a little bothered by the fact that she seemed to be watching him closely.

And not in a friendly way.

He handed her a card, dealt to Del Cycer and himself, then, without looking at his cards, took a tiny sip of *snillik*. "Cards?" he inquired.

The trunk-being nodded, its proboscis flopping obscenely, then threw all three down in disgust. "Thirty-seven!" it exclaimed. "Amazing!"

Lob Doluff stood pat.

Bassi Vobah took another card, said nothing.

Del Cycer accepted a card, laid his hand down gently. "Out, confound it."

"Anybody again?" Lando asked. Bassi Vobah responded, took the card, stared grimly at her hand. This time the centerpiece was not as rich. Lando finally looked at his cards: Nines, of Flasks and Staves. "Dealer takes one."

Sweat began forming on Lob Doluff's shiny pate, his fingers seemed to tremble a little. Finally, in an explosive gesture, he threw his cards on the table, face up. "Twenty-two! Can you beat that?"

Lando glanced at Bassi Vobah.

"Fourteen," she said. "Forget it."

With the Four of Sabres Lando had drawn, he, too, had twenty-two. He displayed the hand, picked up the deck to deal again. "Sudden Demise."

Doluff received the Three of Staves, breaking his hand. Lando could have stopped there, but flipped the next card over. The Idiot, worth exactly zero. The pot was his again.

"Let's take a break."

Since it was his winning streak, he could recommend a rest without engendering resentment. That was easy: he didn't believe in winning streaks, and wasn't afraid of interrupting them. He did need to consider, though, whether to begin losing a few hands deliberately. His livelihood, well-being, ultimately his survival depended on maintaining goodwill—which meant losing on the small bets and winning quietly on the big ones. He'd believed such a ploy to be unnecessary in a rich-man's playground, but was discovering that it wasn't any different from playing in a hard-rock miners' bar. Psychology, human and otherwise, remained the same.

"FIVE MINUTES TO BREAKOUT, MASTER."

Once again, Lando sat in the lounge of the *Millennium Falcon,* riffling through the cards and thinking odd-shaped thoughts to himself. He and Vuffi Raa had repaired the damage to the ship as best they could. Luckily they carried a good many replacement parts in stores, and the boarding ramp seemed to be something that needed fairly constant upkeep in any event. Moving parts.

Then they'd gone over the interior of the *Falcon* centimeter by centimeter, being the untrusting types that they were, looking for additional sabotage. They had found nothing. Vuffi Raa had wanted to climb outside and check the hull, but had been severely vetoed: the fields around a ship in ultralightspeed drive were not only physically dangerous, but the distortions of reality they created could drive even a droid insane. Besides, he'd studied the manuals enough to know that the defense shields flowed along the surface of the ship, in the first few molecules of her skin. A bomb attached outside could only do less than minimal damage.

They'd take their chances. He wasn't a gambler for nothing, and he had a friend's concern for the continued health of his mechanical sidekick.

He realized suddenly that he hadn't replied to the intercom.

"All right, old can-opener, I'll be up in a moment."

This was to be Lando's first planetary landing under the tutelage of the talented robot. His previous attempts, before he'd acquired Vuffi Raa, had been fiascoes. Perhaps setting down on the surface ("*next* to the surface" might be a more accurate description) of an asteroid wasn't a very spectacular exercise, but he needed the practice.

This time he'd made it to the cockpit *before* the explosion occurred.

Afterward, they spent some time untangling arms and legs from tentacles. Lando hadn't had the time to strap in, and Vuffi Raa had momentarily unstrapped himself to check a gauge at the rear of the control deck. They both wound up between the pilots' seats, stuffed under the control panels.

The *Millennium Falcon* turned lazily, end over end.

"Master, I hate to point this out, but that explosion was on the *outside* of the ship, in the outboard phase-shift adaptor."

Lando studied the boards, while rubbing several bruises. "Yes, but I think it may have been spontaneous. Look at the readings on the phase-shift controls—they aren't very far away from where that bomb went off the other day, are they?"

It was the droid's turn to ponder. "I believe you are right. Nonetheless, had we been making a genuine planetary reentry, into a full atmosphere and full gravity, this accident would have destroyed us, Master. Observe the remote cameras; the cowling's been torn and lifted. It would have ablated away, leaving us with—"

"Uh, I think that will do, my friend. I can well imagine us tumbling and burning out of control. How long to fix it?"

"Not more than a few hours, nor will it interfere with our landing now."

LANDO DEALT THE CARDS AGAIN, not quite as honestly as before.

Of course it had turned out to be a second bomb. Whoever had planted it apparently hadn't known their ultimate destination was to be an airless worldlet too small to suck them in and burn them up. Vuffi Raa had found part of the control module, like that in the first bomb, a device built to detect a change in their velocity relative to the speed of light. This one had been set to go off when they dropped below lightspeed.

Somebody really meant to kill him.

He tried to remember all the really big coups he had made at the gaming table. Had he unknowingly pushed someone with enough resources and anger to carry out a vendetta? Well, it appeared that caution might be in order now. And a little sleight of hand.

He dealt the trunk-creature a Two of Staves, Lob Doluff a Ten of Staves, Bassi Vobah the Queen of Air and Darkness, valued at a minus two. Cycer got a Master of Coins; the young gambler dealt himself a Commander of Coins.

Going around a second time, he handed the alien the Star, a negative card worth seventeen; Doluff took a Nine of Sabres; Bassi Vobah got a second negative, the Evil One, which brought her count to minus seventeen. He dealt to Cycer and had scarcely given himself the Nine of Coins for a respectable but unspectacular twenty-one, when the tall, thin retiree shouted, *"Sabacc!"* excitedly and slapped his original Master on the table, along with the Nine of Staves.

Lando breathed a secret sigh of relief and passed the deck over to Cycer for the deal. Sometimes winning included knowing when to lose.

Cycer had the deal for exactly one hand, which Doluff, barely able to contain himself, won. Then the deal passed to the trunk-thing (Lando was beginning to feel a little guilty about not remembering the creature's name—which was humanly unpronounceable in any case), where it stayed for two hands, then back to Del Cycer.

Bassi Vobah didn't seem to be having much luck.

Cycer was dealing the cards when a small spherical droid rolled up beside Lob Doluff and whistled imperatively, then split into a pair of hemispheres.

Doluff looked up from the screen and keyboard thus revealed, all color drained from his face.

"Captain Calrissian, I believe you'd better hurry to the spaceport. I have a message here that your ship, the *Millennium Falcon,* is on fire."

VI

T HE ASTEROID OSEON 6845 had been artificially accelerated to complete a rotation every twenty-five hours, giving its inhabitants a comforting sense of day and night—and those whose task it was to land spaceships there a severe headache. Touching down upon a surface moving at eighty-eight kilometers an hour in the tight and tiny circle that was the planetoid's circumference doesn't seem a difficult job until one tries it.

Consequently, from the Administrator Senior's equatorial garden home, Lando took a pneumatic tubeway to the north pole of Oseon 6845. There a small and relatively stationary spaceport had been leveled out of the barren rock.

Unfortunately, the tube car had no communicator of its own, nor did Lando make a habit of carrying one. Momentarily, he regretted it: he could learn no more in transit about the fate of the *Millennium Falcon*. All he had with him was the forty-seven-odd thousand credits he'd acquired that evening, and a tiny, unobtrusive five-shot stingbeam pistol tucked into his velvoid cummerbund.

It was all the personal weapon he allowed himself in a dark and perilous universe; he preferred to rely on his brains for the heavy firepower.

The tubeway shot him northward through a chord beneath the curvature of the asteroid's surface at several thousand kilometers an hour. Lando fidgeted every second, every centimeter.

He'd sent Vuffi Raa to the space terminal to continue repairs on the *Falcon*. And to keep a big red glassy eye on her.

What had gone wrong?

The little robot was a pacifist by nature. It was ineradicably programmed into him. Could some saboteur have taken advantage of this handicap, overpowered him, and set fire to the ship?

With a plastic-gasketed wheeze, the tubeway lurched to a halt. Its transparent doors opened to let Lando out into a maze of service corridors underneath the landing field. He ran down seemingly endless crossing and countercrossing passageways until he reached one numbered 17-W. A temporary holosign in a bracket on the wall displayed in six languages the legend:

MILLENNIUM FALCON
LANDO CALRISSIAN, CAPT. & PROP.

Overhead, a large circular pressure door hung open, connected by a short accordion-pleated tube to the underside of the *Falcon*. A metal ladder led upward through it. Oddly, there was no one else about in the harshly lit cylinder of the service corridor. The only sounds Lando could hear were those of small mechanical things going about their business.

Shaking his head, Lando climbed the ladder.

He emerged in the curving companionway of the *Falcon*, the somewhat dimmer light and familiar clutter something of a comfort after the stark, brightly lit port corridor. Everything was perfectly quiet. He stalked along the passage until he came to the first intertalkie panel he found set in a bulkhead.

Nervously, he pressed a button. "Vuffi Raa?"

"Yes, Master?" a cheerful voice replied. *"I'm out on the hull, finishing up with the phase-shift adaptor."*

"Oh. Well, I'm aboard, very confused. You didn't happen to have a fire here tonight, did you?"

"Master? Why, no, aside from some welding—and that was vacuum-synergetic, no open flame of any kind. Why do you ask?"

Suspicions of several and various distinct flavors began to fill Lando's mind. "Er, this may sound silly, but how do I know it's really *you* I'm talking to?"

"Master, what's wrong? Of course it is really I. Please come to the starboard gun-blister and I'll show you."

That could be an altogether different kind of invitation than it sounded. Lando drew his stingbeam, every nerve on edge. He crept into the short tunnel leading to the gun-blister, his back tight against the low, curving wall, and slid sideways until he could see out past the quad-guns through the hemispheric plastic.

Outside, the Oseon sun shone garishly on a stark and rocky scene.

The spaceport had begun as a huge natural crater many kilometers in diameter. The *Falcon* sat in its approximate center. Here and there a ship lay, positioned over its own assigned service hatchway. Pleasure yachts, company vessels, those of traders, distributors, and caterers. Halfway across the crater to the rim, Lando could make out the impressive bulk of an elderly but well-maintained battle cruiser. Well, everyone to his own taste. Stars beat feebly downward, making a minuscule contribution to the solar brilliance.

A flicker of movement at the corner of his eye sent Lando into a tense crouch, both hands wrapped professionally around the small grip of his pocketgun, its muzzle seeking, sniffing after something to bite.

A chromium tentacle rasped across the plastic before him. Lando found himself staring into Vuffi Raa's eye as the robot swung down in front of the blister and hung on one manipulator.

The gambler punched the intercom button beside the gun chair.

"Sorry, old bolt cutter, I'm a touch paranoid tonight. Some thoughtful individual interrupted my game—and quite a profitable one, I might add—with a fire alarm. Anything at all exciting happening at your end of the planet?"

Through the plastic, the droid gave as much shrug as it was

capable of. *"I've simply been tidying up here, Master. There have been no communications, visitors, nor have I so much as seen anybody within a hundred meters of the ship except a few of the spaceport automata. Shall I come in and—"*

"Don't trouble yourself. Perhaps I still have time to return to my game."

The robot waggled a free tentacle in farewell. *"Very good, Master, I'll see you at the hotel."*

"Good night, Vuffi Raa."

The light flickered momentarily, as if a ship had flown between the *Falcon* and the sun.

Out of the blister and around the passageway, Lando went directly to the hatch he'd entered through. He clambered down the ladder, more careful this time not to get his semiformals greasy. On the next-to-last rung, he heard the sharp grit of a footstep behind him, twisted to see who it—

CRUMMMP!

Something hard and traveling fast smashed savagely across his lower back. Grunting with shock and pain, he released his hold on the ladder, fell rapidly in the artificial gradient, scraping his face on the ladder.

A second swipe missed him, zipping over his head to clang noisily on the metal rungs.

Hitting the floor with a gasp, Lando rolled over in desperate haste, clawing at his middle. A pair of dirty boots tromped toward him. They were all he had time to see before something came swooshing downward toward his head.

He fired the stingbeam upward.

There was a high-pitched piercing whistle from the weapon, a high-pitched scream of agony from the target. The club—whatever it was—clattered noisily to the surface: Lando's adversary fell backward, the chest area of his jacket bursting into flame. Smoke and the nauseating stench of flaming synthetic fabric began to fill the corridor.

Lando rose stiffly, millimeter by tortured millimeter, pulling on the rungs of the ladder. There were tears in his eyes from smoke and pain. Leaning hard against the ladder, he reached around behind himself, felt his back where he'd been struck. His life had probably been saved by the forty-seven thousand credits distributed in his compartmented cummerbund.

Stingbeam hanging limply along his thigh, he staggered over to see who had attacked him. The figure lay still. The brief-lived flames—accidental byproduct of a close-range discharge—had died.

So had the assailant.

A soldier of some kind. That's how he appeared to Lando. The gambler tugged a soft leather helmet off the fellow's unresisting head, the kind of headgear customarily worn under the larger bubble of a spacesuit during extended periods in hard vacuum. The club, a two-meter section of titanium pipe, was the only weapon visible, although Lando detected wear across the dead man's trousers where a gunbelt had abraded the fabric.

The uniform, if that's what it was (hard to tell with only one of the things around), was patched and faded, many times mended. It seemed to match the wearer's condition. He was a large man, gray and weathered, his face deeply furrowed with age. Lando didn't recognize the insignia. In a million-system civilization, chances were he wouldn't.

What to do now?

In the big cities of many a civilized planet, one was far wiser, having disposed of a mugger or burglar, simply to pass on, leaving a small mystery behind for the authorities. Such was Lando's inclination. They were accustomed to it, as they had every right to be. They were the ones who had made the act of self-defense a worse offense than the crime that had provoked it.

In the Oseon, would that be the case? Lando didn't know. He couldn't very well afford simply to walk away. A dead body, at the docking entrance of his ship, plenty of other physical evidence scattered around, and a partially discharged energy-weapon in his hand. Embarrassing, to say the least.

Well, down the corridor there was a public communicator.

He climbed back up the ladder.

Vuffi Raa, back now from the hull, met him at the top of the ladder. In the dimly lit corridor, his eye glowed like the coal of a cigar.

"Master, what is going on? I heard shouting, and—"

"I've just killed a man, old thing. Be a good sort and com Lob Doluff. We may have a bit of pull in this system; I suspect we're going to need it." He sat down suddenly on the decking, leaned against the wall, and collapsed, sliding over sideways.

It wasn't bad, as jails go.

The life of a gambler was somewhat checkered. Often people took offense when they lost money. Sometimes they were in a position to do something about it *outside* the rules of whatever game they'd lost money at.

The suite was semitastefully decorated in cheery plastic colors that did not quite make up for the colorless music drifting blandly from a speaker in the ceiling. A separate bathroom offered modest privacy—as long as one overlooked the large mirror over the sink that was undoubtedly a window from another point of view. There was a genuine skylight, heavily barred and shielded, that served to reduce claustrophobia and gave a fine, undistorted picture of the stars overhead. There had even been a band of plastic around one of the ceramic facilities stating that it had been sanitized for Lando's protection.

Somehow, he couldn't quite summon up the appropriate gratitude.

His injuries had been properly attended to. They weren't many: a couple of cracked (or at least severely bent) ribs, some abrasions. The tape was supposed to fall off of its own accord sometime in the next fifty hours.

They'd confiscated his clothing and personal papers, his cummerbund with the forty-seven thousand credits, and, of course, his stingbeam, leaving him a set of shapeless drab pajamas with a number on the back and front in six languages and a pair of step-in slippers that threatened to deposit him on his head every time he took more than three paces.

There was only the one bed, and it wouldn't turn itself down when Lando told it to. Technically, he was in solitary confinement. That was all right with him: the acquaintances one makes in jail are seldom broadening, nor was he enamored of any sort of company at the moment. There was nothing to read, nothing to watch, nothing to do—but think. Lando was good at that.

LOB DOLUFF HAD answered the call himself.

The Administrator Senior expressed gratification that Lando's ship hadn't actually been on fire. He couldn't understand the false alarm, however. Such criminal offenses were prosecuted harshly in the Oseon.

"There is one small complication," Lando added, "however."

"However? And what is it, Captain?"

In the background, Lando could make out the figure of Bassi Vobah, drink in hand. They were still in the starlit garden dome. He wondered whether the other players were still there as well, and if not, what else might be going on in the upper echelons of Oseon Administration.

"Well, sir, the false alarm seems to have been intended as a trap. Someone ambushed me as I was preparing to return to the *sabacc* game—a stranger.

"I'm rather afraid I've killed him, Administrator Senior."

The older man's eyebrows danced up a fraction of an inch and he leaned into the video pickup. "You aren't joking, are you, Captain Calrissian?"

Lando sighed. "I don't believe I'd joke about something like this. He surprised me, attacked me with a piece of pipe, and I was forced to shoot him."

The Administrator Senior's eyes widened and his eyebrows

soared impossibly close to the crown of his naked scalp. "*Shoot him?* Did you say—"

"Hold on a moment, Captain . . ."

Bassi Vobah leaned over and whispered something. Doluff looked puzzled a moment, then nodded.

"Captain Calrissian—Lando, my boy, stay right where you are. I'm going to send Miss Vobah directly over to you. I believe she can be of help to both of us in this affair. In the meantime, leave everything exactly as it is; I'll order access to your service corridor closed off. We'll get this over with as quickly and discreetly as possible."

Another whispered conference.

"Yes, and by the way, it is perhaps better that you tell Miss Vobah and myself nothing further about what happened. We are duty-bound to testify in court about it, being administrative personnel, the both of us. You understand."

Lando understood. He nodded, signaled off, slouched back in his pilot's chair disconsolately. Outside, the light seemed unnaturally harsh, even for an airless asteroid, and flickered now and again as if a fleet of ships were passing overhead. The colors all seemed a bit off, as well, but that may have been explainable by the mood of the observer. Finally he turned to Vuffi Raa.

"Well, old vegetable-slicer, it looks as though we're in for it again. I must be losing my touch."

"Now, Master," the robot replied, patting the gambler on the shoulder with a gentle tentacle, "I'm sure everything will work out. You would not have done what you did, had you not been forced to."

He extracted a cigar from beneath the control panel, trimmed it, handed it to Lando, and lit it with a glowing tentacle tip.

"I didn't know you could do that. Do you suppose he was the party behind the bombings, the fellow I shot?"

"The idea had crossed my mind, Master. I do not know." A glum silence settled over the pair.

The control panel beeped. Lando flipped a switch. "Yes?"

"It's Bassi Vobah here, Lando. I'm in the service accessway beneath you. Come down and meet me, will you?"

"Very well. Shall I bring a toothbrush?"

Her voice was apologetic. "It might be a good idea."

Lando gave the robot a few instructions, then turned and retraced his steps to the bottom of the ladder. When he turned around, she was bending down, dispassionately examining the body.

She was wearing the uniform of the Oseon police.

In his cell a few hours later, Lando once again resisted the urge to get up and pace. He'd never taken very well to confinement. It was well past local midnight, there on a different spot on the equator, closer to the small city of which the Esplanade formed the core. Yet the lights had been left on—more or less standard practice in jails everywhere. Worse yet, the syrupy music still dribbled from the overhead. Resentfully, he looked up—

—and was nearly blinded by a flash of overwhelming brilliance in the sky. As his eyes began to readjust, he saw that long streamers of color had begun to creep across the zenith, deepening every second in hue, like mutant fingers closing over the transparent bowl of the heavens.

Crimson flared. Yellow seethed. Blue and green pulsed steadily against a syncopated counterpoint of violet.

The Flamewind had begun.

VII

A POLICEPERSON'S LOT IS not a happy one.

Sometimes, it was downright discouraging, thought Peacekeeper Bassi Vobah as she wrote up her report on the *Millennium Falcon* killing. What a time for something like this to happen!

Flamewind had begun, and she was going to miss it.

Born in the Oseon System, she was one of the many who served the few, her function—not terribly different from that of the countless robots that populated the asteroids—was to spare her masters all possible inconvenience. That this has been the essential task of police officers everywhere in time and space, she was unaware. Her education had been specific and to a point. It had not been noticeably cosmopolitan or analytical.

Her parents, even less well off than she was, had originally immigrated as merchants after passing batteries of examinations, probes into their backgrounds and intentions, studies of their attitudes and goals. Nevertheless, they had not been terribly successful. In the end, she had worked to support them, and by the time it was no longer necessary, what she did for a living had become a habit with her, although not a particularly comfortable one.

Her one relief, her one vacation every year, was Flamewind.

It was a deadly and spectacular time. Brightly colored streamers of gaseous ionization filled the open spaces—a thousand kilometers on average—between floating mountains. Fantastic lightnings blasted from rock to rock. The seven belts of the Oseon fluoresced madly.

Radiation, static discharges, and swirling, colored fogs distorted navigational references, drove instruments and men alike insane. All interasteroidal commerce was grounded by law for the duration, averaging three weeks, to protect would-be sojourners from their own folly. The sleet of particles that lashed the system was only one opportunity for misadventure and destruction. Communications of any sort between the asteroids or with the rest of the galaxy were physically impossible, blotted out by wailing electrons.

No one went anywhere. Or wanted to.

And there were spooky stories of a less scientifically verifiable nature that circulated every year during Flamewind. Legendary disappearances, ominous apparitions, phenomena of the oddest, ghastliest, most relishably gossipable sort.

Yet—or consequently—tourists flocked to the Oseon just before the cataclysmic display. It had become a carnival of continuous parties, public and private, unceasing gaiety. Hundreds of different intelligent species intermingled from a million systems, giving some meaning and adventure to the otherwise humdrum life of a small-town girl.

Like Bassi Vobah.

And now this. Aside from the arrest itself and the keyboard-work it engendered, there were the impoundment documents, to be completed in nanolicate, it seemed. This Lando Calrissian, a wandering tramp who hadn't filled out so much as a single visa form, had so far collected one hundred seventy-three thousand credits from his betters (and hers) without lifting a finger to do any honest work. That had been confiscated, of course, and, whether he was ultimately found innocent or guilty, would go to pay the expenses he'd imposed on the administrative services of the Oseon.

That much money would have supported half a hundred families like Bassi Vobah's for a year. It was simply indecent for an individual to gain so much so easily. At least justice reached a long arm out to punish evil-doers *sometimes*. This was one occasion when her job generated a great deal of satisfaction.

And then there was the broken-down smuggling vessel he claimed was a freighter. That was worth fifteen or twenty thousand. If she could think of additional appropriate charges, the ship would go on auction to pay for them. Also that pilot/repair droid. It was worth considerably more than the ship and would have a much more enthusiastic market in the Oseon. Mark it down at fifty thousand credits.

Incidental personal items of property, worthless—and, of course, the murder weapon. *No*, she wasn't legally justified calling it that. Yet. The confiscated stingbeam, then. It would make a nice addition to her tiny department's "museum." Such killings didn't happen often in the fat, complacent community she served. It would make an interesting story to tell.

But that scarcely made up for the trouble Calrissian was causing, and if possible, she'd see him fried for that. The other complication was his fault, indirectly, as well. She'd argued with her superior, Lob Doluff, about it, but pressure was being put on him, and the pressure worked its way down onto her shoulders. Calrissian would pay for that, as well.

Flamewind had begun, and she was going to miss it.

VUFFI RAA PACED the curved companionways of the *Millennium Falcon*. He was a most unhappy machine. Below, the hatchway to service corridor 17-W was closed, clamped with an impound seal, and it had been all he could do to persuade the authorities not to stencil a seizure notice on his body—or take him away and lock him up in some warehouse.

Maintaining a modest silence about his manifold additional capabilities, he'd convinced them that, as a pilot, navigator, and repairbot, he was essentially part of the ship. As a consequence, they had affixed to his torso a restraining bolt—a bit of electronic mischief that was supposed to inflict enormous pain on his nervous system should he attempt to leave the *Falcon*.

It had taken him all of thirty seconds to disable it, once the police had departed. Nonetheless, prudence dictated that he stay there unless he could think of something useful to do for himself and his master.

Outside, huge sheets of polychrome gas filled the sky, punctuated every few minutes by terrifying displays of lightning. Flamewind was barely underway and yet, for most observers, the phenomenon was overwhelming.

Vuffi Raa didn't even notice it.

He supposed that Lando had offered at least a hundred times to set him legally free. For some reason it bothered the gambler deeply to own another sapient being, even a mechanical one. Vuffi Raa had always turned him down, preferring to stay with his adventurous master. Now he wondered—very briefly— whether it mightn't have been a better idea to accept. As a manumitted droid, he would have been at liberty to deal with the situation.

Although what, specifically, he would have done remained a mystery.

As an article of property, he was told nothing by the authorities about Lando's fate or that of himself and the *Falcon*. However, from long, long experience with human culture, the robot could make a fairly accurate guess. Somehow all of that must be prevented, some bargain struck that would at least leave them even, leave them in the condition in which they'd arrived.

Vuffi Raa had very little experience making deals.

Outside, the sky writhed with the seven colors of the spectrum—and with every possible mixture in between. For Vuffi Raa, there were more than a hundred basic colors, from lowest infrared to highest ultraviolet, and the permutations and combinations possible had to be expressed in exponentials.

Yet the spectacle was lost on him, and not from any lack of aesthetic sensitivity.

He *liked* Lando Calrissian. The little droid had a deceptive appearance; he always looked brand-new, and his mere meter of height made people think diminutive thoughts about him. In reality, he had a powerful mind and a lifetime that stretched back centuries, even further than he could remember.

Apparently, that was the result of a pirate attack on a freighter in whose hold he'd occupied a commercial shipping crate. It was his first clear memory, the jarring, shouting, screaming. The groaning of the fabric of the victimized ship. He hadn't been supposed to awaken until arrival at his destination. The premature activation was a survival mechanism, but it had cost him something. He could remember nothing of his origins; had only the vaguest impression that the race who had created him looked something like him.

In all the time since, through hundreds of owners, hundreds of systems, planets, cultures, he'd never grown so fond of a human being. He couldn't exactly say why Lando Calrissian affected him so, but affection was the truth. They laughed together; Vuffi Raa's separating tentacles (once the robot had disclosed this capability) had become the basis for a number of Lando's rare but elaborate practical jokes. They prospered together, and in financial extremes, Lando had divided his small fortunes between buying food for himself and whatever small electronic items the robot's maintenance required.

They were friends.

And now, Vuffi Raa was helpless to aid his master.

Outside, a braid of raspberry red, lemon yellow, and orange orange twisted through the heavens, across a constellation locals called the Silly Rabbit.

No sentient sighted being could have cared less than Vuffi Raa.

ROKUR GEPTA FLOATED in an utter blackness not half so dark as the secret contemplations of his soul.

Deep underground, where the final traces of the minuscule natural gravity of the asteroid were canceled, he hung suspended in the center of an artificial cavern, momentarily free of all sensation, free of the annoyances attendant upon suffering the incompetence of his underlings, free of the steady, grinding presence of the warmth and bustle of life.

His plans were well in motion. The *Wennis* was some distance away, its crew performing drill after endless drill, not so much to sharpen their abilities—they were, after all, only the best of a hopeless lot—as to keep them out of the kind of trouble that uncontrolled individuality never fails to generate. Gepta smugly affirmed to himself that chance favors the prepared mind: a happy turn of fate had placed his enemy, Lando Calrissian, in the custody of Oseon officialdom. Since that officialdom was a government, and he was who he was, Calrissian was already three-quarters of the way into his hands.

They would be cruel hands, once they received their prey. And deservedly so. Who had kept the sorcerer from obtaining and using the Mindharp of Sharu, an instrument of total mental control over others? Lando Calrissian. Who now owned the ancient enigmatic robot that seemed the key to yet another sheaf of tantalizing unanswered questions—and limitless power? Lando Calrissian. Who had evaded trap after trap, including that prepared for him on Dilonexa XXIII and the device planted aboard that cursed wreck, the *Millennium Falcon*? Lando Calrissian.

How he hated that name! How he would make its owner squirm and writhe until he learned the secret of his weird luck, or the other, hidden powers for which he was a front! How he would crush the life—slowly, very slowly—out of Lando Calrissian's frail body, after first destroying most of the mind (but not enough so that its owner couldn't appreciate the final moments).

Gepta thought back to an earlier, a happier time, to his first years as an adept among the ancient Sorcerers of Tund. How he had deceived the doddering fools, even while stealing their esoteric and sequestered learnings. As intended, they had mistaken him for a young apprentice and had been unable to penetrate his disguise. Already, he had been, even those thousands of years ago, far older than the most ancient of the sorcerers, and *they* knew how to stretch a life span!

Ah, yes. The galaxy still believed that somewhere the hidden planet Tund was home to the mysterious Order. Only Gepta knew it was a sterile ball. Not so much as a tiny fingerbone was left. The thought—the memory of what he had done on that final day—filled him with delight and satisfaction.

Someday he'd do it to the entire universe!

Meanwhile, that universe wasn't big enough for Rokur Gepta and Lando Calrissian. As Lando Calrissian was going to discover very soon.

Slowly, with elaborate precision, the sorcerer everted his body—turned inside out on the axis of his digestive system as a form of meditative relaxation—and resumed a true appearance only slightly less disgusting than the one he had given a few seconds before. No human being had ever seen him thus, none ever would—and live to relate the horror of it. He relaxed his numberless alien appendages, stretched them, and relaxed, then spun about himself the appearance of the gray-swathed presumably humanoid sorcerer the world knew.

Summoning a power of which the universe was equally ignorant, he drifted slowly, deliberately, toward the floor of the cavern. There was work to do, and he must be about it.

And yes . . . he must feed his pet.

KLYN SHANGA CONCEALED his grief. Year after year, it never got any easier to bear. Now, Colonel Kenow, his old and valued companion, was dead. Dead and gone. Forevermore.

They had fought in the battle of the Rood together as boys. It had been an insignificant sideshow in a vastly greater war, but to them, it had been a life path–altering cusp. They had survived, toughened by the ghastly experience, transformed from callow farm boys into soldiers.

And friends.

And now, Colonel Kenow was dead.

The worst of it was that it had been a senseless, purposeless death spurred by an impetuosity Shanga wouldn't have believed possible in a man of Kenow's age and battle experience. The stringent rich-man's laws of the Oseon had forced the veteran to abandon the weapon he was used to in favor of a crude length of pipe. Then he had been shot down by a stranger only tangentially involved with the enemy they sought, an accidental, not altogether innocent bystander. If only Kenow had listened . . .

Lightning flared, shaking the entire fabric of the odd assembly of fighters. Keeping station off the asteroid was growing more difficult by the minute. He could scarcely see across the few hundred meters that separated him from the farthest ship in his tiny fleet, thanks to the colored vapor that smoked and roiled around them. The radiation-counter needles climbed inexorably, despite the fact that they were in the shadow of a billion tons of iron-based rock. How much longer they could keep it up . . .

Well, in the end, it wouldn't matter. The giant engine still pulsed reliably, the cables connecting it to the fighters were sound. They'd had to rebalance to make up for Kenow's missing ship, but that had been simple, really. If they could just hold on long enough to do their work, it wouldn't make a bit of difference whether they survived the fury of the Flamewind, whether their skin flaked off and they lost their hair and vomited up the last drop of their lives. Those lives would have been well accounted for, the loss well worth it.

Shanga, like the rest of his companions, bided his time, hid his grief. The sleet of energy around them was making even line-bound communication impossible. The cables acted like a huge antenna, gathering up a howling cacophony that ground on the nerves, eroded morale and resolve. It was as if all the dead the universe had ever seen gathered in an unholy chorus once a year in the Oseon.

And now there was a new voice, that of Colonel Kenow, Klyn Shanga's old friend.

Well, soon there would be other voices, Shanga thought. His among them.

LOB DOLUFF WASN'T any happier than anyone else that carnival season. He regarded the whole Flamewind foofaraw as an enormous, unnecessary pain in the neck. He had never liked it, never understood why anybody else did.

Lob Doluff was color-blind.

He was also worried—half to death. Dressed as he was in lightweight indoor clothing, his head uncovered, his plump arms bare to the chill of the special section of his garden, standing in the middle of half a hectare of snow, his hands were sweating.

The Administrator Senior's visual disability did not affect his appreciation for flowering plants, although his reasons for collecting them may have been a bit different from those others might have. He loved their perfume and their persistence. To him a weed that cracked a ferroconcrete walkway was something of a miracle, and here, where tiny, almost microscopic flowers poked their small, courageous heads up through snow and ice, there was something especially miraculous.

It did little to cheer him now, however. He was in a bind.

Unlike his subordinate, Bassi Vobah, he was one of the *few* who served the few, while making an unusually honest effort to serve the many. He was quite as wealthy as anyone in the Oseon, and yet a sense of civic duty, personal pride, drove him to sit in the Administrator Senior's office and attempt to govern the essentially ungovernable millions upon millions of falling worldlets that comprised the system. He kept the peace. He maintained minimal social services. He acted as a buffer between the Oseon's inhabitants and a galaxy that often clamored for their attention, in response to either their great wealth, their enormous fame—or their criminal reputation.

At all of this he was very good, and his independent wealth allowed him a certain latitude denied the average civil servant. He might not *quite* be able to tell his superiors to take a flaming jump into the Core, but he had *thought* about it more than once and made the recommendation to many of their representatives.

Unfortunately, he was unable to indulge himself on this occasion. Pressure—greater pressure than he had known existed—was being placed on him to betray many of the things he stood for. If he complied, it was distinctly possible that no one would ever learn of it. But he, Lob Doluff, would know, and it would remove a great deal of the satisfaction from his life.

At the other end of the proposition, he stood to lose his position, his wealth, his reputation, even his life if he insisted on pushing things to their extreme. In addition, many, many others would suffer. It was ugly, and he hadn't thought such things could happen in a civilized universe.

Now he knew different.

He turned from his absent contemplation of the snowflowers of a hundred systems, walked through an invisible air curtain into a semitropical wedge of the dome, strode to a tree stump, and flipped the top upward. Reaching in, he seized a communicator and brought it to his lips.

"This is the Administrator Senior," he said after asking for the correct extension number. "Have Captain Calrissian brought to my office in an hour."

His hands were sweating again. He'd never sent a man to certain death before.

VIII

I T WAS TWO and a half meters tall, had an orange beak and scaly three-toed feet, was covered with bright yellow feathers, spoke in an annoying high-pitched effeminate voice despite its repulsively obvious masculinity, and answered to the name of Waywa Fybot.

It was also an undercover narcotics agent.

Lando hadn't learned any of this yet as a pair of robots, spray-painted the same color as Bassi Vobah's uniform, dragged him from his comfortable cell to confront the Administrator Senior.

"The charge is carrying a deadly weapon, Captain Calrissian, and the customary sentence, upon conviction, is death by exposure."

Lob Doluff paced back and forth before the floor-to-ceiling window in his office. Outside, the Flamewind filled the sky with racing garishness, but most of it was obscured by the dozens of hanging plants that turned the window into a vertical carpet of shaggy greenery. Other plants were scattered about in pots, in long narrow planters, in aquaria, even drifted in the air on lacy pale wings. A gentle frond brushed Lando's cheek as a flying plant passed over his head.

Lob Doluff didn't have a desk. He didn't need one. Tucked away in an alcove was a datalink with its screen and keyboard; a pair of secretaries awaited his summons in an anteroom. What he had were several comfortable chairs, none of which had been offered to Lando, and the enormous bird-thing that none of the mobile plant life would even approach.

And Bassi Vobah herself, looking prim and starched and heavily armed.

Lando reached downward to thrust his hands in his pants pockets, discovered once again he hadn't any, and folded his arms across his chest. He looked from Bassi to the Administrator Senior, spent a moment on the weird creature in the corner, then back to the humans.

"I take it, then, that you're not charging me with murder."

Bassi Vobah nodded. "That would be irrelevant. In the first place, there's ample evidence that you killed him in self-defense. In the second place, we have no record of him having entered the Oseon by legal channels, and therefore, at least in legal terms, he doesn't—never did—exist."

Lando shook his head. "Nice government you have here. Why is carrying a weapon a capital offense, and what have I got to do to get out of it? I take it that I wouldn't be here if you weren't going to offer me some nasty alternative to being shoved out an airlock."

The gambler had been in this position before, on more than one occasion. Odd, how government people needed extra governmental people to manage their dirty work on occasion. The things that he'd been asked to do, however, could scarcely be classified under civil service job descriptions.

Bassi Vobah had stiffened at Lando's reply, and only steely nerves and training had kept her hand away from the gigantic military blaster hanging at her hip.

Lob Doluff, however, seemed relieved. He nodded toward the nonhuman observer, introduced the creature to Lando. Waywa Fybot flapped his short arms as if in greeting, ruffled his feathers, and settled back into silence.

"In one sense, Captain, you are mistaken. You have been arrested and are soon to be tried and duly convicted of the offense."

The Administrator Senior made a gesture, and robots on each side of Lando stepped back. Lando was signaled to a chair facing those in which Lob Doluff was seated and Bassi Vobah stood behind at a sort of parade rest.

"As I said, the punishment as prescribed by law is exposure to the heat, cold, and vacuum of interplanetary space. There is, however, no provision for the precise method to be employed, and I am moved, my boy, to suggest a means by which the law may be obeyed and yet spare you from the unpleasantness such an experience ordinarily brings."

"I get it. You're going to shoot me before you stuff me out the airlock. By the way, Administrator Senior, have you ever *seen* somebody after they were spaced?" (Lando hadn't either, but he had a good imagination and hoped that Doluff did as well.) "Pretty messy."

He made a face, eyes bulging out, tongue lolling at the corner of his mouth.

Lob Doluff grimaced painfully, gulped, and placed a protective hand on his large stomach. "That's exactly what we're trying to prevent, my boy. To my knowledge, there has never been a formal execution in the Oseon, and I have no desire to be the first—"

"Nor I," Lando agreed. "I suppose this is where our avian friend comes in, isn't it?" He indicated Waywa Fybot, taking up a great deal of room in the corner.

Fybot stepped forward. "Tell me, Captain"—the creature squeaked ridiculously, especially considering its size—"have you ever heard the name Bohhuah Mutdah?"

"Sounds like somebody bawling for his mommy." Lando was sick of being the eternal patsy. He knew by then that they needed him, and had become determined to make things as difficult as he could for them.

The humor of the response—what little there was of it—was lost on everybody present. Lando even detected a little shudder from Lob Doluff. The Administrator Senior shut his eyes, wiped sweaty palms on the creases of his trousers.

The big bird took another step forward, towering over Lando.

"Bohhuah Mutdah is a retired industrialist, a trillionaire. His holdings in the Oseon are the largest in the system by a single individual, and it is possible that he is the wealthiest person in the civilized galaxy."

"He is also thoroughly addicted to *lesai*."

Lesai. Lando shut the bird-being out of his mind for a moment, summoning up what he knew of the rare and extremely illegal drug.

The product of a mold that grew only on the backs of a single species of lizard in the Zebitrope System, *lesai* had many desirable qualities. In the first place, it eliminated the necessity for sleep, thus effectively lengthening the human life span by a third. Unlike other stimulants, which consumed something vital in the human brain, *lesai* provided that something vital itself, meaning it could be taken indefinitely.

Yet it was not without its cost. It turned the user into an emotionless, amoral calculating machine. In the end, family and friends, the lives of thousands or millions of other individuals—at least so the authorities claimed—counted as nothing, compared to whatever goals the addicted mind had set itself. One had to be careful; those in power often lied about things like the effect of drugs, and even Lando, who was strongly predisposed against any mind-altering substances, took what the government said with a very large grain of salt.

Nonetheless, some of this made sense. He could understand how *lesai* and the richest individual in the known universe might be associated. There wasn't any particular trick to becoming rich—as long as one devoted his whole life to it to the exclusion of everything else. Lando wasn't capable of it; to him, money was a means to an end. It became meaningless when it was an end in itself.

But not everybody felt that way. Perhaps Bohhuah Mutdah was a person like that.

"Okay," he interrupted the avian creature, "so we have a fabulously wealthy *lesai* addict, and you're a drug cop. What's the matter, didn't he pay his protection money on time?"

Waywa Fybot stood up even straighter than before, his feathers fluffed straight outward as if in shock. "Captain Calrissian, you forget yourself! I, after all, am a—"

"An agent of a government fully as corrupt as any government that ever existed. Don't kid me, worm-breath. Vice laws are always written to be selectively enforced, to serve other purposes. What have you people got against this Mutdah character—or is it simply that you don't like the size of his bank account?"

The bird-creature blinked, began to tremble with rage. It opened its beak to reply, shut it again, opened it again, and subsided into the corner, speechless. Lando grinned at the Administrator Senior and his Peacekeeper, spread a hand that was half a shrug.

Bassi Vobah was nearly as scandalized as her professional colleague.

Lob Doluff, however, chuckled and appeared to relax for the first time since the interview had started. His smile became a grin to match the gambler's, then became outright laughter. He glanced, guiltily at first, at the feathered VIP, then shook his head and laughed again, this time without qualms.

"By the Core, Captain Calrissian—Lando, if I may—I *do* admire you! You're a gambler through and through, not just at the table. Please allow me to make this unpleasantness more comfortable. Have you had anything to eat?"

Lando nodded. "Best food I've ever had in jail. I could use some coffeine, though, and maybe a cigar."

"And by Core, Edge, and Disc, so shall you have them! Bassi, see to it immediately!"

The police officer stared at her boss indignantly, decided he was serious, and stalked out of the room to attend to the chore. Doluff snapped a finger at one of the guard-robots who had retired to the corners of the room behind Lando.

"Bring this gentleman his clothing, this very minute! By the Eternal, if I have to go through with this charade, I'll bloody well go through with it in my own way!"

Lando had sat quietly through it all. Now he sat up a little straighter as the Administrator Senior settled back, fully relaxed. Coffeine and tobacco arrived in due course, delivered by a seething Bassi Vobah. A police-robot brought Lando's personal property, which the gambler ignored for the time being as more interesting matters occupied his attention.

"Now," Lob Doluff said, when everyone was settled in again. At his insistence, a strange-looking rack the size and shape of a pair of sawhorses had been brought in by a robot, and Waywa Fybot encouraged—at the Administrator Senior's insistence—to perch on it. The bird got a dreamy look on its face, its feathers smoothed once again, and it was quiet.

"Now, sir, I will tell you the plain truth—as much as I have been told, in any case—and we will *all* understand. You're quite right, of course. Bohhuah Mutdah's corporate enemies and business rivals are preparing to overthrow his commercial empire. But they fear him greatly, sir, as I would in their place, and, accordingly, are seeking to put him personally and physically out of the way.

"I rather guess they hope he will resist arrest, providing them with an excuse to make things permanent. But that is only a surmise. The point is, Lando, I must ask you to help make all of this possible, and there is no way I can refuse to do so. I have what amounts to direct orders—by Gadfrey, it feels good to tell the truth!

"Were it simply my position, I would tell them—well, I hold this office quite voluntarily—quite unnecessarily if the truth were told. I like it, but not so much that I'd betray a fellow *sabacc* enthusiast and gentleman adventurer I admire."

Bassi Vobah squirmed uncomfortably in the chair she'd been ordered to take.

"Why do I have the feeling you're going to find another reason to betray me, then, old bureaucrat?" Lando asked. "That's what you're leading up to, isn't it?"

The Administrator Senior sighed. "I'm afraid so, my dear fellow. I offer no excuse. Means have been found to exert leverage upon me which my scruples cannot withstand. I do not ask you even to understand my position. I am attempting to arrange things so as to minimize the damage the situation inflicts on us both. I'll thank you to believe that much, at least."

Lando shrugged again, noncommittally. "How much does a hangman's apology count for, Administrator Senior?"

Doluff grimaced uncomfortably, then nodded. "You're quite right, sir. But look here, this is how I am prepared to hold up my end of a bad bargain." He turned to Waywa Fybot.

"Listen to me, you ridiculous creature, and listen well—"

"Adminis—" interrupted a shocked and outraged Bassi Vobah.

"Hush, child, I'll get to you in a moment. Are you listening to me, you absurd collection of flightless feathers?"

The Imperial narcotics agent blinked stupidly. Apparently the position it had been forced to assume triggered some reflexive sleep reaction. It shook its head, peered at the Administrator Senior, but said nothing.

"Very well, then, and you can inform your mercantile-class sponsors that I gave you this direct order: you may arrest Bohhuah Mutdah—I haven't the power to stop you. But you will return him to *me*, alive and in condition to stand trial in the Oseon, or I'll have you plucked, dressed, and roasted for Founder's Day. Am I making myself clear?"

The bird-creature nodded, a look of hatred latent in its large blue eyes.

Doluff turned to Bassi Vobah. "And as for you, my dear, remember who it is you work for. Your orders are to see that my orders are carried out. And you are to use that oversized chicken-roaster of yours"—he indicated her energy pistol—"if the occasion calls for it, on whosoever merits it."

He nodded significantly toward Waywa Fybot.

"Now, Captain Calrissian—Lando—this is what you are to do. As you probably are aware, it is perilous in the extreme, and also illegal, for ships to travel from asteroid to asteroid in the Oseon during Flamewind."

As if to underline the Administrator Senior's words, lightning flared briefly outside the window, washing the colors from every object in the room. The flash subsided.

"Nonetheless, I am required to instruct you to take this pair of law-enforcement officers to Oseon 5792, the home and estate of Bohhuah Mutdah, so that they may make their arrest."

Lando shook his head. "I don't get it. Why not just—"

"Because, my dear Captain, it seems he must be caught in the act. His enemies lack sufficient evidence at the moment, and even they dare not move without it. You are the goat because of your avocation as captain of a tramp freighter. It must appear that you are taking him his regular shipment of the drug; apparently he supplies himself every year under the cover of the Flamewind, and—"

Lando stood up suddenly. "Now wait just a minute, Admin—"

The bureaucrat slammed his large hands down on the arms of his chair. "*You* wait a minute, Captain! I have no latitude in this; my instructions are clear, detailed, and unavoidable. We will provide you with a large amount of *lesai*, which has been seized from Mutdah's regular connection. You will make transit to the next Belt inward, to the particular rock owned by Bohhuah Mutdah, and sell him the drug. You will be observed doing so by Officer Waywa Fybot and Oseon Peacekeeper Bassi Vobah, who will then seize both drug shipment and payment and take Mutdah into custody. That is how it has been ordained; that is how it shall be done." Doluff subsided once again and took two or three deep breaths.

Lando sat quietly for a moment, thinking, then asked a question. "All right, so we're boxed in, if I'm to believe your word. But—well, I've won rather a deal of money here in the Oseon in the last few days, nearly two hundred thousand creds. I can anticipate that it would suit certain interests if *I'm* arrested in the same illegal exchange, wouldn't it?"

A predatory gleam became visible in Bassi Vobah's eyes.

Lob Doluff, on the other hand, simply smiled sadly. "Lando, we already have you on the weapons charge; I repeat, a capital offense. Those whose interests I serve desire that no one besides themselves possess the means of deadly self-defense, and they enforce the rule—or expect me to, which amounts to the same thing—quite severely.

"Besides, although you have been quite fortunate—no, let us acknowledge your skill—at the gaming table, I assure you that no one you played with, excepting Miss Vobah here, who was appropriately subsidized, will miss so much as a micro of your winnings. We are a wealthy people.

"However, if it will make you feel more comfortable, you'll recall I offered you an additional assurance of my goodwill in this awkward matter. This is what I had in mind: transport these two individuals and help them make the arrest. In return, I shall see that you take your winnings with you, along with every other item of your property, and you may depart the system directly from Bohhuah Mutdah's estate. He owns a large number of small interasteroidal craft, and I believe that the Flamewind may have quieted enough that Bassi, here, and Officer Fybot can make their way with evidence and prisoner back to this place unassisted. Is that fair enough?"

Lando thought it over, nodded reluctantly.

"And you, my dear, have I made myself sufficiently clear to you? Should you oppose my will in this, inconvenience Captain Calrissian in any way, I shall expect you to leave the system directly from Mutdah's asteroid, in his place."

The policewoman gulped visibly and nodded fully as reluctantly as Lando.

Once more Lob Doluff frowned at Waywa Fybot. "And as for you, you hyperthyroid whooping crane, should you interfere in my wishes concerning the good captain here, after you have been plucked and roasted, I shall stuff a cushion with your feathers and rest my fundament upon it for the remainder of my life. Do you understand?"

The bird nodded, adding a third portion to the general grudging atmosphere in the room.

Doluff folded his hands across his paunch, a satisfied expression on his face. "Very well, then, we are agreed, and everything is settled. By the Center, it is good doing business with a group as straightforward and understanding as you all are. I am feeling extremely fond of the three of you. Shall we see about having lunch, then?"

IX

IN THE OSEON System during Flamewind, the inhabitants and their guests have little to do but party and watch the fireworks. But even the most spectacular display in the known universe begins to pall after sufficient time, and attending parties has its limits—and its consequences.

Thus it is an interesting fact of demographics that, although the majority of Oseoni, owing to what is required of them to achieve their high place in the general scale of galactic society, are long beyond childbearing age, yet the human birthrate in the system inevitably jumps every year nine months after Flamewind.

One reason for the increase is the peril of traveling during Flamewind. The deadly rain of radiation accompanying the display vastly accelerates the decay of electronics that control navigation and life-support equipment.

Even travel on the surface of an asteroid is dangerous.

And yet, Lando Calrissian, once resigned to the journey, was anxious to be underway. Freedom in the Oseon, he was discovering rapidly, had its severe drawbacks. There would be no more *sabacc* games for a variety of reasons: he had effectively cleaned out the available talent, not so much depriving them of their discretionary funds as convincing them that it was pointless to oppose him at the gaming table. In this he had been, if not directly careless, then overly enthusiastic. It was not a mistake he would have made in less opulent surroundings; he had yet fully to appreciate how much more tenaciously the rich hold on to what they have.

Had he been a waitress or a bell-bot, no one would have needed to tell him. The wealthy are notoriously lousy tippers.

What was worse, given the local standard of living, the fact that there were so many wealthy inhabitants and that the commercial overhead was so high, he was once again watching his money—his winnings—being eaten up. Everything was expensive, from a simple meal in the humblest eatery to the equipment and supplies his ship required for the journey ahead.

As usual, Lando's luck, both good and bad, was operating at full blast.

The day after his revealing conference in the Administrator Senior's office, he and Vuffi Raa were bolting down the weirdly shaped seating rack that had been sent over for Waywa Fybot.

"One more turn ought to do it!" Lando grunted. "I wish there was room for an autowrench in this corner—unh!"

The head of the bolt had twisted and torn off. This meant they had to undo all the other bolts and move the rack while Vuffi Raa drilled out the broken hardware and removed it for a second try.

"Master, why is the installation necessary? We could override the gravfield in this part of the ship and let Officer Fybot spend the trip in free-fall. It would be much more comfortable." Having drilled a hole through the soft metal of the bolt, he inserted a broken-screw remover, the twist of its threads being opposite those of the bolt, and tightened it, turning the offending artifact neatly out of the deck.

"What, and have his birdseed floating everywhere? Not a chance. Besides, his physiology is supposed to be delicate or something, like a canary's. Don't ask me why they made somebody like that a cop—that would require an assumption that logic functions at some level of government."

Together, they moved the distorted chair back into place over the boltholes drilled for it in the decking. Somehow, thought

Lando, the parties responsible for this—the final straw of messing up his nice, neat spaceship—would be brought to a reckoning.

The first three bolts went in perfectly. Again. Lando and Vuffi Raa looked at each other with resigned expressions (Lando reading the little droid's body posture since it had no face), placed the fourth bolt in its hole, and locked the wrench around its hexagonal head.

"If it doesn't work this time, old power-tool, we're going to send for a big wire cage!"

DEEP WITHIN THE HONEYCOMBED recesses of Oseon 6845, down where enormous pipes the diameter of a man's height conveyed air and water and other vital substances from fission-powered machinery to hotels and offices and stores and other places habituated by human beings, down where no one but an occasional robot made its perfunctory rounds, a meeting was being held.

"So you came," a gray-clad figure whispered. The clothing had the look of a uniform, although it was barren of the insignia of rank or unit markings. The face above the stiff collar, below the cap, was young. It was the first officer of the *Wennis,* lurking in the shadows of a ship-sized power transformer, his voice drowned within a meter or two by its titanic humming.

The other figure was even less conspicuous, hidden more deeply in shadows, cloaked for anonymity in many yards of billowy fabric. It was taller than the *Wennis* second-in-command, and stood there silently, acknowledging the greeting with a nod.

"Good," the officer hissed. "And do you understand what you are supposed to do when you get to 5792? There must be no mistake, no hesitation. The Administrator Senior has found a legal means of circumventing our intentions in this matter, and it must not work! The orders come from very nearly as high as they can."

Once again, the tall disguised figure nodded.

"All right, then. In return, you will be richly rewarded. Our, er . . . principal understands the pragmatic value of gratitude. Be sure *you* understand the consequences of failure."

The cloaked form shuddered slightly, but that may have been the cold. Even with the machinery in full operation, there was a chill in the air that converted both their breaths into clouds of barely visible vapor.

It shuddered again. And it may not have been the cold.

The gray-uniformed officer departed without further conversation. He was in a hurry. Before he returned to the *Wennis,* he had another meeting, even deeper in the planetoid's core, and it was not one he was looking forward to particularly.

Behind him the tall, cloaked figure departed as well, leaving a single downy yellow feather that trembled in the cold draft along the floor, then was still.

WITH UNDERSTANDABLY MIXED FEELINGS, Lando tucked his freshly recharged stingbeam into the waistband of his shipsuit. Mere possession of the thing inside the Oseon System was a capital offense, and the manner of execution made hanging, gassing, perhaps even the nerve rack seem desirable ways to end it all.

On the other hand, he was operating under the direct verbal orders of Administrator Senior Lob Doluff, whose concern for Lando's continued existence, it appeared, was sincere and rivaled only by his desire that Bassi Vobah and Waywa Fybot carry out the mission precisely as the administrator had instructed. Lando's pistol was a small but additional guarantee he had insisted upon.

On the third hand (Lando looked at Vuffi Raa, whose capable tentacles were flicking switches, turning knobs, and doing other things mandated by the preflight checklist), the Administrator Senior had adamantly refused to issue the young gambler a written permit to carry the weapon, fearing, perhaps, that his original leverage on Lando would be weakened thereby.

Ah, well, Lando thought, if things went according to plan (he had no great confidence that they would, being a cynic by inclination and having lived long enough to see his natural suspicions confirmed more often than not), he and Vuffi Raa would be out of the confounded system in a few days, and the whole issue would be irrelevant.

He had taken some pains of his own to assure this.

He intended to take even more.

As Lando and his mechanical partner warmed things up in the cockpit of the *Millennium Falcon*—illuminated through the forward canopy by the multicolored glare and flash of the Flamewind—their passengers were in the lounge area, each keeping his or her trepidations about the coming voyage to him- or herself. Bassi Vobah, having reluctantly abandoned the psychological protection of her police uniform, sat in a sort of semi-circular booth with an electronic table in its center, glumly watching an entertainment tape from the *Falcon*'s meager library. It was the saga of some early star travelers, marooned on a harsh and barren world through the failure of their spacecraft during a magnetic storm. At present, the characters were casting lots to determine which of them would eat the others.

Somehow it failed to elevate her mood.

Waywa Fybot was essentially a bird in his anatomy and physiology, although no more bound by the characteristics of such creatures than are men by their fundamental origins. While he was nervous, he could remind himself that what he was about to endure was in the line of duty, what Emperor and Empire expected of him, and consistent with future promotion and increases in salary. While he felt murderously angry at the local administrator who had verbally savaged him (Fybot's own people had plenty of snappy remarks applicable to mammalian species in general and simian ones in particular, but Doluff's office hadn't seemed the place to trot them out), the prospect of bigger game and future rewards helped him smooth his ruffled feathers.

Damn! He'd done it to *himself* that time.

Beneath the long thick plumage of his stubby left arm—a vestigial wing useless for flight long ages before his people had chipped their first crude stone tools—Fybot wore a small energy-projector that was something of an advance on Bassi Vobah's openly sported blaster. Half the military weapon's size, it had six times the power, coming close, in theory, to one of the modules of Lando's four-barreled quad-gun. The projector was a Service Special and a closely guarded secret, even from the regular military.

It didn't need to be drawn to be used, which was a blessing, as nature had not provided Fybot's people with the quickest or most adroit of manipulators.

He looked over at Bassi Vobah as she tried hard to keep her attention on the entertainment tape. It wasn't easy. Calrissian and his robot were running the *Falcon*'s engines through a series of tests that shook the vessel like a leaf at irregular intervals and left stunning silences between. Their caution in assuring themselves of the ship's operating condition only served as a grim reminder of what risks they were all about to take.

Which brought Waywa Fybot around again to his nervousness. He settled deeper into his resting rack, enjoying the reflexive drowsiness that came with the action, and wished his species still had sufficient flexibility to tuck their heads under their wings.

Come to think of it, he'd only bruise himself on the weapon he carried.

A gentle snoring sound began to issue from the small round nostrils pierced through the narcotics officer's beak.

"ITEM ONE NINETY-SIX," Lando quoted from the manual, "navigational receivers on standby. Well, old can-opener, we can skip that one. How'd that dead-reckoning program of yours turn out, or do you want to say?"

Vuffi Raa paused, a tentacle tip over a switch on the panel before them. "I wish, Master, that there was another name for it.

It sounds awfully final, doesn't it?" He flipped the switch, watched the panel indicators go crazy as the Flamewind's ionization attacked the navigation beam receivers.

He flipped the switch to OFF again. Both partners felt relieved.

"Item one ninety-seven," Lando said, ignoring Vuffi Raa's rhetorical squeamishness. "This begins a subseries of thirteen intermediate items before we get to one ninety-eight. First item: check main reactor core-temperature, which should be up to optimum by now. Check. Second item: make sure that moderator fluid is circulating freely in the heat exchangers. Check—at least according to the instruments. Third item . . ."

Administrator Senior Lob Doluff had stoically suffered the indignity of ordering the datalink, normally tucked inoffensively away in an alcove and concealed by a hanging fern, rolled out into the center of what was supposed to be his office and what was, in reality, a miniature of his greenhouse home.

By landline he was having a view transmitted to him of the north polar spaceport, specifically, the central area where the *Millennium Falcon* vibrated in readiness.

Maybe, he thought to himself, he hadn't the intestinal fortitude to be a first-rank administrator. He found it difficult in the extreme to order those beings, Lando Calrissian and his doughty little Class Two droid, into the fury of the Flamewind at its most colorful and dangerous moment. His heart would be traveling with them, he knew, and might never return to its proper location.

He wished them well.

However, he sighed, he did know a cure for the anxiety and guilt he was experiencing. In another alcove, across the room from that in which the datalink normally was exiled, he kept a terrarium filled with odd spongy growths from a planet a quarter of a galaxy away. Even to him, the great lover of green, growing things, they were utterly repulsive. But they were necessary to nurture and conceal an even more repulsive specimen of lizard that lived in symbiosis with them and shared the planet Zebi-trope IV.

On the back of the lizard, another symbiont, there grew a rather disgusting purple mold.

Lob Doluff locked his office doors, extracted a small plastic spatula from beneath the datalink, trod over to the terrarium, seized the lizard, and scraped a bit of mold from its back. This he rubbed with thumb and forefinger into the hollow at the base of his throat, covering the resulting stain, which looked rather like a bruise, with some flesh-colored powder he kept for just that purpose.

He settled back in his chair.

They were wrong, thought the governor, those "experts." He watched the *Falcon* detach itself from the accordion tube beneath it and seal up its belly hatch. *Lesai* didn't stop you from caring.

Lob Doluff wished it did.

SEVERAL THOUSAND KILOMETERS AWAY, a missile streaked past an odd conglomeration of battered and obsolete fighting craft attached with long and brightly pulsing cables to the core of a starship engine.

It was a signal, the only means of conveying information across space during the Flamewind of Oseon. Klyn Shanga watched it sizzle past his canopy, began punching buttons to place himself in wire-communications with his companions.

"That's it, men," he said in a grim, determined voice. "Now it begins, and it will not end until *we* have ended it. Call off your status when I say your name. We have to get this damned mess synchronized just right or we'll wind up slamming into a rock somewhere between here and there.

"Den Sait Glass!"

"*On the tick,*" came the reply.

"Glee Jun!"

"Hot and ready!"
"Stec Eddis!"
"On the mark!"
"Mors Eth!"

"ITEM TWO TWENTY-THREE," Lando read. "At long last. Landing tractors out, prepare to lift."

"Landing tractors offline," Vuffi Raa answered. "Zero weight on the landing jacks, negative weight, we're clear! Ease forward on the throttle, sublight drives engaged at three percent power. Altitude—if that's the word for it—twelve thousand meters and rising."

"Good!" the gambler/spaceship captain replied. He hit a button, spoke toward a small grill in the arm of his acceleration chair.

"This is Captain Calrissian speaking. Hope you two are thoroughly uncomfortable over there. We're off the ground and headed toward the Fifth Belt. If we arrive in one piece, it won't be any fault of yours!"

X

VIOLET FRINGES LASHED at the *Millennium Falcon*, purple flames licking at her hull as lavender-colored lightning flashed in a sky that was infinitely mauve.

"Vuffi Raa, according to these instruments, we're spinning like a top and following a course that's essentially a giant figure eight!" Lando shook his head. The plum-colored glare through the cockpit's canopy was souring his stomach, and the hard vacuum of space, which supposedly was incapable of conveying sound waves, rocked as if with the laughter of malicious giants.

He could scarcely hear the droid's reply.

"I'm sorry, Master, there isn't any help for it. We must trust the program I fed into the engines and attitude controls. I can't see a single instrument on the panel that's reliable." Even the robot's voice had the faintest hint of a hysterical edge. Or perhaps it was Lando's ears, battered by the screaming of a universe tearing itself into bits.

In the passenger lounge, Waywa Fybot was aroused from a sleep unusually deep even for his deep-dreaming species. He stirred, felt the feathers on his long neck ruffling themselves, and tried to close his eyes again. A glimpse through a small round port across the room caught his attention. His gaze became involuntarily fixed upon it, as, one by one, his feathers lifted, stood perpendicular to his body.

Bassi Vobah's hands covered her eyes.

Had she been capable of a single linear thought, she would

have wished for a second pair to cover up her ears. It seemed to her that the very Core of the galaxy was shrieking at her for some terrible thing she'd done and somehow forgotten. With a sob, she collapsed sideways on the curving couch, squeezed herself into a huddled ball, knees up to her chin, eyes shut so tightly that they were slowly blackening under the self-inflicted pressure.

Her hands were on her ears now, so that the titanic bellowing of a sun gone mad and its resonating orbital companions transmitted itself through her very bones.

Beneath her face, the cushion of the couch was soaked with tears.

What end was there to madness?

Starboard, in the cockpit, Vuffi Raa switched off another bank of useless instruments. They were distracting and therefore worse than useless. In a similar disgruntled humor and for identical reasons, he had shut off his hearing, but it hadn't done quite as much good. Where humans had a small cluster of senses, seven or eight at most, he had nearly a hundred, and at the moment, every one of them seemed to be his enemy.

Unlike Lando, who could suffer the effects but never feel the machine-gun sputter of ionizing particles through his body, part of Vuffi Raa's sensorium was a sophisticated scintillation counter. He could *experience* the density and frequency with which a dozen distinct kinds of particle drilled through him. For the first time in his long existence, he wished sincerely that he had the same limits to his awareness as his master. For the first time in a very long existence indeed, he entertained the notion that what he didn't know mightn't hurt him.

Lando had finished being sick—or at least with having something to be sick with. Fortunately the cockpit sanitation unit was still functioning. Of course it wasn't electronic and had almost no moving parts. Lando, wishing for the impossible like everybody else, was wishing *he* didn't have any moving parts, because, every time he moved something, it sent waves of nausea up whatever limb it happened to be, waves that zeroed in on his solar plexus and waggled it back and forth until he had to inspect the sanitation unit again.

Closely.

He didn't think he ever wanted to see anything purple again as long as he lived. If he lived. Or wanted to.

A BLUENESS THAT was more than blue seeped in through every port, window, blister, bubble, and televisor on the ship. With the same delightful irony that determines every other day-to-day event in a malicious universe, the only electronic devices on the ship that worked perfectly were the outside visual pickups and their repeaters inside the hull.

Navy blue, robin's-egg blue, sky blue (the sky of a million different planets, all mixed together indiscriminately in agate whirls), powder blue, denym blue, velvet blue, true blue.

Lando blew his nose.

His stomach seemed to have subsided a little. He glanced at Vuffi Raa, who bristled with alertness, tentacles on the controls and his big red eye fastened on the cockpit transparency.

"How are you feeling, Master? Better?"

"Don't call me master. Yes, I'm feeling better. How are you feeling, old trash-compactor?" Lando thought about lighting a cigar—and immediately had to lean over to the sanitation unit again. False alarm, but it very nearly made him stop smoking for the rest of his life.

"I don't know, Master. I'm afraid I had to shut my feelings off in order to function. Please forgive me if I don't seem quite myself for the duration of this journey."

Lando laughed. "I'm never going to be myself again! What can I do to help? You look like you have your tentacles pretty full."

"There is really nothing either of us can do, Master. The

course is logged in and—one trusts—being followed. I am merely monitoring life-support and other housekeeping functions. And wondering how reliable even *those* indicators are."

"We could always go back and look—you *or* I, I mean, whichever you think best." He tightened his chair harness a little, straightened up. He'd always wondered why sadness was described as being "blue." Now he knew: much more of this, and he'd be looking around for something sharp to cut his wrists with.

He'd never known there were so many shades of blue, all of them ugly.

"I think not, Master. If something goes wrong up here, I believe it will require the attention of both of us to correct it. You might try asking one of our passengers how things are elsewhere in the ship, though."

"Good idea." He pushed an intertalkie button. "Hello, over there! Anybody listening? We just want to know if the air and lighting and heat are all working. Hello? Can you hear me? Bassi? Fybot?"

Nothing could be heard over the roar of static in the system. Lando looked at Vuffi Raa and shrugged. The instruments said everything was all right in the lounge and elsewhere in the ship. Other instruments, however, said that they were traveling in a spiral now, looping the loop as if riding down the coils of a cosmic corkscrew.

Everything was blue outside. Lando felt a tear creep down his cheek and, for the first time, in a long, long time, thought about a dog he'd had once. It had been run over by a hovercraft.

BASSI VOBAH FELT green inside.

As a matter of fact, she felt green outside, as well. The leaf-colored radiation then battering at the *Falcon*'s viewports seemed to penetrate to her very marrow, turning it and the blood it produced green, too.

It didn't make sense. Nothing made sense, and that alarmed her far worse than the light or radiation. She was a person of certain bounds, of linearity, of rationality, of rules. She was a person—an upholder, a maintainer—of law and order.

Now see what had become of her. The penetrating green light let her do exactly that. She could see her own heart beating, deep green muscle fibers pumping bright green blood to medium green tissues and organs—all of which she could watch functioning—and returning, gray-green, to be reoxygenated in her spongy green lungs.

With transparent green oxygen.

VUFFI RAA EXAMINED his tentacles one by one. Reflecting bright yellow light from the cockpit canopy, they gleamed back at him as if made of gold. He had been silver-colored all his life. Now he was a golden droid, glittering at every joint. He rather liked it.

A beeping on the control panel indicated another set of instruments gone mad. Irritably, he shut them off, then returned to a pleased and fascinated contemplation of his highly polished self. Perhaps when it was over, he'd have himself gold plated. Tastefully, mind you, nothing ostentatious. How would gold and the red of his eye look together? Rather nice, he thought.

A yellow light began blinking on the console. It clashed with the yellow streaming in the windows, so he flicked a tentacle down and squashed it. There was a *pop!*, a fizzle, and—blast it all, he had soot on his tentacle tip! He searched around for something to clean it with, found a tissue beneath the panel, and began tidying up. Must be perfectly clean, he thought, unless I want the plating to peel on me, and that would be atrocious!

Absently, he reached down to turn off another half dozen switches, and suddenly became aware of a sallow pinkish starfish of a being sitting right on the dash in front of him. Vermin! How in the name of—

"Vuffi Raa! What are you doing, old cybernaut?"

"What did you call me, you—"

"Vuffi Raa, listen to me! You've busted up the intercom, and you were starting to turn off the life-support monitors. Get hold of yourself, droid! What's the matter?"

With considerable effort, Vuffi Raa forced himself back into something resembling a normal frame of reference. "My word, I'm sorry, Master, I must be taking radiation damage! I don't know what to do about it, though; it's so hard to think. Would you like me better if I had myself gold plated, or would it be too garish?"

Lando stared in blank amazement at his friend. "Can you turn yourself off temporarily? If you removed your tentacles, I could put you in the safe—the one under the panel where I keep my cigars. Would that work?"

"Er, *what*? You want me to *what*, you organic slug, you blind, groping grub, you sniveling, hydrocarbonated—*yawp!*"

Lando snatched the robot from the pilot's chair and, tentacles trailing, crammed his pentagonal body into the safe.

"I hope you appreciate what I'm doing, old geiger counter. I've ruined my entire supply of cigars—crushed them to a . . . Vuffi Raa, are you all right?"

The robot responded groggily. "I think so, Master. Did I really call you all those things?" The heavy genuine steel antique safe— left by a previous owner of the *Falcon*—surrounded him on all sides but one and seemed fairly effective at shielding him from the radiation. Lando swung the door as far shut as the robot's tentacles would allow and chuckled.

"I believe that's the most gumption you've shown since I met you. I rather liked it—but don't make a habit of it. And don't call me master!"

"Master, I'm still feeling the effects of the radiation. Can you get by without me for a while? I'm going to disconnect my manipulators, and ask you to close the door. I'm terribly sorry, but—"

"Don't have another thought about it. That's right, I'll take care of your legs. I'm closing the door now. Have a nice nap. I'll wake you when it's over."

He shut the door, suddenly feeling very lonely, and carefully placed the little robot's tentacles on the pilot's seat, strapping them down. He took a look at the instruments, decided there wasn't very much he could do about them, and sat for a while, wishing he had a cigar.

WAYWA FYBOT AWOKE suddenly with the oddest feeling that he was home.

Familiar orange light poured in from somewhere, and suddenly the world felt better, looked better than it had since he'd left his native planet decades ago to join the police.

Why, yes! There was his hometown, a lovely place, not too large yet not so small it didn't have all the conveniences a being could want. He could see it now, wavering a little on the horizon as the sun beat down upon it. He kept walking . . .

Egad, it had been a long, lonely time out among all those weird alien races. Everywhere he went, they made bird jokes. Could he help it if his people were evolved—and proudly so—from avians?

He only wished that somewhere along the track of time they hadn't lost the knack of—

—but what was this? He was *flying*! A glance to either side assured him that his arms had somehow lengthened, broadened, strengthened. Well, it was all in the genes somewhere, he supposed. Recapitulation, he recalled, recapitulation. He banked steeply, enjoying the sensation, banked the other way to get himself headed right, and passed over the rooftops of the town to the house that he'd been hatched in, a large place of cement and steel beams with a thatched roof. He saw now that the place had been reroofed with genuine straw. His folks were nothing if not stylish. Those checks he was sending home were going to a good cause, then!

He hopped over the fence, stirring the lawn lice with the power of his wings and making them complain in their mewling tones. There were thousands of them, of course. It was a well-kept lawn of a lovely shade of magenta, alive with crawling, rustling legs.

He went inside the house.

THE *FALCON* SEEMED to be flying in right triangles as the Flamewind shifted from orange to red. Lando caught it in the act that time, blinked as many-branched lightning bolts blasted all around the ship.

He fought the urge to seize the controls as the apparent geometry of the *Falcon*'s flight path shifted with the colors from triangles to something indescribable that would nauseate a pretzel-bender. Well, I'll be damned, he thought, we're traveling on the inside surface of a Klein bottle.

Or so it felt.

Satisfied that the ship was flying true to course (or at least resigned to trusting its computer), he bent down and put his head next to the safe.

"Vuffi Raa?"

"Yes, Master?" the robot answered meekly, its voice severely muffled by the metal door and barely audible over the Flamewind's titanic howling.

"Are you all right?"

"I'm all right," the box said. "How are things with you?"

"I'm having a wonderful time, wish you were here. I—*by the Galaxy Itself!* Hold on, I'll get back to you if we live!"

Directly ahead of the *Millennium Falcon* was a vision out of a nightmare. But it was no illusion. Half a kilometer wide, the thing loomed up out of the glowing star-fog and ominous red glow like an impossible spider with too many legs.

It seemed to be a starship engine attached to a great number of obsolete one-man fighters. Even as he watched, the smaller craft detached themselves, leaped toward the freighter, their energy-guns spewing destruction.

These were no remote-control pirate drones. These were the real thing.

And they were ready and eager to kill.

XI

S TEADILY THE MOTLEY fighter squadron bore down on the *Millennium Falcon*. Its instruments unreliable, bound to a predetermined course, the converted freighter was a helpless target. Lando reached to the panel without hesitation, flipped a bank of switches, cutting off the artificial gravity and inertial buffers. Loose items in the cockpit swirled and floated as he punched the override and took control of the ship from the computer.

He couldn't see—not with the dials and gauges acting the way they were—but he could feel. He could con her by the seat of his pants. Whether or not they reached their destination was of secondary importance; survival came first.

A pair of fighters streaked by, spitting fire. The *Falcon*'s shields glowed and pulsed, absorbing the energy, feeding it into the reactors. There were limits to the amount that could be absorbed that way—in which case the reactor would come apart, taking the ship and everything within a thousand kilometers with it—but for now, each unsuccessful pass fed the *Millennium Falcon*'s engines.

And her guns.

Rolling to defeat another run by the fighters, he slapped the intercom switch. "Bassi Vobah, try and reach the starboard gunblister! I need some help with the shooting!"

Silence.

Diving steeply, finishing up with a flip that left four fighters soaring helplessly past the freighter, Lando realized that Vuffi

Raa, in a moment of demented frustration, had wrecked the inter-talkie. He was on his own, for the first time since acquiring the little robot.

He wasn't liking it much.

A pair of smaller weapons on the upper hull was controllable from the cockpit. Lando started keyboarding until he had established fire control through a pair of auxiliary pedals beneath the console. Then, turning sharply—and feeling for the first time the stresses of acceleration as it piled his blood up in odd parts of his body—he trod on the pedals, blasting away at three of the enemy as they passed.

They kept on passing. Either Lando had missed, distracted by maneuvering the ship, or he didn't have the firepower to do the job. It was like a nightmare where you shoot the bad guy and he doesn't fall down.

Half a dozen fighters overtook the *Falcon* from behind, their energy-cannon raking her. She shuddered, staggered. Lando brought her back under control, rode the shock waves out, and continued to pour fire at an enemy he saw—to no effect at all. He slewed the ship around, getting angry, and found he faced at least a dozen of the fast, vicious little craft, coming head-on.

He picked out the leader, got it in the canopy cross-hairs, and stamped on both pedals. Every move the fellow made, he matched, keeping the fighter centered, keeping the guns going. The enemy's nose cowling suddenly disintegrated, and the small craft burst into flames, showering debris over the *Falcon* and his squadron-mates. One of the companion vessels staggered suddenly and veered off, trailing sparks and rapidly dispersing smoke. Two with one—rather prolonged, Lando admitted to himself—shot.

The *Falcon* lurched, as if lifted suddenly from behind, then stabilized as Lando applied counterthrust. Something solid had smacked her in the underside vicinity of the boarding ramp, always a weak point. He skated her in a broad horizontal loop, gave her half a roll as she came around, and there it was: another fighter, its fuselage accordioned, its engines spouting flames.

Ramming? In this century? They must be pretty desperate.

And certainly not pirates, Lando thought as he fought the ship into a better attitude to fire from. No profit in ramming. The bombers, then? The man he'd killed on 6845 could have been a fighter pilot. What had he done to get an entire squadron of fighter pilots angry with him?

The *Falcon* jumped again. This time the instruments—if they could be relied upon—showed heavy fire being poured into the hull about where the fighter had rammed her. Sure enough, the shields, never at their strongest there, were steadily deteriorating. He rolled the ship, only to be attacked in the same place by another group of fighters. The battle was getting serious.

All right, then: he hadn't anyone to help him, and a battle by attrition was a losing proposition. He only had one ship to lose. He'd taken the measure of the fighters. They were maneuverable and fast—more maneuverable than the freighter, which was only natural. But not as fast, either, not on a straight course. Trusting his feel for direction, he ironed out the circle he'd been making, rolled through three-quarters of a turn to bring him parallel to the Oseon ecliptic, and shoved all throttles to the ends of their tracks.

Behind him, the sublight thrusters outshone the Flamewind for a moment. Then, from the viewpoint of the fighters, they were gone, lost in the multicolored mist.

Lando knew his enemies—whoever they were, confound it!—would not be long in following. They'd had that gigantic antique battleship engine they were using as a collective booster. He had to think of something clever, and he had to do it *fast*.

Momentarily, the Flamewind paled. They were out of the Sixth Belt, where they'd begun, and crossing the narrow space between it and the Fifth Belt, their destination.

Either that or they were headed from Six to Seven—Lando didn't trust his navigational capacities at the best of times, let alone now.

No, they were headed toward the Oseon's fractious primary.

His hand swept instrument switches. The screens still showed an indecipherable hash, but coming up a little to the starboard was a small cluster of asteroids, irregulars, following their own course through the belt. He modified his course to meet them.

As he switched the instruments back off, he could see the tiny fleet of fighter craft behind him.

The screen had shown him half a hundred asteroids. His naked eyes showed him half a hundred more, all small—none greater than a few kilometers—all very tightly bunched together. Taking a great chance, Lando cut straight through them until he saw a sort of miracle ahead.

Whether it had been a single rock, struck and not quite split in half, or a pair of floating worldlets that upon colliding had not quite wholly fused, there was a deep crack around its circumference, seventy or eighty kilometers long, no more than twenty meters wide.

Using everything he had to stand her on her nose—without smearing everybody aboard into roseberry jam in the absence of inertial buffering—he steered for the crack, orienting himself correctly and establishing a tangent course to the double asteroid. At the last moment he killed everything but the attitude controls and the docking jets, brought her to a gentle stop deep within the crevasse.

The portside windows showed a half a dozen fighters streaking past without noticing where he'd hidden. Puffing little bursts of attitude reactant, he ground the *Falcon* gently into place. The guns he could control he aimed at open sky. The Flamewind pulsed luridly, looking like a far-off fireworks display.

Which is when he noticed the instruments.

One by one, as he checked them, most of his instrumentation seemed to turn reliable again. He guessed his hidey-hole was an iron-nickel asteroid that acted as a shield against the storm of radiation. The protection wasn't perfect, but it was within the abilities of the ship's electronics to correct.

He ducked his head beneath the panel, spoke loudly and distinctly.

"Vuffi Raa, come out of there! Coffeine break's over!"

RECONNECTING THE LITTLE robot's tentacles was not as easy as it was under ordinary circumstances. They themselves were sophisticated mechanisms, the equal of the fully equipped droids that drove buses and typed stories in newsrooms everywhere in the galaxy. Even deactivated, they had taken a lot of radiation, and their self-repair circuits, set in motion once they were attached to their owner, would require some hours to bring them to full efficiency.

Lando left Vuffi Raa in the cockpit to watch for enemy strays, and wended his way around the corridor to the passenger lounge.

Where he was greeted by utter chaos.

It looked as though a herd of house-sized animals had stomped through. Freed of the restraint of artificial gravity, impelled by sudden changes of direction without inertial damping, everything loose in the room had collided with everything stationary at least once. Perhaps more than once.

And that included Waywa Fybot and Bassi Vobah.

Wires hung loose from ceiling and walls. Small articles of furniture had ended up in extremely strange places. The female police officer was beginning to stir. She moaned heartily, lifted herself up on an elbow, and shook her head.

"What happened? Where are we?"

"Two very good questions," the captain responded. "We were attacked—I don't know by whom—and we escaped. But I don't know to where. Are you all right?" He stopped beside her, assisted her in righting herself. She breathed deeply, made a sketchy self-examination.

"I don't think anything is broken—although to look at this room, that would require a small miracle. Ohhh, my head!"

"Take it easy, you're not expected anywhere very soon. That's me: Lando Calrissian, miracles made to order. You stay there. I'm going to look at our fine feathered fuzz."

He rose and stepped over the debris toward Waywa Fybot's sleeping rack. In the bird-being's case, there had been something less than a miracle. Both the creature's legs were broken, in exactly the same place, apparently where a bar of the rack crossed them. The arrangement had never been intended for free-fall *and* high acceleration.

Nonetheless, the avian officer seemed to have a blissful expression on his face, if Lando could rely on his interpretation of it. The gambler felt a presence at his elbow. Bassi Vobah had made it to her feet and across the room. She stood a bit unsteadily, but she wasn't leaning on anything or anybody.

Lando liked her a little bit more for that, but not much.

"What's wrong with Officer Fybot, and why in the name of the Eternal is he smiling in that idiotic way?"

"Shock, perhaps," Lando answered her. "He's broken both his legs—rather, I've broken both his legs. I'm having a bit of trouble regretting it very much, considering the circumstances. Although I wish I knew how to examine him for further damage. I don't know where he's *supposed* to bend, let alone where he isn't."

Bassi seemed a bit hysterical all of a sudden, and Lando subtracted a few of the points he'd given her. "Well, can't you do something? We can't just leave him lying there!"

He shook his head. "That's exactly what we're going to do, after I splint those legs. I don't think we'd better move him."

The birdlike creature sat up suddenly, opened his great blue eyes, and said delightedly, "Yes, I'll have another centipede, Mother, if you don't mind!"

XII

"AND THIS ONE is worth a *negative* eighteen—am I clear, so far?" the robot asked. The gigantic yellow avian towering over him at the lounge table nodded, trying to shift to a more comfortable position.

Lando looked up from the covered free-fall dish that contained his long-overdue meal and chuckled, wondering who was going to take whom to the laundry when the bird and the droid had the rules of *sabacc* straight between them. Vuffi Raa's literal-mindedness could be a handicap; on the other hand, Waywa Fybot was a bit preoccupied at present, between his injuries and whatever it was he'd seen during the onslaught of the Flamewind.

They'd gotten the narcotics officer splinted up all right: tinkle-wood fishing rods had turned out to be good for something, after all. Lando had never been able to sell the blasted things back in the Dilonexa. He still had a bundle of them stacked in one of the auxiliary holds.

Ah, well. Things could be worse.

They could all be dead.

Looking up again, he winked and smiled at Bassi Vobah, likewise feeding herself from a covered tray. It had taken them the better part of an hour to manhandle the bird into a position where his broken legs could be treated, even in free-fall. Then, all at once, it seemed they had a million things to attend to, and it hadn't been until later that they could think of food.

The first order of business had been the *Falcon* herself.

She'd been pretty badly battered by the desperate flight through the Flamewind and the battle with those tramp fighters—Lando still didn't know who the Core they were or why they had attacked him. She'd never been constructed for astrobatics with her inertial dampers shut down. The stresses to her hull and frame must have been titanic.

In addition, she'd been shot at and even rammed, albeit by a tiny, lightweight single-seater with insufficient mass to do very much except momentarily overload her dynamic shielding. That was the key, of course: her force fields had held her together through everything; she was basically a loose pile of nuts and bolts kept in one place by electromagnetogravitic gimcrackery.

But—like his girlfriend the bootlegger's daughter—he loved her still.

"MASTER, THAT SHOULD *be another centimeter to starboard, I believe.*"

Vuffi Raa had been on the other side of the hull—the inside—measuring the effects of Lando's exhausting labor on the outside. There was a huge ugly dent—but no more than that—in the underside of the boarding ramp where the fighter had smacked it. Lando laughed to himself. You shoulda seen the other guy!

There was nothing he could do right now about the purely mechanical battering. Her seals were intact, the ramp would work perfectly (although there'd be a slight bulge to stumble over, exiting the ship), and what really counted was the shielding.

He moved the micropole another centimeter to the right, waited for the robot's confirmation, and riveted it in place. He didn't understand why the *Falcon*'s previous operators hadn't done this long ago. They had the parts in stores. Just lazy, perhaps. When he was done, the effective density of her defenses would be doubled—of course with a correlative increase in what the shields pulled out of the power plant. Maybe that explained things.

It was hot and sweaty in the vacuum suit, and he was hungry again. Worse, it was extremely claustrophobic working in the skinny wedge of space between the *Falcon*'s belly and the face of the asteroidal crevasse. Well, he had no one but himself to blame for that: he'd sheared half a dozen communications and sensory antennae wiggling her in there, items that by their very nature had to protrude through the defenses in order to operate.

The fact that they hadn't been operating at all, on account of the Flamewind, had helped to guide his instantaneous decision. That and the twenty-odd hostile spacecraft determined to blow the *Falcon* to smithereens.

He began to back from the cramped enclosure. "Let's see about those soft spots on the upper hull now. Then I'm going to have to quit for a while. This is rather tiring, I'm afraid."

The little droid's response was laden with apologetic overtones. "*Master, if it were possible, I would be doing that for you right now. I—*"

"Vuffi Raa, for once shut up and let somebody else do the donkeywork. You come out here and the blasted sun will start frying your brains again. It's like that safe in the cockpit: we're shielded by the asteroid, but not perfectly. You need the extra protection of the hull."

"*Yes, Master. How lucky it was that this crevice runs perpendicular to the direction of the Flamewind. Were it a few degrees the other way, it would function as a funnel or a wave guide and concentrate the—*"

"Yes," said Lando with a shudder, "how well I know!" He hadn't been thinking about all that when he'd ducked the *Falcon* in there. He'd simply been trying to get away from the fighters. He'd been flying and fighting by the seat of his pants. Even now it gave him a chill to contemplate.

"All right, I'm out from under. Start the lock cycling. I'll rest for five minutes and then get out on the upper hull." This may be hard work, Lando thought, but when I'm finished, my ship and passengers—and *I*!—will be as well protected from the Flamewind as we are now. *Without* having to hide inside an asteroid and go wherever it feels like taking us.

"*SABACC!*" VUFFI RAA CRIED, displaying his cards to the bewildered bird. "You see, this comes under a special rule: whenever you have the Idiot—that's worth zero, you know—then a Two of anything and a Three of anything are considered an automatic twenty-three."

Dejectedly, Waywa Fybot handed over a few credits. "But that's ridiculous," he said in his ridiculous voice. "It doesn't make sense. Two and three are five, not twenty-three, and besides, the addition of a zero—"

"That's why it's called the Idiot's Array, old passenger pigeon," Lando supplied. If things kept going that way, he was going to fly the ship and let Vuffi Raa do the gambling. Lando opened a flap in his tray, took a final bite of whatever it was, and slid the container into the mass recycler. "Why don't you play with them, Bassi? A three-handed game's more interesting."

"Not on your life!" She shook her head ruefully. "I've played enough *sabacc* to last me a lifetime, thank you."

"*MASTER, WOULD IT be presumptuous of me to say that your piloting of the ship earlier today was highly proficient?*"

"Only if you don't call me master when you're doing it." Lando could not have been more pleased by this modest praise. He had been a perfectly terrible flyer when Vuffi Raa had taken him in hand—rather, in tentacle. Now, at least sometimes, it was as if he were *wearing* the *Millennium Falcon* instead of riding in her. The little droid had been mortified about his own failure to stand up to the sleet of radiation, at his momentary irrational irresponsibility. But Lando had pointed out that even a diamond, subjected to the proper stress at the proper angle, would shatter.

HE TIGHTENED DOWN another micropole, this time on the upper surface of the *Falcon,* and went on to the next designated location. No bloody wonder the vessel was so vulnerable; there were a dozen spots where the fields failed to overlap properly.

Carefully he pulled his arm out of the suit sleeve, pulling at the glove with his other hand, snaked his fingers up through the collar into the helmet, and wiped perspiration off his nose. You'd think that after all the centuries people had been wearing pressure suits that someone would have invented—

A red light lit up on the surface just below his chin. Now what the devil did that mean? Great Edge! It meant a heat-sink overload! He was cooking himself to death! He examined the readouts on his left arm; everything looked nominal there. What was the matter, then? He keyed the suit's transmitter.

"Vuffi Raa, you'd better start the lock going. I've got to get out of this suit. There's something—"

No response.

"Vuffi Raa, do you copy?"

Still no response.

Again he checked the indicators on the panel inset in his sleeve. The communicator pilot was burning steadily. He hoped that his little friend was all right. The difficulty there lay in the fact that the high point of the *Falcon*'s hull was precisely at the upper airlock. He'd had to crawl out from below, climb around the edge of the ship, to get to where he was. Now, with an apparently malfunctioning suit, he was going to have to repeat the procedure in reverse, with no guarantee he could do it in time to keep from being poached in the shell.

Vuffi Raa could save him a critical few minutes—if only he'd answer!

"Captain to *Millennium Falcon,* do you read?"

Nothing.

He sat as still as possible, thinking as hard as he could. It seemed to be getting hotter inside the suit by the second.

Suddenly, he glanced at the riveting gun in his hand and at the airlock wheel wedged against the rock that formed a roof over his head. Crawling slowly forward a meter, he rapped against the shank of the wheel. The *clank!*, transmitted by the hull, reverberated in his suit. He tried it again. And again.

A few moments later, there was another kind of reverberation in his suit.

"Master, is that you making that noise? I can't raise you on the comlink."

Uncertain whether Vuffi Raa could hear him, he bashed the riveter against the wheel again, once.

"Are you in some kind of trouble other than communications being down?"

Good guess, Vuffi Raa. *Clank!*

"I'll come and get you, right—"

Clank! Clank!

"But, Master . . . !"

Clank! Clank!

A few sweaty minutes later, another suited figure clambered toward Lando over the edge of the ship. Bassi Vobah—her pistol strapped to the outside of her borrowed vacuum-wear—crawled beside him, placed her helmet in contact with his.

"Once a cop, always a cop," Lando said before she got a chance to open her mouth.

"Don't be an idiot. What's wrong with your suit?"

He shook the sweat out of his eyes. It floated in tiny droplets inside the helmet, distracting him. "Coolant failure of some kind. I was worried about getting dinner; now it looks like I'm going to *be* din—"

"Oh, shut up! You relax and lie still. I'll pull you out of here. Your little five-armed friend and Officer Fybot are at the downside lock right now, waiting for us."

"Not the bird, he's accident prone!"

"You should talk!"

Lando was approaching unconsciousness when they cycled through the lock. Vuffi Raa practically tore the helmet off his master—and his ears with it. The resultant blast of fresh air in Lando's face was like an arctic gale.

"Well, another small adventure," the gambler observed as the three of them stripped him down to his underwear and handed him a plastic bag of water, "when what I really needed was a few days in a sensory-deprivation tank. That's the universe for you. Anybody think of slapping something in the food-fixer?"

Bassi Vobah huffed and stomped her way out of the lock area, not an easy thing to do in the absence of gravity. "You're welcome!" she said over her shoulder.

The alien officer followed her, limping awkwardly on his splinted and bandaged legs.

Vuffi Raa looked up at Lando from where he was minutely examining the vacuum suit. "Master," he said cautiously, and in a very quiet voice, "did you remove this suit between the time you were working down below and when you went topside?"

Lando floated on his back beside the airlock hatch, thinking—but only thinking—about getting up and going forward. The cold metal felt extremely good to him at the moment.

"Had to," he replied, hoping the robot wasn't headed where he thought he was headed. "Call of nature."

"So that's when it was done. Master, somebody—"

"Sabotaged the suit when I wasn't looking, is that it?"

"I'm afraid so. They cross-programmed the communicator with the cooling system. Oddly enough, if you'd continued trying to call me on the radio, it would have saved you from being roasted."

Lando shook his head, grabbed a stanchion, and sat up stiffly. "That's a little obscure, even as practical jokes go. Which one of them do you suppose it is?"

"Bassi Vobah helped to save your life."

"When she couldn't avoid it. Come on, I want a smoke. Do you suppose I could roll a cigarette out of one of those crushed cigars in the safe?"

"Why would you want to, Master?"

"Because it's there."

THE NEXT ORDER of business—after getting something to eat— was figuring out where they were. Lando's running battle with the fighter squadron had taken him through many turns and twists, and across what distances he couldn't guess. He and Vuffi Raa spent a good deal of time pondering all that over the navigational computer.

"The device is useless, Master. The radiation's finished it off. That gives me an eerie feeling, I must confess. However, the catalog has some information: this asteroid is uninhabited, but it isn't uncharted."

In the seat beside the robot in the cockpit, Lando's shoulders jerked in surprise. "What? You mean you know where we are?"

"I know the catalog number and some other characteristics of the asteroid we're on—or in, if you prefer. Its configuration is unique, and has been noticed in the past. On the other hand, I can't say precisely where the *asteroid* is at the moment. I have its orbital elements, but everything in this system is subject to everything else, gravitywise—"

" 'Gravitywise'?"

"Yes, Master, and predicting where anything will be at any given moment amounts to a billion-body geometry problem. At any other time than Flamewind, there are continuous long-range sensor inventories, and the system's databanks are updated hourly, but you see—"

"I see." Lando turned a knob, activating the deck plates at their lowest intensity so he'd have just enough gravity to roll a cigarette. He lit it, kicked them off again, and reclined in his chair, mind working furiously.

"Once we get out in that mess again, we won't be able to navigate," he said, more to himself than to the robot.

Vuffi Raa agreed, adding, "However, I shall be of more assistance, now that you have increased the shielding, Master. The trouble is that we don't know where to go."

"We still have that dead-reckoning program of yours?" Reflexively, he flicked ash off his cigarette. It drifted in the cabin, finally settling on Vuffi Raa's carapace. The droid, equally absently, flicked it off. It broke up and they both lost sight of it.

"Yes, Master—with what amounts to a big ball of unknown squiggles at the end of it where you evaded those fighters."

"Can you estimate how big a ball?"

"Yes, certainly. From the power consumption, if nothing else."

"Then that's our margin for error. We simply follow the course as if we'd never deviated and hunt through a sphere of space the same size for Bohhuah Mutdah's estate."

"I'm afraid not, Master, if for no other reason than that the sphere doesn't stay the same size. It increases as a function of probable error as we travel sunward. During Flamewind, there's no way of accurately estimating drift, and—"

"Does that catalog of yours give details on Mutdah's asteroid?"

"Fifty-seven ninety-two? Yes, Master, I—"

"Then it should give us some hints about the other asteroids around there; it's interested in the weird shape of this one. Let's get as close as we can, then pick our way, rock by rock, until we find the right one."

"Very well, Master, I see no other alternative."

"Neither do I. Now, while we're still up here and have some privacy, we're going to talk about who it is *this* time that's trying to kill me."

"WE'RE NEARLY A DAY behind schedule!" Bassi Vobah protested. They were sitting in the lounge again. Lando had powered up the gravity, assuring himself beforehand that his passenger with the broken legs was settled comfortably, and asked Vuffi Raa to prepare another meal before they started.

"Do you realize," the female officer continued to an unappreciative audience in general and an increasingly irritated Lando in particular, "that, under ordinary conditions, this trip would have required a little over two hours?"

"As an inhabitant of the Oseon System, my dear hired gun, you should appreciate better than anyone else the inapplicability of the expression 'ordinary conditions.' There's a storm going on out there, and although I'm not altogether unwilling to venture out in it again, some preparation is essential."

"Captain, may I remind you that the discretion in this matter isn't wholly yours to—"

"Officer, may I remind you that I am the captain, and that, if you continue nagging me, I'm going to take that blaster away from you and stuff it up your nose?"

The policewoman blinked, sat back in stunned outrage. Even her superiors had never spoken to her like that! Lando grinned—not altogether unironically, and laid down the law:

"Now see here: one of you attempted to murder me when I was outside the ship. I'm going to be rather busy when we quit this refuge, both Vuffi Raa and I are, and I don't want to have to watch my back. Therefore, until we can arrive at an agreement concerning arrangements, we will sit right here. My inclination—and if you think I'm joking, you're woefully deceived—is to handcuff the pair of you together until we get to 5792. Unless you can think of an alternative that suits you better—and will satisfy me—that is what we'll do.

"Or we'll park here until the Core freezes over."

Bassi Vobah sat in angry silence, her arms folded across her chest, a sour expression on her face. Waywa Fybot blinked his huge blue eyes, looked thoughtful, but in the end said no more than did his colleague.

Finally: "Now look, you two, I'm not kidding! I haven't figured out who's doing what to whom and why, yet, but there's something—possibly *several* somethings—going on. I make it a practice to avoid getting killed. One of you get out your handcuffs and lock yourself to the other immediately, or—"

"*Master!*" came a shout over the intercom. "*We've got trouble—big trouble! I need you on the flight deck!*"

Rising quickly, Lando glanced from one cop to the other, smashed a frustrated fist into the palm of his other hand, turned, and hurried to the cockpit.

"What is it, Vuffi Raa? Just now I've got—"

"Look forward, Master, to the edge of the crevasse."

Lando settled in his chair, strapped himself in, and, as a happy afterthought, turned the local gravity in the lounge up to approximately three times the normal pull. "*That* ought to keep them in one place! I—*oh, no!*"

"Oh, yes, Master. You can make out the reflections from their hulls. The fighter squadron has found us. They'll be firing into this canyon—without any chance of missing—in a very few seconds!"

XIII

"MASTER, I HAVE failed you again! We cannot escape. My pilot skills are therefore useless. Nor can I man the guns—my programming forbids it!"

Lando waggled back and forth at the controls, loosening the *Falcon* in its rocky nest. He was wishing he could bring the starboard quad-guns to bear, but that was asking too much.

Aside: "We all have our limits, Vuffi Raa. Remember what I told you about diamonds. Just—"

Diamonds? That gave the gambler an idea—a *gambler's* idea, to be sure, but it was all he had at the moment.

"Get out of there, old automaton, strap yourself in the jump-seat behind us, and warn me if anybody comes up the tunnel to the cockpit. I may be able to get us out of this mess, but I want my back safe and my elbows unjogged."

As soon as the droid had restationed himself, Lando began hitting switches. He had some time: the crevasse was deep, composed mostly of metal-bearing rock. It would take the enemy a while to find the *Falcon,* especially since they were out in that impossible . . .

Taking his first risk, he cut the gravity in the lounge. A needle on a power-consumption gauge dropped slightly to the left. Next, he began robbing power from every other system. Out went every light in the ship. Off went the life-support—they'd all be fine for a few minutes without it, and, if his plan didn't work, they wouldn't need it. He'd never reactivated the inertial damping; he placed it on standby, contingent on what happened next. When he was finished, only the panel lights were glowing, that and Vuffi Raa's great eye behind him. The ship was deadly silent.

With enormous reluctance, he cut the standby power to every gun on the ship. It made him feel naked, but they were useless for what he had in mind.

"All right, Vuffi Raa, everything quiet back there?"

"I can hear the pair of them wondering what's going on, Master."

"Let them wonder."

He reached across the instrument array and flipped the shields on. Lights sprang into bright existence, making him feel better. Then he unlatched a metal cover over a graduated knob. Normally it was set at a tiny minus value, placing the main strength of the shields just under the first few molecules of the ship's skin. There were sound reasons for this, but Lando didn't care about them now.

He turned the knob, slowly, very carefully.

The ship's structure groaned as the shields expanded, first a millimeter, then a centimeter away from the surface of the hull. Stresses were transmitted through the hull members to the heavily buttressed casing of the field generator. Lando turned the knob a little more.

The *Falcon* had been tightly wedged within the rock, the wheel of her upper airlock hatch scraping one side of the crevice, the bottom of her hull abraded by the other. There hadn't been a millimeter to spare.

Now Lando was demanding more room, expanding the shields against the asteroid's substance. He turned the knob again; something groaned like a living—dying—thing aft of the cockpit, but the panel lights still showed everything intact.

Half a dozen fighters shot by the lip of the crevasse, seeking, searching, probing. One of them fired an experimental shot. It penetrated and rebounded half a dozen times within the walls before it faded.

Another group of fighters swooped past.

And another.

They were circling the asteroid, searching the long canyon, hundreds of kilometers in extent, for the hidden freighter that had burned at least two of their number out of the polychrome skies of the Oseon.

Their flybys were becoming more frequent as they narrowed the search.

Lando turned the knob a little more, a little more.

A brilliant beam of energy cascaded across the forward shields. By accident or design, the enemy had found its prey. The power needle jumped. Lando slammed the knob to the right as far as it would go.

There was a deafening exploding sound. Multicolored light showered in on Lando and the robot as the asteroid burst under the stresses of the shields and the Flamewind swept around them again.

Secondary explosions punctuated the space around them: one, three, five—Lando lost count as the hurtling rock fragments smashed and scattered the fighter squadron—seven, eight. Perhaps more, he wasn't sure. No one turned to fight. He diverted a little power to the inertial dampers, cut the shields back to normal, fired up the drives, and kicked in the dead-reckoner.

They were on their way again.

He turned up the gravity in the lounge. Even he could hear the thump and a curse from Bassi Vobah. He grinned and shook his head.

THE IMPROVED SHIELDS seemed to help considerably. Vuffi Raa retained his reason. Bassi Vobah was as rational as she ever was. Waywa Fybot dozed in his rack, recovering from his injuries with the aid of an electronic bone-knitter from the *Falcon*'s medical bag of tricks. He ought to be completely well in a few more hours, just in time to arrest the trillionaire addict.

Swell.

Lando, for the most part, stayed up in the cockpit. He was tired of having police for company, preferred the company of Vuffi Raa. The little robot scurried around, tidying up and doing minor repairs. He reported that the hull was perfectly sound, despite the torture inflicted on it, and, in a spare hour, checked the mountings of the shield generator for stress crystallization.

There wasn't any.

NOW THAT HE had time to think about it again, Lando realized that his life had become very complicated.

He'd had many of the same thoughts in jail back on Oseon 6845, but things had been simpler, even as recently as then.

He was a simple man, he told himself, a relatively honest gambler who usually only cheated to avoid winning too conspicuously. Yet someone—several someones, it would appear—kept trying pretty hard to kill him. First with a bomb. Then with another bomb. Then, just to show a little versatility, with a big piece of titanium pipe. Finally, most recently, with a cleverly jimmied spacesuit. He didn't even count the pirate attack or the two encounters with the fighter squadron, although the latter seemed at least tangentially connected. He simply didn't know where it all fit in.

Everybody has enemies, especially a gambler who makes a habit of winning. But the vendetta was ridiculous. For the hundredth time, he reviewed his life over the past few years, trying to discover some person he'd known and hurt badly enough to merit such attention.

He was a skillful *and* fortunate man with the cards, and, despite his failings as a merchant captain, he was becoming a pretty good ship-handler, as well. If he did say so himself. Vuffi Raa said so himself.

Unfortunately, when closely examined, his proficiency was a talent of no practical value. All it seemed to do was get him into trouble. He belonged on a luxury interstellar liner as a passenger, educating other passengers about the follies of trying to fill an inside straight. The soldier-of-fortune routine was beginning to pall.

Well, if by some slim chance he got out of this mess, he'd see about rearranging his life. He had come to love the *Falcon*, but it was a dangerous affair, one that threatened to get him killed at just about any moment. Vuffi Raa was quite another matter, a good friend and partner, an astute adviser. But this captain business . . .

WITH A SINKING HEART, Klyn Shanga inspected the remnants of his command. One lost at Oseon 6845. Two lost in the first engagement with that tramp freighter. And now, between the Flamewind and that exploding asteroid, a mere five fighters left. It was possible that more had survived, were even now trying to find their way back to the squadron through storm and radiation. Some of them might even live past the misadventure *because* they'd lost touch with their comrades.

Five tiny fighting craft, no two alike, except in general size, range, and firepower. They drew on the battle-cruiser engine, restoring their own power even as it pulled them through the nightmarish void.

Well, each of the men had known from the beginning what he faced: a cruel and cunning enemy; a being that took delight in human misery; a creature willing to sacrifice whole cultures, entire planets to satisfy whatever unknowably evil objectives it set for itself.

And each had understood, when he had assembled them in his home system from the ragtags of a dozen armies, how little chance there was of surviving the quest. To them, it had been worth it.

Five out of twenty-four.

It still was.

———

Bohhuah Mutdah lounged in a gel-filled recliner, watching a performance of surpassing obscenity. On the lawn before him, all manner of sentient beings mingled, progressing through every permutation of activity possible to them. He had hired them— over three hundred of them—for that express purpose. They were following his detailed instructions.

He found it boring.

Bohhuah Mutdah found very nearly everything boring. There was little he cared to participate in directly, owing either to security considerations—even now he was surrounded by an unobtrusive force field to protect him from potential assassins among his employees—or to his physical condition. He had seen too much of life, had too much of life. Still he clung to it, although he didn't know why.

To say that Bohhuah Mutdah was obese would be to engage in understatement. He had begun, a hundred years ago, with a large frame, a little over two meters tall, broad-shouldered, long-legged. That had been only the beginning, an armature on which he molded a grotesque parody of heroic sculpture. He was heroically obese, monumentally obese, cosmically . . .

On a genuine planet, with a real gravitic pull, he would have weighed three hundred kilos, perhaps three-fifty. He hadn't entered such a field for a quarter of a century. He was bigger around the waist than two large men could reach and working on three. His own arms looked stubby, his legs like cones turned over on the ends into absurdly tiny baby feet. His face was a bushel basket full of suet, dotted with impossibly tiny features: a pair of map-pin eyes, a pair of pinprick nostrils, a miniature blossom of a mouth.

He hadn't used his own hands for any purpose for five years.

He could afford to use the hands of others. He had no real notion of what he was worth. No truly rich man does. He'd heard it said he was the wealthiest human in the known galaxy. He wasn't sure about that, either, and didn't care.

He didn't care about anything at all—except, perhaps, *lesai*.

Maybe it was the drug that kept him going, maintained the mild interest he experienced in remaining alive. Everything else, the world, the entire universe, resembled a bleak gray plain to him. The Flamewind, lashing and snarling above his heavily shielded dome, seemed colorless to him, although the hirelings on the lawn paused long enough, now and again, to look up in awe at the display.

It wasn't being rich that had done this to him. As long as he could remember, since he was a child in rather ordinary circumstances, he'd puzzled over the phrase "will to live" and wondered what drove others to the bizarre extremes they sometimes reached while struggling merely to remain in existence. Mutdah's wealth had been the casual result of a decade's desultory application of his incredible intelligence, directing his modest substance toward a path of inevitable, automatic growth.

Nor did that intelligence provide him with an answer to his real problem. He knew submorons, many of them working for him, whose capacity to enjoy life was infinite compared to his. He simply lived on, whether he cared to or not, like a machine— no, even the machines who worked for him appeared to relish the mockery of life they possessed with greater fervor and satisfaction than their master.

It was a puzzle. Luckily, he didn't care enough about solving it to let it worry him unduly. He watched the sky, he watched his performers. He watched reflections of it all in the fist-sized Rafa life-crystal he wore upon a yard of silken cord about his neck, wondering why he'd bothered to obtain the thing in the first place.

That philosopher, whoever he had been, had been right: the greatest mystery of life was life itself. And the question that best stated it was: why bother?

A tear rolled down Bohhuah Mutdah's pillow of cheek, but he was far too numb to notice it.

IN A HIDDEN PLACE, Rokur Gepta thought upon the art of deception. How ironic it was, and yet how fitting, that the surest way to lie to others is to lie to oneself first. If you can convince the single soul who *knows* the falsehood for what it is, then everyone else is an easy mark.

Salesmen had known this simple wisdom for ten thousand years, but Rokur Gepta had never known a salesman. Politicians knew it, too, but politicians were Gepta's natural prey, and while the spider knows the ways of the fly in many respects, she never asks him what he thinks of the weather.

Gepta, isolated by necessity now, from his cruiser, from his underlings, even from his beloved pet—they'd better be taking proper care of it, or they themselves would face a greater appetite!—did not regret the rigors that fulfillment of his plans required. Long centuries before an infant Bohhuah Mutdah moaned that life meant nothing, Gepta was consumed by an overwhelming lust for all the things life meant to him: power; hunger filled; power; humiliation of enemies; power.

He let himself be warmed, in his stifling concealment, by memories of triumphs past, by extrapolation to future victories. He saw himself astride the universe, whipping it on to exhaustion in his service. In a linear progression, he would make vassals of emperors, servants of gods. Nothing was beyond the scope of his ambition, nothing.

And his certain destruction of Lando Calrissian would be but a microscopic footnote, a token of good luck, a single four-leaf clover in an infinite field. It was an exercise in determination to Rokur Gepta, an example of taking minute pains to assure that everything, absolutely everything, was right.

———

THE SUBJECT OF a microscopic footnote to the future history of intergalactic space was pleased.

He rolled another cigarette and lit it while Vuffi Raa checked references against the Oseon ephemeris. Exactly as the gambler had anticipated, they'd wound up, at the end of the program, in a flock of asteroids that were well cataloged and identifiable.

And not too very far away from Oseon 5792.

A gambler's life had taught him to take satisfaction from success without being cocky or becoming careless. Well outside the range of the best-known ship-detection systems, and despite the fact that the Flamewind howling outside had blinded any such devices, he ordered Bassi Vobah and her feathered colleague into hiding. Examining the blueprints of the *Falcon,* it had occurred to him that there was space below the corridor decking that might be perfect for installing hidden lockers. Smuggling was merely an interest with him; it might someday rise high enough among his priorities to become a hobby. In the meantime, he had not as yet taken time or gone to the expense of building the lockers. He might never get around to it.

As a consequence, the two police officers were extremely uncomfortable just then, zipped into their spacesuits and stuffed beneath the decking. They clung to stanchions, cursing Lando and their jobs, wishing they had become clerk typists or shoe salespersons.

Which suited their chauffeur right down to the ground.

"Fifty-seven ninety-two coming up, Master. I believe it's that big blob over there on the right."

"That's *starboard,* old binnacle; don't let's disillusion the tourists. Yo, ho, ho and a bottle of— You've got the package ready?"

The little robot turned from the controls, reached behind himself adroitly, and took a vacuum-wrapped parcel from the jumpseat. "I inspected it and analyzed it as you requested, although I don't quite understand why that was necessary. It's genuine *lesai,* all right, in its most potent form, enough for six months' use by even the most habituated addict, and worth more than—"

"Fine, fine. The reason why I wanted you to check it is that I didn't want to be caught delivering a shipment of phony goods. The recipients would likely find a way to reprimand me. Terminally. Also, I didn't want to be exposed to the stuff myself. I don't know how addictive it is, but it's potent applied to the skin."

Lando checked the lightweight vacuum suit he was wearing, made sure his stingbeam was handy in an outside pocket. The part of the mission that had always worried him was coming up. His gambler's wisdom told him it was a bad bet: when the owner of a big, well-defended estate found out he'd brought the law, there were bound to be some recriminations.

The *Falcon* drifted closer to Oseon 5792.

At approximately a hundred kilometers—farther than Lando would have expected under the current "weather" conditions—they were hailed by a cruising ship. It was small, like the fighters Lando had fought off, but brand-new and nearly as heavily armed as his own. Radio being out of the question, it was using a modulated laser to communicate. Unfortunately, Lando didn't have a *de*-modulator.

"They say we're supposed to stop here," Vuffi Raa supplied. "They say they'll fry us out of the firmament if we don't heave to for boarding. Good heavens, Master, they're listing the weaponry they carry! If they're only lying about ninety-five percent of it, we're done for."

"That's all right, old electrodiplomat. How do we tell them that we're stopping for inspection?" Lando had a password, but—with all the other details in his mind the past few days—it hadn't occurred to him that there might be a problem using it.

"I can tell them, Master." The robot leaned forward, directed his big red-faceted eye toward the security ship, and *blat!* a beam of scarlet coherency leaped through the canopy.

"Tell them the secret word is *'dubesor'*—I understand that's a native insult on Antipose XII." Lando took a final, not altogether relaxed, drag on his cigarette and put it out. Vuffi Raa's laser beam winked out almost at the same moment, and he turned to his master.

"They say we're late. I told them, who wouldn't be, considering the Flamewind and everything, and gave them a little edited version of our trouble with the fighters—presumed to be pirates. Did I act correctly, Master?"

"First *sabacc,* and now bluffing your way past the bouncers. I'm not sure whether to be proud of you or worried. I think I'm a bad influence. What did they say?"

"That we're expected and should set down on the small field opposite the surface mansion complex—but not to try any dirty tricks. They gave me another list of engines of destruction they can employ with pinpoint accuracy against a ground target."

"That guy must have been a drummer for an arms company. All right, let's set her down. You do it, won't you? I'm a little too nervous to risk it, considering my amateur status as a pilot."

"Very well, Master."

I wonder what the folks on Antipose XII are doing tonight, Lando thought, whooping it up in the local saloon and calling each other *dubesor?*

It beat hell out of what he was about to do.

XIV

O SEON 5792 WAS not particularly large as asteroids in the
Oseon go.

It was perhaps fifteen kilometers across its widest span, a flat-
tened disk-shaped accretion of many smaller bodies or a peculiar
fragment from a shattered planet. To Lando it rather resembled
an island, floating on a sea of impossible blue—that being the
color the Flamewind was concentrating on at the moment.

Yet it was an island with two personalities.

The top side, as the gambler thought of it—perhaps because it
was the first view that he had of it—was a mythological garden,
dotted with small lakes, spread with rolling lawns, and punctuated here and there by groves of trees, all held down by high
transparent domes and artificial gravity. As the *Falcon* approached, Lando could make out clumps of beings on the grass
before a huge old-fashioned palace, doing something. He couldn't
make out quite what it was.

The underside of 5792 was an impressive miniature spaceport, cluttered parking grounds to an enormous motley fleet of
spacecraft, almost as if it were a hobbyist's collection, rather than
a working landing field. The port was ringed, at the asteroid's
edge, with heavy armament; Lando began taking the security
picket's boasts more seriously. These folks believed in firepower
and had the hardware to back up their belief.

Vuffi Raa settled the *Falcon* in a berth designated for him with
a pulsing beacon. As the freighter's landing legs came into gentle

contact with the surface, and the robot began slapping power-down switches, Lando slapped his safety-belt release.

"I'm going to finish suiting up. You understand what you're supposed to do?"

He pulled on a lightweight space glove, gave his stingbeam another check. It shouldn't look too obvious. No point making things easy for the opposition.

"Yes, Master, I'm to conceal myself in the main control-cable conduit between here and the engine area. I'll tap into the lines there and keep the *Falcon* ticking over for an instant getaway."

The little droid paused as if reluctant to continue. "I'm to stay here, no matter what, and blast off for deep space if you're not back within eight hours. Why do you ask me to repeat these things like a child? You know I have a perfect memory."

"Yeah? Well, I'd feel a lot better about that if you remembered not to call me master. Besides, you've been known to improvise."

The robot considered this gravely. "You could be right, Master. I certainly won't depart as you've instructed me to. Not without looking for you first."

Though inwardly pleased at the response, Lando scowled. "To hell with you then," he snarled. "I've logged your manumission into the *Falcon*'s memories, just in case I don't get back. You'll be a free machine, my little friend, like it or not, with a fully operational commercial starship of your very own."

He was halfway through the rear door of the cabin when he turned and spoke again. "By the way, I've also made you my legal heir. I wish you better luck with this space-going collection of debris than I've had."

The droid said nothing, but his eye dimmed very slightly in a manner that indicated he'd been touched emotionally. Then: "Good luck to you, too, Master. I'll be waiting . . ." But Lando was already gone.

He followed his master off the tiny bridge.

In the passageway, the robot loosened a ceiling panel, hoisted himself up inside, and drew the panel into place beneath himself.

Within a few seconds, he was a part of the *Millennium Falcon*. A very expensive, highly unconventional, and sullenly (for the moment, anyway) independent one.

CARRYING HIS HELMET under one arm, the parcel of *lesai* under the other, Lando reached a certain point in the ship's main corridor where, transferring both burdens clumsily to one hand, he stooped down and rapped, not very gently, on the floor.

A section of roughly sawn decking parted upward and an angry and uncomfortable-looking Bassi Vobah raised her helmeted head.

"I'll take my money now," Lando said. His own helmet began to slip from between his gloved fingers. He gave it an irritated hitch. He doubted he'd really need the thing anyway, but he was a man who took precautions. He was taking one now.

"You can whistle for it, lowlife!" Bassi Vobah's spacesuit served a different and more certain purpose. It was a common quarantine practice to flood a visiting ship with poison gas. Hard on insects, germs, and furry creeping things of a million species, it also discouraged smuggling of certain types and illegal immigration where such phenomena were regarded as a problem by the authorities. "I don't keep bargains with criminals!"

"Then why do you work for politicians?" He thrust a determined hand out. "Give me my money, or I'll suddenly and to my innocent amazement discover a pair of stowaways. Just in time for Bohhuah Mutdah's security goons to take them into custody."

"You *wouldn't*!"

Lando smiled sweetly. "Try me."

Breathing heavily, and from more than exertion, Bassi Vobah struggled among the pipes and wires in the cramped, disorganized space beneath her. She fetched up a bundle, threw it at Lando's feet.

"Take it then, you mercenary anarchist!"

"That's me all over," he agreed charmingly, counting the credits. One hundred seventy-three thousand, four hundred eighty-seven of them. Well, at least Lob Doluff was an *honest* criminal. Better than that, by returning everything he'd won to Lando, the Administrator Senior had, in effect, underwritten the gambler's expenses on the mission.

"Thanks, fuzzikins. Try and understand it takes all kinds. *I* certainly do."

Bassi Vobah slumped back into the floor space, slammed the improvised lid down on top of herself. Lando took an angry step forward, stamping on the slab, ostensibly to seat it flush with the rest of the floor, but more as if afraid that some vindictive spirit would rise from its grave to haunt him.

Then he chuckled at his own annoyance with the lady cop, dismissed it, and continued along the passageway. A few meters farther, he bent again, tapped the beginning of shave-and-a-haircut on the deck, got the final two notes from Waywa Fybot, straightened, and went on.

Near the ship's main entrance, he used a screwdriver to good effect, stashing the wad of money behind an intercom panel. He let down the boarding ramp and stepped onto the "soil" of Oseon 5792.

BOHHUAH MUTDAH MET him halfway.

The trillionaire's private planetoid, while more than a dozen kilometers in diameter, was less than three in thickness. Like nearly every other human-developed rock in the system, it had been steadily honeycombed over the decades of its occupation with storerooms, living quarters, utility areas, and spaces for every other conceivable use.

Two armed guards in stylish livery—and heavy body armor—met Lando at the foot of the boarding ramp, each stationing himself at one of the gambler's elbows. For what had appeared to be a bustling port facility from a few thousand meters overhead, the place seemed remarkably deserted just then. No one else was about, organic or mechanical, as far as the eye could see.

The guards bracketed Lando for a brisk walk across the ferroconcrete apron, into a corrugated plastic service building, through the door of an industrial-grade elevator, and down into the innards of the asteroid. He needn't have bothered with his helmet. There was enough artificial pull to hold a generous atmosphere. The helmet's transparent bubble made a not-too-terribly-convenient receptacle and carrying case for the package of *lesai*.

"Well, fellows," Lando offered conversationally halfway through the elevator ride, "everybody here enjoying Flamewind? Where is everybody, by the way?"

A stony silence followed, during which the gambler spent a futile several moments attempting to peer through the mirror-reflective visor on the riot helmet of the guard at his left elbow. Instead, he saw the swollen and distorted image of a gambler with a mustache, lamely trying to make conversation.

The elevator halted with knee-bending alacrity, its door whooshed open, the guards escorted Lando into what appeared to be a titanic library. The spherical chamber, half a klick from wall to wall, was lined with every known variety of book produced by any sentient race anywhere in the galaxy: chips, memory rods, cassettes and tapes of various compatibilities, bound and jacketed hard- and soft-cover publications, scrolls, folios, clay, wood, and bamboo tablets, stones, bones, hides stretched wide on wooden poles, clumps of knotted rope, and a good many other artifacts whose identity the young captain could only infer from their presence with those other objects he *did* recognize.

The only things missing were librarians and browsers. The place seemed utterly devoid of life.

Bohhuah Mutdah, Lando surmised, was addicted to the printed (written, punched-in, hieroglyphed) word as much as to *lesai*—either that or he had carried pretension to a new extreme. Perhaps it was a tax write-off.

The three, Lando and his personal bookends, were whisked by a length of fluorescent monofilament—one of hundreds drifting handily around the cavernous room—to the center, where an obese giant took his ease.

The trillionaire was being read to by a frail, elderly male servant in a long white robe. Mutdah himself wore nothing but a pair of purple velvoid shorts that would have made a three-piece suit for Lando with an extra pair of trousers.

"Ah, Captain Calrissian," hissed the enormous figure floating effortlessly in midair. His flesh billowed as he made a slight gesture. "I am given to understand you have a delivery for me and that you braved the perils of a solar storm to accomplish the swift completion of your appointed rounds, is that correct?"

Lando, angered by the condescension, cleared his throat, nodded in a way that someone foolish might have interpreted as a slight bow. He reached across his spacesuited chest to extract the *lesai* from his helmet.

"Hold it! Freeze where you stand!"

That from a guy who wouldn't even discuss the weather with a fellow. He and his companion had their blasters drawn, pointed at the gambler's head. The first guard looked to Mutdah. His employer nodded microscopically. The guard took the drugs, helmet and all, examined them one-handed without reholstering his weapon, gave them back to Lando.

The second gunman thrust a palm out. "Okay, let's have it!"

Lando blinked. "What are you talking about?"

A wheezy chuckle emanated from the trillionaire. "Your pistol, Captain. Give him your pistol. You were thoroughly scanned in the elevator."

With a disgruntled expression, the gambler carefully extracted his stingbeam, handed it to the security man.

"The other one as well, please, Captain."

Lando shrugged, grinned at Mutdah, bent over, and removed an identical weapon from his boot. Straightening, he gave it to the guard on his right, who was having trouble handling three guns with two hands.

"What happens now?" the gambler asked mildly.

"That will be all, sergeant, thank you," Bohhuah Mutdah said cheerfully, then, turning to the servant, who had remained impassive, added, "You may go as well, Ekisp."

That left Lando and the trillionaire sitting all alone in thin air in the center of the cavern.

"I thank you sincerely for the trouble you have gone to on my behalf, Captain Calrissian. I ask you to forgive the concern for my continued health which my employees often demonstrate. It is personally gratifying, but sometimes a nuisance. Your property will be returned when you depart."

Not knowing what to say, Lando said nothing.

"On that table, beneath the book old Ekisp left behind, you will discover another package. Please open and examine it; assure yourself that it contains what it is supposed to. The package you have brought may then be left in its place. Will you do that now, please?"

Pulling lightly on part of the monofilament mesh surrounding them, Lando drifted to the table, the sort usually found at either end of a sofa, incongruous there in free-fall. The book, a heavy double roll of vellum written in an alphabet he didn't recognize, had been tucked beneath an elastic band that stretched across the tabletop from edge to edge.

Beneath band and book, as the trillionaire had said, was indeed a bundle. Lando stripped opaque brown plastic from it, attempting to control his eyebrows when he saw the stack of hundred-thousand-credit certificates it contained. With an experienced thumb, he riffled through the pile, estimated that there were at least two hundred of them. Twenty million credits—the gambler suppressed a whistle.

What price lizard mold?

He placed the package of *lesai* under the restraining band, replaced the scroll, and pushed himself back from the table. "Thank you, sir," the gambler said. "If that will be all, I'll be getting back to my—"

Mutdah had opened his mouth to reply, but whatever he had been going to say was muffled by a

BRAAAMM!

Beneath them, the elevator door bulged and split, impelled by a highly directional charge. Two mutilated bodies—the security men who'd stationed themselves on the wrong side of the door—spun end over end across the great library.

Through a cloud of smoke two figures swooped on suit jets, braked to an airborne halt in the center of the chamber, their weapons out and leveled at the trillionaire.

"Bohhuah Mutdah," Bassi Vobah stated formally, "you are under arrest on the authority of the Administrator Senior of the Oseon System, for trafficking and use of illegal substances!"

Mutdah smiled. The explosion hadn't startled him. Nothing seemed to take the obese trillionaire by surprise. He looked at Bassi, looked at Lando speculatively, then looked at Waywa Fybot, ridiculous in his outsize bird-shaped spacesuit.

Waywa Fybot looked back.

Mutdah nodded to the avian. Fybot changed the direction of his blaster, pulled the trigger, and neatly blew off Bassi Vobah's head.

XV

BASSI VOBAH'S BODY slowly tilted backward, its legs projecting rigidly. One arm caught briefly at a filament that turned the corpse as it moved. It drifted away to join those of the guards in the book-lined void.

Bohhuah Mutdah turned his mildly amused attention back to the feathered law enforcer. "Your report, Officer Fybot, if you please."

The creature gave him a salute.

"The order for your arrest, sir, originated in the highest possible echelons. The very highest possible echelons. In addition, shortly before I was dispatched to this system, I was given purely verbal instructions, sir, that you were not intended to survive the process. As insurance, pressure was applied to the local governor through his family, his business interests, and by virtue of his . . . er . . . his . . . ."

The trillionaire's raisin eyes twinkled pleasantly. He lifted a negligent hand, sending waves of obscene motion through his bloated flesh. "Pray go on, my friend, you may speak frankly. The truth does not offend a rational being."

"Very good, sir: through his habituation to *lesai.*

"Somehow Lob Doluff knew or guessed about my secret orders and sent *her*"—Fybot pointed in the approximate direction of the drifting body, now several dozen meters away and dwindling rapidly—"to see that they were not carried out."

The bird-being had been speaking more and more rapidly, a hysterical edge growing in his already high-pitched voice. Now he paused, caught his breath before continuing.

"Captain Calrissian was induced, under threat of prosecution on a capital charge, to provide us transportation and to assist in your entrapment. No one, however, not the Administrator Senior, not his police chief, not Calrissian, and I most fervently hope not my superiors, seems to have been aware of our . . . er, arrangement, sir."

Mutdah smiled. "An excellent report, Officer Fybot. Most succinctly delivered. All in all, I am highly pleased at the outcome.

"But tell me: you are very nearly twenty hours later arriving than either of us anticipated at the outset. I appreciate the difficulties of negotiating the Flamewind, but . . . twenty hours, Fybot? Really!"

The alien blinked, finally thought to reholster his blaster. He fastened down the flap. "In transit to this place, sir, many queer events transpired. I myself suffered deep hallucinations, although my Imperial conditioning is supposed to have rendered me resistant to most . . . Well, that's as may be, sir. In any case, we were attacked, by a collection of odd military spacecraft. We took refuge. Some repairs were required."

Here, the alien hesitated, visibly nervous about the next part of his report. Lando thought he knew why, and doubled both his fists in anticipation.

"Sir, believing—on account of our pursuers—that Calrissian had become a liability, I took the initiative in attempting to dispose of him by sabotaging his vacuum suit. I also thought perhaps this would disrupt the plans of Bassi Vobah when it came time for your arrest. I was reasonably confident that I could get the *Millennium Falcon* here myself. Calrissian has a pilot droid that—"

"Yes, yes," Bohhuah Mutdah answered, for the first time betraying a touch of impatience. Lando relaxed, started breathing again. He'd hoped his little five-legged ace in the hole wouldn't come up in casual conversation.

"But tell me more about these raiders," Mutdah continued. "Who were they? What did they want?"

"Sir, they made no demands, they simply—I have no idea, sir."

"Captain? Surely you must—"

Lando shrugged. "I've been trying to figure it out myself for days. There might be some connection with a pirate ship I fought off between Dilonexa and the Oseon. Then again, it might just be another sore loser."

Mutdah contemplated Lando's reply for a rather longer time than Lando could see any reason for, muttered, "Possibly," more to himself than anyone else, then ". . . and possibly not."

Finally he shook his massive head and turned very slightly to face Lando again. "I might explain that Officer Fybot has never been particularly happy in his line of work. He was, I ascertained when my intelligence sources informed me of this scheme, conscripted to pay tribute owed by treaty by his system to the central galactic government.

"A gentle being, our Waywa; at heart he nurtures no ambition greater than to become a gourmet chef. I suspect that you and I would find his culinary efforts quite resistible. Nonetheless, he possesses no small talent, in the view of his fellow avians, and fondly wishes to resume his education where he was forced to abandon it upon being drafted into service.

"Have I stated your case correctly, Waywa?"

The bird-being reached up, gave his helmet a quarter turn, detached it from its shoulder ring, and tucked it under an arm. He wrinkled up the few mobile portions of his face in a grimace Lando had learned to recognize as representing happiness.

"Oh yes, quite correctly, sir!"

The trillionaire addressed Lando again. "In return for his cooperation, I have personally assured Waywa that he will no longer be required to suffer involuntary servitude at the behest of the government. I fully intend to make good upon that promise, keep my part of the bargain."

Abruptly, Mutdah raised a tiny pistol from where he'd concealed it in the deep folds of his corpulent body, drilled Waywa Fybot cleanly through the abdomen. The beam of energy pierced both suit and bird. A surprised expression froze on Fybot's face as his inert form wafted away slowly from the center of the room.

That made *four* corpses in the library. Things are getting pretty messy around here, the gambler thought.

"The anatomy," Bohhuah Mutdah said incongruously, "is somewhat differently arranged than one might anticipate. That was, believe it or not, a clean shot through the creature's heart."

His fat hand, which supposedly hadn't been used for years, adroitly tucked the pistol into the waistband of its owner's shorts, then hovered there, ready to draw and use the gun again in a fraction of a second.

Lando had noticed that the fat man's reflexes were incredible. Now he noticed something else: a glow of cruel satisfaction that suffused the trillionaire's decadent face. The man *liked* killing.

He looked at Lando appraisingly. "The question now, my dear Captain Calrissian, is what I ought to do with you. As you are aware, I have eliminated—have caused to be eliminated—two duly sworn officers of the law. They will doubtless be missed. I have illicitly purchased a substantial amount of a highly illegal substance. I have suborned an agent of the government. In short, nothing I couldn't easily pay to have taken care of."

The obese figure pointed toward the table once again. "There is a box of excellent cigars in the top drawer of the end table. Would you kindly remove two of them, light them with the lighter you will also discover there, give one of them to me, and enjoy the other yourself?"

The fat hand stayed near the gun.

Lando followed the instructions—with the exception of lighting the cigars. He handed one to Mutdah, offered to light it for him.

"Oh, come now, Captain. I suppose you are afraid of being poisoned or something silly like that. Here: If you don't mind, I'll puff on both cigars while you apply the flame—no, don't let the flame touch them. That's right, just hold it there until the ends begin to glow. That's the way to enjoy a fine cigar. Please choose either one you wish."

Lando was a gambler, a professional manipulator of cards. He knew how to "force" a draw, determine which card another person took while appearing to encourage a free choice. Mutdah wasn't doing it to him.

He took a cigar. It was very, very good.

"Well," he said after a couple of satisfying draws. He'd missed the cigars he'd accidentally crushed aboard the *Falcon,* and the crude cigarettes he'd rolled from their tobacco had been no substitute. "I don't suppose you can just let me go my own way. Believe me, I don't care *what* substances you find enjoyable, and these two"—he waved a hand broadly to indicate the room in which the remains of Vobah and Fybot were floating somewhere— "were no friends of mine."

Bohhuah Mutdah slowly exhaled smoke. "I'd be a great deal more inclined to take that seriously, my boy, if I hadn't seen the expression on your face when they were killed. I suspect that you pretend to be a blasé Core-may-care, live-and-let-live sort of rogue, Captain. But you are a moralist at heart, and I would always have to be looking over my shoulder for you."

He waggled his massive, bloated shoulders. "As you can see, I would find that quite a burdensome task."

Lando's chest began to tighten. He hadn't any illusions about what was about to happen, not since he'd seen Waywa Fybot burned down, but here it was, unmistakably. Soon *five* corpses would drift on the air currents in the chamber, and the next few seconds would determine whether the fifth body was slim and uniformed or gross and nearly naked.

"So I guess we can't make a deal, then?" Lando asked rhetorically. The second pistol hadn't been his only cautious preparation, but he was damned if he could see what good his others would do now.

"I'm afraid not," Bohhuah Mutdah answered sadly. "And for more than one reason. In the second drawer of the end table, you will find a pair of manacles." He drew the gun, leveled it at the gambler. "I wish you to put them on. If you do not, then I will slowly roast you with this weapon, rather than kill you outright. The first shot will pierce your lower spine so that you will be helpless to resist the subsequent agony. Get the manacles and put them on, please."

Lando thought about it, looked at the muzzle of the pistol, looked into Mutdah's unwavering beady eyes, and got the manacles. They were force shackles, a pair of cuff bands connected by an adjustable miniature tractor beam. First class and very expensive. That figured.

"That's right," the trillionaire said encouragingly. "Now put them on."

Shrugging to himself, the gambler snapped the bands around his wrists. He wasn't altogether resigned; Mutdah had something in mind. After all, he hadn't handcuffed Bassi Vobah or her partner.

"Thank you very much, Captain. Now place the shackle beam in this loop of monofilament. Yes. You see, I mentioned that there was more than one reason why I cannot let you go? You recall that?"

An exasperated expression on his face, Lando asked, "Why do jerks like you always have to go into this thespian routine? If you're going to kill me, do it with the gun instead of boredom, there's a good fellow."

A flush spread itself across the vastness of Bohhuah Mutdah's face. With a gargantuan effort, he forced himself erect, pointed the weapon at Lando.

"The first reason I have explained. My enemies are hounding me and would see my power and fortune redistributed. Parenthetically, I must tell you that I do not care a whit about any of that. The continuation of the Bohhuah Mutdah 'empire' is of considerably less than no interest to me at all. I am constitutionally incapable of feeling any concern about it.

"The real reason, Captain, is that I don't *want* to let you go."

The obese trillionaire's body began to blur, its colors swirling together, its outline dissolving. It was replaced by the somewhat smaller form of an individual swathed in gray from top to toe. Only his insanely hungry eyes showed through the wrappings of his headpiece.

"For I am Rokur Gepta, and I'm going to torture you until you *beg* for death!"

XVI

"*S*ABACC!"

Lando Calrissian slapped down the cards in triumph—a triumph that turned to embarrassed agony when he saw he'd hesitated too long between shouting out his victory and sealing it in the stasis field of the gaming table.

In the brief interval between the acts, his perfect twenty-three had transmuted itself into a losing hand.

The seventeen-year-old would-be professional gambler writhed inwardly. He'd practically begged for a chance to join the game in the back room of the local saloon. He'd lied to his family, ducked out on school, broken or severely bent several ordinances about minors and environments such as the one he found himself in now.

He wished that he was home in bed. He wished that he was home *under* his bed. He wished he'd never seen a deck of card-chips in his life, never practiced with them, never imagined himself a dashing rogue and scoundrel.

It was all a dream, a foolish, idiotic dream.

"ALL IS ILLUSION, Captain Calrissian!"

Lando shook his head. The back room of the sleazy hometown saloon had vanished, and with it the embarrassed memory of humiliation and mistake. Actually, he'd gone on to win that game, taking home more money than he'd ever had together in one place before. Why hadn't he remembered that?

Replacing the saloon in his field of vision was a broad rich lawn, trees at the horizon, Flamewind spouting, roiling, and coruscating overhead. That was where he'd seen all those people on the approach to Oseon 5792. Where had they gone?

"The sights you see at this very moment are no more real, no more substantial than the memories you have just experienced so vividly, my boy! *That* is the fundamental truth the universe has to teach us, and like nearly everybody else, you have not managed to learn it until the uttermost end of your life!"

The hiss in that voice was unpleasantly familiar. Lando twisted his head around—he was tied up!—but couldn't find the source. The range of his vision was limited by the upended picnic table, a cold, synthetic marble of some kind, to which he had been bound. All he could see was the garden before him.

And the Flamewind.

The soft sound of slippered feet on grass. A shadow passed around the table—from the angle, Lando guessed it had been propped up on a bench—and turned to confront him.

"Rokur Gepta!"

The voice was filtered through a smile behind the turban windings. "And you thought I was dead, victim of the uprising on Rafa IV. No, Captain, I have been quite thoroughly alive for a vastly longer time than you could guess. I am hard to kill and highly reluctant to let strangers terminate my existence."

Lando bit back a witty reply. In the first place, this was not the time for it, not when he was staked down and helpless. The tractor cuffs were anchored to the table, the beam of force between them lying in close and inseparable contact with the marble surface above his head. Likewise, another pair of manacles had been added to his spacesuited ankles. He and Gepta had moved from the bubblecavern in the asteroid's free-fall center to the surface, beneath the domes.

And he couldn't remember a moment of it.

"No remarks?" the sorcerer taunted. "I see that you have at least learned *some* discretion. This is not a moment for repartee, but a time for contemplation. You are about to experience an agony so excruciating, so unprecedented in the history of intelligent life, that being one of its first experimental subjects is a privilege and a signal honor.

"You have had a sample of it: *torture by chagrin*."

The sorcerer waved a leather-gloved hand.

A JAIL CELL ON Rafa IV at dawn. The open-fronted chamber looked out on a graveled yard. The noise was deafening: they were waking up the prisoners for a day of murderous labor in the life-orchards.

The guards beat on the bars. Lando had awoken with a start; now the fear of what was about to happen filled his being to the core. He backed into the cell, trying to escape the noise, his unsteady breathing slowly turning into a whimper.

BLAAASSSST!

The fire hose caught him unprepared. It dashed him against the wall, the icy water sluicing over him, blinding him, forcing itself into his mouth and nose. He fell to his knees, his head battered against the wall. He ducked it, trying to breathe, trying to stay alive against the killing force of—

"BUT, YOU PROTEST, it wasn't like that at all?"

Gepta paced back and forth in front of Lando, relishing the gambler's agony. Despite the sweat on every centimeter of his skin, Lando was freezing, simply from the memory.

But Gepta was right: it hadn't been like that at all.

"It—it only lasted a few moments," Lando stuttered. Perhaps it was a surrender of some kind; he hated to give the madman any satisfaction at all. But he had to understand what was happening here.

"I wasn't nearly that frightened. I'd already worked out a way to escape. And it only lasted a few seconds—not the *hours* I just . . ." He tapered off, unable to continue because of his shaking. Shaking merely at the remembrance of something that hadn't bothered him all that much when it was actually happening.

"You're a brave man, Captain Calrissian. You don't like to think of it that way. What do you call it, 'creative cowardice'? You regard yourself a pragmatist, one not given to heroics."

The sorcerer had paused, stood now nearly motionless before the gambler. In the background, the Flamewind whorled around the demented sky, casting many-colored shadows. Lando shook his head to get the sweat out of his eyes, tried his bonds. As he'd expected, they were there to stay.

"And yet," Gepta continued, "what is bravery but the capacity to *reject* our fears, ignore and suppress them, then go on to do whatever it is we are afraid to do. What you are experiencing now, dear Captain, is the fear you *refused* to experience the first time. Now you have no choice!"

Surprise attack!

Wrestling the *Falcon* with one hand, Lando desperately tried to fire the cockpit guns with the other as the weird ragtag fighter-squadron bore down on him. It was a nightmare: they were too well shielded for his inconsequential guns to trouble, yet he couldn't operate the quad-guns without leaving the bridge.

Vuffi Raa, insane and helpless, couldn't assist him.

He fired again. He might as well have been shooting streams of pink lemonade as the pale, ineffectual fire that was all he could manage. The enemy fleet bore down on him, bore down, bore down . . .

LANDO FINISHED THROWING UP, coughed, choked, cleared his throat.

"Obviously," Gepta hissed cheerfully, "you survived the peril that you just reexperienced. Otherwise, you wouldn't be here now—it's only logical. It is a logic which enables us to live with our unpleasant memories, is it not? An integrative, healing contextualization which we all require to survive."

"Sure," the gambler gasped. "Sure, you rotten—anything you say!"

"Ahh! Resistance at last! As I was saying, however, the art of torture-by-chagrin lies in *denying* the mind that integration, that perspective. As you relive the minor horrors of your life, you don't recall that you survived, eventually triumphed. You see, even at moments of extreme peril, there are defenses, distractions, digressions which dilute the passions. What is more, my method does not allow its subject to experience anything *but* the fear. You can think of nothing else. The experience goes on and on, in circles, until the ego and the will are utterly crushed.

"Resistance," the lecturer trudged on relentlessly, "only adds the *brisance*, the, how shall I express it, the *snap!* which makes the quashing of the human personality possible. Get angry by all means, Captain. Insult me. Not only will it speed the process—without rendering your eventual agony any shorter in duration, I assure you—but I relish it, as you shall see to your dismay!"

Lando's breath was sour, the taste in his mouth bitter, but he managed a reply. "I'm betting that you're bluffing, Gepta. I'm betting that you're lying about that part. It would be like you. I think I'll continue hating your guts for a while, just as a matter of form. I think I'll imagine them pulled out through your navel and roasted over a slow—"

LANDO'S WORLD WAS a forest of giant legs.

All around him, grown-ups on their private hurried errands jostled him, threatening to knock him down and trample him. There wasn't anything he could do. He was only three years old.

And he had lost his mommy.

The frightening alien city streets were crowded for the holidays, wet and dirty, dark with early evening. The lighted windows of the giant stores along the sidewalk didn't help. He stumbled in the slush and nearly fell, sagged instead against the wall below a window filled with toys, and fought back the tears rolling down his terrified little face.

"Mommy!" Where was she? Why didn't she come and get him? She'd left him at one of the windows—he'd wanted to watch the animated display—when he'd promised he wouldn't move. He was tired of the inside of the store; everything was up too high; there were too many people; and it hadn't been an interesting department anyway, where the lady had given Mommy too much money back.

"Mommy?"

"*Your mommy isn't here, Lando. You're all alone, and always will be.*"

"Who's that talking?"

"*I'm your fear, little Lando, I'm your terror. I'm an eternity of anguish and I'm going to get you!*"

"Mommy!"

Somehow the voice sounded familiar. Somehow he knew the voice hated him and wanted to hurt him. He didn't know what those big words were, terror, eternity, anguish, but they didn't sound very nice. He wanted his mommy.

But he was lost forever in the forest of legs.

"AHHH, THAT WAS a deep and fundamentally traumatic one, wasn't it, little Lando? I could barely stand it myself."

Gasping, Lando shook the tears from his eyes, tried to catch his breath. It felt like he'd been crying for a thousand years. He remembered the incident very well. It had lasted, in reality, all of ten minutes, but somehow, he had never quite trusted the universe afterward.

"What do you mean *you* could barely stand it?" shouted Lando, then: "*You!* You were the voice! What are you doing to me?"

"Only beginning, my dear boy, only beginning. We've been at this, what? Half an hour? It will go on for days, Captain Calrissian, with any luck for weeks! I may attempt to prolong it for—But I see that you are puzzled, Lando."

Gepta had resumed pacing. Lando moved, tried to stretch, and discovered that he'd hurt himself. Where the force cuffs held him, where the marble table bore against his back, he was in pure, unadulterated physical agony.

It felt good by comparison.

"You see, the art of torture-by-chagrin requires that its practitioner experience what the subject experiences. He must guide the mind of the subject into always deeper, always more terrifying waters. He must suffer the experiences himself, in order to assure the quality, the depth, the texture of it.

"And in your case, Captain, and in mine, to make sure it is suitable as revenge!

"Yes, I have a way of living in your head, and yes, I am willing to suffer every bit of pain you suffer, so that I will know that I am torturing you enough!"

Overhead, the Flamewind sheeted the sky with a demented rainbow. Interplanetary lightning crackled across ionized paths. A hurricane of color whirled around the asteroid.

Gepta whispered, "The next little nostalgic digression will concern your business failures, Captain. But before we begin, I wish to tell you that they are not altogether the product of a malicious universe or your incompetence."

Gepta had been pacing back and forth a couple of meters in front of the tilted table where Lando was restrained. Now, for the first time, the sorcerer stepped forward until his eyes burned into those of the gambler.

"*I hounded you!*"

Lando shook his head, too groggy from pain of several kinds to comprehend fully what Rokur Gepta was telling him.

"I dogged your footsteps! Everywhere you went, I saw to it that the prices were a little higher, the rates you could resell at were a little lower! I warned the authorities anonymously that you were a smuggler, increasing the number of fees you had to pay, raising the amount in bribes! I devoured you by attrition—and then arranged for you to be invited to the Oseon!"

"What?" It didn't make sense. Hadn't the government wanted to destroy Bohhuah Mutdah? Hadn't—

"I anticipate the questions you are asking yourself, Captain. I and I alone arranged for that decadent leviathan to be harassed by the government, then had him killed and took his place. All so I would be here when you arrived. I saw to it that more money was placed in your hands than you have ever had before—tens of millions!—money you will now never have the chance to spend."

Here, Gepta reached behind the table, took the thick sheaf of bills, and placed it on the ground at Lando's feet.

"Enjoy it, Captain Lando Calrissian, in the limited way that you are able. Enjoy it as you shall enjoy the memories of every sickening, humiliating, painful event in your life—including this one! I shall enjoy it all with you, purify it, help you to concentrate upon it to the exclusion of all else.

"And we shall see, as I have never had the opportunity to determine before, whether an individual can die of shame . . ."

He lifted a hand; Lando could feel something like drowsiness steal over him, just as he had in each instant before. He fought it, wrenching himself in the restraints, but his mind kept getting fuzzier, his eyes refused to focus on anything but his own terrifying inner realities. He fought it—

But he was losing.

XVII

MAGENTA CURTAINS SHIMMERED against a stationary tapestry of pale stars as lightning exploded above Bohhuah Mutdah's crystalline dome.

And exploded again.

Startled, Rokur Gepta whirled in mid-gesture as a flash bleached his surroundings for a third time in as many seconds. Somewhere, far away, there was a roar of matching thunder—which should have been impossible—and a breeze began sifting toward its distant source. The broad lawn rippled like the pelt of an angry predator.

The wind was fully as impossible as the thunder. Yet it rose from an initial flutter to gale force in a twinkling, whipping at the sorcerer's gray cloak, hurling dust and loose papers along with it.

Lando squinted. The dead trillionaire's lofty architecture had been breached somewhere near the edge of the worldlet. The artificial pull of gravity this side of the asteroid was indolently kinder than at the spaceport, and consequently insufficient to maintain the present atmospheric pressure without help. That help was departing rapidly. The hurricane would roar until things equalized.

He hoped he'd be able to breathe by then.

Battered by the powerful current, Gepta lurched against its strength, trying to reach Lando. The gambler realized this was his only chance—and that perhaps the preparations he had made, however elaborate, might be worthwhile, after all.

Beneath his spacesuit, under the sleeves of his shipclothes, he was wearing his own set of tinklewood splints. In fact, it had been this idea that later served as inspiration when Waywa Fybot broke his legs.

In Lando's case the intention was to *prevent* injury. There were half a dozen twenty-centimeter rods, half a centimeter in diameter, running parallel to each of his forearms, tucked through small fabric loops in three neat circumferential rows, near the elbow, wrist, and in between. Vuffi Raa, thrilled at the chance to do some valeting at last, had sewn them on a heavy shirt for his master. Lando had speculated that they might be handy stopping a blow or parrying a blade. They were X-ray transparent, non-metallic, indetectable by the usual run of security scanners.

Unlike his pistols.

He wore similar crude armor around his lower legs, knee to ankle.

Wriggling an elbow, he finagled one of the rod ends until it was free of the force cuff on that wrist. This would have been a futile effort while Gepta had the upper hand. Now, fighting the incredible wind blowing into space through the broken dome, the sorcerer was too busy to interfere.

The rods had added enough girth to Lando's wrist that he was able—very painfully—to tear his hand through the manacle just as Gepta reached him. Quickly, he slipped one of the rods out of his sleeve, *jammed* it through the turban slit into the sorcerer's eye.

Gepta screamed, clapped a hand to his shrouded face, and stumbled backward. The wind caught his voluminous cloak and took him away in a tumbling, fabric-covered ball of curses. He vanished into a nearby grove of thorn trees. There was more screaming.

Liberating the feet was more difficult. Lando finally pulled his suit boots off, scraped his way past the restraints, and had begun to gather up his shoes and wits and Mutdah's money, when a silvery snake appeared in the grass before him. It had fingers for a face and a red glassy eye in the palm.

It couldn't bite; it was programmed not to.

"Vuffi Raa, you've got to pull yourself together!" There was no response; the independent appendage couldn't talk, and vulgar gestures were beneath the robot's dignity. "I don't know exactly what's going on around here, but it's our chance to get out! Move!"

Behind the uptilted table, Lando found his suit helmet. He also found a complex pile of electronic equipment, cables leading to a large flat, complexly braided coil that had been situated at the back of his head.

"I'm a little disappointed," he said to the tentacle. "And here I'd thought he was doing all that spellbinding by sheer force of personality!"

Somehow the chromium appendage managed to convey impatience as Lando dawdled. It lay on the ground fidgeting while he pulled on his boots. Overhead—directly overhead—there was a resounding bellow. Jagged sheets of curved plastic began falling.

"Relax, old boy, I'm pedaling as fast as I can! I wish you could tell me what the deuce is going on!"

As he shoved his foot into the boot, snapped the vacuum clasps tight, Lando saw the lightning flash of high-powered energy weapons above them.

And several of the fighter craft he'd battled on the way to 5792.

"Edge take me, *that* makes things a little clearer!"

Together the gambler and the disembodied tentacle hurried into the deceased trillionaire's deserted mansion, robot appendage in the lead and seeming to know where it was going. Inside, they took an elevator down into the planetoid. Even as they let it bury them, they could feel the asteroid shake and shudder from the assault overhead.

In the blink of an eye, the carriage passed the ruined door of the library, swung on its gimbals, turning at least one startled occupant on his head, and whisked onward in this new orientation. Adding injury to insult, Lando was nearly dashed to the floor as the machine crashed to a stop inside the spaceport service building.

Rasping on damage-distorted ways, the pneumatic door ground halfway open, then froze. The gambler squeezed through, chrome snake underfoot, and the pair leaped from the building a fraction of a second before it collapsed in flames.

Fire and explosions rocked the airport as more fighters strafed and bombed it. A scarlet beam lashed the waiting *Millennium Falcon* as they approached her. The backsplash nearly fried the gambler. But her shields held.

Gasping, Lando ran up the boarding ramp, pausing only to punch buttons to retract it, then sprinted forward around the corridor, momentarily outdistancing even the tentacle as it hastened back to its owner. Vuffi Raa had climbed down out of the ceiling access and was strapped into the pilot's seat.

Lando took the right-hand position without complaint. "Let's get the devil out of here!" he screamed above the chaos roaring outside.

Reclaiming his leg, Vuffi Raa spared a split second of attention for the gambler while he helped it connect itself. "You're a hard being to rescue, Master. You don't wait for help. I'll ask you how you got loose from Rokur Gepta later, if we live. Meanwhile, hadn't you better man the quad-guns?"

"*You* suggesting an aggressive act? I think you're right." Lando was gone before he'd finished the last sentence. Sliding into the gun chair, he flipped switches and pushed buttons, grabbed the handles of the ungainly weapon, and rested restless digits on the triggers.

A fighter made a pass at the larger ship as she lifted, her thrusters glowing blue-white.

Lando made life hell for him.

The *Falcon* soared into the multicolored sky, two of the fighters harrying her like angry hornets. They were fast, maneuverable, and *good*. Too good: Lando hadn't any easy dodge available there, as he had at the fissured asteroid. Nor was he experiencing much success smoking his tormentors. But his steady, accurate, occasionally inspired shooting kept them from having very much luck, either.

Another frantic pass, another exchange of energy bolts, to little effect except in generating adrenaline on both sides.

Oseon 5792 dwindled rapidly beneath them.

Then somebody manhandling a fighter made a mistake, zigging when he should have zagged. Aboard the *Falcon*, crosshairs rested firmly on his midsection, waiting for exactly such an error. They were still on him as Lando mashed both triggers, tracking all the while, following through.

The fighter burst into a tumbling ball of sparks and greasy smoke.

Vuffi Raa rolled the *Falcon*, skidded, bringing Lando's guns to bear again. He poured her fury into the remaining fighter as it swerved to avoid the fate of its companion.

Freighters weren't supposed to be able to do that!

The unnaturally agile saucer suddenly performed a maneuver that, in another place and time, would be called a Lufbery circle, placing her smack on the fighter's back again. Her quad-guns pounded.

The enemy wriggled off the hook once more, but this one made an error, too: he got sore. Veering in a wide, angry, predictable loop, he came back to have his vengeance. Instead, he got four parallel pulsed beams of raw fusion-reactor output straight in the helmet visor.

And exploded: showering space with incandescent atoms.

Beneath them, there was a sudden streak of light.

Something left the asteroid *faaassst!*, headed for interstellar space. At very nearly the same instant, the surviving three fighters, having reconnected themselves with their battleship engine, bored directly for Bohhuah Mutdah's miniature world, fanatically intent on taking their victim with them—and unaware that (whoever it was) he was gone. Detaching themselves at the last second, they slung the giant, throbbing power plant at Oseon 5792.

One of them had a mechanical failure. His cable wouldn't release. He was pulled down with the engine into hell.

The other two sheered off frantically.

Vuffi Raa raced tentacle tips over the *Falcon*'s keyboards. The resulting acceleration could be felt by her captain even through her powerful inertial dampers. His gun seat slewed around violently, slamming itself and its occupant hard against the stops as the guns swung wildly. The asteroid dwindled to a pinprick—

—and blossomed into a glowing cloud, consuming one of the fighters who thought he'd gotten away, tumbling the other. Even the Flamewind paled momentarily as the ravening fireball expanded, growing brighter, brighter.

Then, from the inside out, it began to dim.

Lando took a deep breath—discovered he'd already taken one he didn't remember—and let it out.

"Brace yourself, Master!" screamed the intercom beside his ear.

BLANG! ZOONG! GRAT!

It was like being inside a titanium drum being beaten by a tribe of savages. Debris showered past the *Falcon*, mostly ricocheting off her shields, some pieces actually getting through at a reduced and harmless velocity.

The freighter shook and danced, then steadied.

Lando released a second breath he didn't recall taking, unstrapped himself from the quad-gun chair, rubbed a couple of sore places on his back, and shambled forward to the cockpit.

DEEP IN INTERSTELLAR SPACE, far from the Oseon and getting farther by the nanosecond, a brand-new one-seat fighter, bruised and battered by the Flamewind and the destruction of a world, took its badly shaken pilot home.

Rokur Gepta laughed bitterly. The best deception is the one that first deceives the deceiver. Blood stained the voluminous gray robes he wore, and agony pulsed through his ruined eye—another debt he owed Lando Calrissian. Yet Rokur Gepta was a being who took precautions, too. For example, his private fighter, one of the tiniest craft capable of interstellar flight ever constructed. It had saved his life in the Rafa System; now it guaranteed his continued existence once again.

In a universe that was all illusion, deception was a double-edged sword. As Bohhuah Mutdah, he had nearly sunk into that flaccid degenerate's depression so thoroughly had he absorbed the role. Only an all-consuming passion for vengeance had helped him to maintain his true identity. Similarly, when attacked by Calrissian, the disguise that he had worn for centuries had nearly been his undoing.

He endured the pain a while longer as a lesson to himself. There was no truth, no objective reality. Yet it would serve him, as a master of deception, to keep his illusions sorted out better. He would meditate upon this lesson while waiting at the Tund System for the scheduled arrival of the *Wennis,* due to rendezvous with him after the passing of the Flamewind. He'd left her and her crew on Oseon 6845 and flown the fighter to 5792 to assume the role of Bohhuah Mutdah.

A pulse of raw anger nearly overwhelmed him, and he concentrated on the pain again to maintain self-control. He'd lost his pet on 5792—another debt he owed the vagabond gambler, one that he would pay with interest when the opportunity presented itself again. Correction: when he *made* the opportunity.

Well, enough was enough. He set his tiny ship on automatic, let the gray-swathed form he usually assumed fade. At long last he occupied the pilot's seat in his true appearance.

The tinklewood rod dropped to the floor of the small cabin,

the blood smears along its length vanishing before it hit. Gepta's pain, fully as illusory as his common worldly manifestation, vanished even more quickly.

Then another rearrangement, another shift of shapes and colors. Once again the charcoal-cloaked, mysteriously masked entity appeared, clean of bloodstains, free of pain.

He cut out the autopilot, took the grips of the fighter's controls, and punched in the overdrive.

The ship became a fading streak against a starry sky and was gone.

"THERE IT IS, MASTER!" an excited Vuffi Raa called.

Lando peered into the transparent canopy of the *Falcon*'s cockpit. The radar and proximity indicators were still nonfunctional and would remain so as long as the Flamewind raked the Oseon. He longed for an old-time primitive optical telescope. The electronic magnifier aboard the *Falcon* was worse than useless here.

"You've got a sharp eye, little friend. But keep the shields up—we don't know whether he's really helpless or just faking." Lando took another puff on the crudely rolled cigarette. Someday he'd get the chance to buy some more cigars.

The *Falcon* swayed and dipped, matching the velocity of the tumbling fighter. Not only had the droid insisted on rescuing its occupant—if said occupant had survived the beating his craft had received—but Lando had agreed in the hope that it might answer a few nagging questions.

Exactly *whom* had he offended sufficiently to merit the fantastic vendetta that—he hoped—was drawing to a close this very minute? He'd certainly never won enough money from any single individual to make it understandable.

The streamers of the Flamewind and the starry background began whirling crazily as Vuffi Raa rolled the ship to match the motion of the disabled fighter. Lando took a final drag, groaned, and cranked himself out of the seat, staggering a little at the disorienting sight. The *Falcon's* artificial gravity and inertia compensators were functioning perfectly, but his sight was fooling his middle ear. He squinted.

"I'll get topside. Hold her steady, will you?"

"Be assured, Master—and be careful. I'll join you as quickly as I can."

"Right."

On the way to the upper hatch, Lando reclaimed his helmet. He hadn't had time to take off his pressure suit, which was just as well. He placed the bubble on his head, gave it the slight push downward and the fractional turn that locked it into place, and checked the telltales on his arm to make sure he had a perfect seal.

One more stop. He seized a meter-long breaker bar from a socket-wrench set in the engine area. He'd lost his stingbeams on 5792, kept no other small arms aboard the *Falcon*. Hefting the length of titanium, he swung it experimentally. Not as good as steel would have been, too light, but it would do to crack a helmet faceplate or a skull.

A muffled *clank!* reverberated gently through the entire ship. Almost as quickly, the robot's voice crackled in his earphones. *"We're locked on, Master. I'll just stabilize our attitude and be right with you."*

Lando didn't feel the maneuver. When things were working right (and he couldn't see out a window), he wasn't supposed to. In any case, he was busy turning a large metal wheel set in the hatch over his head. The seal was supposed to be tight with the escape aperture of the fighter; his suit was only a precaution. But he had closed an airtight door behind him when he entered this area of the ship.

Lando was a man who took precautions.

The wheel hit its stop, the door slumped downward a couple of centimeters, and Lando swung it aside. Pocked and abraded metal greeted him, a circle of it, set in a broader area that matched it in long, hard wear. The circle had an inset ring at its edge. Lando dug a gloved pair of fingers under it, pulled hard, and a strip of sealant followed it down through the *Falcon*'s hatch.

The circle popped out—slightly higher pressure inside the fighter. Lando tossed the emergency access plate down to the chamber floor, stuck a cautious wrench handle through the port, followed it with his head and shoulders. A booted foot hung on either side of his head. The boots were connected to a pair of legs that rose to a body slumped in an acceleration chair and strapped in. The body didn't move.

Straining a little, Lando stretched up and hit the harness quick-release. Tugging gently on the figure's ankles, he got the body started down through the hatch, having to drop his breaker bar to the floor to make room and gain an extra hand. The shoulders jammed momentarily, then slid through.

Lando was glad he'd adjusted the gravity in the room to one-tenth normal. The guy would have squashed him on the way down the hatch ladder. He was huge.

With the rescued pilot lying unconscious on the floor, Lando heaved the hatch back into place, turned the wheel until a green light winked from a small panel beside it, and dropped back to the floor. He read what he could of the pilot's suit telltales. Appearances could be deceptive; the pilot looked human, but it could be ammonia he was breathing inside his suit.

That wasn't the case. As he detached his own helmet and began on that of the disabled fighter pilot, he heard another clank as Vuffi Raa cast off the ruined craft. Inside the helmet was an aged rugged face, elaborately scarred, and covered with a grizzled week-old beard. Even in repose the face looked tough and wise and experienced.

An eyelid fluttered.

Lando recovered the wrench handle, just in case, then had a second thought. This fellow looked strong enough to take the handle away from the gambler and shove it right up his—

A hiss sounded across the chamber. Vuffi Raa stepped through the door just as the pilot began to stir. The tough old man shook his gray head slightly, looked up groggily at Lando, blinked, and looked around the room.

His gaze stopped at the droid, froze there. A look of passionate hatred suffused the pilot's face, and his body tensed for combat.

"*You!*" the pilot screamed. "Destroyer of my world! Kill me now, or you shall surely escape death no more!"

XVIII

WITH A VICIOUS tentacle slash at the bulkhead behind him, the robot launched himself across the room, straight at the astounded fighter pilot. The pilot leaped up just as four chrome-plated manipulators seized him in their mechanical embrace, joined by a belated fifth.

The pilot heaved his forearms up and outward in a hold-breaking maneuver, fended off a tentacle with a forearm block that would have snapped radius and ulna of a human antagonist, delivered a powerful turning backfist blow to Vuffi Raa's pentagonal torso.

The little robot flew back the way he'd come, smashed into the wall, and was on the way back into combat again before Lando could so much as blink.

"Master!" the droid shouted, once again wrapping his limbs about those of the pilot. "Use your medikit!"

Fumbling at the belly of his suit, Lando grabbed the kit's injector, a flat thick coin of an object with a red side and a green side laminated over silvery plating. As Vuffi Raa held the fighter pilot momentarily, Lando slapped the injector on his neck.

There was a *hisssss*, the pilot slumped, and Vuffi Raa released him.

The robot seemed to slink into a corner, his red eye growing dimmer, his tentacles spreading and curling until the little fellow was a simple metallic sphere. The light pulsed feebly once and went out.

"Vuffi Raa!" the gambler exclaimed, shaken with surprise and grief. He hurried to the robot's side, without the faintest idea what to do for his friend. A tiny hint of eye-glow still could be made out. Lando stood as anger began to fill him.

He walked over to the pilot. The sedation hadn't rendered him unconscious. He lay, breathing deeply, his eyes swimming in and out of focus, in and out of burning lunatic hatred for the helpless droid across the room.

Lando turned him over roughly, tore the somewhat antiquated blaster from the man's military holster, flipped him on his back again. Poking around in the small cramped chamber, he found some scraps, odds and ends from maintenance projects, among them a two-meter length of heavy wire. Holding it against the shield-saturated upper hull, he burned it in half with the blaster on its lowest setting, and, without waiting for the fused ends to cool, returned to the recumbent pilot, twisting one piece around his suited wrists, the other around his ankles.

Then, uncaring about what physiological damage he might be doing the soldier, he twisted the knurled edge of the injector until a small arrow was opposite the engraved legend STIM, and clapped it firmly to the man's face.

The device made its subtle noise. The fellow flushed, groaned, but his eyes grew clearer immediately. Lando pressed the still-warm muzzle of the blaster against the man's left kneecap.

"All right, Ace: tell me your story and make it short. By all means *don't* cooperate. I'd love an excuse to use you up, one joint at a time!" The knuckle of his index finger tightened on the trigger, and the pilot saw it.

"I'm Klyn Shanga," the trussed-up figure said with a sigh. "I'll tell you anything you want to know, as long as you promise to use that blaster on me afterward. One clean, effective shot for an old soldier, what do you say?"

Taken aback, Lando let the muzzle drop to the floor. "I say I'll let you know after I hear what you have to say. 'Klyn Shanga': what kind of name is that?" He squatted on the deck beside Shanga, one eye on Vuffi Raa. The robot didn't stir.

Shanga shook his head and sighed again, trying to accept defeat. He'd had a good deal of practice. "It's the name of a dead man, friend, the name of a dead man. Who in the Name are you, and what are you doing fighting *men* like yourself with that fiend over there?"

"I'm Captain Lando Calrissian of the *Millennium Falcon*," Lando replied evenly, "and that 'fiend' is my pilot-droid and *friend*, friend. His name is Vuffi Raa and he never hurt the tiniest insectoid in his life. He's programmed against it."

The pilot blinked. "A droid? Is that what it told you? That explains the fancy chrome—I almost didn't recognize it. But I *did*! You don't forget the devil that destroys your civilization!"

Lando scratched his head. "Be sensible, man. How could one little droid . . . and anyway, what I've told you is true. He *is* a droid. I've seen him partially disassembled. Let me tell you, if he's been permanently harmed— Do you know why he's curled up like that and deactivated? Well, it's because he was forced to attack and restrain a sentient being, I'd guess, to defend himself and me."

Shanga slumped back on the deck, laid his head down, and groaned. "I don't know what the Name is going on here! Partially disassembled? Programmed against aggression? You don't happen to have a cigarette, do you?"

Lando smiled grimly. "I was about to ask you the same thing, Klyn Shanga."

"Klyn Shanga?" said a small voice from across the room. "Is that what you're called? Master, I believe I can clear up some of this confusion, now."

"*Vuffi Raa!*" Lando shouted joyfully.

The pilot stiffened. "You don't know me, creature, but I know you! Remember the Renatasia System?"

The robot uncurled himself, stepped slowly and gracefully toward the two men, and lowered his torso to the floor, letting his tentacles relax. It was one of the few times Lando had ever seen the robot rest. It was one of the few times he had ever needed to.

"Yes, Klyn Shanga, I remember it very well. And with more shame and regret than I can ever express. Master, the Renatasia is a prehistoric colony. No one knows how long ago human beings settled there. Long before the Republic, certainly. Long before any historian is willing to admit there was spaceflight. But it *exists,* and was totally isolated from the rest of civilization, not aware of it any more than we were aware of them."

"YOU WILL RECALL," the droid explained, "that my former master, the fellow you won me from in the Rafa, was an anthropologist and government spy. Well, I was with him for many years, a condition of mutual discomfort and dissatisfaction, I assure you.

"An independent trader, much like yourself, Master, had stumbled across the Renatasia, and my master was designated to check out his findings, reported because there is a standing reward for such discoveries.

"Forgive me, Freeman Shanga—oh, it's Colonel, is it?—well, forgive me, sir, but the Renatasia was a backward place in the technological sense. My master surmised that, sometime after the original colonization, it had been cut off from whatever system the settlers had come from, and, over the next dozen generations, had slid back into barbarism—perhaps even further. As it turned out, they had climbed back high enough to have commercial interplanetary travel within their own system, but had not discovered faster-than-light modalities.

"It was this which was their undoing. The government had classified them as socially retarded and suitable for forcible redevelopment—a variety of wholesale 'therapy' that is a thin euphemism for ruthless exploitation. The Renatasia System, unable to defend itself, was to be *used.* To be used *up,* if desirable.

"But first it had to be surveyed, analyzed, inspected for hidden strengths.

"My master believed that the best deception was the truth—suitably edited. He ordered me to cover my metallic surface with a latoprene coating of an organic appearance, had me make suitable clothing to fit over my admittedly rather unconventional shape, and accompanied me to the surface of Renatasia III in an open, highly conspicuous landing. We announced ourselves to the local government—the system was divided at the time into separate nation-states that often fought vicious wars with one another—as representatives, envoys, from a galaxy-wide civilization.

"Renatasia, after a suitable interval, was going to be invited to join.

"There were parades, Master, and celebrations. We traveled widely in the system, the honored guests of a people who hoped that this fresh contact with a higher civilization would put an end to war and poverty among them. We went to banquets, we made speeches. And always, always, *I* was the Chief Delegate. My master played the role of secretary and assistant.

"We were there for seven hundred standard days, during which we helped them organize a single system-wide government, organized their defense force under a unitary command, then greatly reduced its size. We gave them new technology—trivialities that would aid them not at all when our true purposes were revealed.

"The Imperial Fleet arrived on the seven hundred first day.

"In the beginning, the rejoicing was only redoubled—until the fleet began collecting slave levies, demanding taxes, closing schools, and forcing the Renatasians to teach their children the major galactic tongues to the exclusion of their own. Whole cities, whole nations resisted. Whole cities, whole nations were leveled.

"Two-thirds of the population were exterminated in the bungled pacification operations that followed.

"Stunned and embarrassed, the government left the Renatasia System. The entire matter was covered up and what was termed an 'incident' was forgotten as quickly as possible."

———

"WE DIDN'T FORGET!" Klyn Shanga cried from his supine position on the deck of the *Millennium Falcon*. "We had nothing left but our dreams of retribution! And now we have failed!"

Vuffi Raa propped himself a little higher, began untwisting the wires around Klyn Shanga's wrists. "You gathered warcraft. I didn't recognize you for what you were. There were fighters from at least twenty civilizations in your squadron, and that booster engine was from a scrapped dreadnaught."

"Yes! It took us a decade to put the operation together, cost us everything we had! And in the end, it came to nothing!" He turned his face to the floor; his shoulders shook briefly.

Lando untied the soldier's ankles, helped him to his feet. "I trust, old man, that you understand: Vuffi Raa is many things, but he is only a droid. He has no choice but to do exactly what he is ordered to do. Did you ever see him personally harm anyone?"

Shanga turned to face the gambler. "No, no I didn't. What has that got to do with it?"

"A very great deal. You saw how he reacted, simply to passively restraining you?"

The warrior set his mouth grimly. "So what? You can kill a man by *ordering* it done. You don't have to bloody your own hands. Yet you'll be just as guilty!"

Lando took a firmer grip on Shanga's blaster. "Then I suppose that means you won't give your word not to—"

"You're bloody well *right* I won't!" roared Klyn Shanga.

"Very well." Lando, holding the weapon on the man, reached up and reprogrammed the airlock hatch. "Come along, Vuffi Raa."

Stepping through the bulkhead door, the gambler spoke again. "We'll bring you a cot and some food. I intend to drop you off at the nearest system, and you won't be harmed. I hope to convince you on the way, sometime in the next few days, that this vendetta is irrational. Vuffi Raa is a thoroughly good being, and would have died rather than destroy your culture, but he is also a robot who, even in the vilest of hands, must obey. I'm trying to do something constructive about that, too."

"You are?" a dazed Vuffi Raa asked from the corridor outside. "What, Master?"

"Don't call me master!"

He shut the door, programmed it to restrain the fighter pilot, and shoved the blaster into a slash pocket on the outside of his suit. "Let's get forward, old thing. We need to decide where next to head for."

"That would depend, Master, on whether we are freight haulers or gamblers, wouldn't it?"

"Indeed it would, except that, at the moment, we are gentlebeings of leisure. We have a hundred seventy-three-odd thousand credits I won on Oseon 6845, after all."

Halfway to the cockpit, the droid turned and looked at Lando. "I hate to say this, Master, but from past experience *that* won't last very long."

Lando stopped in midstride, a scowl on his face. He wanted desperately to shuck out of his increasingly uncomfortable spacesuit, get a shower, and lie down for a couple of eons. "Thanks for the vote of confidence. But we also have twenty *million* credits I sort of accidentally brought along with me from Bohhuah Mutdah's place. He won't be needing it anymore!"

They continued along to the control deck, where Vuffi Raa began the procedure necessary to setting a course. Lando was glumly rolling another cigarette with crushed cigar tobacco and highly unsuitable paper.

"Twenty million credits, and I don't have any decent smokes!"

The robot paused. "Master, may I ask you a question?"

"As long as you don't call me master when you do it."

"I'll try. Lando, Klyn Shanga's people, the Renatasians—I feel responsible for them. Their civilization has been all but obliterated. If they recover at all, it will be centuries before they're finished."

Lando nodded solemnly. "That's true. On the other hand, everybody has to start again, fresh every day, from wherever they are."

"Well, Mas—I mean, Lando, we have your winnings from the Oseon. Wouldn't the Renatasians recover a good deal more quickly if they had some help? After all, we're gamblers and adventurers. Being rich would only get in our way. I think we ought to give Klyn Shanga the twenty million."

Lando looked at Vuffi Raa, lit his cigarette, and leaned back in his acceleration couch. It was a long time before he spoke.

"Vuffi Raa, you're a decent, humane droid at heart. And, when you get right down to it, I'm not too bad a sort myself. Compared to the rest of the universe, we're the good guys.

"But as far as the twenty million is concerned, my little mechanical friend, forget it.

"I'm going to *enjoy* being rich."

LANDO CALRISSIAN
AND THE STARCAVE OF THONBOKA

I

LEHESU SWAM THE ENDLESS Open Sea.

He was large for a young adult, although there were Elders of his species twice his size and mass. An alien observer in a different place and time would have pointed out his resemblance to an enormous manta ray—broad and streamlined, powerfully winged, and somehow pleasingly sinister. His sleek dorsal surface was domed high with muscle.

Others would have been reminded of the Portugese man-o'-war, seeing the tentacular ribbons hanging from his ventral side, marveling at the perfect glassy transparency of his body with its hints and flashes of inner color.

Yet, naturally enough, such comparisons would have been misleading. Lehesu had been born among the people who call themselves the Oswaft. He was, unlike ray or jellyfish, penetratingly intelligent. Unlike most others of his kind, he was also aggressively curious.

He dwelt in a place the Oswaft called the ThonBoka, which, in Lehesu's language, brought to mind visions of a cozy harbor on the margins of a stormy ocean. It was a haven of peace and plenty, a refuge.

There were those among the Oswaft, principally family and friends, who had warned him smugly that he would regret adventuring beyond the safe retreat of the ThonBoka into the dark perils of the Open Sea. Few of them actually dared speculate precisely what those perils might consist of, what he might find, what might find him—except a quick, unpleasant death. For all their intelligence, the Oswaft were not remarkably imaginative, particularly when it came to the topic of death. They were a long-lived people and patiently, even fatally, conservative in their outlook.

Others hadn't even cared enough to scold him. Lehesu, himself, was a nuisance and a danger, whose very presence was somehow inappropriate to the warm sanctum of the ThonBoka, a hint of the darker ugliness that lurked beyond its confines. To their credit, it would have been completely uncharacteristic of them to expel him, just as it would never have occurred to any one of them, regardless of personal opinion, to attempt to stop Lehesu from sacrificing himself to his incomprehensible exploratory itch.

At that moment, he was beginning to wish he had listened to *someone*. The Open Sea was slowly starving him to death.

He flapped his great manta wings reflexively to achieve calm. It was an awe-inspiring, majestic gesture—had there been anyone to see it—among his kind, the equivalent of breathing slowly and deliberately. And for Lehesu, it was every bit as effective: it didn't help in the slightest. If anything, it only reminded him that he *had* a plight to worry about.

He was not really frightened. For all their conservatism, fear came slowly to the Oswaft, panic not at all. It was just that curiosity was not a common characteristic among them, either. They had their ancient, venerable, time-tested, firmly established, customary, and honored traditions. Such redundancy was necessary, Lehesu thought, to convey the suffocating stuffiness of it all. Yes, there were ways of accepting innovation. After all, his people weren't savages. It happened gradually, over several dozen generations. The culture of the Oswaft was far from stagnant. It was simply, excruciatingly, *boring*.

Lehesu, on the other fin, was a genius of curiosity—or a totally demented mutation. The conclusion depended on whom you sought for an opinion, Lehesu or any other individual of his species. In his thirst to know what unlooked-for wonders lay beyond the cloying safety of the ThonBoka, he was utterly alone. He could not so much as begin to explain the burning need that drove him into the Open Sea—not to anyone his own age, certainly not to any of the Elders, no, not even to the younger ones.

Well, perhaps one day he would have young of his own. And if curiosity were something that could be passed on, they would understand and share his thirst. He chuckled to himself: how he would ever find a mate who could tolerate him might constitute something of a problem.

Then again, it might not. It was highly unlikely he would survive traversing what amounted to a desert. Every fiber in his great and graceful body ached with hunger. He had been cruising for what seemed an eternity without encountering a molecule of nutriment, and it was far too late to go back. He lifted his enormous wings once more, unable to ignore their rapidly failing strength.

Lehesu had never seen or even heard of a cat, but he would have understood what killed it, how, and why. Still, he couldn't really bring himself to regret what he had done. Curiosity may have killed him already, but it was vastly better than dying from boredom.

Perhaps.

Lehesu estimated that he had, at most, only a few hours before he expired. His people fed continually as they moved about through life, automatically, almost unconsciously. There was little capacity in his gigantic body for storage of nutrients. As he weakened, and the effect was increasingly noticeable, increasingly painful to him, he reflected that at least he was dying in the Open Sea, away from all the—

But wait! What was that? There was something else in the desolation! Far beneath him in the depths, another entity swam, one that pulsed with life and power. Stretching his sensory abilities to their limit, he could feel that it was comparatively tiny, yet it virtually sang with strength—which meant there had to be sustenance around somewhere.

He did another uncharacteristic thing then, something no

other Oswaft would have done: he dived for the object. Lehesu was not a predator. Nor was he herbivorous. Such distinctions had no meaning in his time and place, under those circumstances. It was the habit of the Oswaft to eat whatever they found edible, leave everything else alone. They knew of no other intelligent species, and the entirety of creation was their dinner plate.

At least he could discover what the thing had found to eat. He realized there was a possibility that it would find *him,* and he had little strength for fighting left, even if he had been inclined to fighting, which he was not. Yet he had less hope, even, than strength.

Down and down he went. Yes, there it was, a mote less than a tenth his size, yet he could feel that it was stronger than he was by a substantial margin. Better armored, as well, much like the small carapace-creatures that swam the calmer currents of the ThonBoka.

They were delicious.

As he approached the thing, he could see that it was not shaped terribly differently from himself. To judge from its direction of travel, it was a bit broader than it was long, more rounded in its major contours than he was. Like Lehesu, it had two nondescript projections on its frontal surface, although whether they were sensory arrays, like his, was another question.

Lehesu's senses were not strictly limited to straight lines. He could "see" that the creature possessed no manipulators on its underside. He had hundreds. Yet it appeared that part of the surface was capable of opening; perhaps its tentacles folded into its belly. He knew of organisms that—

Lehesu recoiled in shock! He was near enough now to make out and be astounded by a major difference between himself and the . . . the thing. It was completely *opaque,* like a corpse! His people lost their transparency upon dying and, until they decomposed into the dust of which all life is made, remained visually impenetrable. This creature looked like a dead thing, yet moved with confidence and fleetness. There were those among his people who . . . But Lehesu was not superstitious. With a mental snort, he rejected such foolish notions. Almost completely.

Another milder surprise awaited him. Drawing even nearer—any other Oswaft would have known then and there that Lehesu was quite insane—he felt the thing trying to say something. The ThonBoka was vast and its people many, but neither so vast nor numerous that separate languages had ever developed. Within their limits, the Oswaft were far too wide-ranging, too swift. And they could speak over distances that would only seem incredible to another race.

And so he felt the tingling of communication, for the first time in his life without being able to understand it. He broadcast a beacon of good wishes himself and waited. His own message was repeated back to him. He repeated the first greeting the small armored creature had sent him.

Each now knew the other to be an intelligent organism. That was as far as communication could proceed. The armored creature began counting—that was silly, thought Lehesu; if it were intelligent, of *course* he could deduce that it would be able to count. Thinking hard, he spoke a picture-message, one meant to convey visual reality rather than pure ideas. Lacking any better image, the wave front he transmitted was that of the small armored object before him.

A rather long pause followed. Deep within Lehesu, he experienced a brief sensation of satisfaction that *he* could surprise *it*. Then he received a picture-message of himself. Fine! Now he could convey the essence of his disastrous situation to it, and perhaps it would help him. If in no other way, perhaps it could help pull him into richer currents.

He spoke a picture of himself, then modified it in his imagination until he showed a pitiable scene in which he was growing increasingly opaque, increasingly withered. Finally, just to do things properly and in full, he imagined himself dissolving, his molecular constituents wafting away. It made him feel very strange to imagine such a thing, but it was necessary.

Finally, he started the image over again, but this time had himself feeding richly on what drifted in the currents of the Thon-Boka. He pictured himself growing stronger, healthier, sleeker, more transparent. He pictured himself growing to become a giant Elder. For some reason this made him feel worse than did the idea of dying, although whether the feeling came from imagining a feast while he was starving, or imagining himself in the image of his stuffy forebears, he was not quite certain.

In any case, the creature hung motionless before him in the void, nor did it reply for a long, long time. As he waited, Lehesu examined it carefully. Numerous spots glowed on its outer surface, much like the courting glow pigments of some of the Thon-Boka wildlife. One in particular, a large globular spot at the front end, displayed odd, changing patterns. All the while, the creature pulsed and throbbed with indecently good health. It had come to a halt when the communications began, and continued to be still though obviously restless and thrumming to be on its way.

Finally, it sent him a picture-speech. That caught him by surprise, as his mind had wandered—another dangerous sign of imminent starvation. He had been gazing at the stars, wondering what they were, how far away they lay, and how he might, if he lived, contrive to reach them, as he had reached the Open Sea.

The armored creature asked him, in effect, if *these* were what he liked to eat. It then began displaying pictures of every imaginable variety of wonderfully delicious nutriment, from the incidental nutrient haze that drifted on the currents and was gobbled up by Oswaft as they passed, to the most succulent of complex culinary creations. The trouble was, these images were mixed incomprehensibly with things he didn't even remotely recognize—and with downright garbage.

Excitedly he shouted confirmation when the images were right, withheld comment when they were not. He and the creature hadn't gotten around to establishing the symbols for "yes" and "no." He wondered what the thing had in mind. Would it lead him to this banquet it was promising? Would he have the strength to follow? Or was it merely mocking him?

He was beginning not to care. There were only minutes left for him, anyway.

Suddenly, the greatest shock of all. The belly of the creature split open and vomited out everything it had shown him. It filled the currents around them, forming an almost impenetrable fog. Shouting joyously, he swooped and dived and soared through it all, plowing great clean swaths where he had passed. The creature stood off, watching, doing, and saying nothing.

One pass took him very near the thing. It was not smooth but was covered with knobs and bulges. Only portions of the thing showed any signs of transparency, and they simply admitted the sensory probes into an internal darkness that revealed nothing.

But for once, Lehesu's curiosity was abated. He fed, perhaps more richly than he ever had in his life. Each pass brought him nearer the creature, but he was not afraid of it; it had saved his life. His senses passed over a spot that might have told him a great deal more, except that the Oswaft had no written language, no need for one. It was a plate, a plaque, attached with rivets to the creature's hide. On it were enameled five words that would have shocked him deeply, for this was not a living creature at all.

The sign read:

MILLENNIUM FALCON
LANDO CALRISSIAN, CAPT.

Lehesu the Oswaft, swimmer of the starry void, was content merely to soar and graze about the *Falcon*, singing out his gratitude to her every second he did so, with the natural radio waves generated by the speech centers of his mighty brain.

The formaldehyde was *delicious*!

II

L ANDO CALRISSIAN, gambler, rogue, scoundrel—and *humanitarian?*

It didn't seem very likely, even to him. But the undeniable truth was that, several months after her initial encounter with that remarkable spacebreathing being, Lehesu of the Oswaft, circumstances found the *Millennium Falcon* stolidly boring her way through the interstellar void straight toward the ThonBoka, which translated roughly into human languages as the StarCave.

Lehesu's people were in trouble: Lando was bringing help.

He *was* the help, and he was furious. His anger had nothing directly to do with Lehesu, the Oswaft, *or* the ThonBoka, but was rather more closely connected with the broken arm he was nursing at the moment. It was not quite so onerous nor prolonged an ordeal as it might have been in a more primitive place and time. He wore a complex lightweight brace consisting of a series of electrical coils that generated a field that would encourage his fractured humerus to knit up nicely in two or three days. Yet the appliance was cumbersome and inconvenient, particularly in free-fall. And Lando had grown particularly fond of free-fall. It helped him think.

With the deck-plate gravity switched off, he would sit in the middle of a room—equidistant not only from its walls, but from its floor and ceiling as well—parked comfortably on a cushion of thin air, cogitating. But the cast got in the way.

Lando also had a black eye and a broken toe. But, considering everything else that had happened, those were minor annoyances. He flicked expensive cigar ash at a vacuum hose he'd arranged to hang conveniently nearby, and spoke in the direction of an intercom panel set in a table somewhere beneath him.

"Vuffi Raa, what's our ETA again?"

The instrument returned a voice to him, soft-spoken and polite, fully as mechanical in its origins as the instrument itself, yet rich with humorous, astute inflection.

"Seventy-six hours, Master. That's a new correction: this region is so clean we've gained another four hours since I made the last estimate. I apologize for my previous inexactitude."

Inexactitude! Lando thought. The Core-blessed thing talks prettier than I do, and *I'm* supposed to be the con *artiste* around here!

The *Millennium Falcon*'s velocity, many times greater than that of light, was limited only by the density of the interstellar medium she traversed. Ordinary space is mostly emptiness, yet there are almost always a few stray molecules of gas, sometimes in surprisingly complex chemical organization, per cubic kilometer. Any modern starship's magnetogravitic shielding kept it from burning to an incandescent cinder and smoothed the way through what amounted to a galaxy-wide cluttering of hyperthin atmosphere. But the resistance of the gas was still appreciable through a reduction in the ship's theoretical top speed.

The particular area the *Falcon* was then passing through seemed to be an exception. Bereft of the usual molecular drag, the *Falcon* was outdoing even her own legendary performance.

The captain pondered that, then addressed the intercom again. "Better back her off a few megaknots. I need more time than that before this confounded dingus comes off my arm. And you've still got a dent or two yourself that needs ironing out. And Vuffi Raa?"

"Yes, Master?" was the cheerful reply. Lando could hear the

clack-clack-clack of keyboard buttons being punched as per his instructions. The vessel slowed, but that could not be felt through her inertial dampers.

"Don't call me master!"

That had been very nearly reflexive. He'd long since given up wondering what the robot's motivation was for the small but chronic disobedience. Actually, Lando was concerned about his little mechanical friend, and not just because Vuffi Raa was such a terrific pilot droid. Or at least not entirely. These sporadic violent attacks they'd been suffering lately were getting to be a serious matter where they had only been minor nuisances before, and knowing *why* they were happening, to Lando's great surprise, hadn't helped a bit.

The gambler sneered down at his foot where another tinier set of coils pulsed healing energies into his flesh. Somehow, *that* was the final insult—that and the black eye. It was one thing to attempt to murder an enemy. That was what a vendetta was all about, after all. But to do him in by millimeters, an abrasion here, a contusion there? Fiendish, Lando was forced to admit—if it wasn't simple ineptitude. Somehow the enemy realized that a man otherwise willing and capable of bare-handedly confronting a ravening predator his own size sometimes panics at the sound of a stinging insect barnstorming around his ears.

Well, the gambler told himself, that's why we're on this socalled errand of mercy. I'm going to put a twelve-gee stop to all of this juvenile assassination nonsense, one way or the other, once and for all.

Sure, it was a risky proposition; the stakes were as high as they could be. But above and beyond every other consideration, Lando Calrissian—he told himself again—was a sport who'd wager anything and everything on the turn of a single card-chip.

That's how he'd gotten into the mess in the first place.

It seemed that, some time before, a talented but essentially prospectless young conscientious-objector-of-fortune had won himself a starship—actually a converted smuggling freighter—in a game of seventy-eight-card *sabacc*. A little while later he had, quite unintentionally, acquired a pretty peculiar robot in much the same fashion. Together, the two machines and their man had set out upon a series of adventures, some more profitable than others. In the process, they had made a number of enemies, one of them a self-proclaimed sorcerer who had plotted to Rule the Galaxy, and had tripped over Lando on his way to the top. Twice.

The fellow had resented that, blamed Lando for his own bumbling and bad luck, and the vendetta had begun. Until now, it had been an unrequited, entirely one-sided relationship. All Lando wanted was to be left alone. He'd tried explaining, via various media, that he didn't care who ran the universe—he'd break whatever rules it suited him to disobey in any case, whoever was in charge—and that the sorcerer was perfectly welcome to all the power and glory he could grab. Alas, these blandishments, reasonable as they sounded to the gambler, had fallen upon inoperative auditory organs.

Just to make things really complicated, Vuffi Raa had already had enemies of his own. Although the robot hadn't known it. His previous master, while spectacularly untalented at games of chance, had been a highly effective government employee in the spy business. This fellow, ostensibly an itinerant anthropologist, had used the little robot, forced him to help undermine a previously undiscovered system-wide civilization in a manner that had resulted in the brutal military extermination of two-thirds of its citizens. The remaining third, understandably perturbed, had sworn eternal hatred for the droid, and had enthusiastically begun to do something about it.

Subsequent attempts at negotiation, as in Lando's case, had been nearly lethally futile. Some people just won't listen.

Well, life is like that, Lando thought as he hovered in what had been designed as the passenger lounge of the *Millennium Falcon*. It served as their living room; just then, it was the gambler's private thinking-parlor, and the thoughts he was thinking were reasonably ironic. He took another puff on his cigar.

The trouble with two partners having separate sets of mortal enemies is that said enemies don't always make distinctions. Particularly when using fragmentation grenades. Poor Vuffi Raa had gotten badly dented by an assassin in the employ of the sorcerer at their last port of call. The idiot had confessed before expiring; with the nervousness of a beginner, he'd thrown the pin instead of the grenade. The robot's injuries would work themselves out after a while. He had excellent self-repair mechanisms.

In another incident, Lando had been pushed over a rail into a vat of vitamin paste he had considered acquiring for that very trip, somehow fracturing both arm and toe and picking up a shiner. What really hurt was that he'd simply *ruined* his second-best velvoid semiformal captain's uniform. He was certain Vuffi Raa's enemies were responsible. It felt like their style. Clumsy.

Nor was the *Millennium Falcon* considered immune. In fact, she'd rather taken the brunt of things, with bombs planted inside her (two of which had actually gone off) and having felt the fury of several small space battles in recent months. A fighter pilot had deliberately rammed her, crumpling her boarding ramp. She'd strained her engines getting them in and out of various places in a hurry. Her battery of quad-guns, under Lando's capable direction, had staved off the occasional pirate vessel, who probably hadn't anything at all to do with vendettas. Surprised at the ferocity with which her captain had taken it all out on their hides, defeated pirates were giving the battered old freighter quite a reputation.

Pirates they could handle. The *Falcon* was a good deal faster than she looked, terrifyingly well armed; he and the robot were pretty hot pilots, but Vuffi Raa had taught Lando everything he knew in this regard. Lando told himself again that the business at the StarCave would pay off all other debts, as well. He was thoroughly fed up, loaded for whatever furry omnivorous quadruped the fates cared to place in his path.

Tugging gently at the vacuum ashtray hose, Lando drifted to the ceiling of the lounge, gave a little shove against the overhead, which propelled him near the floor. He switched on the gravity and walked both forward and starboard around the *Falcon*'s curving inner corridor, to the cockpit, which was set in a tubelike construction projecting from the front of the ship.

In the left-hand pilot's seat, an equally weird construction perched, a five-limbed chromium-plated starfish with a single glowing red eye set atop its pentagonal torso. Its tentacles were at rest just then, having reduced the *Falcon*'s speed as Lando had requested.

The meter-high entity turned to its master. "I believe you'll be able to make out the nebula now, Master. See, that blurry spot ahead?"

Lando strained his eyes, then gave up and punched the electronic telescope into activation. Yes, there it was: the ThonBoka, as its inhabitants called it. It was a sack-shaped cloud of dust and gas, enterable only from one direction, rich with preorganic molecules even up to and including amino acids. Inside that haven, life had evolved without benefit of star or planet, life adapted to living in open empty space. Some of that life had eventually acquired intelligence and called itself the Oswaft. But at the moment, they were under seige.

"What about the blockade, can you locate that?" Lando strapped himself into the right-hand seat, ran a practiced eye over various gauges and screens, relaxed, and plucked a cigar out of the open safe beneath the main control panel.

"Yes, Master, I'm overlaying those data now."

Vuffi Raa's tentacles flicked over the panel with a life of their own. He was a Class Two droid, with a level of intelligence and emotional reaction comparable to those of human beings. He had a good many other talents, as well. To Lando's occasional disgust, however, the robot was deeply programmed never to harm organic or mechanical sapience and was thus an automatic pacifist. There had been times when that had been inconvenient.

On the main viewscreen, showing the sack-like ThonBoka nebula, a hundred tiny yellow dots sprang to life.

Lando whistled. "That's quite a fleet for bottling up one undefended dust cloud. What do they think this is, the Clone Wars?" He leaned forward to light his cigar but was stopped by the offer of a glowing tentacle tip. Yes, Vuffi Raa had a lot of useful talents.

"That isn't even half of them, Master. Although I can't understand why, some of the fleet out there have modified their defense shielding into camouflage to conceal themselves. I also believe they've mined the mouth of the nebula."

Puffing on his cigar, Lando forced calm. "And we're going to run that blockade. Oh, well, it's been a short life but a brief one. Can you do anything about shield camouflage for us?"

The robot wiped the screen display. "I'm afraid not, Master. It's very sophisticated technology."

"Which means that everybody in the universe is using it except civilians. Well, then, what's our plan?"

There was a startled pause that might have been filled with a blinking red eye had Vuffi Raa been capable of such a thing. "I thought *you* had the plan, Master."

Lando sighed resignedly. "I was afraid you'd say that. To tell the truth, I had a plan, but it seems pretty insubstantial, here and now. I shall repair to my free-fall cogitorium once more and reconsider. I'll get back to you as soon as possible. Don't hold your breath, it may very well be a century or three."

He unstrapped himself from his chair, took a final disgusted look through the sectioned canopy, and removed himself from the control area with his cigar. Around the long, heavily padded corridor, out into the cluttered lounge, off with the artificial gravity, and back to the geometric center of the room, where he sat and smoked and tried to think.

It wasn't one of his better days for that.

"*Master?*" The voice coming over the intercom was agitated. It startled the gambler out of a dream in which, no matter what *sabacc* hand he held, his cards kept changing to garbage, while a faceless gray opponent held a newly invented one, the Final Trump, which was an automatic twenty-three.

"Zzzzzz—what?"

Lando blinked, discovered that he was covered with sweat. His velvoid semiformals were soaked through, and he smelled like a bantha someone had ridden half to death. He stretched, trying to remove kinks from his muscles that shouldn't have been there in zero gee.

"Vuffi Raa, how many times have I told you never to call me—"

"*Master,*" the robot interrupted, sounding both worried and eager at the same time, "*it's been nearly three hours. Have you come up with a plan?*"

"Uh, not exactly," the gambler replied, shaking his head in an unsuccessful attempt to clear it. "I'm working on it. I said I'd call you when—"

"*Well, I think we'd better talk it over now, if you don't mind. You see, there's a picket cruiser sitting not more than a hundred kilometers off our starboard bow. I didn't see them, so well camouflaged were they, and they've fired two warning shots already. Master, they say they'll cut us in half with the next shot unless we stand by to receive boarders.*"

Lando grunted. His mouth tasted like a mynock cave. "That's the navy for you, no consideration at all."

III

CONCEALED BEYOND THE REACH of civilization lay a place called Tund, a name of legendary repute, one seldom spoken above a whisper. That whispered word named a planet, a system, or a cluster of stars—no one was quite certain which— rumored for ten thousand years to be the home of powerful and subtle mages. Fear was associated with the name, the sort of fear that inhibits mentioning, even thinking about, the thing it represents, so as not to invoke its omniscient, omnipotent, and malevolent attention. Almost no one knew the even more hideous truth.

The planet Tund was sterile, devoid of native life, its surface roasted to a fine, gray, powdered ash where evergreen forests, tropical jungles, and continent-broad prairies had once stretched for countless kilometers. It was a world destroyed by magic.

Or by belief in magic.

At night the planet's face glowed softly, not merely with the pale blue fire of decaying atoms, but with a ghostly greenish residue of energies as yet unknown to the rest of galactic civilization. Where it flickered balefully, nothing lived, or ever would again. It had been partially to preserve the secret of such power that Rokur Gepta, last of the fabled Sorcerers of Tund, had utterly obliterated every living thing upon the planet, from submicroscopic wigglers to full-flowering sentience. His was a terrible, cosmically unfeeling precaution.

The rest had been sheer malice.

Here and there an oasis of sorts had been permitted its closely regulated probational existence, areas reseeded from which, some billions of years hence, when the evil emerald fires had at long last died, life might resume its pitiably humbled march. Massive force fields were essential to press the flickering death away from those few havens.

In one such crouched the cruiser *Wennis,* a decommissioned, obsolete, and thoroughly effective instrument of pitiless warfare, being refitted to her master's precise specifications. Her crew was an odd but deliberate mixture of the cream of the galaxy's technical and military elite and its dregs, often represented in the same individual. Her weaponry and defenses ran the gamut from continent-destroying hell projectors to small teams of unarmed combat experts. She had been a gift of prudence from the highest and consequently most vulnerable of sources in the galaxy.

The *Wennis* would not be recognizable when Rokur Gepta was through with her.

The sorcerer had that way with ships, and planets, and people. The only value anything possessed for him was its utility relative to his inexorable rise to power. Wealth meant nothing more to him than that, nor the companionship of his fellow beings, even—owing to the most peculiar and repulsive of physical circumstances—that of females. He was empty, as devoid of life and warmth as his handiwork, the planet Tund itself. Such an emptiness requires endless volumes of power to fill it even momentarily.

Someday he, too, would bestow gifts of decommissioned battle cruisers—although he would exercise considerably more care to see that they were employed strictly in his interests. And even *that* lofty seat of power was only a feeble beginning. The million-system civilization ruled from it, after all, was only a small wedge of the galaxy.

And the galaxy itself only a small part of . . .

Deep within the twisted caverns of the murdered planet Tund, where Rokur Gepta had once personally searched out and exterminated every one of his ancient mentors—the original sorcerers, who had lovingly instructed him in the ways of power that had been their ultimate undoing—the treacherous former pupil sat, immersed in thought. He brooded in a blackness utterly unbroken by the glimmer of so much as a single passing photon. That was the way he preferred it; he had other means of observing reality.

Even in the full light of a healthy planet's daytime surface, another individual would be less fortunate: Rokur Gepta was simply impossible to come to terms with visually. He was a blur, a vagueness more psychological than perceptual in character, perhaps because his color was that of terror.

On the very rare occasions he was spoken of by others, descriptions varied: he was a malignant dwarf; a being of average though preternaturally imposing stature; a frightening giant of a figure over two meters tall, perhaps three. All accounts agreed that he was perpetually swathed in cloaks and windings of the same hue as his lifeless domain, an ashy gray from the tips of his (presumed) toes to the top of his (apparent) head. He wore a turban-like headdress whose final lengths were wound around the place his face should be, obscuring all his features save the eyes, twin pools of whirling, insatiable, merciless voracity.

Understandably, the sorcerer had enemies, although he had outlived—often by design—the small minority of them with the capacity to do him harm. He had outlived many others as well, simply by surviving centuries of time. His long life was in grave and constant danger, however, from those few who still survived and the continually fresh crop of victims who wished him ill. And that was what produced his present quandary.

Word had been conveyed, through several layers of underlings, of an emissary, a messenger whose credentials offered a potentially profitable alliance. Should he trust the individual sufficiently to hear him out, as per request, in total privacy?

The sorcerer pondered. The risk of a personal audience was great, especially as the representative came from a principal powerful enough to preclude extensive security measures, which could be interpreted as an affront. There were limits to the precautions that could be taken, but none to the cleverness of assassins. He ought to know; he had employed enough of them himself.

Reaching a decision, he gestured with a gray-gloved hand. Feeble light began to glow within the monstrous cavern, swelling until it filled the place. Small black hairy things within the walls squeaked a protest, rustled in their niches, then settled back into troubled somnolence.

He would make up this discomfort to his pets, Gepta thought, and if the audience turned out to be less than advertised, so would the emissary make restitution, most slowly.

A faint electronic chirp from a panel in the left arm of his basaltic throne alerted him of visitors. He firmed up his visual appearance; no sense alarming the messenger unduly at the outset. The time for intimidation, confusion, and betrayal would come later. It always did.

From a passageway far to the right, across a kilometer or more of cavern floor, a small procession wended its way, composed of minions in uniform, their marks of rank and organization stripped away to preserve the fiction that they were civilians. In truth, they were the same sort of gift the *Wennis* had been, and served their original master by serving Rokur Gepta.

The honor guard consisted of a half dozen heavily armed and smartly groomed beings, every fiber bristling at attention as they marched. In their midst was a giant, a large, heavyset man in a battered spacesuit, carrying his helmet under one arm. The group wound carefully among the cavern floor's many stalagmites, following a hidden pattern that, if strayed from, would precipitate their immediate and total destruction.

Gepta waited on his throne, three meters above the floor.

As the column reached its base, Gepta's soldiers snapped to a halt. The visitor technically stood at attention, too, but he was the sort of being who, when the time came, would look as if he were lounging indolently in his own coffin. He was utterly relaxed, utterly alert. He was utterly unafraid of anything, most especially death.

If Rokur Gepta feared anything himself, it was men such as this.

"Sir!" the leader of the guardsmen said, "we present Klyn Shanga, Fleet Admiral of the Renatasian Confederation, sir!"

Gepta would accept no title or honorific. Such were for lesser beings. He tolerated being called "sir" because his underlings, of military background, seemed to grow increasingly uncomfortable and uninformative unless they could insert it at least once in every sentence they addressed to him.

Gepta nodded minutely, looking down on the craggy giant. "Admiral, welcome to the planet Tund," he hissed. "Few have seen it, save my minions, and even fewer have lived to say they've seen it."

Shanga grinned broadly from a face that was one scar overlaid upon another until nothing of the original flesh remained. Yet an ordinary human being would have found the effect somehow pleasing. Klyn Shanga was everybody's adventurous uncle, the one who'd been everywhere, done everything, and had it done back to him.

He ignored the threat: "That 'Admiral' is something in the nature of a joke, Sorcerer. In your terms I'm more of a squadron leader, and it's not much of a squadron. Core—for that matter, it's not much of a Confederation, either! But we have our points, as my letters of introduction demonstrated, I'm sure. You know about the Renatasia?"

Gepta nodded once again. Upon receiving the communication in question, he'd consulted references and had a conference with his kennel of government spies. What was to be learned was skimpy; there had been a highly energetic cover-up. Yet the essential facts were clear.

"It was a system and a culture colonized long before the current political status quo was achieved. It developed independently, unknown to the rest of the galaxy, and at a somewhat slower pace technologically. It was discovered, subverted, exploited, and obliterated by certain commercial interests acting in concert with the navy. You, your squadron, and your Confederation are some of the rare survivors. Are these the fundamental elements of the story, Admiral Shanga?" The sibilance of Gepta's whisper echoed in the cavern.

Shanga's turn to nod. "That's it. About a third of the population lived, reduced further by starvation and disease." He leaned against a stalagmite, casually swinging his helmet by a strap around his finger. "Get rid of the flunkies and we'll talk a deal, how about it?"

Gepta savagely repressed a wave of rage and nausea that swept through him at the man's impudence. Time, he told himself, there would be time to deal with him appropriately later. He gestured and the men, with uncertainty on their faces, brought themselves back to attention, turned in place, and marched back the way they'd come. It took them a long while, so indirect and lengthy was the route. All the while, Shanga leaned against his stony outcrop with a grin across his battered face.

"What have you got against Lando Calrissian, anyway, Gepta?"

The sorcerer's gaze jerked upward across the chamber to assure that no one else was present to witness the gibe. Then he settled back in his throne and stared coldly at the fighter pilot before him, struggling to maintain an even tone.

"It is sufficient that he has offended me—primarily with his impudence, Klyn Shanga, a fact you would do well to bear in mind. We have agreed upon the history of your woebegone system; tell me, what is *your* interest in a vagabond gambler. What has he to do with—"

In an instant, Shanga's facade of relaxation dropped away. He stood rigidly beside the stalagmite, his body trembling with anger. Rather a long time passed before he was able to reply.

"Calrissian doesn't figure in it. He has a partner—"

"The robot? Surely, Admiral—"

"Robot!" Shanga shot back hotly. "In the Renatasia it wasn't a robot, but a five-limbed organic sapient! I saw it then—nobody could avoid it! It was treated to parades and banquets, in the media every minute! It was an emissary from a long-lost galactic civilization that . . . that . . . that ultimately destroyed us! It was a spy, Gepta! It infiltrated us, observed our weaknesses, planned our downfall with ruthless precision! Robot? Oh yes, I saw it again after the battle of Oseon, disguised as a harmless droid, but I wasn't fooled, not for a nano! Robot? What would a robot have to gain from—"

Gepta raised an interrupting hand. He knew perfectly well why a droid might help destroy a system. Programmed to obey, it wouldn't have a choice, and properly disguised with an organic-appearing plastic coating, it would be a perfect spy. The sorcerer, however, wasn't about to argue with the man and possibly lose an ally. Shanga would have his uses—and his ultimate disposition.

"Very well, Admiral, we each of us have personal reasons for wishing a conclusion to this hunt, and your offer of assistance is welcome. But your communication hinted at more; there was a claim that you know where the *Millennium Falcon* may be found?"

"And *trapped*!" the warrior added with a snap in his voice. "Imagine the sweetness of it: trapped between us and the navy!" He began laughing, the edge in his voice growing increasingly hysterical until he leaned heavily against the stone column, wiping his eyes and coughing. When he could speak again, it was only one word: "StarCave!"

Rokur Gepta kept his peace, offering no reply. The term was meaningless to him, but given an hour of privacy and access to his sources of information it would not remain so. Finally he replied. "StarCave, you say."

The fighter pilot nodded. "Yes, we have our spies, too, Gepta—we have to. After all, they're the ones who—but never mind that. The navy's keeping a heavy blockade there. We don't know why. There are rumors, but most of them are so silly that we think they're an Intelligence cover. Whatever the reason, we also know that Calrissian's planning to run the blockade, in fact may be there as we speak. We have things you need: information, a rebuilt fighter squadron. You have something we need: passage through the blockade. With Calrissian bottled up there, we can . . ."

There was a very prolonged silence during which each of the figures savored his personal revenge. Gepta was secretly surprised that the military could mount a major action of that type without his knowing of it. On the other hand, he hadn't known about the Renatasian affair until years after it had happened. He was equally surprised at the depth—and enthusiasm—of Shanga's intelligence sources. After it was over, if he, the sorcerer, could incorporate . . . But that was for later. This was now, and the culmination of a very long, very annoying episode in the gray magician's otherwise unopposed rise to total power.

"Very well, Admiral Shanga, let us make an agreement between us. We shall go to this, this StarCave and see what may be seen. The refitting of the *Wennis* is nearly complete, and I will hurry the work. Your squadron will rendezvous with her at a place convenient to us both. I shall take us through the blockade, and you shall assist with the destruction of the *Millennium Falcon* and her owners. And afterward . . ."

Shanga stood, his right hand flexing where his blaster would have been hanging had it not been taken from him by Gepta's security people. He felt incomplete without it. There was a worn diagonal area across the lower half of his pressure suit, from high behind the left hip where the heavy belt ordinarily settled itself, to the middle of his right thigh where the weapon would have been strapped down.

"Yes," said the Admiral, "and afterward: what?"

The sorcerer smiled, an expression that manifested itself only in the sarcastic tone of his voice. Inside the dark gray windings about his hidden face, it was a far from pleasant expression.

"Afterward, my dear Admiral Shanga, we two shall go our separate ways, you to rebuild Renatasian civilization to glorious, dizzying new heights, while I, on the other hand—"

"Mynock muffins!" Shanga raised his gauntleted hand in a mocking salute. Then, without further ceremony, he turned on his space-booted heel and began the trek across the damp cavern floor to the elevator.

He itched to have his blaster once again—an itch he felt between his shoulder blades as he turned his back on the perfidious sorcerer—to get in his small fighter and rejoin the squadron hovering at the edge of the barren Tund System. The dead planet was giving him the creeps.

For his part, Gepta watched the figure of the Renatasian soldier diminish in the twilit distance, kneaded his gray-gloved hands together, once more stifling rage that bordered on gibbering insanity. To be walked out on by a mere underling! And especially one who possessed the gall to consider himself an equal partner in the sorcerer's affairs!

It was almost more than the ancient magician could bear. Almost.

There are rituals, however, formulae for calming both the mind and body under such nerve-shredding circumstances, venerable practices of the long-dead Sorcerers of Tund.

Rokur Gepta applied them all with a will.

IV

LANDO SAT IN the copilot's seat, smoking a cigar and thinking. The navy cruiser wasn't naked-eye visible and he had no desire to crank up the telescope. He'd seen a cruiser before.

They'd been given ten minutes to make up their minds: prepare for boarders or be obliterated. Lando was using every second of those minutes, trying to produce a third alternative. He wasn't having much luck. He'd known from the beginning that a moment like this was going to arrive, sooner or later—although he hadn't imagined it arriving quite so soon. The plans he'd sketched out in the leisure and safety at their last port of call seemed fragile and silly now, however detailed and astute they had appeared at the time.

The trouble, of course, arose from the fact that Lehesu hadn't gone straight home. Fortune or coincidence hadn't had very much to do with his rescue. Lando and Vuffi Raa had stumbled across the same "desert" that had threatened to kill the young Oswaft. What it meant for them and the *Falcon* was a sudden drop to below lightspeed while Vuffi Raa recalibrated the engines. In the empty sector, the engines had met almost no resistance and they threatened to race wildly until they tore themselves and their operators apart, atom by atom.

Thus they had been poking along on their reaction drive when they'd encountered a five-hundred-meter monster soaring out of nowhere. At first they'd taken Lehesu for a weird ship from an unknown culture. They'd been half right, but then Lehesu had mistaken the *Falcon* for a being something like himself. It had taken much longer to straighten out *that* misunderstanding than to puzzle out the vacuum-breather's plight and do something about it.

Vuffi Raa had, as usual, been at the controls, as Lando kept a suspicious eye on Lehesu and a nervous thumb on the trigger from the quad-gun blister.

"*Master, I have communications on a very unconventional frequency.*"

"What's being said?" Lando shifted the stump of his cigar to the other side of his mouth, hunched over the receiver of the quad-gun even farther, and strained to see the weird object floating half a klick away. It was transparent, and didn't show up very well on the detectors, as if it were made of plastic instead of metal. There was no sign of shielding, and he'd seen much bigger ships. Nevertheless, its casual proximity raised the fine hair on the back of his neck and gave him the impulse to jam the triggers down and keep them down until it was reduced to harmless vapor.

"*I've got the* Falcon's *computers working on it—they're not very well suited to translation, I'm afraid—and I'm also plugged into things myself. It would appear—wait! We're starting to receive a visual array. Repeating that first greeting seems to have done the . . . yes . . . yes . . . Master! It's sending us a picture of ourselves!*"

Great, Lando thought, here we are, parsecs from any known civilization, and we've stumbled across an itinerant portrait photographer. Usually they brought a pony or a young bantha with them, but . . . He let the sarcastic thoughts dribble away. They weren't doing any good. He trusted Vuffi Raa to handle things in general but hated to put his life in *anybody's* hands but his own.

"Well, send them back a picture of themselves, for Core's sake! Pretend we're a pair of tourists taking each other's snapshots. It beats shooting it out."

"*Yes, Master, I had already arrived at that conclusion and am transmitting a slow-scan with the proper characteristics. I can put it on one of your gunnery screens if you think it's worth the risk."*

"Go ahead. I can do better with the naked eye anyway, given our range and this thing's weird composition."

On a display to his left, the outline of the *Falcon*, as seen by the alien object, faded away to be replaced with an enhanced representation of the object itself. Vuffi Raa's vision was better than Lando's. He was making out or inferring a good deal more detail. The thing remarkably resembled some marine creatures Lando had seen in his travels although it was too large by at least an order of magnitude. It was also somewhat like a bird—

The picture jerked, the viewpoint changed, the object curled and uncurled its "wings."

"Master, this picture's coming from them! Master, I don't think this is a spaceship! I think it's a—"

At this point, Lehesu began his little video drama, showing himself starving to death and dying, then changing things to show himself feeding and prospering. By the time he was finished, Lando and Vuffi Raa had a much better idea of what they had encountered in that odd, empty region of interstellar space.

Lando knew that it was theoretically possible for organisms to evolve in free space. Chemical compounds formed spontaneously there, many of them very sophisticated and much like those that had preceded life in the oceans of millions of worlds. There were even substances that scientists argued *were* ultrasimple life, somewhere below the level of viruses on a scale of organization.

What bothered Lando was that they'd encountered Lehesu in a region utterly devoid of the chemical soup that was supposed to give rise to life. It didn't make sense. One didn't expect to find human beings in places where there was no light, no heat, no oxygen, no—then he remembered where he was, the same lifeless, empty stretch of nothingness the odd creature was navigating, and liked the situation even less than before.

"Master, I think it's asking for help!"

"Tell it we gave at the office!"

"Master, those symbols! They're atomic nuclei! It's telling us what it needs. That settles it: those aren't fuel compounds, they're food. It's a living creature, and it's been starving to death!"

Lando thought about it. "What does it want, Vuffi Raa? We're not very likely to have anything this alien can eat, are we?"

"Simple organic compounds, amino acids. Master, the contents of the ship's recyclers are almost made for its requirements. Could we . . ."

"Oh, very well, go ahead. We could always use a friend who breathes vacuum and can cross interstellar space by sheer force of personality. Let him have what he—"

The *Falcon* gave a small lurch as Vuffi Raa vented the recyclers. The creature reacted immediately, swooping and soaring ecstatically through the haze of muck they'd released into the void. Lando nearly went crazy trying to keep the energy weapons trained on it, then gave up. The thing wasn't going to harm them; it ate garbage and had been starving to death. They'd made a friend, and friends don't point guns at one another.

He switched off the gunnery circuits, unstrapped himself from the swiveling chair, and lumbered forward to join Vuffi Raa in the cockpit.

THEY'D REMAINED IN that one spot for several days, learning Lehesu's language while Vuffi Raa adjusted the engines. At one point it had become necessary for the gambler to suit up and step outside so that the giant Oswaft could be made to understand that the *Falcon* was a *thing* containing people of a different size and shape than the Oswaft had been capable of imagining. For all his size and the idiotic fix he'd gotten himself into out there, the alien was not stupid. Artifacts were not entirely unknown to his culture, and, as soon as he'd grasped the concept of a spaceship, he'd come up with an idea of his own.

Which meant that Vuffi Raa had to go to work again. In the end, the robot had cobbled up a huge tank out of metal and sheet plastic and filled it with recycler contents. Now Lehesu could travel without running out of nutriment. It had taken both man and droid to maneuver the tank into position beneath the enormous space-going creature. He grasped it in several dozen of his tentacles, gently stroking his new friends with a couple of others as his voice filtered through Lando's suit-helmet radio.

"Many thanks to you, for you have given me life twice. My regret is that there is nothing I can do for you, you who can make food out of nothingness in the middle of nothingness."

Lando was about to say a perfunctory "forget it" when Vuffi Raa raised a cautionary tentacle. *"Master, he's making pictures again. I can see them in my mind!"*

"You're a droid of many talents, and there are advantages to having an electronic brain. What's he showing you, naked dancing-droids?"

"Master! *On the contrary, he's displaying things which he can fabricate from the chemicals he doesn't need in his food. Apparently he does it atom by atom. Master! He's showing me opals, sapphires, flame gems and sun-stones. Why, that's a life-crystal from the Rafa System! Lehesu, can you truly—"*

"Yes, my little friend, if these objects interest you. There is more, much more that I can make. But tell me, is it true that Master cannot see what I am showing you this moment, without an artifact to assist him?"

Lando interrupted. "Core blast you, Vuffi Raa, now you've got *him* calling me master! I want him to stop it immediately, do you hear me, Lehesu? And Vuffi Raa?"

"Yes, Master?"

"Come on inside and we'll take a look at what Lehesu's offering over a screen."

LEHESU'S PEOPLE, the Oswaft, had had yet another talent, and that was what had gotten the young vacuum-breather into trouble the second time.

The interior of the StarCave, over a dozen light-years in extent, was huge even for the relatively enormous organisms and the rest of the complex ecology that inhabited it. Simply boring along at sublight velocities, as Lehesu had been doing on his last (figurative) legs when the *Falcon* had found him, wasn't enough.

Lehesu hadn't gone straight home when he left the *Falcon*. His curiosity hadn't been satisfied—in fact it had been sharpened exponentially by contact with the human and the droid. He wanted to see what things were like in the regions of space that had produced them.

Holding firmly onto his canister of nutrients, he'd bidden them farewell and exchanged promises to get in touch again someday. The gambler had taken these no more seriously than any frequent traveler does with the strangers he gets to know superficially for a short time. He and Vuffi Raa had gone on about their own business, flipping switches and turning knobs to bring the *Falcon* up to full power once more when they reached the margin of the "desert."

Lehesu had gone in search of civilization.

Unfortunately for the Oswaft and the subsequent security of his people, he had done his searching in a region patrolled by the navy, whose sensors, acquired at the unwilling expense of quadrillions of taxpayers, were more sophisticated than those of the *Falcon*. They'd ferreted out the truth about the strange being upon first spotting him, noticing an ability Lando and Vuffi Raa had missed: not only to soar through space in a linear fashion, but to "skip" vast distances when it suited him, as hyperdrive starships do. They'd tracked him back to the ThonBoka when he'd returned with joyous news of his discoveries.

The navy, of course, had recognized a threat when they saw one: a race of beings at home in space, capable of faster-than-light travel—a terrible thing to contemplate. Their scouts' estimate of the number of Oswaft was even more terrifying. It was like encountering a previously unknown superpower with millions of fully operational starships. There was only one thing to do.

The ThonBoka was an open system. It had to be, or exhaust its resources rapidly. The idea was to starve the Oswaft to death, denying them the chemicals drifting in on the galactic tide. Once the vacuum-breathers were sufficiently weakened, they could be finished off neatly, their threat erased forever.

But the navy didn't know that Vuffi Raa's canister handiwork had included a radio relay and transducer—he had truly meant to stay in touch—through which Lehesu had shouted a cry for help across the parsecs. Lando, seeing in the creature's problems a solution to problems of his own, had loaded his ship and come arunning. Now he was having second thoughts.

Less than a hundred kilometers away, point-blank range as distances in space are reckoned, a battle cruiser waited impatiently for an answer. The *Falcon* was fast, but not fast enough to evade the vessel's tractor beams or destructive weaponry. As freighters go, she was well armed and heavily shielded against impecunious pirates and the usual run of freelance riffraff one was likely to encounter in interstellar space. But her quad-guns and other weaponry were no match for the armament sprouting from what seemed like every square meter of the warship that confronted them. And worse, at that range, the Falcon's shields would buy her only seconds of extended life.

Lando considered running—not away from the nebula, but toward it—until he realized that a simple message from the picket vessel would have a hundred more just like it primed and ready by the time the *Falcon* got to the StarCave's mouth. He evaluated very carefully a slim number of other alternatives, compared them with his original plan, and shook his head. No two ways about it: the idea had been lousy to begin with, was still lousy, but it was the only one he had.

"Vuffi Raa," he said at last, closing his eyes as if that could shut out the images of disaster forming in his mind, "shut down all weapons systems as we discussed. Also power down the shields and make sure they can see what we've done over there on their scopes, will you?" He flipped a fifty-credit coin and caught it in the air.

Beside him, the robot sounded dubious. "But, Master, that will leave us completely helpless." His tentacles fidgeted on the control panels.

Lando grinned. "A long time ago, a machine of my acquaintance pointed out that a person who believes that violence is the first or only alternative is morally bankrupt." Up went the coin again, down into the gambler's palm, and up again.

Vuffi Raa stood silent. *He* had been the machine, and the occasion Lando's learning that the little droid was programmed against causing harm to any intelligent being.

"Right now, old can-opener," the gambler continued, "our mechanical defenses are a liability, the appearance of helplessness an asset. Long before I became a starship captain, I was a grifter and a hornswoggler. I guess it's time to see if I retain the skills." Lando walked the coin across the backs of his knuckles and put it away.

The sound of chromium-plated metal tapping on plastic was loud as Vuffi Raa began the process of rendering the ship harmless. Lando sat, deep in thought, weighing his next words carefully.

At last: "All right, raise that cruiser out there; get them on the line. And cheer up—I know what I'm doing. I think."

The robot was incapable of facial expression, but his voice was ripe with worried skepticism. "What should I say, Master?"

Lando chuckled. "Don't call me master. Tell them we received their earlier messages, and that it's *they* who should be prepared to take on boarders!"

V

LANDO CALRISSIAN HAD never particularly liked spacesuits.

Not only were they bulky and uncomfortable, they lacked elegance. His was maintained in the best condition possible, but the color combinations were egregious, the line was execrable, and it clashed with every formal and semiformal shipsuit he owned. And wrinkled them, as well.

Nevertheless, he was suited up and waiting by the topside lock as the *Falcon*, under Vuffi Raa's deft maneuvering, backed and filled to a designated place under the belly of the cruiser *Respectable*. Beside him on the deck plates was a large soft-sided carrying case loaded with supplies and samples he'd purchased for just the occasion. It was one of those times when thorough preparation and a detailed plan instilled no confidence whatever.

"*Locking on, Master,*" came the doubly electronic voice from the cockpit.

"All right, Vuffi Raa, don't wait up for me."

Lando gave the wheel above his head a full turn, another half turn, and cringed, as he always did, when it popped heavily out of its threads. He swung it to one side, reached down for his case, and made his clumsy way up the metal rungs of the ladder, through the *Falcon*'s hull, and into the receiving area aboard the *Respectable*.

To discover he was staring straight into the muzzles of half a dozen high-powered blasters.

Gulping—and happy that it was concealed by his helmet—

Lando keyed his suit radio as he swung the heavy bag onto the deck of the cruiser, lifted himself up, and straightened.

"Good afternoon, gentlebeings. Lando Calrissian, interstellar trader at your service. What can I do you for?" He laughed heartily at his lame joke.

He'd climbed into a hangar bay. Lando thought it a little stupid that they hadn't been invited inside, freighter and all—the navy certainly had the room for it. The ceiling was invisible far above, drowned out by the harsh lights glaring down onto the deck. The chamber was at least two hundred meters from its broad, curving, and presently tightly shut doors to the complicated-looking rear wall where half a hundred windows lit in various colors showed control and maintenance areas behind a pressure bulkhead.

The squad of security guards didn't relax a millimeter. Their leader, identifiable by the insignia on his battle armor, crackled forward, slapped the weapon he was carrying across his chest.

"*Quiet, civilian! You are ordered to report, under arrest, to the sector security chief. Your baggage will be taken for inspection and decontamination!*"

"Decontamination?" Lando feigned dismay. "You want to decontaminate a dozen cartons of fine Dilnlexan cigars, Oseoni cigarettes, Trammistan chocolates—"

"*Cigars?*" the head goon asked in a rather different tone of voice than before. He looked right and left, slapped a pair of switches on his arm panel, grabbed Lando's arm, and similarly rendered the gambler's suit radio inoperative. He touched his opaque-visored helmet to Lando's bubble.

"Cigars, you say? Do you know how long the Ship's Exchange has been out of cigars? We've been on picket at this Core-forsaken nebula since—*ahem!*" The man seemed to regain control of himself momentarily. "Report, with this escort, to the sector chief. I'll take custody of your sample case and make certain that its contents are undamaged."

"Although they may be somewhat depleted when I get them back?" Lando grinned and winked through two layers of plastic at the invisible face next to his. "Just keep in mind, Sergeant, that there's a lot more where this came from if we establish an amenable relationship, all right?"

The sergeant snapped to attention after switching on both radios again.

"Message received and understood, trader! I trust you'll enjoy your stay aboard the Respectable.*"*

"Oh," Lando said, "I'm sure I will. Shall we be moving along?"

THE SECTOR CHIEF was a grizzled, overweight warrant officer with hash marks on his uniform sleeves that threatened to dribble off his cuffs and onto the metal deck plates of his office. He scratched a crew-cut head and then shifted his hand to rub a bulbous, well-veined nose.

"Well, I ain't never heard of nothing like this before—a civilian merchant plyin' his wares to vessels on blockade duty. And friend, if I ain't heard of it before, you've got a problem, cause this man's navy operates on precedent."

Lando, having been examined, searched, scrutinized, peered at and into by human eyes and hands and the sensory ends of countless pieces of nastily suspicious equipment, leaned back in the chair across from the warrant officer's desk and nodded pleasantly. He was glad he'd selected his plainest, least colorful shipsuit to wear beneath his pressure outfit, which was hanging neatly in a locker near the hangar, and even gladder he'd left his tiny five-shot stingbeam aboard the *Falcon*. It was the only personal weapon he ordinarily allowed himself, but at the moment it would have been as conspicuous and counterproductive as his freighter's quad-guns.

"Believe me, Chief, I understand tradition. My family tree is full of it. But there ought to be room for a little enterprise and innovation, shouldn't there? As long as it doesn't jeopardize the mission, and is conducted through the proper channels?"

"*Errhem!*" The sector chief cleared his throat, inhaled from one of Lando's expensive cigars. The gambler's case lay on the floor beside his chair, as thoroughly inspected for weapons and instruments of sabotage as himself, and considerably lighter in weight than when he'd brought it aboard the cruiser. At each level of inspection, from the guard sergeant to the warrant officer, it had become slightly more empty, in proportion to the rank of the emptier.

"My precise sentiments, Chief. Now, about our arrangements. I suggest we route our marketing *around* the Ship's Exchange. In the first place, my overhead won't allow me to offer what I have at wholesale. In the second, I suspect buying from an itinerant peddler such as myself might provide an agreeable diversion for your troops. In the third—well, do you think there might be any interest aboard in games of chance?"

The warrant officer blinked. He fancied himself a sharp gambler and regarded all civilians everywhere as easy pickings, having spent decades taking things from them at large-bore gunpoint. He wasn't able to distinguish between this and situations where civilians had an even chance; could not, in fact, conceive of such circumstances.

"Games of chance? Such as . . ."

"Such as *sabacc*." Lando smiled. "I'm something of an enthusiast, and it would offer you and yours a small opportunity to get your money back for whatever you happen to buy—'you' being a figurative expression in this instance, on account of your commission."

"Commission?" The sector chief looked confusedly at the stripes on his sleeve, then suddenly at the cigar he was smoking. "Oh, *commission*! I get it! Actually, it's a warrant. But no matter! Very funny!"

Lando hadn't intended it to be, but he laughed heartily along until the creature subsided. Then the sector chief adopted an expression that he imagined was shrewd, having practiced it before a mirror since he was a rating.

"I'm sure a few games might be arranged, for a suitable *commission*!" He broke into guffaws again, and Lando stifled a self-destructive urge to strangle the uniformed baboon with his own hash marks.

"Very well. Now there's one more thing I'd like to ask about. I hesitate, because I have some idea of the importance of your mission here—"

"*You do?*" The chief surged forward, leaning avidly across his desk. Only the artificial gravity of the floor-plates kept him planted on his swivel chair.

A wave of alarm swept through the gambler's body. He'd said the wrong thing. This mission was supposed to be top secret and, furthermore, was an unusually shameful one, even for the current government. His mind raced, trying to find a way to salvage something from the mess his careless tongue had created.

"Tell me," the chief said before Lando could speak. "It's the ranks that always know the least, and the folks back home who have a better picture of what's going on." He peered about the room, rose, slid a picture of the fleet commodore aside, seized a small plastic bulb hanging from a wire behind the picture, and closed his hand around it, covering it completely.

"Bugs," the chief said. "We can speak freely now. What *is* so important about this mission?"

Lando almost wept with relief. Then he had to do some fast thinking. "I've heard they have more pirate ships bottled up inside the nebula than have ever been seen in one place before. Apparently Intelligence tricked them into some kind of rendezvous, and you're keeping them trapped until they can be destroyed."

The chief nodded sagely. "That makes some sense of the scuttlebutt I've heard. Any idea when we're going in?"

Lando shook his head. "You know the navy: 'hurry up and wait.'"

Again the knowing, comradely nod. Lando had a friend, now; he revised his prices upward 20 percent. "Sounds like you were maybe a navy man yourself," the chief suggested.

Lando returned the nod. "Just a swabbie, when I was a kid," he lied. "Never made it big, like you, Chief."

"Well, we all have our place in the scheme of things, son. They also serve who only—"

"Sell cigars? And while we're speaking of cigars, why don't you have half a dozen of these for later, Chief. A man only gets so many luxuries, out here on the front line."

"*SABACC!*" THE EXCITED rating cried, gathering in a pot that wouldn't have paid for one of Lando's cigars. The gambler made a practice of losing loudly on the small bets and raking in the winnings as inconspicuously as possible when the stakes were high. Now he was following a policy of steady losses on nearly every hand, in order to win the larger game that awaited him in the ThonBoka.

It was the fourth cruiser he and Vuffi Raa had visited in as many days, using the original warrant officer's connections. Each transfer, ship-to-ship, with its attendant docking and security procedures growing laxer and more perfunctory, brought the *Millennium Falcon* and her real cargo closer to the StarCave and its waiting denizens.

The freighter hadn't been immune to searches, but nobody wastes much time—or olfactory sensibilities—on the trash and toilet recyclers, especially when they were genuinely full of substances that everyone heartily regarded as filth. And especially when no one below the rank of admiral seemed to know the reason behind the stupid blockade.

Lando was rapidly coming to love military security procedures.

With inexpert hands made clumsier by petty greed, the rating dealt the cards out. There were seventy-eight of them, divided into five suits: Sabres, Staves, Flasks, and Coins, arrayed from Aces to Masters, and a special suit of face cards with negative values and more profound meanings. The object of the game was simplicity itself: acquire cards until the value of your hand was exactly twenty-three, or as close as you could get without going over. A perfect zero or a minus twenty-three was as bad as a twenty-four, and there were certain special hands, such as that combining a Two of anything, a Three of anything, and an Idiot from the special suit, which ritual decreed were the equivalent of twenty-three.

The game being played in the cruiser *Reliable*'s MessRec area included Lando, two cooks, and a pair of low-ranking gunners. Lando wore his most tattered clothing, pressed with razor creases, for the occasion.

What made *sabacc* really interesting—and destroyed the nerves of most amateurs who tried to play it—was that each card was an electronic chip, capable of changing face and value at any random moment until the card-chip was lying flat on a gaming table or upon the electronic mat Lando had provided. Thus a winning hand, held too long, could change spontaneously to garbage, or, more rarely, a mess of meaningless numbers could become a palladium mine.

Lando found the game relaxing and a welcome change from the exigencies of interstellar freight-hauling. He'd always enjoyed it, no matter the stakes, possibly because he found it quite difficult to lose. Even honestly.

The older of the two cooks took the hand and the deal shifted to him accordingly. He'd won perhaps half what the previous winner had and was looking inordinately pleased with himself. Lando inwardly shook his head, remembering times when the ransom for a princess or the price of a starship had rested before him on a table in the most exclusive and luxurious settings imaginable. It was difficult to keep the right perspective, to remember from moment to moment that the real stakes here were the highest he'd ever played for: the survival of an entire race, and whatever he might demand in fabricated precious stones indistinguishable from nature's best.

With pitiable awkwardness, the cook dealt Lando a pair of card-chips from the bottom of the deck, attempting to cheat the others in the process as well. Not only wasn't he good at it, he wasn't *any* good at it. Lando received a Master of Staves, worth fourteen points, and a Nine of Flasks: a natural two-card twenty-three. The gambler held them back, hoping one or the other would metamorphose into something worthless. He wasn't after the pay of those miserable sailors, but information.

"Well," he said casually, "I've almost sold my quota here on the *Reliable*. You swabbies have any suggestions where I might find greener pastures?"

His connections, compliments of the *Respectable*'s sector chief, had about run dry, and he needed not only the name of the next ship closer to the mouth of the ThonBoka, but the name of someone aboard in a position to do him some good. As bets were placed and extra cards were passed around, Lando asked for one, giving up the Commander. He received an Ace of Coins just as the Nine in his hand transformed itself into an Eight—*another* pestiferous twenty-three!

All right, then: "*Sabacc!*" the gambler said for the first time that afternoon. You lose some, you win some; you gotta take the good with the bad. He raked in a few millicredits and promptly engineered a loss again. It was simpler to do when he had control of the cards.

"You might try the *Courteous*," the younger of the two cooks suggested, pushing his white hat back from his sweaty forehead. He smelled of onions and had a missing tooth. "Those boys been on the line longer'n anybody here. I got a cousin-in-law over there who says—*OW!*"

"Oh he does, does he?" observed Lando, watching the older cook kick the younger under the table. "Accident-prone or just sensitive to pain?"

"You gotta keep your flapping lip buttoned, Merle," the older cook said. "There's sucha thing as security."

"Aww, Clive, Lando's all right. Usta be a rating hisself, didn't you, Lando? He just wants to sell stuff over on the *Courteous,* like he done here, ain't that right, Lando? An' seein' as it's the closest ship in, he might be able to get a look at what the fuss is—*OW!*"

The older cook looked apologetic. "No offense, Mr. Calrissian."

Lando grinned as he watched the younger cook rub a tender shin. "None taken."

IT WAS A CHEERFUL tune the young gambler was whistling as he shinnied down the ladder into the airlock of the *Millennium Falcon.* "Honey, I'm home!"

"Are you referring to me, Master?" Vuffi Raa asked, maneuvering his tentacles over the hatchway coaming. He took Lando's helmet, helped his master raise the circular overhead hatch and screw it into place.

"Did you take care of that little job I asked you about?" the gambler inquired. They passed along the corridor to the cockpit. Lando stopped to inspect his quad-guns. The fleet security force's seals were still in place; the weapons were theoretically inoperable. Vuffi Raa had cheated around them the first hour they'd been installed.

"Why yes, Master, I have. Can you tell me now why you wanted such an odd thing done?" Strapping himself into place, the robot received clearance from the *Respectable* and detached the *Falcon* from her belly.

Lando glanced suspiciously around the cabin. "You tell me: can I let you in on it without informing the boys in gray up there?"

The little droid sounded a bit scandalized. "Master, I removed a total of twenty-three listening devices from this vessel, put there by at least three separate agencies in the last seventy-one hours. We're completely clean. What I'd like to know is why you wanted—"

"Simple. I want you to raise the *Courteous,* confirm we're on our way, and set a course for her. Then I want you to be ready to punch everything we've got into the drives, and everything else into the aft shield generators, as soon as we pass by her and light out for the ThonBoka. Got that?" He reached under the control panel, extracted a cigar of a quality much higher than the ones he had been selling. Vuffi Raa lit it for him with a tentacle tip.

"Aye, aye, Master. But that device you had me construct while you were aboard the *Respectable:* it projects at least a meter beyond the after shields, and it's—"

"*Courteous,* this is Millennium Falcon if you're reading. As per previous permission, we're on our way over. I've got a hundred gallons of beebleberry ice cream I've been saving especially for you. Over."

"But, Master, we don't have any—"

"Em Falcon, *this is* Courteous. *We haven't had* any *kind of ice cream aboard for weeks. You're highly welcome, and we hear you have an interest in statistics.*"

Lando laughed at the universal gambler's code. "Permutations and combinations of the number seventy-eight, *Courteous*—fives are wild. Watch for us at your airlock any minute now. Out."

The *Falcon* soared under reaction drive across the distance between the two warships, Lando worrying every moment that his idea and the device he'd had Vuffi Raa construct would actually work. It was the most terrible risk he'd ever taken, with no time to experiment, and technologies were not exactly his bailiwick. If it failed, then they'd be little metal splinters scattered from there to the Rafa System.

"Millennium Falcon, *you're off the beacon! Where'd you learn to fly that overstuffed horseshoe, you confounded feather merchant, some charm school somewhere?*"

Critical moments ticked by, during which the *Falcon* refrained from replying to the innuendo—and precious kilometers toward her goal racked themselves up on the boards.

"Em Falcon, *now hear this! Correct course immediately! Our guns are bearing on you, do you copy?*"

Gritting his teeth and clamping nervous hands securely over the arms of his chair, Lando sat motionless, watching the dials. A trickle of sweat ran down the side of his neck into his collar, but he said nothing.

Once more: "Millennium Eff, *you've got five seconds from the mark, and then you'll be nothing but incandescent atoms! Mark: five, four, three . . .*"

"Okay, Vuffi, this is it! As soon as the drives are hot, punch everything she's got!"

"Very well, Master."

The robot's tentacles were a confusing blur over the ship's control console as he diverted power to the after shields until the gauges screamed at the incipient overload. Lights began twinkling cheeringly across the section of the panels labeled FTL; the powerful interstellar drives awoke from several days' unwilling somnolence. Finally, all boards were green. Drives and shields were ready as the navy voice in the com reached zero.

Lando hoped his invention was ready, too.

"*Millennium Falcon,*" the communicator warned a final, unnecessary time—giving the gambler and the droid an extra few seconds—"*you're a dead—*"

"*Now!*" Lando and Vuffi Raa screamed at the same time.

The voice chopped off. The after shields blossomed into an invisible protective canopy while the ultralightspeed generators began to throb—just as the leading wave front of the first meter-thick destructor beam from the cruiser struck the *Falcon* squarely in the center of her stern.

Her shields held . . . and held . . . and—

Suddenly the *Millennium Falcon* burst into an enormous blinding cloud of rapidly dispersing gases; a rain of metallic particles glittered, occupying the space where she had been.

VI

THE ONE ADDRESSED the Other: "At long last, it is nearly time."

Like Lehesu of the Oswaft, he swam comfortably in emptiness absently contemplating the surrounding stars. Unlike Lehesu, he knew everything about them, had been to visit many of them himself. Nor was that the only way that he was not like the Thon-Boka vacuum-breather. Even Lando Calrissian, accustomed to many strange and wonderful sights, would have had trouble recognizing the entity as a living being.

"Yes," the Other replied, although his companion's statement had been rhetorical. "All things are now as they have been planned. I shall gather the Rest, and they shall accompany us."

He took action to accomplish just that. Such were the distances involved that, even at communications speeds exponential to that of light, it would require several days to achieve the desired transfer of information.

"Indeed," the One agreed. "That, too, is as it has been planned. It is very strange, my friend, this 'not-knowing,' stranger than I had anticipated. Quite an uncomfortable feeling, really. It has been so long since . . ." He let what served him for a voice trail off, contemplating a gulf of time the mere thought of which might have driven a lesser being to gibbering disconnection.

The Other indicated silent sympathy. He, too, had experienced the discomfort of uncertainty, and, despite his almost unimaginable life span, and the relatively recent character of the events, for far too long. Uncertainty was like that. However, that had been the very purpose of the plan. Over the countless eons of their existence, the One, the Other, and the Rest had become, in a manner of speaking, too perfect, too well informed. It had become all too easy to anticipate events simply from long experience with reality, excellent sources of information, and well-practiced logic.

Ironically, it was in that manner that the One had originally foreseen racial stagnation and eventual death did these comfortable circumstances continue. He had advised all concerned that an element of the unknown be reintroduced. They, of course, had seen the sense of it and agreed (with a cordiality that was itself symptomatic; a more vital, lusty people would have included a number of individuals who were contrary just for the sake of contrariness). Their first experiment in guesswork, partial knowledge, and risk was maturing now, a process some thousands of years in the making.

"Do you suppose . . ." the Other began, unconsciously reviving a long-unused turn of phrase as he let the unproductive thought trickle away. At that point speculation was futile. He knew as well as the One what consequences, in all their manifest likelihoods, were possible, from a vast unprecedented enrichment of their ancient, already lavishly complex culture, to its uttermost destruction. These were not beings to whom such gambling came easily or naturally—which was yet another reason why it had become necessary. "Do you suppose . . ."

The One replied, "I do not know— How truly unsubstantial a sensation! For the first time in eons we shall learn New Things, regardless of the outcome. These we shall have to integrate with the old, producing syntheses unlooked for. I feel . . . this emotion must be very much as our ancestors experienced when scarcely anything was known, and everything remained yet to be learned. It is little wonder they were half mad and came close, times without number, to destroying themselves."

After a long period of silence, the Other said, "I have learned a New Thing already." In the tone of his voice there was an odd, semiforgotten, yet somehow familiar difference.

But excitement tinged the voice of the One: "Please tell me—what is it? I, too, must learn this New Thing, and we must pass it on to—"

"I have learned that the prospect of learning New Things makes you unreasonably loquacious. I am not certain—there it is again, that 'not knowing'—that this is altogether good."

"I believe," the One replied rather stiffly, "that you have reinvented humor. And I am not certain whether *that* is good."

KLYN SHANGA RACED through endless night to join his makeshift squadron. Considering his three careers—soldier for his nation-state, farmer upon military retirement, soldier again for a hastily united and inevitably defeated Renatasian System—this last, the seeking of ultimate vengeance, was quite the strangest.

Shanga leaned back in his patched and shabby acceleration couch, carefully placing his feet between control pedals, stretching his long legs and arching his back to relieve an aching stiffness born more, on this occasion, of emotional tension than of lengthy travel. He was well practiced at that, having logged an incredible number of intersystem parsecs in his unlikely machine.

His blaster, its grips polished smooth by use, its muzzle bright with holster wear and pitted by many more firings than it had been designed for, once again clung comfortingly to his thigh. It was not that having the weapon made him a whole man; like most professional soldiers, he was revolted by killing and avoided it whenever he could. Besides, he could do more damage to an opponent with his left elbow than most individuals could with an entire arsenal. But, like the battered, ancient ship he flew, it was an accustomed extension of his body, a companion and friend.

He had very few others left.

Somewhere ahead, hovering at the deep-frozen margin of the Tund System, his tiny fleet awaited the news he carried. They had towed themselves originally into this sector of the galaxy—a long, long way from home—by means of a scrapped and resurrected Centrality battleship engine that had been left among the ruins of their civilization by the departing marauders. To this they had attached, by cable, craft bought, stolen, and traded from a hundred cultures. Ultimately, the engine had become a weapon of despair, a fusion-powered battering ram. Even so, they had failed to accomplish their purpose for it, the destruction of Vuffi Raa.

Now, deprived of an independent method of ultralightspeed travel, they had to rely upon an uncertain ally. One who, without question, would betray them in the end.

Alone in the cramped cockpit of his fighter, Shanga reviewed the words he would employ to persuade his men that he had made the best of a bad bargain—those few who had survived the voyage to the Tund System and their first bloody encounter with the enemy at the Oseon. More had joined them afterward, dribbling out in the filthy holds of ancient freighters, hitching rides aboard the interstellar garbage scows.

Ironically, it was Rokur Gepta who, more than anybody else, represented the malign spirit that had destroyed the Renatasia. Somehow, too, it was fitting that they plotted together to use the navy as a sort of backstop against which they could crush their common foes. That same navy had been the direct agent of his home system's destruction. At the beginning of his vindictive adventure, Klyn Shanga had been fatalistically resigned to throwing away his life and the lives of his threadbare command in order to avenge their titanic losses. Now he realized with increasing clarity and weariness that there was more—much more—to live for. The capture and slow termination of the five-legged infiltrator would only begin the process. Somehow they must make their mark upon the navy, upon the Centrality itself, upon everyone responsible in any way for the murder of a civilization.

Hopelessness breeds desperate measures. A partnership with the Sorcerer of Tund necessarily included a risk that the pitiable remains of Renatasian manhood might be used to some surpassingly evil purpose, to fulfill some objective even more hideous than the obliteration of a system-wide culture. If anyone was capable of engineering such a cataclysm, it was Rokur Gepta.

There was a Renatasian animal that planted itself by the waterside and, in the process of giving birth, provided fodder for a predacious toothy swimmer. Gepta was very much like that toothy swimmer, circling expectantly. Shanga, with his tiny fleet (call it, rather, a "school") felt very much like that hapless littoral creature who must die herself—sacrificing, as well, a certain percentage of her young—in order to give whatever microscopic meaning to life that it was capable of possessing.

On the other hand, only sapient beings were foolish enough to imagine that the universe was anything but a sadistic battlefield where brutality was the natural order and agonized screaming provided the background music. Not even a man as bitterly demoralized as Klyn Shanga believed there was any meaning to death.

Perhaps he should never have retired from the military, he thought with a deeply felt sigh uncharacteristic of the role he presently played or the place he found himself now. All those years on his farm, amid fresh, growing things under a kindly sky, had made him far too philosophical to be a good soldier ever again. But he was all his world had left, so he would have to do.

Klyn Shanga flew onward through the star-strewn darkness, reviewing the words he would employ to persuade his men. He wished fervently they were of some use persuading himself.

ROKUR GEPTA, traveling aboard the refitted cruiser *Wennis,* was receiving an alarming report from one of his advance escorts. The flyer had returned in a one-seat fighter approximating the size and combat capabilities of Klyn Shanga's, but which was equipped—and this was rare, even for the navy—to exceed the speed of light. The little ship was half engine, virtually unarmed, and a tight fit, even for a slender youth. Piloting such a vehicle for more than a few minutes brought new meaning to the word "discomfort."

It and its occupant had been to the ThonBoka and back again already while the lumbering *Wennis*, considered a very sprightly vessel for its class, was still many days' journey from the nebula.

Gepta had such a fighter for his personal use. It had saved his life at least twice. He came as close to feeling fond of it as he came to feeling fond of anything—aside from the grim denizens from the darker recesses of his cavern on Tund. Fondness was not an emotion ordinarily to be discovered within the similarly stygian depths of Rokur Gepta's soul, although whether it had never lived within him, or had been ruthlessly exterminated early in his life, was a question that perhaps even the sorcerer was not prepared to answer.

Thus it was with something of a shock, in the brief instant before he regained control of himself, that Gepta experienced an unfamiliar, transient, and microscopic pang of personal regret as he learned of the destruction of the *Millennium Falcon* and her crew by the blockade cruiser. While the sorcerer wasn't watching, Lando Calrissian had somehow risen unbidden from the ranks of petty annoyance to that of worthy opponent and honored enemy.

"I saw it myself, sir!" the breathless scout gasped as moisture from the surrounding air condensed upon his space-cold armor and trickled off into a little pool on the deck plates. Like those of all his comrades attached to the mysterious *Wennis,* his gray uniform was unadorned by signs of rank or unit in order to preserve certain political fictions that his masters cherished. That no creature wiser than a sponge was taken in by such an exercise constituted no good reason not to pursue it.

Likewise, the slowly warming pressure suit he wore over his uniform, having just a few moments before leaped out of his cramped, ultrafast spacecraft into the cavernous hangar deck of the supposedly civilian cruiser, was without markings. Most of the personnel aboard the *Wennis,* being professional soldiers, resented the shallow deception but, with understandable circumspection, seldom got around to mentioning it aloud.

While in command of the *Wennis,* Rokur Gepta did not affect the basaltic throne and the splendid isolation he preferred on Tund. He occupied the captain's acceleration chair (although there was an officer on board who claimed the title) and supervised his underlings on the bridge as they manipulated the controls at his bidding. He pitilessly examined the incoming scout, wondering whether, after all the time, all the effort, someone else had casually robbed him of victory over his prey.

"What ship, again?" the sorcerer hissed, briefly contemplating punishing its captain and crew. "Which ship destroyed the *Millennium Falcon,* and by what means?" The sorcerer hunched over like a scavenger bird, peering through the windings of his headdress, his eyes a pair of glowing, pulsating coals.

The rest of the bridge crew paid close attention to their consoles, cringing at the pilot's plight, but unwilling to interfere with his presumed destiny. They had seen a captain stripped of dignity and all but killed in that very place. They held out little hope for a mere lieutenant.

The scout gulped visibly, wishing he was back inside the claustrophobic confines of his craft. He was the best pilot aboard the *Wennis,* possibly one of the best in the service. That was not going to do him any good with the sorcerer. Nor had he been educated to say or do the diplomatic thing when confronted with malevolent and arbitrary authority, at least of such potency. He felt he would have been better served had such a skill been part of his otherwise exhaustive military survival training—seldom had the need arisen for making a fire with flint and steel or using a signal mirror to summon help.

"The *Courteous,* sir," he answered finally, "part of the blockade line at the ThonBoka. In fact, sir, at the time, she was the closest vessel to the nebula. I listened to the traffic, sir, as I had been about to report aboard the flagship on your orders, and was awaiting docking clearance. This *Em Falcon,* an ugly old tub of a tramp freighter, was supposed to rendezvous with *Courteous* for purposes of trade. She'd been through the whole fleet that way, peddling tobacco and other civilian stuff like a vendor droid at a ball game. Instead, she attempted to evade the cruiser and made high speed for the mouth of the nebula. That's when *Courteous* caught her. I never saw a beam like that before, sir. Must be something new."

Gepta leaned forward even farther, towering from his pedestaled chair over the young officer. "And the *Millennium Falcon?* What of her?"

The pilot gulped again, appreciating well the fate of innocent bearers of bad tidings. "Vaporized, sir. She took the full force on her after shields and overloaded. It was visible all over the fleet. Sir."

"So . . ." The sorcerer considered these data, the scout virtually forgotten as the young man stood before him, trembling at attention, his helmet under his arm. A runnel of sweat slowly crept down the side of the pilot's neck into the metal pressure collar of his suit.

The gray-swathed sorcerer glanced up again a moment later, almost absently. "Are you still here, Lieutenant? I suggest you report back to your section immediately."

The room fairly creaked with sudden relaxation.

An astonished and highly relieved young courier saluted his commander gratefully and departed the bridge amid the silent cheers of the cruiser's conspicuously disinterested crew members.

Looking forward to a good meal and something tall and cool to drink in the pilot's lounge below, the lieutenant passed through the bulkhead doors with a new spring in his step. The panels whispered closed behind him as he stepped into the companionway.

A large security trooper, one of Gepta's personal bodyguards, came up behind him, laid a hand the size of a telecom directory on the young man's shoulder. The lieutenant nearly jumped out of his spacesuit.

"Thought you'd bought the farm there, didn't you, son?" The older man's face crinkled in a grin that was difficult to interpret. "Say, I'm just going off duty, and seeing as how I was aboard the first time we ran into that garbage scow the *Falcon,* and seeing as how *I'm* just as pleased she's a cloud of radioactive dust, what do you say we both go below for some liquid celebration?"

The lieutenant looked up uncertainly into the trooper's face. The clamp-like grip on his shoulder gave him little choice. He nodded without enthusiasm, and the two dwindled and disappeared down the corridor.

A SHORT TIME LATER, Rokur Gepta stirred from futile contemplation, held up a gloved hand, and snapped his fingers.

From somewhere aft and overhead there came a rustle of dry, hairy wings as one of his pets lurched out of its darkened, foul-smelling niche, flapped across the room trailing an indeterminate number of scrawny, many-jointed legs. It came to rest, perching blindly on Gepta's outstretched wrist, salivating in anticipation just as the bodyguard entered the bridge with a small, shallow tray.

With his free hand, Gepta accepted a pair of plastic tongs, reached for something on the tray, and held it up before his pet. The creature had nothing resembling a face, simply a gummy puckered opening toward the front of its body, set between the wings. The cavity distended greedily at the touch of the offered morsel.

There was a moment of enjoyment, some sucking, digestive noises. . . . It belched.

VII

LEHESU CAME AS close to nervous pacing as any Oswaft could.

The giant raylike creature drifted in the relative emptiness of space at what he regarded a prudent distance from the warship-guarded mouth of the ThonBoka.

Watching the watchers.

As always, his estimate of what was prudent differed somewhat from that of his cosapients. None of them could be persuaded to venture within light-years of the spot from which the periodic activities of their new enemies could be observed, if not entirely understood. Restless, Lehesu concentrated a moment, got his bearings in some manner no one but another Oswaft would be able to fathom, and *hopped,* without thinking much more about it, a few hundred thousand kilometers, as if the intervening distance didn't exist. It was a gesture of frustration. He had been brought up to believe such fidgeting was infantile, undignified, not to mention impolite when in the company of others. But at the moment he couldn't help himself. He was impatient, an emotion he shared in common with other species, but that would be beyond the comprehension of most Oswaft. Still he waited.

He wasn't at all certain when Lando, Vuffi Raa, and the *Falcon* would arrive. He had difficulty yet, realizing that the freighter was not a real person. The existence of, and his friendship with, the chromium-plated robot made this realization even more difficult to achieve. That they would not fail to come to his aid he never doubted for an instant, despite the genteel jeering of family and friends. They had not believed the least of his tales about the Open Sea until the evidence had thundered up to the ThonBoka mouth, heavily gunned and, for some reason, angrily disposed toward the vacuum-breathing race.

This, of course, was somehow the adventuring Lehesu's fault.

Concerning Lando Calrissian . . . the Oswaft's brief sojourn into human territory still hadn't educated him about cats; however there were certain aspects of that animal's psychology he might have identified with. Hadn't the gambler and his friends saved his life? Twice?

They were obligated now.

Anxiety shifted Lehesu again, this time a quarter of a light-year, to one side of the nebula mouth, before he fully noticed it. He could "see" better from the vantage anyway. Metallic motes lost against a starry backdrop, the elements of the fleet themselves were invisible at this distance. But the aggregate was *noisy*. A welter of communication darted from ship to ship in a complex net of energies the operators of which fondly imagined was private. Lehesu had learned Lando's language in a matter of hours. It did not occur to him that the stirrings and mixings of ideas that constituted top-secret military codes were anything other than amusing games to those who employed them. He puzzled them out in idle moments, much faster than he'd overcome the initial difficulty presented by communicating with the gambler and the robot.

Had those in command of the fleet, those who had ordered its destructive presence outside the ThonBoka, become aware of that minor Oswaft capability, they would have redoubled their efforts to exterminate the space people. In this instance, ignorance was mutual; Lehesu hadn't a notion of the threat he and his people represented to those who cherished power for its own sake.

A small, thin cloudlet of interstellar plankton drifted by, borne on the complex tide of gravity and photon pressure, tiny pseudo-animals and quasi-plants that formed the basis of the Oswaft diet, indeed for the diet of all the thousands of space-evolved species living in the shelter of the StarCave. Lehesu nibbled at them in a desultory fashion. To the small extent he was aware of them, he realized they didn't taste particularly good. There was a reason for that: they were slowly dying.

The bottom rung of the ThonBoka food ladder was being ruthlessly and deliberately sawed out from under the rest of the nebula's ecology. Every now and again the vessels of the picket fleet outside would blossom into glowing visibility as, in concert, they unleashed titanic energies, saturating the space around themselves with destructive particles and waves. It was at these moments that Lehesu (who had found it necessary to explain to his people something he didn't altogether understand himself: that these were not living organisms that beseiged them, but artifacts *containing* living organisms) could see that the blockading fleet formed a carefully calculated pattern through whose fields of fire not one molecule of preorganic substance could sift unassaulted.

What did come through was spoiled and tasted terrible.

If that were not enough, the ships sprayed a kind of poison—enzymes designed to smash the complex natural molecular arrangements of deep space, reduce them to constituent atoms, and destroy their nutritive value. The Oswaft and their environment were being coldly and systematically starved to death by an implacable enemy they did not know, hadn't picked, had owed no animosity.

Until now.

"YELLOW NINER, this is Hosrel XI Perimeter Control. We have a bandit at coordinates three-five-oh-two-three. Do you copy? Over."

The young rating at the sensor screen had been bored until then. She had been bored for thirty-four solid weeks, and the constant drills, the frontier-duty pay, the promise of a chance at a commission, hadn't helped. Not a bit. But she was no longer bored. If the bogey was a drill, it was something new. At that top-secret navy base on the freeze-dried edge of an already unspec-tacular system, *anything* new, however potentially threatening to life, limb, or the continued wearing of a uniform, was highly wel-come.

"Perimeter Control," the interceptor pilot replied with a stud-ied drawling casualness that belied the fact that he was a year younger than the sensor operator, *"we copy. This is Yellow Nine Leader. Are you requesting a six-sixty-six? Over."*

The operator leafed quickly through her procedures manual. It was so hard remembering . . . yes, there it was: six-sixty-six, scramble and visual checkout of an unidentified target. Scram-bling, in effect, was already taken care of: Hosrel XI Command kept at least one full interceptor squadron spaceborne on the pe-rimeter all the time, and Yellow Niner was *it*, at the moment. She hadn't any idea what was being defended at the Core-forsaken base. Probably the navy was developing something unimportant, but they were giving security all the ruffles and flourishes.

"Yellow Niner, that's affirmative. Give me your ETVC. Over."

"My what? Oh yeah: we ought to be eyeballing your bogey in about, oh, call it seven minutes, give or take. Got it on the scope repeater now. Looks kinda like it's made of plastic, doesn't it? Over."

Both the interceptor pilot and the sensor operator had been briefed, fairly recently, on new developments in camouflaging shields. But neither could discuss it in the clear over an open com-munications band. Security is a sword that cuts both ways, and most often wounds the hand that wields it.

"Yes, yes it does, Yellow Niner. I have your ETVC at six min-utes, now. Is that about right? Over."

"Yeah, yeah. Yellow Nine Squadron, this is Yellow Nine Leader. As far as I know, this is no drill, repeat, no drill. Unlock your arming switches and keep the thumb you aren't sitting on

near the button. *No mistakes, now, or we'll all be plucking crystals in the life-orchards. Out to you, and over to PC."*

PC, thought the Operator, that sounded sort of nice and heroically terse. She said nothing, but simply watched a dozen hard, sharp, shiny blips converge on the single fuzzy, almost invisible one. She had already sent nervous fingers flying over an alphanumeric pad, alerting her superiors to the situation, and other eyes were monitoring other scopes, now, within the subterranean bowels of the installation. She fastened her military collar and straightened a crease. Almost, she hoped, the target would be a genuine pirate attack or rebel uprising. Promotions came fast in times of—

"Perimeter Control, this is Yellow Nine Leader. Where the Core is this thing? We oughta be right on top of it, unless you're—by the Great Lens, there it is! It's huge and clear as glass! We're making our first pass, using prerecorded hailing signals . . . oh yeah; over."

The strange vessel failed to respond, at least on frequencies the interceptors were permitted to receive. Instead, it simply disappeared as the squadron crowded it, leaving the fighters to mill around an empty spot like moths around a light that is suddenly turned out.

It reappeared to one side, a few thousand meters away, just as Yellow Nine Seven passed beneath its transparent wing, which twitched involuntarily as Lehesu struggled to regain his balance. Suddenly Yellow Nine Seven corkscrewed away, a smoking, flaming ball of crumpled metal, its pilot screaming something into his helmet mike about his deflector shields having failed to function properly.

The voice bit off suddenly.

Eleven pilots whipped their ships around savagely. Eleven thumbs mashed down upon their firing studs. Twenty-two eyes widened as eight destructive beams—three had not been maintenanced correctly—converged on empty space. One interceptor, Yellow Nine Four, was caught in the crossfire. He'd failed to make a turn, due to faulty attitude control, and vanished in a flash of energy and atomized debris.

Lehesu stepped off half a light-year, astounded at the hostile reaction he'd encountered, not at all like his first contact with the *Millennium Falcon*. And his people thought *he* was crazy. With the Oswaft equivalent of a shrug, he turned his face toward yet another star whose spectrum showed traces of artificial, highly ordered radiation, and prepared himself for a longer jump this time.

Unaware that a densely cloaked scout vessel was right behind him.

THE NEXT SYSTEM had been much the same, except . . .

They'd been forewarned, somehow, of this bizarre unidentified craft that had managed to destroy three (Yellow Nine Nine had missed the mouth of its Launch/Reentry tunnel and splashed itself all over a mountainside of frozen nitrogen; little squiggles of liquid helium danced with glee at the sight) first-rate fighter-interceptors. The new group also ignored his frantic, placative signaling and suffered forty-three casualties, some of them on the ground, due to an unfortunate change of shift going on between two double-strength squadrons. Lehesu had given up and gone home.

Eventually the fleet had made its appearance. The ordeal was a little more bearable for Lehesu than for the others. He was the only Oswaft in a hundred generations who had come close to dying by starvation once before. As some human philosopher in a different time and place would observe, that which fails to kill us strengthens us. Lehesu knew his limits; he could tell that the pogrom was going to take rather a longer time than either side realized. To his less adventurous comrades, it was already agony, already an unprecedented emergency. They felt, for the first time in their long, long lives, a relatively mild discomfort, and were afraid. Some actually spoke of attempts to negotiate, to establish upon what terms the enemy would let them live, not knowing that their utter destruction was the only success the fleet's mission profile recognized.

Lehesu wished his people would get angry instead.

Thus, he waited.

It was some hours after the last of the energetic nutrient-destroying displays that something unusual happened. Lehesu felt a tight, powerful beam of communications energy coming from the blockaded nebula entrance. While he knew the language, he didn't know the culture; the gulf between planet-bound species and free-fall dwellers was so enormous that *any* understanding was a gigantic tribute to the Oswaft's intellectual capabilities. Whatever they were saying out there, it was frantic, and not at all friendly.

It happened again! Judging from the manner in which this second burst was all bunched up into the higher frequencies, something was headed away from the fleet and toward the Thon-Boka, fast. Lehesu maneuvered that way, both by straight-forward distance-covering flight to keep an "eye" on the incoming signals, and by nonlinear distance-avoiding hops. Whatever was coming, it ought to have *some* kind of reception committee.

Suddenly an impossibly solid bar of unbearably bright light lashed out, connecting the two points in space with each other. There was a brilliant flash, a scattering of reflections, then nothingness. A sparkling hint of metallic debris and smoke lingered at the very edge of Lehesu's sensory capabilities. The galactic drift carried traces of scorched titanium and plastic into the Thon-Boka.

A long, quiet moment followed. Then, without warning, something materialized not far from Lehesu, out of the wherever-it-is that starships go when they're traveling faster than the speed of light.

It was an absurdly shaped object, like something resembling a coral-encrusted horseshoe magnet a tenth the Oswaft's size and possessing none of his fluid grace. The thing was tumbling slowly, end over end, while enormous volumes of dense white smoke billowed from its blast-blackened rear surface.

Naturally, Lehesu recognized her at once.

"Lando! Vuffi Raa! Can you hear me in there? Are you all right?"

The vacuum-breather swam closer, carefully avoiding the foul-smelling effluents issuing from the curved rear edge of the freighter. Nothing indicated that life had ever inhabited the strangely shaped craft. The glow-spots he now knew to be windows lay dark and foreboding along her surfaces as she continued to somersault gently before the space-going sentient, the random motion itself a grim presentiment that nothing rational lived at the controls.

"Vuffi Raa! Lando! Speak to me!" the Oswaft beamed on every frequency he knew. "This is Lehesu!"

Nothing replied.

Much more figuratively than literally, Lehesu cast a backward glance at the fleet besieging his home. He didn't know how he could accomplish it, but he swore, in that moment of grief, a terrible revenge against those who were responsible for the tragedy. To gain and lose new friends, good friends—in some respects the only friends he'd ever had—in what seemed to the extremely long-lived creature like the mere space of minutes . . . it was almost more than a being could bear.

Thrashing frantically back and forth, he peered into the vessel's darkened ports, learning nothing. Gently, he nudged the spaceship, unintentionally adding an additional vector to her tumbling motion.

"Lando! Vuffi Raa! Are you in there?"

He thought a moment, then, despite everything he had struggled to understand about his new companions, added: "*Falcon,* my little friend, *please* talk to me! This is Lehesu the Oswaft! Are Vuffi Raa and Lando still alive?"

VIII

THE REFITTED CRUISER *Wennis* was a trowel-shaped wedge of metal bristling with instrument and weapons implacements arranged to overlap yet not interfere with one another's fields of effectiveness. At an unusual—and unusually heavily shielded—point on her after surface, between the great blinding arrays of drive tubes and deflectors, was a small chamber with windowless walls two meters thick. It could be entered only by a small auxiliary craft, available to the vessel's master alone, and then only when he had ordered the drives temporarily shut down. To navigate the small craft while the cruiser's massive engines were in operation would be instantaneous suicide.

Two hundred centimeters is a great deal of wall, especially when it is composed of the latest state-of-the-art battlewagon armor. Yet the armoring of the special chamber was not intended to protect its contents from the ravening drive radiations of the *Wennis*. It was to protect the *Wennis* from what lay in the chamber. Even so, it was a futile effort, intended more to comfort the one entity who knew what the arrangement was all about, to provide some sense, however illusory, of security.

Inside the chamber, Rokur Gepta stood before a chest-high metal pylon capped with a transparent bubble the size of a man's head. Gepta knew the chamber and controls by memory. No light burned within it. He ran a gray-gloved hand along the surface of the pylon, watching with unseeing eyes as his fingers pressed inset keys. Inside the bubble, he had begun to create an infinitesimal speck of the most dangerous single substance the universe had ever known. A sickly green light began to seep from the bubble, filling the darkened chamber with malignant luminosity.

The trouble with a man like Klyn Shanga, the sorcerer thought, wasn't that he was not afraid to die. It had taken Gepta an unprecedentedly long while to figure that out, so tortuous and alien was the line of reasoning involved. Rokur knew many individuals who were not fearful of death; in fact they seemed to welcome the idea, embrace the opportunity. They were eager to die, for their beliefs, for the government or the numerous causes that opposed it, even for Gepta himself. Such men were easy to control and extremely useful. Down deep somewhere they hated and feared life and were anxious to be relieved of the burden of living in a manner that would not disturb their other contradictory beliefs.

It was clear Klyn Shanga enjoyed being alive, which was what made things confusing. Rokur Gepta was not used to being confused, and it infuriated him. How was it that someone who loved life could be unafraid to die? The first conclusion the sorcerer had reached—not much help in understanding the perverse phenomenon, but of high pragmatic significance—was that the original expedition to Renatasia hadn't done a thorough enough job. They had done only two-thirds of it, and it badly wanted finishing.

Gepta promised himself to assign that matter the highest of priorities once the current operation was over and he could think about other things. If Shanga was representative of Renatasia's people, that system could turn out to be a much greater danger to his plans—and to the government—than even the essentially harmless vacuum-breathers of the ThonBoka.

He gazed into the ghastly glow before him, savoring its destructive potential. One cubic millimeter of the substance, established in a self-sustaining manner, would leap from point to point on a planet's surface, eradicating anything that lived, devouring any organic substrate on which future life depended. It was the ultimate disinfectant, the ultimate sterilizer. There was something wonderfully clean and neat about this substance and the very concept of it.

It cleared up confusion. *Life* was confusion, and intelligent life the most contradictory and confusing of all, realized Gepta. Klyn Shanga wanted to live, yet was unafraid to die. Such a man could not be controlled, and, when he had something that the sorcerer wanted, he became . . . *impossible*! It had not been two hours since he interviewed the man, shortly after the *Wennis* met his ragtag squadron in deep space. The craft of Shanga's squadron were not interstellar vessels, and they were to have waited for Gepta at the edge of his home system. But so eager had they been for the ThonBoka (or desirous of leaving Tund) that they had departed early, confident the cruiser would overtake them before they ran into trouble.

"*It was insubordination!*" the livid Gepta hissed, looking down at Admiral Shanga. Their confrontation was not being held on the bridge because of the possibility that things would be said that would harm discipline.

Shanga threw his head back and laughed. "I am not your *subordinate*, magician, nor is the least senior of my men. We felt like going and we went. Here we are, closer to the ThonBoka than we would have been, the better rested for having done something constructive to get ourselves there. Is it this that you find objectionable?"

Beneath the bridge of the *Wennis* lay the captain's battle quarters, which, like his command chair, had also been preempted by the sorcerer. A duplicate of the command chair was placed in the center of the room before a large viewscreen, which presently showed the depths of interstellar space, as translated by the ship's computers from the hyperdrive hash of what was really to be seen. The light was gray and even, matching the sorcerer's clothing and, somehow, his voice.

"You are a military man, Admiral. I ought not need to explain these matters to you, of all people."

The military man grinned and shook his head. "I *was* a military man. Now I am a mercenary in my own employ, fighting, because it suits me to do so, for the honor of a civilization that no longer exists. I recognize no authority and I desire no authority. My men follow me because it suits them."

He grew tired of standing. The discussion was altogether too much like being called to the school supervisor's office, and it rankled. Shanga looked around, discovered a lounger beside the door to the corridor, tossed his helmet onto another chair, and reclined, stretching his customarily ship-cramped legs and relaxing.

Shanga groped around inside his spacesuit until he found tobacco in a shirt pocket. He withdrew the cigar, put it in his mouth, and lit it with a hundredth-power discharge of his blaster. Gepta's guards hadn't taken his weapon this time. He hadn't let them. Three of them had broken arms and a fourth, who'd gone on insisting, was dead. That was the real reason for the conference.

"Let's put our card-chips in the table-field, Gepta," Shanga said through a cloud of blue smoke. "You're up to something—the way you've redecorated this cruiser is evidence enough of that—and it amounts to more than simple revenge against one lousy gambler. And you need us. I've got twenty-three flyers in a battered assortment of fighters gathered from the scrap heaps of a dozen cultures, and yet any one of them is a match for any three of yours."

The sorcerer gripped the arms of his chair, convulsively fending off the impulse to have the man disintegrated where he sat. There was too much light in the room for his comfort, and increasingly too much smoke. Yet he had always prided himself on an ability, a willingness, to withstand temporary deprivation and discomfort for the sake of future gains. "Oh, and how is it that you reach this conclusion?" he asked evenly. After all, the crew of the *Wennis* was the best the navy had to offer.

Shanga blinked, considering his words. "It's how you throw away good people. Your whole culture places no value on the individual. Funny, because that's all there is: no 'group,' no 'navy,' no 'Empire,' only individuals, who do all the thinking, all the work, that gets done. Waste that, and it'll come back to haunt you, Gepta. People aren't plug-in modules you can use up. That's why my guys are a match for any five of yours. They know they're irreplaceable, and . . . Look: you've got a drive tech who's pretty good, but doesn't have the right family or connections, or espouses the wrong beliefs. Disregard his unique competence, pack him off to the life-orchards or the spice mines, and all that leaves you are the socially acceptable incompetents. Starts to show, after a while; the machinery grinds down."

A tiny portion of the gray-robed sorcerer that was neither illusion nor altogether human shuddered. And controlled himself. Klyn Shanga's time would come later. In the meantime, in order to prevent morale-destroying rumors from spreading through the crew, he would order that "complications" set in among the lesser casualties of Shanga's intransigence. They'd be given space burial with full honors; he needed to shut down the ship's drives briefly, anyway.

"We shall agree," he said to the fighter pilot with forced amiability, "to disagree; it is not necessary that we hold the same philosophy in order to cooperate."

"No," Shanga said, "it isn't. What's important is that I have my squadron, you have this ship and passage through the fleet. Together, we both know Calrissian, have confronted him in the past. He'll become your prisoner—or worse. We'll have Vuffi Raa, the Butcher of Renatasia, to haul back in force shackles for public trial and execution!"

Knowing full well that a very different fate awaited the squadron commander—one not dissimilar to that which he planned for the gambler—Gepta nevertheless replied, "Yes, of course. Then you will be free to rebuild your civilization." A hint of cordiality very nearly made it into his tone.

"Rebuild Renatasia? There's nothing left *to* rebuild! We've become your stinking suburbs! Everything we have, everything we do is a pale, threadbare, plastic imitation of whatever was in fashion ten years ago in the capital! All we have left to aspire to is . . . *justice*!"

Inwardly, Gepta chuckled. How right the admiral was; how much more right he would be. The sorcerer watched Shanga for a moment, sitting in his presence without permission, *smoking*, and enjoyed the unintended irony. Then he pressed a button on one arm of his throne.

"You know Vuffi Raa, Admiral Shanga, and we both have reason to know Lando Calrissian." The name stuck unpleasantly in Gepta's throat; the two words were not the terms on which he was used to thinking of the man, but Shanga would not appreciate or understand the sorcerer's private system of references. "Now let us hear from one who claims to know something about what else awaits us in the ThonBoka, shall we?"

The squadron leader shrugged, looking suddenly old and tired. He needed to get back to his men. He needed—

A door slid aside, and a tall, gangly human being entered, a man with bushy white hair and a permanently sour expression pulled down over his long undertaker's features.

"Fleet Admiral Klyn Shanga of Renatasia," the sorcerer intoned formally, "please meet the *Ottdefa* Osuno Whett, Associate Professor of Comparative Sapient Studies at the University—"

"College boys, now!" the fighter pilot snorted, his energy renewed by contempt. "What's he got to contribute to this palaver, anyway?"

"Rather a good deal, my dear—Admiral, was it?" There was a note of polite disbelief in the man's voice as he examined Shanga's clothing, found a place to seat himself, looking first to Gepta for approval, and sat. "I am the galaxy's foremost expert—by virtue of the fact that I am the only expert, heh, heh—on the Oswaft, the intelligent space-evolved life of the ThonBoka."

"Some expert! According to our friend the magician, here, nobody knew about those creepy-crawlies until a few months ago, nobody. How much could you have learned in—"

Whett looked a bit disturbed, as if Shanga's disrespect for Gepta, or at least its punishment, might be contagious. "Sir, I am an anthropologist, the very same who unraveled the impenetrable mysteries of the Sharu of Rafa. I have lived among and studied the asteroid miners of the Oseon, I—"

"The way I heard it, Mister Associate Professor, the Sharu sort of unraveled themselves!" He blew a puff of smoke from his relit cigar and laughed, particularly to see that mention of the Sharu made even Rokur Gepta appear momentarily uncomfortable. Now *there* was a race of sorcerers!

"My title, *Admiral,* is *Ottdefa,* an honor conferred by my home system, and I would thank you to—"

"Forget it, friend, I got carried away." Shanga looked back to Gepta. He was one of the few men in the known galaxy who could look directly into the sorcerer's face without wincing. "Okay, I'll bite: what's this all about?"

Without a word, Gepta nodded at the *Ottdefa,* who began again.

"The Oswaft are a most unusual people. I began observing them with an electronic telescope, at the behest of Lord Gepta, until it became apparent that they were aware of the instrument's emanations. Then, in a specially fitted meteoroid, I traversed much of their region, making observations with less intrusive devices. They evolved in space out of the clutter of organic molecules to be found there, and reached the pinnacle of intelligence, protected by the nebula that all but encloses them, and unaware that anyone else existed.

"They have a natural ability to enter hyperspace and travel through it. They communicate by modulating radio-frequency waves with their brains. Theirs is a complex, highly sophisticated language, and it is just about all the culture they possess. They have no need of clothing or shelter, and what little food they require drifts past them on a sort of breeze. Hence, they make few artifacts, most of them sculptures or bodily decorations."

Shanga shook his head. "I don't get it. It's stupid enough that the navy is bothering with them. From everything you say, they're no threat to anybody; they don't want anything anybody has. But what's the point of *our* boning up on—"

"Because, my dear Shanga," the sorcerer hissed, "they are allies to our enemies! We shall either win them over and force them to betray Calrissian, or they, too, shall be destroyed!"

Now, in his special secret chamber aft of the *Wennis'* drives, Rokur Gepta contemplated the temporary contents of a force-bubble stronger than the full battle-shielding of the cruiser. Perched upon its pylon, it contained a secret an entire race, the Sorcerers of Tund, had died to protect.

At greater strength now, its ghostly flicker filled the room with evil dancing shadows, all of them Gepta's. He felt at peace. It was the only light he really liked. It reminded him of home. The home he had remodeled with its assistance.

Inside the bubble tiny forms seethed and sizzled at the border of visibility, like dust motes in a sunbeam. They were densest at the bottom of the bubble, yet many thousands more sparkled in the space above the bottom. They were lively, active, *hungry*.

Gepta chuckled to himself. In a manner of thinking, they, too, were his pets. He had harnessed the most dangerous forces in the universe and kept them there in a cage. He made and unmade them at his pleasure. And he had work for them to do. Again. There was enough . . . substance . . . there to eliminate the life in an entire globular cluster.

The ThonBoka, all its inhabitants, Lando Calrissian, Vuffi Raa, Klyn Shanga—yes, and perhaps this arm of the navy, which was, after all, another obstacle to his desire for power—all of them would feel the agony of first contact with this, the most unusual of all his pets.

And then they would feel nothing.

He shut off the switches. Where there had been activity before within the bubble, all movement stopped. The green glow died abruptly. The motes stopped dancing. It was drawing near the time that Gepta had arranged to have the drives shut down again, so that he could steer his small auxiliary through the zone of murderous radiation, back to the main hull of the *Wennis*.

The force-bubble grew smaller until it, too, disappeared, leaving the smooth, mirror-surface top of the pylon, a simple pedestal of polished metal. Gepta smiled to himself, pocketed the one small object he had removed from the pedestal as the force field deactivated, and began cycling the airlock.

How beautiful to contemplate an entire galaxy of worlds glowing sweetly thus, to imagine the whole universe clean and sterile, linear and predictable.

THE ONE SAID to the Other, "I observe that you have brought the Rest."

They were arrayed before him, rank on rank, less for the sake of discipline (a concept utterly alien to those beings) or even orderliness, than for the simple reason that all of them wanted to see and hear what was going to happen next. Uncountable numbers of them bristled with unfamiliar tenseness. They were not altogether certain it was an improvement over their normal state.

"Yes," confirmed the Other, like his companion, like all his companions, glittering in the cold diamond starlight, "and I believe that they wish for you to address them now, explain—"

"But they know as well as you or I," the One protested, rude interruptions and strained emotions coming now with greater frequency, even at so vast a remove from their grand experiment. "They're all perfectly familiar with—"

"Yes," his friend said, but gently, "and yet they wish it as a kind of ceremony, marking the passage of one epoch and the initiation of another, unknown, somehow frightening one. I wish it, too, if you do not mind greatly."

The One hesitated, even though he had already assented within himself. After all, if those he cared for felt the need . . .

and perhaps it would help calm him, as well. What sort of result would issue when this project was mature, however, worried him. Already circumstances were nearly unbearable.

"My friends, as we all know, some while ago, a rather long time, even for we who are perhaps the most longevous race in the galaxy, at my suggestion we caused a being to come into existence among us who was, well, somewhat different, imbuing him with certain minor physical advantages, and a burning desire to know about the universe."

There was a murmuring of remembrance, a stir of suppressed excitement. Change was coming hard and fast to the One, the Other, and the Rest.

"This being was peaceful, unaggressive even by our standards, for we had shaped him in this wise for several reasons that made sense to us and still do. Nonetheless, he has become embroiled in one violent incident after another, brutal, sanguine clashes with primitive cultures. Lives have been lost.

"Yet he has learned much, and the time has arrived for us to learn it from him."

The rumbling of comment from the Rest grew louder. The One gave them time to contemplate, then said at last, "We go now to gather him in. We do not even know whether he will be happy to see us, to learn that his searches, at least for the time being, are over with. Let us greet him in dignity and love, understand the trials he has been through, and treasure what he has to give us, for it is rich.

"And it will change everything."

IX

TUMBLING PONDEROUSLY BOW over stern, and with the slight-est of rolls to starboard, the *Millennium Falcon* slowed microscopically, her attitude burners sputtering at irregular intervals in the eternal darkness. Her roll corrected, her pitch losing its momentum, she stabilized and came to a full stop. There was a fitful, uncertain fluttering of red at her ports, scattered here and there around her battered hull, then the strong, clear crimson of emergency lighting.

From small jets at the rear, streams of milky liquid struck her after hull plates, boiling off noiselessly in thick, gaseous clouds that mingled with the trailing smoke. A still-molten stub of structural metal projecting to the precise edge of her shield radius cooled and dimmed. The smoke ceased pouring; the interior lights and running markers came on full.

From a pressure valve in the circular hatch atop the *Falcon*'s hull, a mast extruded, silvery, slender, obviously being paid out by hand in jerky increments. It stopped with a springy quiver when two meters of it were visible. Lehesu, floating nearby, heard a familiar voice:

"Hello there, old flatfish! Lost the main antenna in all the excitement back there! That is you, isn't it, Lehesu? Glad to be here. If Vuffi Raa had hesitated by a picosecond, you'd be talking to our radioactive ghosts!"

From a rather different culture—one, for example, whose conception of death did not encompass fancies of an ectoplasmic afterlife—Lehesu failed to comprehend at least two-thirds of the greeting. Nevertheless, he understood that his friends had safely arrived in the ThonBoka, and was overjoyed.

"Landocaptainmaster!" the vacuum-breather exclaimed, unconsciously addressing the human occupant of the starship as an Oswaft Elder. "Yes, it is I!" He swam closer to the spacecraft until he could peer into its control room through the canopy. Inside sat Lando Calrissian, con man and sometime gambler (or gambler and sometime con man), and his mechanical would-be servant, Vuffi Raa. Full-time robot.

The two were still busily turning knobs and pushing buttons, attempting to restore the *Millennium Falcon* to some semblance of operational normality. The captain's seat harness lay unfastened, floating in the temporarily gravity-free air about his acceleration couch. So it had been he, most probably, who had erected the antenna, aft and upstairs. The young Oswaft was pleased to have deducted the data, insignificant as they might be. It meant he was beginning to have a feel for what had been a totally alien environment and civilization.

"Greetings and salutations, friend Lehesu," the droid echoed. *"Not one of my better entrances, I'm afraid. And we both apologize for the delay in reaching you."* He looked to Lando, who was nodding, although whether in assent to the apology or as a comment on the robot's flying skills was moot. *"We were within hailing distance,"* Vuffi Raa continued, *"of the StarCave, several days ago, but it was necessary to work our way through the blockading fleet by means of deception."*

There was the slightest hint of distaste in the robot's voice, Lando thought. It annoyed him; deception was supposed to be one of his major stocks-in-trade, and Vuffi Raa understood that as well as anyone. Besides, how else were they supposed to have gotten through the fleet? He lit a cigar and gazed out through the wedge-sectioned port at the Oswaft floating gently ahead of the motionless *Falcon*. Blockade or not, it was good to be out of circulation, beyond the reach of what passed for civilization—

and of hired assassins—however temporarily. Knowing the navy, he had a pessimistic notion just how safe they were within the nebula and for how long. But he had a plan for that, too, and encouraged by his relatively easy victory over the fleet thus far, he intended to relax.

"I do not understand," Lehesu protested in response to something Vuffi Raa had said when Lando wasn't listening. *"I believed that I had seen you and the* Falcon *utterly destroyed. Of course, at the time, I didn't know it was you, but . . ."*

Satisfaction suffused the droid's tone. "It was my master's idea, really. During the time I described to you, while he was spying upon the enemy under the guise of selling things and gambling, I fitted out a cylinder of powdered metallic shavings mixed with various volatiles and attached it to the stern of the *Falcon*. This we left unshielded, so that the cruiser's rays, upon striking it, would convey the illusion that . . ."

I wonder what we would have done if they'd simply used a tractor beam, Lando mused. He'd counted on the guns being manned by trigger-happy jerks, and, as usual, he'd been right. For a while he watched Lehesu, not really paying attention as that being and the little droid communicated. They seemed to get along automatically, he thought, had little trouble achieving understanding. Idly, he wondered why. For all the goodwill in the galaxy, he had to struggle to identify with a creature who had never known a planet's surface, for whom empty space was a comfortable home, who could shift light-years at a time within it, somehow avoiding the necessity for those careful computations the gambler had learned so painfully as an inexperienced captain.

Against the charcoal backdrop of the nebula, a handful of stars twinkled merrily through the transparent innards of the space being. Lando laughed, dismissing every doubt and trouble he was feeling with a shake of his head, took another drag on his cigar through a wide grin, then rose from his seat.

"Pardon me, old gumball machine, if you can, but I'm going aft to change into my bathing togs. Care to join me?" Without waiting for a reply, he stubbed out the cigar and pulled himself between the jumpseats toward the rear of the cockpit.

The robot stirred from his conversation with the Oswaft. "If I interpret you correctly, Master, I think I should like that very much." His five chromium-plated tentacles glittered over the control panels. "I shall inform our friend and place the ship on automatic."

"Swell. Don't call me master."

Ducking through the doorway, Lando floated along the corridor until he reached a locker where he changed from the well-worn shipclothes he'd been wearing for the navy's benefit, into a spacesuit. By the time he'd sealed all the fittings and run through the checklist programmed into it, Vuffi Raa, who hadn't needed to change, caught up with him. Together they made their way to the airlock and cycled out through it into the void.

Lehesu was there to meet them.

It was the gambler's first good look at the ThonBoka from the inside, and the sight was eerie. Behind him, the nearly circular mouth of the nebula displayed the sky as he was accustomed to seeing it, a dense scattering of stars—with the occasional intrusion of an eruption of destructive energies from the fleet.

Everywhere else, the gas and dust shut out the rest of the universe with a solid wall of deep gray that appeared slightly phosphorescent, and through which gigantic bolts of lightning played intermittent natural counterpoint to the unnatural discharges from the navy. The eye, perhaps the mind itself, violently rejected proper proportions in that place. Lando knew that he was gazing across a dozen light-years, something like ten trillion kilometers, to the opposite wall, in reality a finite region of diffuse particles that would be scarcely noticeable to those aboard a ship traveling through it. His eyes told him he was near the entrance to an enormous but comprehensibly sized cavern, one that might require several days to traverse on foot, but a cavern nevertheless.

Billows and folds in the nebula resembled geologic flows, sheets of limestone deposition. All that was missing were stalagmites and stalactites. Illumination was provided by three small planetless blue-white stars that shone in the center of the StarCave, their photon pressure probably accounting for its hollow form, but not for their own presence. One star might have been sensible. Three, spaced a light-year or two apart, would have physicists making excuses to one another well into the next century. Lando was happy to be a gambler, a profession where alibis don't count. Biologists would be unhappy, too—or ecstatic—at the strange life that had evolved in the sheltered space.

Fingering colored plastic control buttons set into a small panel on the arm of his spacesuit, Lando jetted away from the upper hull and retroed to a floating halt a daring few meters away from the impressive young Oswaft. It was something like greeting an ocean liner politely. He circumnavigated the five-hundred-meter creature in a smooth arc, tucked himself into a roll, straightened, and sprang away with arms extended wide, legs spread, and an expression of sudden joy on his face.

"*Yaaahooo!*" he whooped uncharacteristically, rejoicing in the sensation of free movement, open space. He realized he'd been cooped up aboard ship far too long. It felt like his entire life. Or perhaps evolving on a planet, squeezed between the ground and low-hanging sky, made one feel permanently claustrophobic.

Vuffi Raa, propelled by the Core alone knew what, spun like a bright metallic snowflake beside him as Lehesu rotated majestically, then veered off in a huge graceful curve the two smaller beings attempted to emulate. One of them succeeded.

"*Hey, you guys, wait for me!*" Lando shouted unnecessarily; his suit radio carried perfectly well over the kilometer or two he'd missed intercepting them by. Correcting, he tumbled slightly—the free-fall equivalent of tripping over his own feet—stabilized, and swooped to join his friends. By which time, of course, they were somewhere else.

Lando didn't care. On his own, he began essaying ancient patterns, maneuvers that, elsewhere and elsewhen, would be called Lufbery circles, Immelmann turns, imitating the inspired antics of fighting aerocraft of the prespace eras of every culture momentarily infatuated with free flight and glorious death. He dived on Lehesu, showering the vacuum-breather with imaginary reciprocating gun bullets, then pulled up at the last instant as the startled being instinctively rolled to peel the attacking foe off his back.

That didn't save Vuffi Raa. The unfortunate droid was sitting squarely in the bull's-eye etching of Lando's helmet—ordinarily used for the more mundane purpose of orienting oneself before setting off one's suit propellants—when Lando's deadly pointed fingers filled him full of hot-jacketed lead. Caught up in the spirit of the thing, the robot spun out and downward, wishing he could trail smoke for his master's amusement. There were limits, however, even to Vuffi Raa's remarkable capabilities.

Three small blue-white suns glowed against a somber dark-gray backdrop. Lightning licked the folds and billows of the cavern walls.

Three odd beings, Oswaft, droid, and, oddest of all, human, passed an endless hour or so, playing at combat like the young of all intelligent life everywhere. It was both a release and a return at the same time, marred only by the momentarily suppressed dread of what lay outside the StarCave—and the sudden flare of baleful energy as the fleet, on its clockwork schedule of mass murder, sprayed poison and lethal power into the space around the ThonBoka mouth.

Lando cut his spin—that time, *he* had been the victim of Vuffi Raa's machine guns—and halted, hanging in space, resenting being catapulted back into adulthood, watching the stupidly unnecessary fleet operations with an angry grimace clearly visible through his transparent bubble helmet. Life was so simple, he thought bitterly, so thoroughly enjoyable. Why were there always people whose chosen profession was to louse it up for everybody else?

Vuffi Raa swam up beside the gambler, not needing to be telepathic to read his master's thoughts. They were joined by Lehesu. All three stared out through the mouth of the nebula, watching the evil net of beams that did its work of making life impossible for the Oswaft. All knew of the enzymes drifting into the Thon-Boka, as well.

"*The nutrient current grows impoverished, my friends,*" Lehesu observed sadly. He was not actually breathing heavily from the hour's exercise, but the effect was much the same. Lando and Vuffi Raa didn't know his kind quite well enough to understand it was a bad sign.

"Core forgive me!" Lando exclaimed. "I'd almost forgotten why we came here in the first place!" He turned toward the *Millennium Falcon*, applied thrust to his suit. "We'll get you a little snack, old skate, then you can show us where best to place the rest of our cargo."

The robot and the man scooted underneath the starship, began manipulating the locks on a small cargo hatch. In a moment, clinging to the hull, they had it open and delivered of a small canister that Vuffi Raa held out.

"*Here you are,*" Lando heard through his helmet phones. "*Shall I just spray it around, or would you prefer—*"

"*That will be quite suitable, my friend, and many thanks.*" Lehesu tried hard to keep hunger out of his voice. He hadn't noticed until now how famished he'd become. As the specially selected amino acids and other compounds began drifting around the ship, he moved slowly and with dignity, scooping them up and ingesting them. He could feel them sing through his body and knew a joy akin to that which Lando felt at the prospect of freedom.

"*Well, I certainly trust you're enjoying yourself in your selfish gluttony!*"

It was a strange new voice over the ether, one incomprehensible to Lando, but Vuffi Raa understood it—and correctly interpreted its hostile tone. Both of them jetted quickly out from under the hull of the *Falcon*, which was blocking their view, as a pair of titanic monsters slid casually alongside, making even Lehesu appear small and meek.

He may not have had the robot's talent for languages, but the air of sarcastic disapproval hadn't been missed by the gambler, either. Reflexively, he patted the spacesuit pocket where he kept his stingbeam—then laughed inwardly at himself as he thought of pitting its minuscule power against these . . . these . . .

"These are the Elders you told us about, Lehesu?" he asked finally. "Tell them we're here to help them, and that, at the very least, we mean them absolutely no harm." He removed his hand from the pocket and tried to sound sincere.

And almost succeeded.

Easily seven hundred meters from wingtip to wingtip, the pair of Oswaft dwarfed the *Falcon,* and everything else in view. They positioned themselves on either side of Lando's younger vacuum-breathing friend, as if that worthy were being arrested. Or sent to bed without his dinner.

"*No,*" Lehesu replied in words the gambler could understand, *"these are most assuredly not the Elders, and they have no right or authority to interfere with us. Elders are much larger."*

He'd directed the final comment to the two interlopers. Apparently it was some kind of insult, although it was probably lost on the pair, spoken as it had been in human language, Lando thought. If Elders were even larger than these creatures, the gambler reflected, he certainly didn't want to mess with them.

Vuffi Raa put on a burst of speed, whipped around as if to block the progress of the three giant beings—as if a microbe could block the progress of a bantha. "*I suggest,*" the droid radiated in a businesslike tone, "*that you be civil to our friend Lehesu, for he has performed a great service for you and the rest of your—*"

"*Silence, insignificant one!*" one of the creatures replied. "*You know not of what you speak. We are here at the explicit request of the Elders themselves. The three of you are to come to them at once, in order to explain your impertinence and face their mighty judgment!*"

X

"**S**ABACC!" CRIED LANDO CALRISSIAN, gambler, con *artiste*, and interstellar diplomat. He sat back on sheer nothingness with a satisfied look on his face and let the *Millennium Falcon* gather in his winnings, shuffle the "deck," and deal out the "card-chips" once again. It was the weirdest and most profitable game he'd ever played.

Senwannus'gourkahipaff, senior Elder of the Oswaft, let a little ticklish signal be broadcast, indicating amusement and pleasure. "*Truly it is amazing, Captainmasterlandocalrissian.*" Lando gave a mental shrug: if the head vacuum-breather wished to address him with a title longer than his own, indicating deep respect and a relaxed sort of submission, the gambler wasn't going to correct him. There was far too much at stake, and it had very little to do with the game of *sabacc*. "*Amazing,*" the thousand-meter being continued, "*you cannot even see the cards, yet you have won hand after hand under fair and impartial conditions. I abase myself to your skill and intellect.*"

Lando congratulated himself a little, too, principally on his luck. They were playing in the center of the Cave of the Elders, the only architectural structure, as far as he knew, within the ThonBoka, very probably the only such the Oswaft had ever constructed. Or thought to construct.

Located in the middle of the triangular plane formed by the three blue-white stars in the center of the nebula, the Cave of the Elders was a meticulous replica of the StarCave itself. From where he sat—hung might be a better word, as they were relaxing in free-fall—he could make out the folds and tucks he'd seen outside, duplicated in exact detail a mere ten kilometers away. A circular doorway repeated the pattern of the mouth of the Thon-Boka (sans, he was happy for small favors, the blockading fleet), and what he'd seen of the detail outside spoke exceptionally well for the inferential powers of the Oswaft. With the exception of the adventurous Lehesu, they had never actually seen the outside of their nebula, yet they knew just what it had to look like.

The only flaw observable in the titanic modeling effort, and what made the Cave of the Elders *really* interesting, was that it was constructed entirely, all twenty klicks of its diameter, of precious gems.

From outside the entrance of the Cave, the *Falcon*'s computers pinged in his helmet phones, indicating two cards each had been dealt to Sen (Lando irreverently abbreviated the being's name for the sake of his overworked tongue muscles), to Feytihennasraof, the second Elder, on the senior's left, and to Lehesu, who was also sitting in.

"You have a Three of Staves and a Commander of Sabres, Master," Vuffi Raa informed him from the ship, *"total value, fifteen."* The others would be "seeing" their cards by means of television signals produced by the computer. He wished the robot would let him count his own cards, almost as much as he wished the robot would stop calling him master, but there didn't seem to be much he could do about it. To protect the privacy of Lando's hand, they spoke in Old High Trammic, the ancient language of the Toka/Sharu of the Rafa System.

The Oswaft were too polite to mention that they'd "decoded" the language within five minutes of the game's beginning. They'd play fair in any case, ignoring the robot's signals. Both the translation and the refusal to take advantage were reflexive with the creatures; none of them had thought about the matter consciously. Honor and solving puzzles were instinctive with them.

"I'll take one card," Sen intoned, indicating thanks once the

Falcon had electronically dealt it. Fey, too, required a card, while the precocious Lehesu stood pat. Lando asked for a card, receiving Moderation, a minus fourteen, which made his hand worth one point.

"Master, the computer has randomly altered your last card to an Eight of Flasks! That means—"

"Sabacc!" Lando said before the robot could finish. That made a hundred and eighty million credits the Oswaft owed him, if he'd kept his accounts straight. If he ever got out of that mess, life was going to be very, very different.

"This is a most diverting occupation," Fey said. *"Shall we have another hand, Captainmasterlandocalrissiansir?"*

Swell: he'd been promoted by a syllable. At that rate, it would soon take all day to say his name. Maybe he should contrive to lose a few hands. It wouldn't be easy, seeing that the computer was actually controlling the cards, but he'd think of something.

Just like he had when they'd been summoned to confront the Elders.

AUTHORITY COMES IN many packages, and the contents seem to vary just as much as the outer trappings. Imperial power was based on naked, lethal, brute force, pure and simple and no shilly-shallying. The position of decision-makers in the Oseon, to choose just one example, depended on wealth. In the Rafa System, some deference seemed to be paid to religious leadership, although in that system, things were so tied up in ancient science that what looked like high priests might actually be senior technicians.

The Oswaft were a conservative people. They deferred to age and experience. Lando had tried to ascertain how old the Oswaft got to be, but couldn't. Like many lower species, they kept on growing throughout their lives. Lehesu was a young adult, say the equivalent of late teens or early twenties. He was about five hundred meters across the wingtips, and growing.

The pair of yes-men who'd picked them up near the Thon-Boka mouth were apparently of middle years (or centuries or millennia), seven hundred or seven hundred fifty meters in diameter and set in their ways. They hadn't much liked calling on tiny strangers or having tiny strangers calling on them, and they'd liked it less that a youngster like Lehesu had gone and changed the nice, smooth, boring flow of life in the StarCave.

The three had pointed out that Lando and Vuffi Raa couldn't simply go swimming off to meet the Elders. Lehesu wasn't prepared to say what would happen if he attempted to transport them as he had his nutrient cylinder back in the foodless desert. Nor was Lando prepared to risk such a venture. With some haggling, the pair of outsiders was permitted to return to the *Falcon* where, with faster-than-light drives activated, they followed the Oswaft down into the hollow center of the nebula.

Under the triple suns of the StarCave, the Cave of the Elders was an impressive sight, glittering and gleaming from billions of points as it rotated slowly. Vuffi Raa, using the ship's sensors, informed the gambler that there wasn't a valuable stone in the known galaxy that wasn't represented in huge quantities in the walls of the Cave. Moreover, the size of the gems would have sent a jeweler into a dead faint.

Senwannus'gourkahipaff and Feytihennasraof had awaited them within the Cave of the Elders. Lehesu, with his excellent grasp of Lando's language, had spelled the names for the gambler and the robot, explaining that the apostrophe in Sen's name represented another dozen or so minor syllables the Elder was too modest to insist upon, and that there was a third Elder around somewhere who was busy and would join them later.

"Our most cordial greetings, Captainmasterlando" had been Sen's first words in the new form of speech Lehesu had taught the Elder in a matter of seconds. *"I abjure you to forgive the somewhat overzealous invitation issued to you by our juniors."*

The senior Elder administered a mental nudge of admonishment to the pair—a maser bolt that would have holed the *Falcon,* deflectors and all.

"Think nothing of it, Senwannus'gourkahipaff, your Eldership; they're not the first underlings to get carried away with borrowed authority. What can we do for you?"

"*We are,*" Fey replied, "*given to understand that you have brought nutrients to replace those being destroyed by others of your kind outside the StarCave. Is this correct?*"

Lando nodded, a gesture he wasn't sure the Oswaft could see or understand. They'd left the *Falcon* parked outside—although now he wondered why he'd bothered as there was plenty of room for her in the Cave—and jetted in to meet the Elders. "That's right, sir. Not very much, but it's only a beginning. And besides, I think I've figured out a way to get the navy off your back."

"*But why should you bother yourself?*" Fey asked. "*And why should you oppose the actions and interests of your own kind in this matter? I'm afraid we do not understand you, Captain-master; and until we do, we cannot accept this gift you offer.*"

The Elders were at least a kilometer across, Fey being slightly smaller than Sen. Lando felt silly negotiating with them—it was rather like carrying on a conversation with a large apartment building. But from earlier conversations with Lehesu, he was prepared for their attitude and these very questions.

"Well, aside from the fact that Vuffi Raa and I have grown rather fond of young Lehesu, here, we consider it a sort of a game." Lando wished, as he hung in space beside the huge ray-like creature, that there was some provision for smoking a cigar in a spacesuit. He felt better making business talk if he could smoke.

"*A game? Please explain what you mean.*"

"Sure, Sen. I understand that you folks like mental puzzles. Well, my folks do, too. Only we've found a way to make them more interesting and challenging: we turn them into *games.* That's where somebody else tries to solve the puzzle first or better, or opposes your solution of it while he tries to work out his own."

"*Fascinating,*" Sen mused, almost to himself. He turned to Fey. "*Have you ever conceived of such a thing?*"

No answer came from the Elder. To a being so ancient, a new concept came as something of a shock.

"Right," Lando said, jetting closer to the pair of aliens. "And just to make it more fascinating, we try to play for something a little better than the sheer joy of solving the puzzle."

"*Such as what?*" both Elders said at once.

"Well, permit me to demonstrate, friends. Now take the game of *sabacc . . .*"

"AM I MISSING something obvious here," Lando offered conversationally as he took another "card" and the others considered their hands, "or are you people completely resigned to dying?"

A pale pink tinge suffused through Lehesu at Lando's boldness toward the Elders, but he kept his peace, trusting the gambler. Sen and Fey both performed the equivalent of looking up from their cards. Lando's helmet indicators said he was being brushed lightly by twin radar beams.

He knew the beings were far from stupid. Their transparent bodies made it easier and more difficult at the same time to figure out their internal arrangements, but from what he'd seen, he guessed that about two-thirds of their mass was brain, and pretty astute brain at that.

"*Ah yes,*" Sen answered finally, "*that was the reason you were demonstrating* sabacc *to us. I had become so fascinated with the game itself, I had quite forgotten that its purpose was explaining why you wished to help us. So, you play a great sa-bacc game with your own kind out there, and we are a part of it. No, my friend, we do not wish to die, but there seems little alternative. I'll take a card, Starshipmillenniumfalcon, if you please.*"

The ship, apparently unimpressed that it had been granted

status not only as a person but as an Elder among the Oswaft, duly blipped out a signal representing one of the seventy-eight *sabacc* cards, and fell silent again.

"There are plenty of alternatives, friend, there always are. The first, of course, is that you can give up and die. I'm glad to hear you reject it. That's a beginning, anyway. *Sabacc!* That makes twenty-three million you owe me. Can we take a break? I have to visit certain facilities aboard my ship, and we can carry on this conversation from there."

He jetted across the Cave of the Elders, leaving the Oswaft behind, climbed onto the hull of the *Falcon* and into the airlock hatch, where Vuffi Raa greeted him. "Patch the intercom into the ship-to-ship, will you? I need a cigar to think properly, and the powwow has reached a critical point."

"Yes, Master, I've been listening. What are we going to do with twenty-three million credits worth of precious stones? I don't believe we have room in the—"

"We'll figure that out when there's a point to it. Right now staying alive gets top priority." He'd unsealed his helmet and hung it on a rack, and, retaining the rest of his suit, climbed down into the lounge, where for once he left the gravity on, enjoying the feel of some weight under him.

"The second alternative," he continued, once contact was re-established, "is to fight. You folks have some impressive talents; your size alone is pretty terrifying, at least for people of my size, but I think—"

"*Captainmasterlandocalrissian,*" interrupted Sen, "*we are not a fighting people. In fact the concept is nearly as new to us as that of gaming—and somewhat related, I would guess. In any event, there is a third way . . .*"

"And what would that be?" the gambler asked as he slowly and deliberately singed the business end of a cigar, keeping the flame well away from the tip.

"*Negotiation. You will recall mention of a third Elder, Bhoggihalysahonues? At this moment, she and a delegation of other*

*Oswaft have appeared at the mouth of the StarCave and are sig-
naling for a peace-conference with your fleet. We wish to ask
upon what terms—"*

"You bet your apostrophe I remember Boggy, and I can predict *exactly* what's going to happen, Sen. The navy wants you
dead, old beanbag, and that's the only terms they're going to
settle for. I've seen their work on other occasions, and you can
believe me when I—"

"This is much as I had surmised," the second Elder said, *"and
I opposed the attempt, yet we are an open and free people and
would not prevent our third Elder from trying what she might.
Yet you have mentioned other alternatives to dying, fighting, and
negotiating."*

"There's running away."

"What, and leave the ThonBoka?" So much emotion loaded
the response that Lando couldn't tell which Oswaft it had come
from. He poured himself a glass of fruit juice (spacesuits tend to
dehydrate one a bit) and sat back down, puffing on his cigar. Vuffi
Raa was forward, keeping his big red eye on the controls. It was
difficult but important to remember that they were still in deep
space. He could see how the Oswaft thought of the place as a safe
haven.

"I don't know," he said at last. "I gather from Lehesu's experiences that you folks aren't biologically tied to the place. It's an
alternative to dying, isn't it?"

A long, long silence ensued while the massive brains outside
processed his heresy. Finally: *"I am not sure, Lando, that it is a
desirable alternative. We are the ThonBoka; the Thonboka is the
Oswaft. Would you willingly be driven out of your home, accept
an eternity of wandering—"*

He laughed. "Sen, I accepted wandering as a way of life a long
time ago. It beats the Core out of working for a living." The gambler mused. There were a lot of strange life-forms in the galaxy,
ranging, in the matter of size alone, from these gigantic creatures,

the largest he'd ever heard of, down to the tiny Crokes of . . . well, something-or-other. He couldn't remember the system. What made it interesting was that in his travels he'd observed that the biggest critters were almost invariably the most gentle and timid. Well, it made sense: if you were little, you had to learn to be tough. If you were big, it didn't matter. He guessed he'd always thought of himself as somewhere in the middle.

"Okay, yeah. Well, what if you appeared to do one or another of these things—sort of like the way I taught you to bluff in *sabacc*? Say you looked like you were going to destroy the fleet. Or, say you looked like you were all dead? I hate to bring up a touchy subject, but Lehesu tells me you folks sort of disintegrate when you die, drift away in a cloud of dust?"

Another long, uncomfortable silence. At long last, the daring Lehesu spoke for his Elders. *"That's correct, Lando, we return to our constituent molecules. Not the happiest of thoughts. Why, is it important?"*

Finishing his cigar, Lando stood, walked back to the ladder and up to the airlock, screwed on his helmet, and went outside. The Cave of the Elders floated beside the *Falcon* like a fantastic decorated egg, a million brilliant colors, a billion gleaming facets. He drifted toward the entrance and faced the three giant beings who waited for him there.

"Yes, it could be very important. It means you don't leave any remains behind that can be detected against the normal molecular background of space. It means they won't be looking for any stiffs."

"Stiffs?" the three said at once.

"Bodies, corpses, DOAs, meat, Qs—*corpora delicti*. Tell me, what are conditions like out by the wall of the StarCave?"

If Oswaft had been capable of blinking at a rapid change of subject, Sen, at least would have done so. *"Why, not terribly different from here. A bit colder, but not uncomfortably so."*

"Vuffi Raa," Lando said into the radio in his suit, "get me

some scanning data on the nebula wall, will you? I've been working on an idea. Sen, Fey, Lehesu, can you people get *through* the wall at all?"

Lehesu replied, being the only one with any practical experience in the matter. "It is all but impenetrable. One cannot—what is your expression?—'starhop,' because one cannot see where one is going. It is said that attempting it in any case will cause one to burst into flame and vanish."

Lando considered this. "Makes sense. No matter how diffuse the gas and dust is, translight speeds will create that kind of friction. How deep could you—what is your expression?—'swim' into the wall if you had to? Far enough so that sensors couldn't detect you?"

It was Lehesu's turn to think. While he was doing so, a sudden burst of radio transmissions entered the Cave of the Elders. It caused some stir. Lando couldn't understand what was being said, but no one interrupted the conversation for a translation, so the gambler put it out of his mind.

At long last: *"Yes, I believe such might be possible. If I follow your line of reasoning, you would have us conceal ourselves, we and all of the Oswaft, within the folds and billows of the wall until the fleet, believing in their despicable villainy that we had starved to death, gave up and went away to impose misfortune upon someone else. But what would you have us do about the molecular residue that—"*

The gambler grinned. "I have that all figured out, my over-large friend. It wouldn't take very much, would it? How about a little of my cargo, judiciously sprayed all over the place?"

"Lando! I believe the idea might work. Esteemed Elders, may I ask—"

"Silence, young one. Peace! We have something else to ponder at this moment, something very disturbing."

"What's happening, Sen, what's going on?"

The giant spoke: *"Bhoggihalysahonues' attempts to negotiate an end to these insane hostilities have ended in disaster! She, and all of her party—a thousand of our people—were murdered with energy weapons almost the moment they appeared at the mouth of the ThonBoka and greeted the nearest vessel."*

"I'm sorry to hear it, Sen . . . but, well, it doesn't really change things very much, does it?"

"I am afraid, Captainmasterlandocalrissiansir, that it does. You see, unfortunately, and in their consternation—the details aren't very clear—the negotiation party shouted at the . . . 'cruiser,' much as I did in an unthinking moment just now at the two Oswaft who brought you here so ill-usedly."

"Yeah. *I* felt it, and it was a tight beam. The *Courteous*? What happened to her?" He had a bad feeling about this.

Sen gave the broadcast equivalent of a mournful sigh. *"She— your* Courteous *—was not well defended, as is your* Millennium Falcon, *by deflector shields, for they thought our people harmless.*

"Thus was the Courteous *utterly destroyed."*

"Swell," Lando said, more to himself than to the Elders. "Nothing like a premature war on our hands."

"The rest of the fleet, with full shields up now, has entered the ThonBoka mouth to murder us all in retribution."

XI

K LYN SHANGA GRINNED a humorless grin. "Well, Bern, you've
really put your foot in it this time, old friend."

The wiry little man on the fold-down cot spread his skinny
arms and shrugged, returning his commander's rueful smile. He
wore a dark-green military shipsuit with a well-abraded band
around the waist where he was used to carrying a gunbelt. Shanga's low-slung holster was likewise empty; no weapons were permitted in the cellblock of the *Wennis*' detention sector.

"You know what they say, Boss, sometimes you trick the sorcerer, sometimes the sorcerer tricks you." He pursed his lips,
tongue protruding generously, and made a rude and juicy noise.

An alarmed look playing momentarily over his broad and
deeply seamed features, Shanga glanced around reflexively for
listening devices.

His smaller associate laughed. "What're they gonna do, throw
me in the clink for insubordination? That'd be like jailing a mur-
derer for littering." Harsh light from the naked overhead bulb
reflected from the man's equally naked scalp. Where he did have
hair, on the sides and back, it was clipped into a dirty gray stubble.

Shanga sat down on the cot beside his friend, extracted a pair
of cigars from a pocket. There was a brief silence while they got
them lit. "Well, I've got to admit, when you tried hijacking that
auxiliary, you climbed pretty high on the wanted list. I wish to
the Core you'd consulted me before you—"

"What, and have you wind up here yourself? Boss, you *know* you'd have done the same thing I did. There are five pinnaces tucked away aboard this scow with the capability for faster-than-light travel, and our fighters can't hack it. If that blockade fleet moves in before we get to the nebula, we're gonna lose the Butcher!"

And our reason for living, Shanga thought, reading the same thoughts displayed on his friend's face. Bern Nuladeg was the only member of his squadron who went back with him to before his original retirement. They'd served their country together in a brief but bloody conflict with one of its neighbors, earning their wings, both of them becoming aces. When Shanga retired, Nuladeg had gone on to become a flight instructor, finally the commander of his nation-state's flight academy. The invasion from the stars had changed all of that.

Now they flew together in a squadron made up not only of their fellow countrymen but of personnel belonging to their former enemy, individuals from other nations, other planets in their system. They were all Renatasians, and they all wanted the same thing. Vengeance.

"I know, Bern, I know. That's why you did it on your own, didn't take any of the others along. You were going to steal that lighter yourself—then what?"

The small, bald-headed figure chuckled. "Hadn't gotten that far along in my plans. Days before we reach the ThonBoka at this speed, Klyn, *days*! What can Gepta be thinking of, permitting the invasion to begin before we get there? I heard the story—had the ring of truth to it—and acted. Guess I would have swung around and offered you fellows a ride, if I'd had the chance. I dunno. What're they gonna do to me, do you suppose?"

Shanga shook his head. "I have a meeting—an 'audience,' *he'd* like to style it—with our gray-robed cousin in an hour or so. We're going to talk about it then. I won't lie to you, it doesn't look good. You should see the way he treats his own people."

Nuladeg's laughter was practically a giggle now. "I know!

That's what made swiping that machine so blasted easy: everybody was afraid to move for fear of getting terminally reprimanded! Whoever said dictatorship's efficient, Boss? It'd be funny if it weren't so downright stupid." He drew on his cigar, blew a smoke ring toward the bulb in the ceiling. Then his laughter died along with the smile creasing his face.

"Klyn, promise me one thing: don't worry about me enough to stop this mission. Whatever you do. I mean it. I can take whatever they dish out, but I can't stand the thought . . ."

Bern Nuladeg's entire family had been killed by Imperial troopers enjoying a few hours off-duty time. It had been a lark for them, and had only finished what they'd actually been guilty of. The field commander for the group had dismissed it as a prank—the same commander was found the next morning, in his own bed, with a bayonet thrust through his lower jaw into his brain. No one had ever solved the mystery of how it had been done in a heavily guarded building on the grounds of the former flight academy, nor of who had done it or why.

"All right, old friend," Shanga sighed. He'd always thought that Nuladeg, who was the better pilot, experienced with command responsibility, ought to have been running the tattered squadron. The little man had refused even the number-two position, citing an impulsiveness that no one had truly believed in until now. "I'll see what I can do. You're right, I'm afraid. I was thinking about those pinnaces myself, when I heard about the moves against the StarCave. I'll see what I can do and be back with you as soon as possible."

He rapped loudly on the wall, pointedly ignoring the call button beside the force-fielded door. "Guards! Let me out of here! I have to see a toad about a man!"

A QUARTER OF a galaxy away, the One, the Other, and the Rest raced to keep a rendezvous. They had come from even farther, and their speed was something no one in what Lando and his friends regarded as a civilization would have believed.

"We move so slowly!" the Other complained, plunging through hyperspace beside the One. "I fear we shall not get there on time!"

The One allowed himself to be distracted from his headlong course long enough to indicate a smile. "Impatience from you, after all this time, my friend? Truly, this is an era of changes. Never fear, we shall learn what we shall learn, regardless. I, too, would prefer that we—"

The Other interrupted. "Events move of their own accord! What shall come to pass is unpredictable! It is Chaos, I tell you, Chaos!"

"And there ought to be a law? Remember, comrade, that it is this state of unpredictability which nearly every race endures for all of its life span. It is in this state that we began, and we are unusual in surviving it. We very nearly died of boredom; would that have been more desirable?"

"Don't lecture me!" the Other replied with uncharacteristic sharpness. "I know as well as you do of the dangers that confronted us. I was the first to consent to your plan. Do not begrudge me the right to complain of some of its consequences; it assists me in adjusting to the inevitable."

Laughter crackled through the distorted space around them. "Nothing is inevitable anymore, dear comrade, nothing! That is the entire point of the experiment!"

"Well, I hope your experiment will produce a cure for smugness, then. I personally shall take great pleasure in restraining you while it is forcibly administered!"

Once again laughter sundered the twisted ether as the One, the disgruntled Other, and the Rest, in various states of mind, plunged onward.

"NONSENSE!" ROKUR GEPTA hissed from the corner of his apartments below the control deck. "He is mine to deal with, and I tell you he shall be sectioned alive before the entire crew—yours included, Admiral Shanga—as an example!"

It was the first time the fighter commander had ever seen the sorcerer pace nervously. The time was growing near for the resolution of a number of crises, and the Renatasian had a suspicion that Gepta, too, feared he would be robbed of his victory by a trigger-happy fleet commodore.

Carrying disrespect to new heights because he felt the effect was necessary, Shanga flopped into the sorcerer's huge chair. "Gepta, you old charlatan, you know better than that, and if you don't, I'll tell you now. Keep Bern Nuladeg in the brig, if you wish, until we get to the ThonBoka. He could use the rest, and it'll keep him out of trouble. Not to mention saving your well-concealed face. But execute him, and I'm through with you. I'll take my squadron and—"

"*You'll do what you are told!*" Gepta made a threatening magical gesture.

Shanga laughed. "Save your parlor tricks, old man! We stopped doing what we were told when your precious navy destroyed anything we had to lose by disobeying. Twenty-three loose cannon, Gepta, and they're all pointed at you unless you—"

"*Silence!* I have no further need for you, Klyn Shanga. You have foolishly told me where Lando Calrissian might be found. We will soon be there, and he is trapped by the fleet, cannot get away from the justice I shall mete out. You serve no purpose. You are dispensable!"

Shanga obtained another cigar from inside his suit, lit it, and spat out a flake of tobacco onto the carpeted floor.

"Yeah? Well, I spent a little time with your pet professor today. You'll recall you instructed him to be free and easy with information bearing on combat operations in the nebula? What he had to say about the guff relayed this morning from the fleet was very interesting. Very interesting, indeed."

Gepta, his back turned to the squadron commander, spoke to the wall. "And what was that?"

"Ask your own people if you don't believe me. We're up against it, Gepta. There are something like a *billion* Oswaft in that sack, every one of them as dangerous as a fighter ship. Something about folks like us being electrochemical in nature, our nervous systems, anyway. Well, the Oswaft are what your boy is calling 'organoelectronic.' I don't know exactly everything that implies, but they can think and act and maneuver a lot faster than we can. What's more, a flock of them destroyed the *Courteous*. Nobody knows how."

Gepta whirled on Shanga. "What has this to do with disposition of *your* group, *Admiral*?" The way the sorcerer pronounced his title may have been the most sarcastic thing that Shanga had ever heard. With difficulty he shrugged off the implied threat, returned to calculated insult.

"So you think you're going to get anywhere with the clumsy children you've got manning this ship? I told you, Gepta, they're amateurs, and they're so scared at balling things up, they'll ball them up anyway! I think what Bern Nuladeg tried this morning ought to demonstrate pretty well how frightened we are, of you, or of anything else. You need us, you pretentious idiot, and you're going to lose this operation without us. You may have already. Have you heard from the fleet?"

There was a long, long silence while Rokur Gepta gained control of himself. No one, not for perhaps twenty thousand years, had spoken to him in such a manner and lived—or even died a quick and merciful death. In fact some of them had lasted, under one instrument of both torture and regeneration or another, for *centuries*. Klyn Shanga might be one such, after this was over.

Very well, then, the sorcerer reasoned, it should not matter what immediate disposition he made of Shanga or his underlings. They would serve their purpose in the coming conflict, and any who survived . . . But he had one more source of information to consult. He strode rapidly to the chair that Shanga occupied, ignored the man, and pressed a button. "Send me the *Ottdefa* Osuno Whett immediately."

Not three minutes later, the compartment door whisked aside, and the anthropologist stepped in. The tall, emaciated professor took in what was to be seen, sensed conflict momentarily postponed, and vowed to himself to get out of the way as soon as he could manage it.

"You have been following the information from the fleet?" the sorcerer asked without preliminaries.

"Of course, sir, I—"

"What do they tell you of the capabilities of the Oswaft?"

Shanga grinned, but kept his silence.

"Well, sir, it is a confirmation of my earlier studies. In a cellular sense, these beings seem to exist on a sort of solid-state level, something like primitive electronics. This accounts for their communications abilities and—"

"How is this known? Is it merely surmise, or are there data?"

The anthropologist's astonishment grew every time Gepta snapped at him. Along with his fear. "Sir, a number of vessels did a full-range scan at the moment the creatures were destroyed. Most of them were vaporized when the *Courteous* went up. In fact, it's possible that not one of them was injured by fire from the fleet. They simply miscalculated the destructive radius of an exploding cruiser. The *Courteous* did open fire, but there wasn't any time to—"

The sorcerer raised a hand and the scientist halted. "By what means did the Oswaft destroy the cruiser *Courteous,* Ottdefa? And how vulnerable do you suppose they are to the navy's weapons?"

Whett hesitated before he began again: "Sir, as difficult as it may be to believe, it appears that simple microwaves were the method, but at incredible power levels. This is consistent with their ability to hypertravel, since it, too, is an energy-intensive phenomenon. There is also the fact to consider that the *Courteous* was unshielded—I believe the circumstances are referred to as 'garrison discipline'? Shielded, I believe a ship would be quite safe. To answer your second question, there is no reason to believe that the Oswaft would be any more impervious to disintegrator beams, tractor-pressor beams, disruptors, and the like, than any other living thing."

The sorcerer stood deep in thought, one hand where his chin should have been under his wrappings. Shanga sat, apparently relaxed and smoking his cigar, while Whett stood nearly at attention.

"One final question, *Ottdefa:* how many Oswaft are there?"

"Sir, there is no direct way of knowing. Estimates range from several hundred million to a few billion."

Shanga laughed. "Since when do the words 'few' and 'billion' belong in the same sentence. Gepta, they could whittle down the fleet by sheer attrition, and—"

"Silence," the sorcerer said with unusual gentleness. "I must think. *Ottdefa,* I will speak with you later. Thank you for your report." The door whooshed open and closed behind the grateful anthropologist.

Then Gepta addressed Shanga. "Admiral, you are no friend of mine, and, after this operation, will never again be an ally. But you have spoken the truth to me, and I am compelled to recognize it. Very well, we shall do as you have suggested. Your man— what was his name?—will remain confined until we reach the nebula, whereupon he will revert to your command. I trust you and your squadron will serve me as you have implicitly promised."

The fighter pilot rose wearily and stubbed out his cigar. Rearranging his newly recovered blaster on his leg more comfortably, he walked toward the door, turned back to the sorcerer at the last moment.

"I haven't any reason to want to send you flowers, either, old man, but we've got a common enemy. We'll stick with you until that's taken care of. Talk to you later." He stepped through the door and was gone.

Scarcely noticing the man had left this time, Rokur Gepta paced awhile more, then, with a more determined stride than before, turned to his chair. He seated himself and activated several cameras. He pushed a button. "For immediate recording and beamcast to the fleet," he directed unseen technicians:

"Upon my own unanswerable authority, I order you to cease all combat operations upon receipt of this transmission and to return to your positions on the original blockade perimeter.

"Evasion or failure, on the part of any officer, at *any* level, to comply swiftly with this direct order will be punishable by summary revocation of all rank and privileges, judiciary and ceremonial impoverishment, and sale into bondage of all family members within five degrees of consanguinity, and for the perpetrator himself, slow mutilation and death upon public display.

"I, Rokur Gepta, Sorcerer of Tund, command it."

The camera lights went out.

Gepta sat back in his chair, feeling much better. This would buy them all some time, and resolve part of the conflict between Klyn Shanga and himself. Odd, he hadn't had a real adversary stand up to him for thousands of years. No one dared oppose his ruthless exercise of power. Everywhere he went, people in their masses, and as individuals, feared, hated, and served him.

Except for Lando Calrissian.

And now, possibly even worse than the itinerant gambler—because the affront seemed deliberately calculated—there was Klyn Shanga.

The most peculiar aspect of it was that, somehow, it felt good.

XII

THE *OTTDEFA* OSUNO WHETT reflected.

Shuddering in the relative security of his assigned quarters in officer's country, he considered himself extremely lucky just to be alive that morning. He'd seen others broken, figuratively and literally, at the malignant whim of Rokur Gepta, individuals guilty of nothing more than reporting a purely mechanical failure or bringing him information he didn't want to assimilate. To be trapped in the middle of a dispute between the evil sorcerer and his reluctant—and no doubt soon-to-be *former*—partner, that barbarian Shanga . . .

He crossed the cramped living-sleeping space allotted him, noting that he'd forgotten to fold the cot into the wall in his earlier haste to answer Gepta's summons. So—he was still accustomed to depending on a servant after all this time. It was a weakness to make note of and correct.

The gray military wallcoat of the compartment still oppressed him, despite the decorations—ceremonial masks, garish shields, primitive hand-powered weapons—he'd hung up here and there. He'd have to see what else he carried in his luggage down below in the storage hold. It would brighten the place up and strengthen the official "cover" that allowed him to travel thus encumbered in the first place.

Entering the tiny head, he sloughed off the casual civilian ship-suit he'd been wearing, now soaked through with perspiration and smelling foul. He wasn't on the schedule for a shower at this time of day, and hadn't had time for it when the fixtures had been operational. Thank the Core for the mixture of intelligent species whose differences in personal habits and physical characteristics made individual quarters (at least at his level of rank) a necessity rather than a luxury even aboard this spartan vessel. At that, it could be worse: he could be quartered with the noncoms or conscriptees. It wouldn't have been unprecedented; his long career had seen him assume many stranger poses. Now all he desired was a refreshing wash, which he attended to at the small sink (set into the shower stall along with the toilet) with its trickle of lukewarm recycled water. An ironic expression greeted him in the mirror above the sink.

Well, he had *survived,* as he had *always* survived. All it had required was layer upon layer of carefully prepared deception. It was the sole art to which he could truly lay claim, the only way he could expect to get out of *this* mess with his skin intact.

That accursed robot: *it* had been responsible for all his troubles in recent years. Gepta and Shanga were headed toward the ThonBoka nebula—from Tund, on the outskirts of one side of civilization, to the StarCave, on the fringes of the other side—for nothing more than revenge. Perhaps he, himself, the *soi-disant Ottdefa* Osuno Whett, would be enjoying a little vengeance, too, when the *Wennis* finally arrived at its destination.

He splashed water on his thin, elongated face, his neck and bony chest, ran a laser over his stubble, and remembered.

HE'D BEEN YOUNGER THEN, of course, and his appearance considerably different. Afterward, he'd had four centimeters of bonemer grafted into each tibia, fibula, and femur to increase his height, proportionate amounts added to his arms as well, and an extra vertebra interleaved in his spine. It was painful, and it had taken several months just to accustom himself to the new leverages, the new bodily rhythms the surgery imposed. He was *still* learning, and, in the meantime, gave an unnaturally awkward and gangling impression. This he welcomed, as it added to his disguise. He'd also lost some forty kilograms—amazing how much that alone had rendered him unrecognizable. The hair had whitened of its own accord, as whose wouldn't in the knowledge that something of the order of a billion individuals wanted to see him painfully dead, and were willing to do something positive about it. He'd left the hair alone, changing only its style. It, too, served his purpose, which amounted simply to staying alive in a murderous business. He'd already outlived the average life expectancy in his profession by over thirty years.

The tap water shut itself off. He dried himself vigorously with the only towel he'd be permitted on the voyage, picked up the soiled shipsuit from where he'd dropped it, and crossed the cabin to the tiny partitioned alcove where his travel bag hung unfolded. Depositing the old clothes on the closet floor, he got out another set, dressed himself carefully and comfortably, then made another withdrawal from his bag, went to the unfolded bunk with a small electronic device clutched almost desperately in his knobbly fingers.

He lay down, placed the mechanism beside him, drew a small cable from it, and fastened the eye-mask on its free end over his face. His hand hovered over a large green button on the side of the black plastic case.

Then he paused in thought once more.

The Renatasia had been a lovely system.

He recalled it vividly: eight plump planets and a cheerful medium-size yellow star set a surprising number of parsecs outside the then-current margins of the million-system Empire. Apparently they'd been human-colonized in some dim spacefaring prehistory, although no records of the event survived, either there or in "civilized" reaches. For the Administration a million systems, of course, were not enough. A billion wouldn't be. Thus Renatasia must be brought under its kindly influence.

Renatasia III and IV were the jewels in their cozy and conveniently isolated diadem. From space they appeared warm, lush, green, and inhabited by a people who used steel, titanium, and simple organoplastics, who were capable of wringing useful amounts of energy from the core of the atom, and who had not only reached but profitably colonized every one of the remaining six bodies in their system, from freeze-dried outermost to charcoal flambéed innermost—albeit under domes and in burrows, rather than through the total climatic transformation that even the Empire often found too expensive to pursue.

They had not quite reinvented faster-than-light spacedrives, although they were fiddling with its theoretical underpinnings. Nor had they yet made the basic discoveries that would inevitably lead them to such mechanisms as deflector shields, tractor-pressor beams, disruptors, and disintegrators—a fact for which the Centrality navy was later to be rather embarrassedly grateful. For they could also fight, it developed, like the very devil. They'd been doing it for millennia.

Mathilde was the capital city of a nation-state of the same name, located on the second largest continent of Renatasia III. Reception of the system's crude, flat, electronic sound-and-picture transmissions revealed that her citizens spoke a much-corrupted version of the commonest language of the galaxy—this was to serve as justification for the intervention that came later—and were the most prosperous and technologically advanced people in the system, their offworld colonies the most numerous and successful.

The nation-state of Mathilde, along with others like it, was located in the north temperate zone, and divided its activities about equally between agriculture and manufacturing. Just like every other polity in the system, it had forgotten its long-past origins elsewhere in the galaxy. Mathildean writers and scholars speculated about what future explorers would discover among the stars, and whether there was intelligent life in outer space.

A severely damaged civilian star-freighter had first happened upon the Renatasia System by accident. Once it had limped back to port for repairs, her captain had dutifully reported the system's existence to the government. No contact had been made by the freighter, which made things very much easier for the intelligence operative assigned the task of establishing official communications. The *Ottdefa* Osuno Whett.

His academic credentials had always been the perfect cover for a Centrality spy. Where can an anthropologist *not* go and poke his long, thin nose into the most intimate and personal details of a culture?

Before leaving, his superiors had equipped him, more or less against his better judgment, with an assistant, a rather odd little droid of obviously alien manufacture who said his name was Vuffi Raa and that, owing to a mishap of some sort involving a deep-space pirate attack while he was being shipped in a packing crate, he was unable to remember his place of origin or the species who had built him. Whett was scientist enough—and a genuine anthropologist—to be frustrated by the lack of information. Centrality Intelligence was even less helpful. They simply told him to stop asking stupid questions and get on with his assignment. He got on.

Vuffi Raa did prove to be useful in many ways. He was a superb personal valet, had a capacious memory, an astute intelligence with an easy grasp for every cultural nuance. He was utterly obedient—except that Whett couldn't get the little droid to call him master.

Actually, that turned out all to the good. Before landing their small, unarmed entry vessel on the front lawn of the Mathildean chief executive's official residence, among bands and fanfares and uncounted cocked and loaded weapons, Vuffi Raa had been instructed to disguise himself as an organic being with sophisticated plastics simulating skin.

It occurred to Whett that perhaps the droid would then resemble his original manufacturers. It was a galaxy-wide assumption that droids tended to be designed in the image of their makers. However, he shelved the speculation; they had other problems at present.

The robot would pose as the leader of the diplomatic expedition, an envoy from a starry federation Way Out There, ready to welcome the Renatasians into the fold. That was Whett's habitual deception at work. He assumed the role of humble assistant and secretary. This kept him neatly out of a spotlight he felt it would eventually be safer to avoid, knowing standard policy toward unclaimed but occupied territory.

THE *OTTDEFA* OSUNO WHETT, lying in his tiny cabin aboard the decommissioned cruiser *Wennis,* en route to the ThonBoka, paused momentarily in his musings and finally pushed the button on the electronic box beside him on the cot. A tide of relaxation funneled into his brain through the bony wave guides of his eye sockets. It was followed by another and another and another, each successively smaller, yet still soothing. To run the device continuously would put him into deep sleep, a condition he must avoid in the event the sorcerer should call on him again. But the waves of rest were almost as good.

He pushed the button again.

More memories came to him, unbidden.

AFTER THE INITIAL, inevitable awkwardness of first contact, the Mathildeans, along with everybody in the rest of the system, took Vuffi Raa to their hearts. He addressed international conclaves. He presided over formal banquets. He was photographed with scantily clad media personalities. He was compelled to turn down offers involving the endorsement of consumer products. Even so, small replicas of the five-limbed droid began showing up in stores almost from the beginning, and several sizable fortunes were made for their enterprising creators.

All the while, a short, plump, dark-haired *Ottdefa* Osuno Whett made observations and unobtrusive recordings. Estimates

were made and updated concerning the strength of the Renatasian economy, the effectiveness of the system's defenses. It was
accepted as a given that invasion would unite the deeply divided
civilization. Whett would have preferred to play upon those divi-
sions, in effect to let the system conquer itself, but the navy was
beneath such subtleties. Some effort was made by the authorities
to limit the pair's access to high-security installations, but they
didn't take account of a spy technology centuries ahead of Renatasia's.

As he lay in his cot aboard the *Wennis,* Whett's mind was
upon another day, another place. His hand hovered over the button of the electronic relaxer, just as it had hovered, in the small
cabin of their landing vehicle, over a button on the communicator panel. Pushing the button would transmit all the data he had
collected and trigger the invasion by the navy.

"Well, robot, the great moment has arrived! This will alter the
history of Renatasia forever—"

"It will bring history to an end in this system, sir, not alter it."

Whett was sitting in the passenger's seat. Their machine was
stored near the hotel in which they were living, and the excuse
had frequently been offered that Vuffi Raa required certain nutrients and gases in order to subsist in the (to him) foreign atmosphere of Renatasia Ill. There had been some thought of holding
the craft and examining it—the military mind is the same the
universe over—but it had been vetoed by a Mathildean chief executive very much aware of the visitor's popularity.

"Cold feet, from a droid? Why haven't you said anything
about this before?" Whett was annoyed. The creature was spoil-
ing his moment of supreme triumph. Still, there was no specific
way he could fault the machine; it spoke the objective truth, was
in fact incapable of speaking anything else. History *would* end
for Renatasian civilization within a few days of his pressing the
button.

"I am a droid, sir, constructed to obey. Your remark seemed

inferentially to require a reply, that is all." The robot sat in the pilot's chair, its limbs at rest, its eye glowing dully in the dim light of the concrete parking garage.

"I suggest that you address me as master, robot."

"I'm sorry, sir, I am not programmed to respond in that area."

Savagely, Whett jammed his thumb down on the button. A small amber light glowed to life on the panel; no other sign appeared. The deed was done, could not be called back.

Vuffi Raa's eye dimmed almost to extinction, as if the power to transmit the treacherous information was being drained from his supply.

The next few days were bedlam, exactly as Whett had expected. The navy appeared at the fringes of the system, close enough to be fully detectable by Renatasian defense sensors. They even let the local military lob a few primitive thermonuclear weapons at them to demonstrate the utter futility of resistance. The fleet's shields glowed briefly, restoring energy consumed by the voyage out, and that was that. Almost.

Unfortunately for the navy and high-technology aggressors everywhere in space and time, invasions cannot be conducted with continent-destroying weapons or from behind shields. Not unless you're willing to obliterate the enemy, and not at all if you're interested in taking what the enemy has: raw materials, agricultural products, certain manufactured goods, and the potential labor of her citizens. While the fleet sat tight and safe in orbit above the eight planets of Renatasia, 93 percent of the first wave of troopers were savagely massacred by the locals, using chemical bullet projectors, crude high-powered lasers, poison gases, clubs, meat cleavers, and fists. Eighty-seven percent of the second wave died similarly, even though they'd been forewarned, 71 percent of the third, and so on. The navy was winning a glorious, disastrously expensive victory. Troopships carrying replacements began showing up at hourly intervals.

Osuno Whett and Vuffi Raa had gone into hiding briefly after they had summoned the fleet. Nevertheless, they were hunted and hounded across the face of the planet. The relentless natives gleefully cut them off again and again from rescue by their uniformed compatriots.

At long last they joined a force, a remnant of the third wave, which helped them get aboard a shuttle and into the safety of a Centrality battlewagon. But not before the ugly, merciless extermination of two-thirds of the Renatasian population was an evil, personally experienced nightmare they would live with—and sleep with—for the rest of their lives.

WHETT, IN HIS cabin on the *Wennis*, pushed the button again.

Waves of relaxation, but regrettably not of forgetfulness, swept through his tense and tortured body as tears coursed down his face. It was a rare moment: generally he merely hated and feared the remaining Renatasians, having for the most part burnt out his circuitry for shame. He had fled their persistent presence for a long, long time. Nor had he been unhappy when, at long last, his superiors had ordered him to "lose" the robot—both an unwelcome reminder and a dead giveaway to pursuers—to Lando Calrissian in a rigged *sabacc* game.

That had been in the Oseon, and things had not turned out well for either the hopes of his superiors or for those of Rokur Gepta, who had personally supervised that particular operation.

Now, alone with his real pursuers, his memories, Whett realized that it was more than revenge he needed to accomplish in the ThonBoka. He had to see that robot destroyed. It was a dangerous link, in more ways than one, to an even more dangerous past. And he had to see an end, as well, to Captain Lando Calrissian, who could connect his new appearance, adopted before the game, with the robot.

Very well, then: Gepta sought to destroy Calrissian; Shanga sought to destroy Vuffi Raa (because he didn't know the real mastermind was a "harmless" academic he had seen nearly every day); that academic must now seek to destroy them both, gambler and droid.

Still he wondered, after all this time: where *had* that accursed robot come from, anyway?

XIII

T HAT ACCURSED ROBOT scratched his head.

"Politics saved our lives, Master? I'm not altogether sure I understand."

In reality, the gesture was more a matter of flicking a delicate tentacle tip around the bezel that retained the faceted red lens of his eye, mounted on the upper surface of his headless pentacular "torso." But its meaning was clear; he had picked it up from long association with human beings. As usual, certain aspects of that association puzzled him.

"Well, I'm only guessing, mind you, but a massive operation such as that Edge-blasted blockade out there, especially when it's being carried out in secret, presents a lot of opportunities to people envious of the boys on top." Lando pried up his cigar from where he'd secured it to the edge of the bench top, drew deeply on it, expelled the smoke, and squashed it firmly once again, sideways, into the wad of chewing gum that, in the absence of gravity, held it where it wouldn't float away.

"Do you want this end-wrench, Vuffi, or the adjustable spanner?"

The robot glanced back at his master, squatting on the deck plates with one leg thrust under the bench for leverage and security, much like the cigar. Lando leaned on a tool chest, assisting. They'd lifted a repair port and the robot peered now into a complex maze of working and semiworking parts.

"Adjustable, Master. This is a section I rigged after we beefed up the shields in the Oseon. All we had in stock were replacements from the Ringneldia, and everything in *that* system is standardized around the diameter of some native bean or other."

It wasn't just the sudden pullback of the murderous fleet that bothered Vuffi Raa, although it had left thousands of dead Oswaft in its wake. While genuinely ignorant, or at least amnesiac, about his own origins, he could infer certain facts about his makers and their culture, and the trouble was, several of the facts in question were contradictory. And current events were bringing him swiftly to a personal crisis involving those contradictions. It was not a situation that any intelligence—even that of a Class Two droid—finds comfortable.

He detached one of his sinuous manipulators, directing it remotely to thread its way into the starboard reactant-impeller units, deep in the bowels of the *Millennium Falcon*. Nothing was actually *wrong* with the system, but had it been a hair more sluggish, they would have been fried by the *Courteous* instead of cheating their way through hyperspace. It didn't pay to tolerate the slightest malfunction, not when they were the only spaceship the ThonBoka had to put up against the fleet. Those devices fed not only the engines, which was fairly important in itself, but the deflector shields as well. Vuffi Raa and Lando needed every fractional advantage if they weren't going to sell their lives cheaply.

"For example," the gambler continued, craning his neck to see what the robot was doing beneath the floor, "there'll be one group which will loudly—and correctly—proclaim that this undeclared war against the Oswaft constitutes genocide, although they wouldn't hesitate if they'd thought of it first themselves. Then there'll be a gang of middle-of-the-roaders who could do it better or cheaper. Finally, there'll be the ones who regard the action as too gentle and indecisive. They'll want the fleet to sit back and toss in a few planet-wreckers, and *they're* probably the ones we owe for this hiatus."

A little cynical, Vuffi Raa thought before replying. "But Master, there aren't any planets here to wreck, thank the Core."

"Thank three little blue suns out there that went kablooie for that. You're right, although planet-wreckers could make things pretty uncomfortable for our friends the Oswaft—not to mention our tender selves. And besides, in interstellar power politics, it's gestures and appearances that count, not actual results. I've long suspected that's why civilizations rise and fall. Especially fall. Try adjusting that vernier, will you? I thought I heard the field blades wobble a little when you nudged it before." He unstuck his cigar again and took a puff.

Another tentacle clicked at Vuffi Raa's "shoulder" and drifted away to check the readings on the control panels forward. It was possible, the droid thought, that the problem was simply an instrument failure, and it would be stupid to repair something that was already in perfect working order.

Each of the robot's five tentacles, usually tapering smoothly to a rounded tip, could also blossom at the end into a small five-fingered hand. In the center of each rested a miniature replica of the large red eye atop his body; he would see what his tentacles saw. This, and the ability to send his limbs off on various errands, caused him to wonder about his creators.

They were hardly stupid; still, there were counter-indications. Here he was, preparing his master's ship for a battle in which he, himself, dare not participate directly. Early in life, he had experimented: attempting combat, in contravention of his deepest-laid programming, had sent him into a coma that lasted nearly a month. He was extremely clever; he could run and hide; physically he was very tough; he could ally himself with individuals like Lando, *quite* capable of the defensive violence necessary to protect themselves and their mechanical partner, Vuffi Raa. But he, himself, simply could not harm another thinking being, whether organically evolved or artificially constructed.

It just didn't make sense. Vuffi Raa took a certain pride in the fact that he was a highly valuable machine, more so, strictly speaking, than the starship he was servicing. Simply as a market consideration, he had a duty to protect his life; anyone attempting to take it demonstrated, by that very act, that they were less valuable, at least in any moral sense that made sense.

Separating a third tentacle from his body, Vuffi Raa dispatched it to check the readiness of the ship's weapons systems, particularly the quad-guns of which Lando was so fond. The *Millennium Falcon* had always fairly bristled with armament, yet, with only two crew-beings to man her, and one of them a pacifist at that, they'd always meant to tie the weapons together cybernetically somehow. In this brief interlude between confrontations with the fleet, they'd scarcely more than begun the task.

His inhibitions could be stretched, Vuffi Raa had discovered. Knowing full well, for example, that the preparations furthered violent activity, he could nevertheless perform them. Moreover, he could fly the *Falcon* for Lando, maneuvering properly to assure his destruction of the enemy.

How very peculiar, thought the robot. Who made me this way, and what did they intend by it?

"WHAT IN THE NAME of the Edge, the Core, and everything in between are they *waiting* for out there?"

Lando fidgeted at the table as Vuffi Raa watched him disassemble and clean his tiny five-shot stingbeam as a final, albeit somewhat silly, preparation for the coming battle. They were in the passenger lounge. The deck-plate gravity was set at full normal, and that, thought the robot, was a bad sign. His master liked free-fall best for thinking.

"*For somebody else to get here,*" a tinny, electronically relayed voice answered. It was Lehesu, visible in a monitor screen the robot had installed. In reality, the great being hovered outside in the void not far from the *Falcon*. Given his size, and Lando's environmental requirements, this was the closest the three could come to normal face-to-face conversation.

"What?"

Lando stopped what he was doing with a jolt, one hand poised on the cleaning brush, elbow in the air, shoulders suddenly hunched as if someone had punched him in the stomach. He rose. Slowly he turned. Step by step he approached the monitor until his nose nearly rested on the screen. At his side, the half-cleaned weapon dripped solvent on the deck plates.

"*Who?*" he demanded of the manta creature. "And how the deuce do *you* know?" Some sort of fire flickered in the gambler's eyes, but even Vuffi Raa, long acquainted with the man's moods, couldn't guess what it signified now.

"*Why, Lando, somebody named Wennis,*" Lehesu answered in a tone of injured innocence. He'd come a long way, learning to interpret human vocal inflections and the images of facial expressions he received directly in his brain from the ship's transmitter. He was disturbed now because his friend looked and sounded angry with him.

"*As to how I know: it's practically the only thing they're talking about out there. Can't you hear them? Something's going to happen when Wennis gets here, something big. Somebody else named Scuttlebutt has it that—*"

"Oh my aching field density equalizers!" As the robot watched, his master's expression changed, like the face on a *sabacc* card, from puzzled to exasperated to delighted. The gambler crossed the room again in two strides, threw himself into a recliner, dug around in his shipsuit pockets and extracted a cigar.

"No, Lehesu, I *can't* hear them, remember? And even if I could—well, Vuffi Raa can 'hear' radio signals, but the military uses codes that are intended to preclude eavesdropping."

He lit the cigar, heedless of the flammable fluid all over his hands.

"*Dear me!*" cried the Oswaft in real distress, "*have I been doing something unethical? I shall cease immed—*"

Lando sat up abruptly, pointing his cigar at the monitor like a weapon. "You'll do nothing of the sort—you *can't* do anything unethical to those goons, it's philosophically impossible! Here I've been getting ready to die bravely, and now, casually, you've given us all a chance to survive! By gadfrey, Vuffi Raa, old cork-screw, let's break out a bottle of—OUUUUCH!"

Lando's hands glowed a flickering blue as he leaped up from the recliner and began running around the room. Without hesitation, Vuffi Raa thrust out a tentacle and tripped him; he flopped on the deck, yelling, while the robot tossed a jacket that had been hanging on the back of the lounger over the gambler's hands, and wrapped it tight. The fire was out.

"What's the matter over there?" the monitor demanded. "Are you all right?"

"I will be, once I learn not to play with fire," Lando answered as he sat up. He winced as Vuffi Raa unwrapped the jacket. His hands were tender, but not badly burned. The droid was gone a moment, returned with a sprayer of plaskin and coated Lando's hands until they were shiny with it.

The gambler flexed his fingers with satisfaction. "Pretty close, old fire extinguisher. I'd have had to pick a new profession if it weren't for your quick thinking. And if it weren't for this stuff—" With freshly dried digits, he examined the first-aid spray, then his brow furrowed in thought. He helped Vuffi Raa tidy up the gun-cleaning mess while explaining to the Oswaft what had happened, but his voice had an absent quality the robot recognized as the sign of an idea under incubation.

Finally, stubbornly, he relit the cigar he'd flung across the room, sat back in the recliner, and was silent for a solid hour. Vuffi Raa played a few hands of radio *sabacc* with Lehesu and let the gambler think. He was fresh out of ideas himself and, like his master, had been resigned to dying at as high a cost to their assailants as possible.

An odd thing, violence, he pondered, watching the computer change a Commander of Sabres in his "hand" to an Ace of Flasks. He'd inflicted violence on Lando in order to save him from a nasty burn, and hadn't felt a qualm down in his programming.

Yet, had some third person tried to harm Lando, the robot would have been helpless to remove the threat. Definitely a glitch there.

It bothered him.

"THE WENNIS IS A SHIP, Lehesu, like the *Falcon* here," Lando said an hour later over a steaming plate from the food-fixer.

"*So Vuffi Raa tells me. It's a difficult concept to grasp.*"

"Well, grasp this: it's the personal yacht of Rokur Gepta, Sorcerer of Tund. We've run into that fellow twice before, and not nicely either time. Now that I know he's involved, this whole blockade makes sense. The truce'll be over when he gets here."

The gambler suppressed a shudder, remembering previous confrontations. Once, in the Oseon, the sorcerer had used a device to stimulate every unpleasant memory Lando had, then recycle them, over and over, until he nearly went mad. It had been interference from Klyn Shanga, intent on destroying Vuffi Raa, that had accidentally saved him. They'd rescued Shanga from the wreck of his small fighter afterward and turned him over to the authorities in another system. He wondered where the man was now.

"Well, in any case, I think I've got an idea. You know, in order to win a war it isn't necessary to defeat your enemy, just make the fight so expensive he'll give up and go away."

"*I wouldn't know,*" the Oswaft answered, "*but what you say makes sense.*"

"Sure. As I explained to Vuffi Raa, this blockade's bound to have some opposition. It's already expensive, we merely have to make it more so."

"*How can we do that? We have no weapons, and the fleet, with its shields up, is no longer vulnerable to our voices, as was the* Courteous. *It has occurred to me that it was a good thing I was in a weakened condition when I met you, otherwise I might have destroyed you in the same manner.*"

The gambler waved a negligent hand at the monitor. "There

was only one of you, whereas I'm told there were a thousand Oswaft in the party that met the *Courteous*. Never mind that, we're going to let the fleet destroy itself."

"How?" Both Vuffi Raa and Lehesu spoke this time.

"I have some questions to ask you first: it's really true you can understand interfleet communications?"

"*Yes, Lando, so could any of my people, given a few moments' thought.*"

"Hmmm . . . All right, what about this synthesizing business. Can you make *any* substance I ask you to?"

"*As long as it's relatively simple and there are raw materials to hand, as it were.*"

"And the nebula: your elders tell me that there isn't any food there for you, that it was all 'grazed' out, long ago. Yet there are raw materials . . ."

"*Yes, Lando, where is all of this leading?*"

"Out of a mess. One more thing: how long do you have to rest between hyperjumps, and how accurately can you predict where you'll break out?"

"*Lando,*" the Oswaft said in exasperation, "*I think I see where you're going with this. You want us to make bombs or something and plant them on the fleet's vessels. In the first place, from what Vuffi Raa has told me of weaponry, bombs aren't all that simple. In the second—*"

"No, no. Nothing to do with bombs at all, and besides, those ships'll be coming in here shielded to a fare-thee-well. And in the second, I said we'll let them destroy themselves, didn't I? I have a plan to make the war expensive, that's all."

He hunched over the monitor, conspiratorially. Vuffi Raa leaned toward him, consumed by curiosity. Lando was clearly enjoying this part, and the robot wasn't sure that made him happy.

"Now here's what we'll do . . ."

XIV

"GENTLEMEN, MAN YOUR FIGHTERS!"

Klyn Shanga gazed across the cavernous cluttered hangar deck inside the *Wennis* as his squadron climbed into their tiny spacecraft. Even good old Bern was there, snaking up the ladder into his cockpit. He'd served his sentence in durance vile. Gepta had, surprisingly enough, been as good as his word about that.

It worried Shanga. He wondered what the old trickster had up his long gray sleeve. Keeping promises wasn't an expected part of the magician's repertoire, and the fighter commander felt it boded evil.

The noise was deafening as impellers whined, refueling lines were tucked away, commands shouted here and there. There was a constant steady rumble of eager machinery. In a few moments the hangar crew would clear the deck, all inner doors would be sealed, and the huge belly doors of the cruiser would cycle open, giving the Renatasians access to open space.

"THIS IS THE CONFRONTATION we've been waiting a decade for," Shanga had told his men, all twenty-three of them, lined up at a ragged, ill-disciplined attention in their shabby, mismatched uniforms. They represented a dozen old-style nation-states, most of which no longer existed. They flew craft purchased, borrowed, leased, and stolen from as many systems, the ships equally threadbare. In common the flyers shared only a thirst for revenge.

"The Butcher awaits us out there," Shanga had said, pointing vaguely toward the hangar doors overhead. Artificial gravity in the hangar had been reoriented to allow easier servicing and launching of the squadron. "He's laughing at us, you know. His very existence, ten years after his crimes, is a mockery of justice. Well, we will silence that laughter, bring justice back to the universe!"

There was no cheering. Some of the warship's crew members working on the Renatasian squadron had looked up momentarily, impressed more at Shanga's vehemence than at any eloquence he might have possessed. To individuals in a hierarchy such as they served, strong feelings openly expressed were a threat to survival, the highest virtues moderation, compromise, a deaf ear and a blind eye to injustice.

There was nodding among the twenty-three at Shanga's words, acceptance, a grim agreement, a pact. They looked at their commander and at one another, realizing that it might be for the last time.

"And afterward?" Bern Nuladeg lounged against the outstretched wing of one fighter at the end of the line of men, chewing an unlit cigar. "What'll we do then?"

"Afterward, we'll . . ." Shanga tapered off. He hadn't planned for there to *be* any afterward. There were a billion or more Oswaft out there, of uncertain capability, allied with the unspeakable Vuffi Raa. The chances any Renatasian would survive the next few hours were slight. Moreover, their safety afterward, in Gepta's hands, was questionable. The sorcerer would be completely unpredictable once he'd won his victory. There'd be nothing to come back to, not in a fleet commanded from the *Wennis*.

Shanga shook his head as if to clear it of useless speculations. "Afterward you're on your own. Rendezvous with whatever ship will pick you up. Get home the best way you can—if you want to go home. For the time being, my friends, we live only for justice, only for revenge."

There was muttering, but it was in resigned agreement with what their commander had said. If there was any future, let it come on its own terms, its very arrival a surprise.

They boarded their fighting vessels.

SHANGA STRAPPED HIMSELF into his pilot's couch, made sure the canopy seals were good, that all mobile service implements had been properly detached and the access ports dogged down. He watched the hangarmen file out through various oval doorways in an unpanicky haste as the big red lights came on to signal the beginning of the cycling process. In effect, the hanger now became a huge airlock; he knew from long experience that, despite the best efforts to filter and scrub the salvaged air, the rest of the ship, from control deck through officer's country down to the scuppers, would smell of aerospace volatiles for several hours.

It was a good smell, he thought to himself, an agreeable one to die with in your lungs if you couldn't arrange for soft grass and evergreen boughs.

He flipped switches and the whining of his engines raised in pitch, the cockpit vibration skipped a beat and settled in a newer discordance with the other machine noises. Adrenaline was rushing into his bloodstream. By the Core, he was a *warrior.* Say what you like about that, you simpering peace-dogs, he was born and bred to *fight*!

The hangar doors above him ponderously ground aside.

"Five and Eighteen out!" a voice said in his helmet. Two fighters filled the hangar with exhaust mist as they lifted and roared out into space. The vapor cleared quickly.

"Fourteen and Nine out!"

"Six and Seventeen!"

In pairs his men took to the void, as eager for a fight as he was. His onboard computer held a three-dimensional map of the Thon-Boka with probable locations for the *Millennium Falcon* marked therein. It was known that there were three small blue-white stars, and some artificial structure, much larger than the freighter, at their center. That would be the prime area for the search.

The "destroy" part would follow immediately.

"Two and Twenty-one!" another voice shouted, then Shanga himself felt a severe jolt and the blood stress of acceleration as the hangar catapult-pressor latched onto his command ship and flung it into space among his men. Others continued to pour from the *Wennis* in the same manner, in an order tactically determined by the motley mixture of ship types and models available to them. *"Nineteen and Four!"*

They assumed a complicated formation, hovering until all of the squadron was free of the hangar bay. In the center of the group lay Pinnace Number Five, the very auxiliary Bern Nuladeg had been apprehended trying to steal. Her after section glowed and pulsed with pent-up energy. They were still a relatively long way from the nebula, at least where the small fighters' capabilities were concerned. Even once they got there, it was six light-years to the center—approximately twenty-five times their own maximum flying range.

The pinnace, capable of faster-than-light travel, had been fitted with a tractor field. Unmanned, controlled remotely by Klyn Shanga, it would tow them into the heat of battle, returning parsimoniously on its own to the *Wennis*. He and his best computer doctor had checked the lend-lease auxiliary carefully from bow to stern for ugly practical jokes and delayed-action booby traps. He just couldn't bring himself to trust Rokur Gepta's generosity.

That worthy had been unavailable at debarkation time, apparently gone off to meditate or something. Just as well: his orders to release the Renatasian squadron had been there in his place. To the Edge with the sorcerer, Shanga thought. With any luck at all, they'd never see each other again.

He tapped the keyboard, checking the positions of his tiny fleet clustered about the pinnace. "This is Zero Leader," he announced. "Eleven, tighten up a little on Twelve—that's it. Twenty-two, you're idling a little ragged, aren't you? What's your toroid temperature?"

The fusion-powered fighters would conserve reaction mass, relying on the cruiser's auxiliary to do the work, but they must keep their systems up for instant combat readiness. Belt and suspenders, Shanga thought, belt and suspenders. The old saw was wrong about old, bold pilots, but this was the only way it could be done.

"*Nominal,*" Twenty-two replied. He was a young kid from a continent half a world away from Mathilde, Shanga's nation-state. There'd been a time when he'd been supposed to hate that accent. "*I think the trouble's in the telemetry, sir.*"

"Don't call me sir, Twenty-two, and watch that temperature. I want the Butcher just as badly as you do, but charging in there with a malfunctioning ship isn't going to help any of us accomplish that. I don't trust those maintenance people to clean their own fingernails. You'd better be telling me the truth, son."

"*Well, sir—Klyn—maybe I'm a little in the red, but I think this hop will burn out the hot spots.*"

"All right," Shanga replied grudgingly. "Twenty-three, what the Core's wrong with your life-support? I've got red lights all over the readout!"

"Just lit my cigar, boss. The atmo-analyzer don't like it much." Bern Nuladeg laughed. "Can't get into a dogfight without a stogie in my mouth. I'd bite my danged tongue!"

Shanga grinned inside his helmet, suppressed a chuckle. "Roger, Twenty-three, it's your funeral. All right, men, synch your navi-mods to me. We'll move on the tick. Four, three, two, *one—unh!*"

As a unit, the entire squadron lurched forward, propelled by the pinnace, began accelerating smoothly, and moved off toward the ThonBoka. Now, before the coming disorientation of the jump, Shanga and his men had time to look around them.

Ahead, the StarCave looked like a huge eyeball seen in profile. They approached the entrance obliquely to maximize the element

of surprise. It was a stupid ritual, Shanga realized; they'd be seen
coming anyway. But it was something to begin the program with;
it didn't really matter. A huge gray eyeball with no iris, a pupil
that twinkled with three tiny blue-white highlights. Down deep
inside that thing was the Enemy. Deep down inside that thing
was death.

With a joyous shout of violated natural law, the squadron
leaped toward it.

W325 WAS THE DESIGNATION of a very small bathtub-shaped object whose size and power output did not quite earn it the status
of an auxiliary vessel. More than anything else, it was a rigid,
powered spacesuit, used to inspect and repair the hull of the
Wennis while she was in deep space—but most assuredly *not*
under way.

At the moment, W325 was electromagnetically tied in place
well aft of the hull to a boxlike addition to the superstructure
supporting the cruiser's main drive tubes. While their fires were
momentarily quenched to allow the launching of Klyn Shanga's
squadron, they still glowed with waste heat energy. Attached to
the underside of W325 was a decal in the shape of a human
being. More correctly, a human being in the shape of a decal.

The *Ottdefa* Osuno Whett, anthropologist and master spy,
knew he was taking a terrible chance. That was always the case
when serving two masters. He owed Rokur Gepta his assistance
and advice—and stood to benefit by it to the tune of the destruction of his enemies. To one other, he owed everything, including
his life, if need be. His immediate assignment was keeping an eye
on the perfidious sorcerer. Gepta was not trusted as naively as he
may have thought, gift cruiser or no gift cruiser.

Thus, encased in a slim, flexible spacesuit whose color had
been adjusted to match that of W325, the anthropologist lay
spread, arms and legs stretched wide, as tightly as he could to the
undersurface of the little space-faring object while its master was

otherwise occupied. Whett's own attention was elsewhere; he watched the readouts in his helmet closely, his curiosity and excitement mounting.

Above, Rokur Gepta cycled out of the small vessel, moved across to the rear surface of the superstructure addition. Whett had already determined, by means of various probes and rays, that the unconventional add-on was composed of hull armor, thicker than most and impenetrable to his devices. He'd suspected something like this and come forearmed. It had not been easy to strew the sorcerer's path with a dozen information-gathering devices, each the size of a single dust mote, but he had done it. Some of them read out in real time. They would be useless in another moment. But some absorbed what they witnessed and would spew it all out in a fraction of a microsecond once Whett was within receiving range again.

Whett waited.

At the rear of the armored compartment, the sorcerer hung. There was no port within sight, no airlock. Whett wondered mightily about that. He did not believe in the reputed powers of the Sorcerers of Tund. He'd seen far too much primitive mumbo jumbo backed up by trickery and hidden technology to be impressed by such claims. He wished that he dared peek out around the hull of *W325* to see what was happening. Instead, he relied on his devices.

Oddly, the real-time machinery gave the impression that Gepta hadn't bothered with a spacesuit. Strange, but not totally unaccountable. No one was quite sure what species Gepta belonged to although he deliberately gave the impression he was human. And there were a people or two that could stand hard vacuum for several minutes—and of course there were the Oswaft . . . There was also the possibility that the sorcerer concealed life-support equipment beneath his robes. It would be like him, and indeed, the lightweight pressure suit the anthropologist wore could be concealed thus.

Whett waited.

As expected, the telltales in his helmet winked off abruptly. Gepta had entered the compartment and was now shielded by what the spy estimated to be at least a meter of incredibly tough state-of-the-art alloy. Slowly he detached himself from the underside of the maintenance vehicle, worked out a few stiff joints, and peered cautiously around the bulge of the craft.

Gepta was gone. There was no sign of him. Nor was there any sign of the means by which he'd entered. One instrument on Whett's helmet panel flickered fitfully in response to radiation leakage. Something hot was going on inside the shielded compartment, but he couldn't tell what. Whatever it was, it was unfamiliar.

He jetted up smoothly to the rear of the compartment and inspected it closely. As he had guessed, there was no airlock, no door of any kind. He rounded the corner and inspected a side, then another and another and another. No sign. He applied sophisticated instruments, highly developed skills. It was a solid box of metal, approximately ten meters on a side, featureless, except . . .

But that was ridiculous. Precisely in the center of the aftmost surface was a service petcock, opening on a pipeway no more than four centimeters in diameter. He didn't dare lift the cover, but he hung there in free-fall for a dangerously long while pondering, running through a catalog in his head of species and their capabilities.

The Sorcerers of Tund. No investigator—spy or anthropologist—had ever gotten a crack at those mysterious old prunes. He'd regretted Gepta's decision to pick him up in transit; he'd wanted to see Tund, be the first. His employer would have liked that, too.

The Sorcerers of Tund were reputed to have some mighty powers—if you believed in that nonsense—but he couldn't recall any legends about dematerialization or the ability to squeeze through tiny apertures. Magic? Perhaps there was something, after all, to the idea that . . .

But that was ridiculous.

XV

Aboard the *Wennis*, Rokur Gepta prepared himself for
battle.

There were mental exercises peculiar to Tund, disciplines of
ancient ancestry; weapons to inspect, both personal and aboard
the cruiser; personnel to instruct and threaten. Communications
had begun flowing from the fleet. Gepta occupied the bridge,
watching, listening, replying. A steady traffic of messengers
rushed back and forth between the sorcerer and a hundred points
within the ship.

"No," Gepta hissed at the monitor before him, "you will *not*
deviate from your designated position, my dear Captain, even to
pursue escaping vessels—*especially* not to defend yourself. Is my
meaning clear, sir? You are a ship of the line. You are expected to
perform your duty as specified, never to question orders, to consider yourself and your command expendable in the service of
society.

"We have now spoken for two minutes too long on this subject. Out."

He waved a hand; the disappointed features of the captain of
the *Intractable* faded from the screen. It was the third such conversation he'd conducted within the hour, and he was growing
weary of it. Only the thought of what lay aft in its armored compartment, the lovely green death, enabled him to remain calm.

"General Order!"

An electronically equipped secretary hurried to his side, a recording device clutched fearfully in hand. "While it should not be necessary," Gepta dictated, "to instruct officers of the line in their duties, some question has arisen as to the advisability of their writing their own orders upon no other discretion than the wish to preserve their ship or their personal interpretation of their purposes in being here.

"To resolve these uncertainties, and as an example for future individualists, the commanding officers of the *Intractable,* the *Upright,* and the *Vainglorious* are hereby stripped of rank, along with their seconds in command. Said command will revert to the third officer in succession, and the six above-mentioned personnel will be placed unprotected in an airlock, which shall be evacuated into empty space.

"By the authority of Rokur Gepta, Sorcerer of Tund. Did you get all of that, young man?"

The stenographer, his face grown white, nodded dazedly. "Y-Yes, sir."

"Good. Send it out and make sure it's understood that the order is to be carried out immediately. Now run along."

Beneath his headdress windings, Gepta smiled. Aside from his two sessions in the armored compartment aft, this was the best he'd felt all day.

VUFFI RAA SAT in the left-hand seat of the control room of the *Millennium Falcon,* setting up problems on the navigational console and cross-playing them through his master's game computer. He had to admit, Lando had been right. His scheme wouldn't win a war, and it might cost a great many lives on both sides, but it would wear the fleet down and encourage Gepta's political opponents to step in and end the blockade. Had he been capable of shaking his head ironically, he would have done so.

He looked out through the segmented viewport forward, where he saw Lehesu hanging peacefully—at least to all appearances. He keyed the com. "I have completed the modeling exercise, friend Lehesu. I believe we have a good chance. Will you not join the others with their preparations?"

The giant creature swam closer to the *Falcon* and peered in at his little robot friend. "*No, Vuffi Raa. I am aware of what I must do, and I am ready. I was curious as to the projections you are undertaking. Will the fleet truly destroy itself if Lando's plan works?*"

The droid raised a tentacle to indicate certainty since he couldn't nod. "Yes, as unbelievable as it may seem. You are an amazing people, my friend, and that's what makes it possible. The *Falcon* is as ready as she'll ever be, although I—"

"*You are troubled, Vuffi Raa?*" Lehesu could interpret tones of voice even with a mechanical being. "*Please speak to me about it; perhaps that will help.*"

Glancing mentally at the timepiece he carried in his circuitry, the robot gave his equivalent of a shrug. "It is like this, Lehesu . . ." He told the Oswaft of the conflicts he felt in his programming and that he was beginning to disapprove of those who had imposed it on him. It didn't seem right that he should be compelled to stand by idly—at least what he considered to be idly—while the navy exterminated a gentle, admirable people.

"*I see,*" the alien replied at last. "*You know, we are in much the same position. I do not know whether I can take a life in my own defense, either. We are not a fighting people, as you so rightly have observed. Perhaps it is time for us to abandon life to make room for a more successful product of evolution.*"

The robot, not knowing what to say, said nothing.

"*Then again, Vuffi Raa, we should go away only if we cannot change. If we can, we are a successful species, are we not?*"

Momentarily, Vuffi Raa wished he could smoke a cigar like his master. It seemed to help the human think, and it lent a certain dignity to whatever answer he might give the Oswaft. "I do not know, my friend. It seems wrong somehow that the success of a race be measured by its ability to do violence. There are other things in the universe."

The Oswaft was no more capable of nodding than the robot. *"Still, one must consider that none of these things are any good to one if one is dead."*

Vuffi Raa chuckled. "You have a point, there, Lehesu, you have a point."

"WE ARE GOING to be too late!" the Other complained. "I know it!"

"Peace, my old friend," the One replied. "That is not yet a foregone conclusion. There are no foregone conclusions anymore. And even so, it is an experiment. It would not be valid, did we interfere. Any result is a desired result, am I not correct in this?"

They bored through the endless night at a velocity that seemed a crawl to them, although a good many physicists would have been interested to know such a velocity was possible. Behind them stretched an endless line, the Rest who had come to witness the results of the One's experiment.

"However," the Other replied, hesitating in his thought if not in his headlong flight, "I have had a disturbing new thought which—"

"That was the purpose of the experiment, was it not?"

"Yes, yes. But I do not believe you are going to be particularly happy with it. You see, it has occurred to me that, despite the unconventional methods by which you created our experimental subject, and despite the obvious anatomical differences . . ." Here, the Other made a gesture emphasizing the smooth, rounded shape of their kind.

"Yes? Please continue."

"Do not be impatient; this is difficult. I have come to believe we have certain responsibilities toward this entity—specifically that you do—beyond simple scientific inquiry."

There was a long pause as another several parsecs whisked

behind them. Nor did the One reply at all. For once his friend had pursued a line of reasoning where he could not easily follow.

"You are its parent."

"What?"

"You brought it into existence. You sent it out into the universe. We—you—cannot blandly let it be destroyed. Such would be reprehensible."

Again the One failed to respond. The light-years rushed by as he plunged himself deep into thought, pondering not only the question of his responsibility, but the more disturbing thought that he had overlooked the issue entirely. Their experimental subject was a thinking being, not to be trifled with as if it were an inanimate object. Apparently complacency had cost him more than progress and the flavor of life, it had interfered badly with his ethical sensibilities.

At last: "I am afraid you are right, my old friend. Congratulate me, I am a father. And by all means, let us hurry, lest we be too late!"

"IT'S SIMPLE, REALLY," Lando explained for the fifth time with as little hope of success as he'd enjoyed the first four. "You jump into the middle of a pair of ships, do the little trick we've discussed, and jump out. The navy'll do the rest."

The gambler floated in the lotus position in the center of the Cave of the Elders, Sen and Fey on either side of him. Each of the gigantic beings was at least five hundred times larger than he was. He felt like a virus having polite tea with a pair of bacteria.

"But Captainlandocalrissiansir, it is disgusting!" Fey complained. "It is demeaning, beneath the dignity of any—"

"How do you feel about losing your transparency?"

"What do you mean?"

Lando drew on the cigar he'd gotten Vuffi Raa to build a holder for in his suit helmet. There was a slight bulge now in the faceplate, and the air filters had needed overhauling, but at long last he could sit and think properly in hard vacuum.

"Isn't death demeaning, beneath your dignity, disgusting?"

There was the distinct sensation that the younger of the two Elders had blinked with surprise. "Why, I had never thought of it that way before."

Sen had remained silent through this argument. Now he spoke up. "Tell me, Lando, could you perform the physiological equivalent of this act? To excrete bodily wastes in order to—"

"You bet your biffy I could! Look: all that this requires is that you concentrate a certain mix of heavy metals in your systems, hop to the right coordinates, let your pores do their work, and hop out, leaving a sensor-detectable Oswaft-shaped outline behind for the boys in gray to shoot at. Play your cards right and, human reaction-time being what it is, they'll shoot each other, instead."

Sen and Fey thought about that. For rather too long a time, Lando thought.

"Listen, you two, you didn't hesitate to offer me all kinds of precious jewels, and you manufacture them in the same—"

"It's not the same at all!" Fey wailed. "Don't you understand that it's different when one—"

"Not from *my* cultural standpoint. On the other hand, navy humans I know see a big ethical difference between killing animals for food and killing vegetables—although I've met a photosynthetic sentient or two who might give them an argument. Let's leave it that cultures often have blindnesses about themselves where other cultures see more clearly. Can you do this thing?"

The soft twinkling of precious stones gleamed through the transparent Elders. "Those of us who can will rendezvous with you at your signal."

The gambler shrugged. "Guess I can't ask for more than that, can I?"

He sensed that Sen was smiling. "No, I suppose you cannot, unless one wishes to emulate the enemy we are about to fight."

———

As HIS FIGHTER squadron passed through the mouth of the Thon-Boka, Klyn Shanga was fighting a nagging thought. Like a tune that circles through your consciousness all day (whether you like the tune or not—and, more often than not, you don't), he was wondering about the *Ottdefa* Osuno Whett. Why did that son-of-a-mynock seem so familiar? Where had he seen him before?

"Seventeen, square up a little on the mark. You're lagging, and it's putting a strain on the pinnace."

"Roger, Zero Leader. Executing."

He gave a quick glance at the other computer-generated indicators on his boards and settled back in his acceleration couch again. Where had he met the tall, skinny, white-haired anthropologist before, and why did he have trouble thinking of him as an academic. What should he be? A flunky of some kind. Whett was born to be a subordinate.

But why? He came to the conclusion that it wasn't Whett's appearance he remembered so vividly. The voice, then? A high, whiny, nagging voice it was, full of a high opinion of himself that didn't seem to fit the vague memory Shanga had. It was like the false memories one experiences in dreams: you wake up suddenly (and often with relief) knowing that the thing you remembered never happened at all. But Whett was real.

"Twenty-three to Zero Leader, over."

"Go ahead, Bern."

"Sure. How come we're not maintaining comm silence on this run? I thought we were gonna surprise the little—"

"They know we're coming, and there's only one direction we can come from."

"Kinda like that first raid we made south of Mathilde, after the Betrayal, right?" Nuladeg chuckled at the blood-soaked memory. It was the only thing they could do. The reminiscence wasn't that pleasant, although they'd killed a thousand enemies that morning, caught them on the ground before they got set up

for defense. He remembered the shock he'd felt at the invasion, after all the friendly welcoming they'd done for Vuffi Raa and—

Now why did *that* make him think of Whett again?

"Zero Leader to Twenty-three. Bern, have you seen Gepta's pet anthropologist, Osuno Whett?"

"Can't say as I have. How come?" Shanga could see the other fighter's craft on the opposite side of the formation, its cockpit full of cigar smoke. He wondered how the little man breathed in that atmosphere.

"I don't know, Bern, but there's something nagging me, and it seems to be important."

"Stop chewing on it, then, boss. Sleep it over. It'll come to you if it's important. Core, you could use a little shut-eye, anyways. Sit yourself back, and I'll take the con for a while."

"Thanks a lot, Bern, I appreciate it."

"Just so you don't make a habit of it."

"Roger, Twenty-three, and out."

THE OTTDEFA OSUNO WHETT looked over some highly peculiar data as he sat in the cramped confines of his hiding place. Outside, the stars appeared motionless through the ports. It was an illusion.

According to the almost microscopic spy devices he'd planted on Gepta with only partial success, the wizard had indeed entered that armored compartment aft of the *Wennis* through a tube scarcely larger than a child's wrist diameter. And somewhere within that tube, according to these readouts, Gepta had ceased to exist, for the dust-mote-sized recorders had drifted in the tube and remained there, recording nothing, until the sorcerer again became himself.

Whatever *that* was.

Whett shifted uncomfortably on his couch, not daring to show a light that might be seen from the outside, not believing the readouts, their displays stopped down to near invisibility. He'd known others in his field—anthropology, not spying—who'd eventually come to believe in the primitive magic they studied, otherwise serious scholars who thought that dancing, after all, at least when performed a certain way by a certain people, could bring rain. Good minds gone to rot from nothing more than overexposure, some malignant form of osmosis. He'd always resisted that, regarded it as a failure both of scientific detachment and personal integrity. Now, he wasn't sure.

All right, the Sorcerers of Tund were supposed to have been capable of all kinds of magic. No one had ever claimed that they were even human; that was a general assumption and, like all general assumptions, was probably mistaken. Nonetheless . . .

What species was *naturally* capable of the thing his instruments had witnessed? Gepta had returned through the tube, the electronic motes adhering to him again as he, what—materialized? And what was that weird, unknown radiation that, despite armor he now realized was not one but two meters thick, incredibly still leaked out when Gepta had been inside the compartment for a few minutes?

And most of all, what, in the Name of the Core, *was* Rokur Gepta?

XVI

"MASTER, WE'VE GOT COMPANY!"

"All right, Vuffi Raa, I'm coming!"

Lando jumped up from his seat in the lounge where he'd been programming tactics for the Oswaft. Out of over a billion of the creatures, less than a thousand had agreed to play his great game of *sabacc,* live or die. He ran around the corridor to the cockpit and flung himself into the right-hand seat.

"Where away?"

The robot indicated a tightly strung series of blips on the long-range sensors. "Fighters, Master, the same kind we fought in the Oseon. I make it twenty—no, twenty-five. I don't know what that big thing in the middle is."

The gambler nodded. "I wonder if it isn't the same group. They don't look like a tactical fighter wing, and they're using the same formation they did before. Last time it was a battleship engine." He began throwing switches, bringing the *Falcon*'s defensive armament to full readiness.

"Oh my," Vuffi Raa said in a subdued voice, "the Renatasians. Sometimes I think it would be better just to surrender myself to them. If only they knew the truth."

"Cut it out, sprocket-head! They *know* the truth. It's just too hard to let go of a scapegoat once you've got him by the chin whiskers. Let's surprise those mynock-smoochers by going out to meet them, what say?"

The robot's tentacles began dancing over the boards. "My

sentiments exactly, Master. That's what we came here for in the first place, wasn't it?"

Lando rose, steadying himself against a chair as vibrations washed through the ship. "Quite right, although I wasn't sure we'd sucker the Renatasians in, too. Gepta's overdue. How can he resist having us trapped here in the StarCave?"

"Don't worry, Master, he'll show up."

"Swell." The gambler made haste aft to the tunnel connecting with the quad-gun bubble, reached the swiveling chair, and strapped himself in. "Well, old friend, let's go!"

"Yes, Master," the intercom answered. "Full power coming up!"

As the Falcon rushed to meet the foe, Lando reviewed his plans. The Oswaft wouldn't strike the small group of fighters. He'd cranked his ideas through the computer and, from there, directly into their brains. They now knew as much about tactics as he did.

Refocusing on the task at hand, he limbered up, swung the guns up and down, side to side. The chair followed with them, giving him an exhilarating ride that was probably the real reason he liked the weapon so much. He keyed the intertalkie. "Test coming up—and don't call me master."

"Yes, Mas—"

"Got you that time." Using one of the stars for a point of aim, he pressed both thumbs down on the triggers. Bolts of high-intensity energy shot from the guns as they pumped back and forth in their odd pattern, much like the reciprocating machine guns of old. Only now, it was to avoid a backwash of power that would have fused the muzzles of the nonfiring barrels. He fired the guns again, then looked at the repeater screen to see what Vuffi Raa was seeing up ahead.

"One thousand kilometers and closing, Master. That central object is a ship's pinnace. I believe they used it for tow. Shields up at eight-fifty kilometers. They're beginning to cast off the pinnace."

"Hold her steady, little friend. Let them make the first pass."

On his screen, Lando could see that the fighters had erected their deflection, too. Fighter shields were notoriously porous; there just wasn't enough ship—or engine—to support them. That's one thing that made a vessel the size of the *Falcon* so handy.

"Five hundred kilometers, Master."

Now the fighters were visible as tiny dots of light, pseudostars against the starry background of the ThonBoka mouth. Lando brought his guns to bear, swinging to meet the enemies' maneuvers, getting a feel for them. Felt like Klyn Shanga's bunch, all right. Apparently they'd teamed up with the sorcerer and the navy.

Two fighters streaked over the Falcon. Lando poured destructive energy at them, but the pass was too fast for either side to do any damage. They were probably confirming that this was, indeed, the *Millennium Falcon,* Vuffi Raa, a.k.a. the Butcher of Renatasia, first mate.

The robot heeled the ship steeply. *"Two coming up from below!"*

"Let 'em come!" The ship's beefed-up shields would be a surprise. Lando held his fire until the last moment, then pounded into the larger ship of the two. Its shielding lasted all of a millisecond, then there was an explosion and the vessel corkscrewed off, badly damaged.

He swung the guns around, but the second fighter had passed overhead and was gone. One down, he thought, and by Vuffi Raa's estimate, twenty-four to go. "Damage report!"

"Nothing to report, Master. Our shields held fine."

"You do great work. Where'd they go?"

The question was answered as six fighters bored directly for the freighter. Lando sprayed the space in front of them with energy, the ship's lights dimming briefly as he did. They veered sharply, unable to match his fire at that range.

"Master! Bandits straight ahead! Eleven of them!"

"Well, slew the ship! I can't reach them from here! No! Cancel that! I've got trouble enough!"

Four of the original six were back, shooting hard. Lando matched them shot for shot, smoked another, then caught a fighter with a direct hit. It blossomed into an enormous ball of tiny sparks and disappeared. But the others didn't give up yet. Even the wounded ship executed a wide, clumsy circle and came back. Lando centered the lead fighter in his crosshairs, thumbed the ignition, and growled.

Another fireball. Another hit on the crippled ship, which wobbled, skidded off, then suddenly exploded. The remaining fighter fought its way around a corner and lunged out of range. It'd be back.

"Clear, now! Turn the ship!"

"*Too late, Master. I destroyed two fighters and the other nine broke off.*"

There was a long, startled pause that nearly cost the two their lives. A single fighter came in at top speed, fired all its retros, dumped its load of lethal energy directly onto the stern tubes, the weakest portion of the shielding. Lando started, more frightened at his inattention than by the fighter. He swung the quad-guns aft, fired and fired until the single fighter vanished in a cloud of smoke.

The pilot of that vessel couldn't have been more surprised than Lando was. "You say you shot down two fighters, old pacifist?" This much was true: there was a pair of small guns, usually ineffective against anything bigger than a rowboat, located on the upper surface of the ship and controllable from the cockpit. Lando had wanted them synchronized, which would effectively quadruple their power, and Vuffi Raa had gotten around to it in the last few days.

Still, there was no reply from the control deck.

"Vuffi Raa, are you all right?"

No answer.

The fighter group had broken off momentarily, licking their

wounds, no doubt, and sizing up the *Falcon*. If it was Shanga's people, they were probably surprised to meet *two* columns of fire coming in.

Or were they? Tactically, they'd known Vuffi Raa couldn't shoot back, yet politically (psychologically? sociologically?) he was the most murderous villain in their history. How did they resolve a conflict like that?

"Vuffi Raa, speak to me!"

"*Yes, Master. I beg your pardon, and I'll tell you all about it later. No time now—our friends are back!*"

This time they came in force. Lando counted seventeen before he got busy, which agreed approximately with the five kills and one probable they'd scored thus far. Lando wasn't taking trophies; it wasn't in him to do it. He simply wanted to know how near the end of the fight they were getting. He wanted a cigar.

This time they gave it all they had, as well. Lando slugged it out, and he could sense the drain on the ship's engines that meant Vuffi Raa was shooting while he steered the ship. Still, the shields were taking a terrific pounding, and yellow lights, to judge from the robot's shouted reports, were showing up like fireflies on the boards.

Then a bright light bloomed where Lando's guns weren't pointed and Vuffi Raa's couldn't be. Standing off, without the benefit of shields, was Lehesu. He turned slowly, majestically, "shouted" at another fighter, which turned into a knot of greasy smoke, then disappeared himself, to show up on the other side of the ship.

The fighters broke off at some distance; peace reigned momentarily.

"Lehesu, you old ace! I thought you were with your people!"

"*My people are intelligent life everywhere, Captainmaster. I saw you needed help, and—*"

The gambler frowned. "I wouldn't exactly say we needed help, exactly." Retrieving a cigar from where he'd tucked it in his boot top, he lit it and settled back for a moment.

"I would," Vuffi Raa said. *"Thank you, Lehesu, and thank you for the talk. I seem to have resolved the conflict in my programming."*

Keeping an eye on the indicators for further intruders, Lando asked, "Where are your people, Lehesu? Are they waiting to follow my program?"

"No, Captainmaster. Instead, they have followed your example. They have gone to confront the fleet instead of waiting for it."

THE ENTITY WHOM Lando referred to as Sen was gratified. Something far more than a thousand Oswaft swam now behind him, many more than he had counted on, shamed by Captainmaster-landocalrissiansir's valiant example—and possibly his successes against the first wave of the enemy. He directed a thought toward Fey.

"How many would you say we are, old friend?"

"Perhaps as many as a million. The rest have followed another of the human's suggestions: they are concealing themselves in the walls of the StarCave."

A mental shrug. "Well, they may be right, and that may save us from extinction better than doing battle with these monsters. This idea of individual dissent that Lehesu forced upon us may have its uses. Different opinions produce different modes of survival, one or more of which may succeed."

The fleet grew as they approached it.

"I do not know," Fey said. "I believe I would prefer to be playing *sabacc* just now. The notion of being killed—"

"Is faintly refreshing," finished the older of the two Elders. "Lehesu is right: it is better than sitting around becoming stagnant."

"Everyone to his own preferences," Fey answered wryly.

———

ABOARD THE *RELUCTANT,* a gunner's mate finally tore his eyes away from the scope. "A million of 'em! Core save us, there's a million of 'em out there!"

His supervisor hurried over, looked down from the catwalk into the mate's instruments while the mate looked up in fear and wonder at him. "You're wrong, son, the computer's making a new estimate. Make that *two* million."

SEN CHUCKLED TO himself as he hopped out of the artificial skin he'd just generated, leaving it behind to confound the enemy. Their sensors would now be registering three million Oswaft, and even if they fathomed the trick, they wouldn't know which outline to shoot at.

One chance in three of getting killed, instead of unity. You could learn things from *sabacc.* He hopped another hundred meters, paused, and made it one chance in four. Every step his people took this way increased their apparent numbers arithmetically. The real test would come when they reached the fleet and began swimming in its midst.

"Are you ready, old friend?" asked Fey at his side.

"No. Let's go."

Their first leap took them within firing distance of the *Reluctant.* Before she could bring their guns to bear, they were gone. Sen angled his next jump to place him between that vessel and the next in the metallic swarm. He hopped, created a ghost of himself, and hopped again, this time to a safe place where he could watch.

Reluctant belied her name and *fired*! The powerfully huge bolt, a recent Imperial development, sliced through the false Oswaft, scoring a deep and crippling hit on her sister vessel, who had fired only slightly behind the other ship. This bolt was a near miss, but it caught an escort fighter and vaporized him instantly. The Oswaft outline dissolved and was gone.

Sen jumped again, creating another threatening image of himself. It had much the same effect as the first: the enemy counted on a target to absorb the lethal force of his guns before they struck a sister vessel. They were wrong, and discovering it too slowly. A million Oswaft followed Sen and Fey, repeating the same actions. Space was lit with thousands of fierce, futile bolts. Men died by the hundreds until the trick was finally puzzled out.

By then it was too late. Shouting at the top of his voice, Sen crumpled a pair of fighters, then concentrated his energies on a cruiser. Lando was right: her shields were too dense to have any effect. He stopped shouting at everything but the gnatlike fighters, and hopped and hopped, making sure each time to place himself between two capital ships.

For their part, as they saw the destruction of their own numbers by their own guns, the navy slowed even more, trying to aim its fire so as not to endanger the fleet. This was useless: either there was nothing to shoot at, or the bolt would knife through the observed enemy, blasting a cruiser or a dreadnaught instead.

In fifteen minutes, the fleet was reduced by 11 percent. Then the shooting stopped.

By that time, Shanga's diminished squadron had made two more runs against the *Falcon*, losing another fighter. With Vuffi Raa at the controls, the freighter had gradually drawn them nearer where the fleet was busily destroying itself. Fire leaped here and there, lighting up the eternal night. Navy fighters blew up, showering their mother vessels with debris, spreading damage further. The Oswaft darted in and out, their numbers very slightly diminished, too, as the sentients grew tired or careless.

Aboard the *Falcon*, Lando bore down on the quad-gun once again, turning a small spacecraft into drifting junk.

"Say, that wasn't one of our bandits! That was a navy fighter. Where the Core are we, Vuffi Raa?"

From the control room, the robot replied. *"Entering the zone of conflict between the Oswaft and the fleet. I'll try to keep us clear of any large ships, since we—there! got another one!—since we can't maneuver like the spacepeople."*

A cluster of fighters swooped past the *Falcon,* ignoring her while blasting toward a cruiser that was breaking up. Three Oswaft, concentrating all their power, had done that when one of her shields was down momentarily, due to a collision with a fighter.

Suddenly, Shanga's men were back, diving on the *Falcon* by turns, drawing her fire, getting in shots of their own. There was only one of Lando, and his arms were getting weary from their constant work at the quad-guns. The *Falcon* looped and soared, outmaneuvering the fighters again and again. Weapons flared, men died.

Without warning, all action ceased among the fleet. The blast and brilliance of shooting stopped as if someone had turned a switch. Every fighter was recalled.

At the center of things now, Lando and Vuffi Raa and Lehesu watched as a broad corridor was cleared among the ships. Shields up, they were immune to the Oswaft, and, as long as they didn't fire on the vacuum-breathers, they suffered no more losses.

"Something on the scope, Master."

"Keep me advised."

Through the space cleared by the fleet, an older-model cruiser became visible, surface-coated dead black, bristling with an array of unfamiliar equipment. On its underside were emblazoned the arms of Rokur Gepta himself. On its sides were added the ship's name:

WENNIS

"—by edict! You are commanded to cease fire and to surrender to the nearest Imperial vessel immediately."

Apparently, Vuffi Raa had found the navy's frequency—or they had found the *Falcon's* and had patched it through the intercom. As he listened, Lando saw one of his auxiliary target screens go momentarily blank, then fill with the dark and terrifyingly familiar image.

"This in the name and at the order of Rokur Gepta, Sorcerer of Tund."

And then: *"Private to Captain Lando Calrissian of the* Millennium Falcon.*"* The wizard leaned conspiratorially into the pickup. *"You have put up a valiant and brilliantly conceived fight, sir, but one which you shall inevitably lose, if only because I am willing to throw half the resources of civilization at you, should it prove necessary. I could bury you with dead bodies, and fill this entire nebula with the wrecks of ships, and I will.*

"However, I offer you an opportunity to minimize unnecessary bloodshed, to settle things personally and at close hand between ourselves, once and for all. Nor have I need for the resources of half an empire to persuade you. At this very moment the power is mine to exterminate every sentient being in this nebula, every flyspeck of life, every hope that life again will ever flourish here.

"Behold and bear witness!"

He raised a hand, as if in a magician's gesture. Outside, from one of the ungainly projections on the hull of the *Wennis,* there was a faint, fast squirt of brilliant life. Instantly it streaked toward a cluster of gigantic Oswaft who, since ceasing to fight, had been watching and listening. Sen and Fey were among them.

As the light point reached them, they began glowing a pale, sickly green and disappeared without a trace before their dying screams had faded. Whatever the weapon was, it could discriminate between real organic beings and the phony outlines Lando had taught them to create. Those remained like ghosts, hollow and insubstantial.

"That, my dear Captain Calrissian, was a demonstration employing one times ten to the minus seventeenth of the power available to me. The object was an electromagnetic torpedo, scarcely larger than a filterable virus and programmed to self-destruct after it had done its work. Had it not been so, this area

around us would contain no life by now, nor, within a week, would the entire nebula.

"I offer you, however, an alternative. Should you triumph, the entire fleet shall go away. Should I win, I shall release a thousand tons of this destructive agent in the ThonBoka.

"As for ourselves personally, we shall fight a duel to the death."

XVII

"WE HAVE ONE ADVANTAGE, MASTER."

Vuffi Raa had just returned from the *Wennis,* where, at Gepta's command, he had gone as Lando's second to receive the terms for the duel. Frost was turning into water on the little robot's chromium-plated body and dripping off onto the floor of the tiny airlock below the topside hatch.

"That's absolutely peachy, old go-between. Any little boost would be welcome, just now." He looked out through a viewport. On one side the *Falcon* was englobed by the navy, perhaps five hundred enormous capital ships.

From another port, he could see they were hemmed in by Klyn Shanga's squadron, what was left of it, in formation once again about the pinnace. The tractor field was off, and would have been invisible in any case, but the arrangement gave them an instant choice between two modes of movement.

Lando shook his head and went on running down the long-form checklist, getting his best spacesuit up and ready for the coming conflict.

"Yes, Master. You'll recall he was the one responsible for your winning me in the first place? Well, it was he, who, well, supplied me to the *Ottdefa* Osuno Whett. He knows me rather well—and still believes that he can program me to betray you."

The gambler looked up, set the pair of vacuum gauntlets he'd been working on aside, and lit a cigar. Possibly his last. "How very interesting. And can he?"

"Not at all. What's even better is that he still believes me to be bound by my earlier programming. He thinks I cannot fight."

Lando grinned. "You know, I'm not sure I understand that, myself. But of course that's why he offered to let you help me out in this duel, to make up for his powers of magic, so he said."

The robot raised an affirmative tentacle. "What now remains is for us to plan what we will do once we're out there. Have you an idea?"

Lando drew a deep puff, let it out slowly, savoring it. "I do, indeed, old Saturday-night spatial. The terms are one personal weapon apiece?"

"Not precisely, Master. You are allowed one weapon, I am allowed none. He didn't specify what he would use. I didn't ask. It seems we have no choice in this matter."

"No, but tell me, does he know about the way you let your tentacles do their own thinking?"

The gleam in Vuffi Raa's faceted eye grew brighter. "No, Master, I don't believe he does."

"Swell. Then here's what we'll do—and don't call me master."

ROKUR GEPTA STOOD in an airlock of the *Wennis,* watching the *Millennium Falcon* through the bull's-eye in the hatch. He could see her captain and his droid climbing out of their own airlock as he himself suited up. The suit was a deep nonreflective gray, about the color of the walls of the ThonBoka. He turned to the officer beside him, the nominal captain of the cruiser.

"You are certain that you understand my instructions?"

"Yes, sir," the unhappy-looking man replied. "I am to exterminate all life in the nebula, regardless of the outcome of the duel." He gulped at speaking what he felt to be a dishonorable and unmilitary decision, and remained rigidly at attention as the sorcerer donned his helmet.

"Precisely, Captain, and if you are entertaining any ideas of

countermanding that order in the event of my demise, please remember that the continued existence of your family depends on
its being carried out. That was the purpose of sending the courier
to your home system a few minutes ago. Their lives are in your
hands."

"Yes, sir."

"Very well, then, stand aside so that I may exhaust the lock—
unless you care to join me in the airless void?"

KLYN SHANGA WATCHED the accursed Vuffi Raa, Butcher of Renatasia, climb out of the airlock of the *Millennium Falcon*. The
little monster was still wearing that spacesuit he'd affected in the
Oseon that made him appear to be a robot. Shanga began flipping switches; turbines whined as power levels increased. One
trembling hand remained on the button of his weapon system.
Steady, old soldier, he told himself, only a few more minutes.

Suddenly, a fighter across the formation from him slid forward, gaining speed as it approached the *Falcon*. Shanga opened
his mouth to scream "Bern, no!" when a man-thick power beam
from the *Wennis* struck fighter number Twenty-three, blowing it
to bits.

"*Sorry, Admiral Shanga,*" a voice said over the intership.
"*Orders from the Sorcerer of Tund. There is to be no interference.*"

And no revenge, no justice, Shanga realized, unless he could
figure out something quickly. Ten years of his life, of the lives of
all his men, down the drain, unless—

Movement near the *Wennis* caught his eye. Rokur Gepta jetted from the airlock, crossed half the space between the cruiser
and the freighter, and came to a skillful hovering stop. He folded
his spacesuited arms and hung, awaiting his adversaries. Across
the void that had become an arena, Lando Calrissian followed
his example in a bright yellow spacesuit, rocketing to meet the

sorcerer, stopping several dozen meters away. Vuffi Raa was right behind him.

Something on the order of a billion pairs of eyes—or equivalent sensory equipment—watched as the sorcerer inclined his head in a small, grudging bow. Without further warning, his right hand lashed out, and a beam of energy struck the place where Lando—

—had been. He tumbled, spun, and recovered, something small and glittering in his own hand, but didn't return fire. Soaring, he made a complicated figure in the vacuum as Gepta fired twice more, missing both times. While the sorcerer was thus distracted, Vuffi Raa circled warily, working his way behind the gray-clad figure. Two more shots, then Gepta realized that he was being deceived. He whirled, just as the robot's tentacles separated from his pentagonal body, spreading, encircling the sorcerer's position, and moving in.

Almost hysterically, Gepta tried to burn the tentacles, but they wriggled and squirmed as they came toward him, each limb no longer where it had been when the aim was taken. Closer they came, closer.

Lando *fired!* striking Gepta squarely in the back. Incredibly, the stingbeam's energy passed through the sorcerer harmlessly, nearly striking Vuffi Raa's body, which was backing, slowly, clumsily away from the fight while it directed the tentacles to the attack.

Gepta whirled again, getting off three shots at the gambler. The last one hit him in the foot. There was a puff of steam and a hissing audible only to Lando, then the suit sealed, its medical processes already shutting off the pain. He had no idea how badly he'd been hurt, but he knew that he could still fight. He fired a second of his five shots, again taking the sorcerer in the center of the torso. Again the beam sliced through without apparent damage.

Then a tentacle grasped Gepta around the neck.

The gray-suited figure struggled, trying to unwrap the chromium-plated limb, but it hung on grimly. From his vantage point in the squadron, Klyn Shanga watched, then was suddenly struck blind by a thought:

Vuffi Raa, so-called Butcher of Renatasia, really was *a robot!*

Nothing else could explain the independent limbs. But if that was true, then what of their mission of revenge? What of the only purpose they had had for living, since the death of their civilization. What of—

Abruptly, there was a surge of motion as the tenuous hold of tractors at a hundredth power was broken and the pinnace moved forward of its own accord, leaving the fighters behind. No one aboard the vessels of the fleet seemed to notice, so much of their attention was riveted on the duel.

But Shanga did.

"What's going on, there? Who's in the pinnace?"

"*It is I, the* Ottdefa *Osuno Whett,*" came the electronic reply. "*I'm going to end this farce, destroy the robot and the gambler— and perhaps Rokur Gepta, in the bargain! None of them are fit to—*"

Another blinding flash of recognition. It was the voice that did it, separated now from the assumed appearance. Whett was the Butcher's aide! Whett was the Butcher's assistant! Whett was—

—the Butcher himself! It *had* to be! No other explanation was possible.

Heeling his fighter over, Klyn Shanga thumbed his weapons at the pinnace. The larger vessel's shields were up, however, shields designed to protect an admiral's tender person during ship-to-ship and ship-to-planet transfers. Shanga's fire coruscated off the invisible barrier.

"This is Zero Leader!" he shouted on the squadron's frequency. "Get that pinnace—the man we seek is aboard! I'll explain later, if we live!" Desperately, he punched buttons on the remote console that had controlled the pinnace on the trip out. He couldn't prevent Whett from driving it, nor drop its shields, but he could keep it out of hyperdrive and lock the tractor field.

He did the latter. The squadron snapped into formation.

Opening his small ship's engines all the way, he screamed at his men to do the same. Slowly, inexorably, the assemblage of ships achieved headway.

Abruptly, someone aboard the *Wennis* noticed the motion.

"Zero Leader, this is the Wennis! *Halt immediately, or we'll blast you out of the nebula!"* The warning was repeated. Gathering speed now, Shanga steered his squadron and their captive—who was desperately and ineffectually attempting to reverse things from the pinnace—toward the decommissioned cruiser. Faster and faster, skirting the space where the battle between Gepta and Lando and Vuffi Raa still raged, they zeroed in on the larger vessel.

A broad beam of power struck the pinnace squarely on the bow. Her shields held, and the energy, sluicing off the deflectors, missed the lightly shielded fighters as well. As they came within a few hundred meters of the *Wennis,* Shanga abruptly cast off the tractor field and flipped his craft around. Years of reflex allowed his men to follow the motion like a school of fish.

The pinnace struck the *Wennis*—her own shields negligently still powered down to allow the sorcerer to debark—and penetrated her hull. There was a brief instant in which nothing else happened, a suspension of time as inertia was overcome, as systems attempted to control the damage and failed.

Then a titanic explosion as the cruiser belched flaming gases everywhere, consuming herself, the pinnace, and everyone aboard both vessels. Even two of the fleeing fighters were tumbled badly.

Farther away, Rokur Gepta, Vuffi Raa, and Lando were distracted by the explosion. Gepta stared insanely. Lando recovered first, took aim, and—

—was struck by a piece of flying debris. His shot went wild, hitting the sorcerer in the ankle. In shock, Lando recovered and watched as the form of Rokur Gepta withered and faded. He jetted up beside the magician in time to see a heavy military blaster swing around, fire, swing a little farther, and fire again. Vuffi Raa's tentacle floated emptily with nothing left to hold on to. The third shot, cast by an unconscious and dematerializing hand, caught the robot's torso, a hundred meters away, dead in the center.

The metal glowed momentarily. When the incandescence dimmed, so had the single red eye in the body's center. It was flat, glassy, and black.

Lando pawed through Rokur Gepta's empty spacesuit. Down in the leg was a small bundle of ugly, slimy tissue, resembling a half-cooked snail, an escargot with a dozen skinny, hairy black legs. It was one of the most disgusting things the gambler had ever seen, but he'd seen it before.

It was a Croke, from a small, nasty system he'd once visited. The species was intelligent and unvaryingly vicious, and they were all masters of camouflage and illusion.

This one wasn't quite dead. The suit had protected it, and it was nearly impervious to hard vacuum. Lando ripped the suit away, took the stunned and putrid creature that had been Rokur Gepta, and *squeezed*. When he was through, his suit gloves were covered with greasy slime, but no Sorcerer of Tund would ever rule the galaxy.

As if Gepta's death were a signal, the fleet began to open up on the Oswaft within range. In the space of a moment, hundreds died . . . until the fleet had other things to think about; Klyn Shanga's squadron was shooting back, giving the vacuum-breathing sapients covering fire so they could retreat. One fighter exploded, then another, but they were saving Oswaft lives.

"CEASE FIRE IMMEDIATELY OR BE DESTROYED!"

The voice came over everybody's communicators simultaneously, at every frequency. Lando looked up from his little friend's scorched torso—he'd gathered in the tentacles, as well, but they would not attach themselves and lay in his arms like so many dead pieces of jointed metal—to see a figure that dwarfed the departed Elders, even the largest dreadnaughts in the fleet.

It was a starship, but it was at least fifty kilometers in diameter, a smooth, featureless, highly polished ovoid of silvery metal.

Another identical monster followed close behind it. Far to the rear, Lando watched as others, countless others, penetrated the supposedly impenetrable wall of the ThonBoka as if it were so much fog. Hundreds, thousands, hundreds of thousands.

Some fool aboard the *Recalcitrant* opened fire with the new meter-thick destructor beam, deep green and hungry. A red beam from the leading foreign ship met the green one squarely, forced it back a meter at a time until it reached the navy cruiser. A pause, then the *Recalcitrant* became a cloud of incandescent gas.

"CEASE FIRE OR BE DESTROYED! THERE WILL BE NO OTHER WARNING!"

Racked with grief, Lando watched as more and more of the titanic ovoids appeared in the nebula. There was no way to estimate their number. The gambler thought they might fill up the StarCave, twelve light-years across as it might be.

Then a sensation brushed past him. Somehow he knew that only he could hear the tightly beamed message that issued from his helmet phones.

"You are Captain Calrissian, are you not? You have fought valiantly, and not in vain. You grieve for your little friend. I grieve, too, for he was my only son."

XVIII

"*SABACC!*" SAID THE ONE. "By the Center of Everything, Lando, I knew we would learn new and valuable things if only we dared to."

"Yeah, well, you've still got to learn the difference between luck and skill. That's eighteen trillion I'm ahead of you already, counting that last hand, and I don't even know yet what we're using for currency!"

The gambler took a deep drag on his cigar and watched as the One gathered in the seventy-eight-card deck with a sweep of a jointed metallic tentacle. His eye glowed a deep scarlet with delight and anticipation as he dealt them out again, two to Lando, two more to Klyn Shanga, two to the extensor manifesting itself as the Other.

"Too bad," he continued. "This game is a whole lot faster and more interesting five-handed. If only Vuffi Raa . . ."

"Each of us," observed the Other, "sets his own course through the universe and must follow it where it takes us. This is called integrity, and to deviate—"

"Come on, you five-legged clowns, cut the pop philosophy and play cards! You know how long it's been since I sat down at a real table and—"

Lando grinned. "And tried filling inside straights all night long, Admiral? At that, it beats dodging bullets and destructor beams. I'm glad you decided to be on our side, and I'm especially glad you're a better fighter pilot than you are a *sabacc* player."

"I'm only warming up. Give me a chance, and I'll have your hide the easy way: payable in cash!"

Laughter around the table. It was good to have the lounge full of visitors, the gambler thought; a real passenger lounge for a change. But some folks seemed to be missing from his life, missing from places they'd carved for themselves only recently. Or relatively recently.

"Heard from Lehesu yet?" he asked, watching a Commander of Flasks change itself into a Three of Staves. He knew it was an electronic trick, but it never failed to give him goosebumps. Shanga was frowning, a sure sign he had a good hand, Lando had learned quickly. He kept his betting light.

The fighter pilot shook his head, still frowning. "One of the boys said something about seeing a middle-sized Oswaft zooming off during the battle. Said something about a courier he wanted to catch up with. Is it true the spacepeople want to make him High Supreme Galootie or something?"

A mechanical chuckle issued from the extensor representing the One. "It would seem they have decided that leadership—or at least wisdom—do not necessarily correlate positively with age. This is gratifying to me, as I am the youngest of my people . . . that is, I was before Vuffi Raa . . . er, I believe I shall take another card, gentle-beings."

Outside, far away across the StarCave, the actual repositories of the intelligence of the One, the Other, and the Rest lay, as it were, at anchor. They were gigantic fifty-kilometer starships, intergalactically self-propelled droids of ancient origin.

Shanga changed the subject. "I never quite got who it was who built you folks originally—that is, if you don't mind me asking a religious question."

"Not at all," the One replied. "They were a race of individuals who looked rather like these extensors. There are some among us who recall them, although I do not, except through cybernetically handed-down memories. They were not spacefarers; the idea simply didn't appeal to them. They were wiped out in a radiation storm when a nearby star went supernova. Only a few intelligent machines were left, and they were my ancestors. We did explore the stars, at least in our arm. There is a high incidence of unstable stars there, so that organic life is rare."

"Yes," the Other concurred, "it was his idea to seek out organic life to liven up our own culture, and here we are."

Lando shook his head. He wished his little robot friend were there to see this hand; it was a lulu. "Yes, but first you sent out an explorer whose memories were suppressed and who could not act violently. That way he'd generate fresh impressions and not get your civilization into trouble with others unless it was absolutely necessary."

"Correct," the One said. "And while the suppression worked, the conditioning did not. Self-preservation is a powerful motive, even though in the end—*sabacc*!"

"Beginner's luck!" the professional gambler howled, wondering how much he'd lost this time. He heard footsteps behind him, turned and looked down the curving corridor toward the engine area. A figure stood there, covered with grease, a spanner in one of its hands. Its five-sided carapace was still scorched.

"I got the deflectors readjusted, Master," Vuffi Raa said. "Admiral Shanga's men are good shots, but that weakness won't show up again now!"

"Fine. Now will you please stop being dutiful and join the game? And don't call me master in front of your old man, here, it's embarrassing."

HOURS LATER, two days after the battle and departure of the fleet, Lando was dozing in his pilot's chair in the cockpit. Vuffi Raa was out somewhere, visiting his kinfolk.

"*Captainmasterlandocalrissiansir, I have returned*," the ship-to-ship said.

"Zzzzz—*what*? Lehesu! Why so formal all of a sudden—and where the Core have you been?" The gambler had heard it suggested that the young Oswaft had run away from defending the ThonBoka. He didn't believe it for a moment, but he was curious.

"Oh, just before your duel with Rokur Gepta, I heard him tell an officer—his helmet microphone was open, apparently—that he was sending a courier to have that person's family murdered should he disobey a rather ugly order. I hopped after him, but it took me a while to catch up."

Lando stretched, yawned, reached for a cigar. "Oh? What did you do then, ask him to stop politely?"

"Why yes, and he did. In several pieces, I'm afraid: I shouted it at him."

The gambler chuckled. "So now you're home and going to be the Elder of all you survey, is that how it is?"

There was a long pause. *"No, not precisely. I told them I would not be their Elder, and if they wanted my advice, they wouldn't appoint a new one. I don't think they listened to me. I wish neither to give nor receive orders—something I learned from you, Lando my friend."*

Lando his friend scratched his head, a gesture he'd never had habitually until he'd picked it up from Vuffi Raa. "I'm glad to hear it. What are you going to do with yourself, then?"

"Explore, discover the answers to questions. Probably get in trouble again. But tell me, I am very confused on one point: the Millennium Falcon is not really a person, is that correct? Nor the cruiser Wennis?"

"The late, unlamented cruiser *Wennis*. I don't know what that life-destroying stuff was Gepta spewed around, but I'm glad it was destroyed with her. No, friend Lehesu, much as we may love her, the *Falcon* is a machine." He puffed on his cigar, anticipating the Oswaft's next bewildered question. "And before you ask, yes, the One, the Other, and the Rest are indeed persons, of the mechanical persuasion. They think for themselves, the *Falcon* doesn't. In a sense, they are to you what Vuffi Raa is to me: you both live in free space; it's your natural environment. Vuffi Raa and I are arms-and-legs types, born and bred in a gravity well and most comfortable where there's light and heat and atmosphere."

"But Lando, what is Vuffi Raa?"

"A larval starship, if you believe him. The organic people who invented his ancestors looked like him, built machines that looked like him—the same idea as a humanoid robot. Today his people use 'extensors'—manipulators—that still look like him. If he's a good little bot and eats all his spinach, he'll grow up to be a starship, too. If he wants to."

Concern tinged the vacuum-breather's transmission. *"I'm told that he was nearly killed while I was gone. I feel somewhat guilty for—"*

"Forget it, old jellyfish, his daddy repaired him in just a few hours. What counts is the memory, the experiences, the character, and they were all intact, protected in googolicate at the deepest levels of his being. No little blaster was going to do more than freeze him up mechanically."

"What will you do now, Lando?"

"Well, I think it's time I gave up this wandering life, if only for a while. I need to do something responsible, own something, have some obligations. I'll think about it. I've learned a lot, and I have plenty to get started on. The *Falcon*'s holds are full of gigantic gemstones—every variety I've ever seen or heard of, and a few I'm going to have to consult experts on. I could buy an entire city."

"And Vuffi Raa?"

"I don't know, old manta, I don't know."

THE *MILLENNIUM FALCON*'s engines thrummed with pent-up energy. She was eager to go back into intergalactic space, eager for another adventure. In her cockpit, Vuffi Raa was finishing up a lecture: "And be sure to back the engines off at least three percent when initiating the deflector shields, otherwise the surge will overload her, and—"

"I know, I know, I know," her captain replied patiently while trying to suppress tears. "The only thing I don't understand is why you're going back this very minute. Why can't you—"

"Master, it is a bargain I have made. I would much prefer, like you and Lehesu, to continue exploring the universe, to have adventure and savor life. I will again, someday. But I was constructed for the purpose of recording those experiences and relaying them to my people. I feel the need to do this, as you feel the need to breathe. Do you understand, Master?"

"I understand." He patted the little droid's shiny torso. The rest of the blast damage had healed, and the robot looked as new and perfect as the day they'd met. "Well, if you ever get back to this arm of the galaxy, you know how to find me, don't you? I haven't much in the way of a permanent address."

There was an electronic chuckle. "I'll just go where there's the most trouble and noise, and there you'll be, Master."

"Not on your life! I'm going to settle down, be responsible. And Vuffi Raa?"

"Yes, Master?"

"Don't you think, now that you know exactly who and what you are, that you could stop calling me master?"

"Why, I suppose so, Lando. Why didn't you ask me before?"

THE STAR WARS LEGENDS NOVELS TIMELINE

BEFORE THE REPUBLIC
37,000–25,000 YEARS BEFORE *STAR WARS: A NEW HOPE*

c. 25,793 YEARS BEFORE *STAR WARS: A NEW HOPE*

Dawn of the Jedi: Into the Void

OLD REPUBLIC
5,000–67 YEARS BEFORE *STAR WARS: A NEW HOPE*

Lost Tribe of the Sith: The Collected
Stories

3,954 YEARS BEFORE *STAR WARS: A NEW HOPE*

The Old Republic: Revan

3,650 YEARS BEFORE *STAR WARS: A NEW HOPE*

The Old Republic: Deceived
Red Harvest
The Old Republic: Fatal Alliance
The Old Republic: Annihilation

1,032 YEARS BEFORE *STAR WARS: A NEW HOPE*

Knight Errant
Darth Bane: Path of Destruction
Darth Bane: Rule of Two
Darth Bane: Dynasty of Evil

RISE OF THE EMPIRE
67–0 YEARS BEFORE *STAR WARS: A NEW HOPE*

67 YEARS BEFORE *STAR WARS: A NEW HOPE*

Darth Plagueis

33 YEARS BEFORE *STAR WARS: A NEW HOPE*

Cloak of Deception
Darth Maul: Shadow Hunter
Maul: Lockdown

32 YEARS BEFORE *STAR WARS: A NEW HOPE*

STAR WARS: EPISODE I
THE PHANTOM MENACE

Rogue Planet
Outbound Flight
The Approaching Storm

22 YEARS BEFORE *STAR WARS: A NEW HOPE*

STAR WARS: EPISODE II
ATTACK OF THE CLONES

22–19 YEARS BEFORE *STAR WARS: A NEW HOPE*

STAR WARS: THE CLONE WARS

The Clone Wars: Wild Space
The Clone Wars: No Prisoners

Clone Wars Gambit
Stealth
Siege

Republic Commando
Hard Contact
Triple Zero
True Colors
Order 66

Shatterpoint
The Cestus Deception
MedStar I: Battle Surgeons
MedStar II: Jedi Healer
Jedi Trial
Yoda: Dark Rendezvous
Labyrinth of Evil

19 YEARS BEFORE *STAR WARS: A NEW HOPE*

STAR WARS: EPISODE III
REVENGE OF THE SITH

Kenobi
Dark Lord: The Rise of Darth Vader
Imperial Commando 501st

Coruscant Nights
Jedi Twilight
Street of Shadows
Patterns of Force

The Last Jedi

10 YEARS BEFORE *STAR WARS: A NEW HOPE*

The Han Solo Trilogy
The Paradise Snare
The Hutt Gambit
Rebel Dawn

The Adventures of Lando Calrissian
The Force Unleashed
The Han Solo Adventures
Death Troopers
The Force Unleashed II

THE STAR WARS LEGENDS NOVELS TIMELINE

REBELLION
0–5 YEARS AFTER
STAR WARS: A NEW HOPE

NEW REPUBLIC
5–25 YEARS AFTER
STAR WARS: A NEW HOPE

Death Star
Shadow Games

STAR WARS: EPISODE IV
A NEW HOPE

Tales from the Mos Eisley Cantina
Tales from the Empire
Tales from the New Republic
Scoundrels
Allegiance
Choices of One
Honor Among Thieves
Galaxies: The Ruins of Dantooine
Splinter of the Mind's Eye
Razor's Edge

3 YEARS AFTER *STAR WARS: A NEW HOPE*

STAR WARS: EPISODE V
THE EMPIRE STRIKES BACK

Tales of the Bounty Hunters
Shadows of the Empire

4 YEARS AFTER *STAR WARS: A NEW HOPE*

STAR WARS: EPISODE VI
THE RETURN OF THE JEDI

Tales from Jabba's Palace

The Bounty Hunter Wars
  The Mandalorian Armor
  Slave Ship
  Hard Merchandise

The Truce at Bakura
Luke Skywalker and the Shadows of
  Mindor

X-Wing
  Rogue Squadron
  Wedge's Gamble
  The Krytos Trap
  The Bacta War
  Wraith Squadron
  Iron Fist
  Solo Command

The Courtship of Princess Leia
Tatooine Ghost

The Thrawn Trilogy
  Heir to the Empire
  Dark Force Rising
  The Last Command

X-Wing: Isard's Revenge

The Jedi Academy Trilogy
  Jedi Search
  Dark Apprentice
  Champions of the Force

I, Jedi
Children of the Jedi
Darksaber
Planet of Twilight
X-Wing: Starfighters of Adumar
The Crystal Star

The Black Fleet Crisis Trilogy
  Before the Storm
  Shield of Lies
  Tyrant's Test

The New Rebellion

The Corellian Trilogy
  Ambush at Corellia
  Assault at Selonia
  Showdown at Centerpoint

The Hand of Thrawn Duology
  Specter of the Past
  Vision of the Future

Scourge
Survivor's Quest

NEW JEDI ORDER
25–40 YEARS AFTER
STAR WARS: A NEW HOPE

The New Jedi Order
Vector Prime
Dark Tide I: Onslaught
Dark Tide II: Ruin
Agents of Chaos I: Hero's Trial
Agents of Chaos II: Jedi Eclipse
Balance Point
Edge of Victory I: Conquest
Edge of Victory II: Rebirth
Star by Star
Dark Journey
Enemy Lines I: Rebel Dream
Enemy Lines II: Rebel Stand
Traitor
Destiny's Way
Force Heretic I: Remnant
Force Heretic II: Refugee
Force Heretic III: Reunion
The Final Prophecy
The Unifying Force

35 YEARS AFTER *STAR WARS: A NEW HOPE*

The Dark Nest Trilogy
The Joiner King
The Unseen Queen
The Swarm War

LEGACY
40+ YEARS AFTER
STAR WARS: A NEW HOPE

Legacy of the Force
Betrayal
Bloodlines
Tempest
Exile
Sacrifice
Inferno
Fury
Revelation
Invincible

Crosscurrent
Riptide
Millennium Falcon

43 YEARS AFTER *STAR WARS: A NEW HOPE*

Fate of the Jedi
Outcast
Omen
Abyss
Backlash
Allies
Vortex
Conviction
Ascension
Apocalypse

X-Wing: Mercy Kill

45 YEARS AFTER *STAR WARS: A NEW HOPE*

Crucible

ABOUT THE AUTHOR

L. Neil Smith was the two-time winner of the Prometheus Award for Best Libertarian Fiction for his novels *Pallas* (1993) and *The Probability Broach* (1980).

Read on for an excerpt from

LAST SHOT

BY DANIEL JOSÉ OLDER

PROLOGUE

BESPIN, NOW

THE DARKENING SKY stretched out forever and ever around Cloud City. Cumulus kingdoms rose and fell in the purple-blue haze below, parting now and then to reveal the twinkling lights of Ugnorgrad.

Protocol droid DRX-7 chortled to himself. It had been a good day. Impresario Calrissian had entertained an entire diplomatic brigade of young Twi'leks, and the little fellows had been enthusiastic and eager to learn—full of questions, in fact. And of course the new head of Calrissian Enterprises, with his trademark charm, had been happy to comply. This meant that plenty of translating had been needed, and with more than four million languages at his disposal, DRX considered translation his favorite part of being a protocol droid.

Why is Cloud City in the clouds? asked one tiny girl with long eyelashes and her two lekku wrapped into a dazzling swirl above her head.

This most basic of questions would normally have elicited an eye roll or sarcastic reply from the impresario. He would deliver it with a winning smile, and the shine of those perfect teeth would somehow counteract whatever slight could've been perceived. In fact, DRX had wondered if that would happen, and if the girl would somehow take offense. Then he'd have to go into diplomatic overdrive to make sure she felt better, and DRX considered *that* his least favorite part of being a protocol droid.

"Beena," one of the Twi'lek guardians had said, with a touch of menace in her voice, "we covered Cloud City history in class on the flight here; I'm sure Mr. Calrissian has more important matters to attend to."

"Not at all," Calrissian had interrupted with a lively chuckle before DRX could finish translating. "I'm not even the baron administrator anymore, technically. I still get to live in the fancy house, though." With that, his grin had widened amiably. "But anyway, what could be more important than imparting knowledge to the future generations of our friends the Twi'leks?"

And then the guardian, Kaasha Bateen was her name, had shot the impresario a look that DRX was pretty sure indicated extreme skepticism with a hint of possible attraction. But Calrissian hadn't seemed to notice, instead launching into a lengthy and impressively detailed rendering of the travails and adventures of the diminutive Ugnaughts, Cloud City's original architects, and their partnership with Corellian space explorer Ecclessis Figg.

The little Twi'lek eyes had lit up as Calrissian went on to detail his own escapades. Even Kaasha Bateen, who had been standing with her arms crossed over her chest, mouth twisted to one side of her face, seemed to lose herself in the story, and even corrected DRX on a translation matter. (It had been one open to interpretation, like most translation issues, and DRX had opted to concede the point rather than launch into a lengthy discussion of its nuances. Anyway, he loved a good challenge.)

And now the little ones had all been tucked into their sleeping quarters and the Bespin night was sweeping slowly across the sky. DRX was alone, accompanied only by the gentle hum of Cloud City and occasional blips and whirs from the nearby gas mining rigs. At any moment, the Bespin Wing Guard would be zipping past in their bright-orange twin-pod cloud cars, making sure the city was safe and sound.

In fact, now that DRX thought about it, they should've already zipped past. He'd been standing at the rail of his favorite platform for exactly fourteen minutes and twenty-nine seconds. It was nine thirteen.

He gazed out into the gathering night; nothing stirred, no lights blinked.

Odd.

Perhaps, DRX thought, *Master Calrissian knows what's going on.* He raised him on the comm and received a curt and immediate response from Lobot, the city's computer liaison officer: *Calrissian is busy. Relay message through me, Dee-Arrex.*

How rude, DRX thought. *Status check on Bespin Wing Guard,* he messaged back.

And then: nothing. Minute after minute passed with no reply. Very odd.

He turned back to the night sky, the clouds, the faraway stars, and then took a step backward, arms raised. A tall figure in a dark-green hooded cloak stood at the edge of the platform.

"Greetings," DRX said. "I am protocol droid Dee-Arrex Seven, at your service." He didn't really feel like putting himself at the service of this stranger, who had, after all, appeared without so much as a noise of warning and seemed to care not a whit for the basic mores of decent interaction. But rules were rules.

"Is there anything I can do for you this evening?" DRX asked, when a few moments had gone by without a reply to his initial salutation.

"Oh yes indeed," a gravelly voice said.

The stranger did something with his hands, and DRX felt all his gears, wiring, and synapses tighten at the same time. A hazy shade of red covered the world. And then everything was very simple: He had to kill.

The vast night sky, the teeming galaxy beyond, the billion blips and clacks of Cloud City: All spiraled together and resolved into a single, pulsing need. Somewhere in that complex, Impresario Calrissian dwelled. Probably asleep in his chambers. *Perfect,* DRX thought. A tiny voice cried out from the depths of his programming, a notion, a desperate wail, the single word: *No.* But it was too distant and tiny to bother with, and DRX had a singular mission: *Kill.*

He pushed forward, barely aware of the dark figure slinking along just behind him. He entered the bright hallways of the central throughway, swerved into a side corridor reserved for staff and administrators, and then bustled along past servers, soldiers, and casino droids until he reached the shadowy side entrance to the baron administrator's palace.

"Protocol droid Dee-Arrex Seven for the impresario," DRX said to the two guards. "With one guest."

They saluted and stepped to the side and the wide door slid open. DRX whirred in and navigated quickly through the narrow back hallways, past the kitchen, and up into an elaborate front room where Calrissian received guests.

Kill.

A simple, shrill mandate that pulsed unceasingly through him. *Kill.*

And he would, he would. But first he had to get to Calrissian, and that was about to become difficult: Lobot stepped out from a curtain, face creased beneath his bald head, the red light of his cyborg tech headgear blinking in the shadows.

Lobot's expression indicated disappointment and ire, DRX knew, and a memory surfaced from somewhere deep inside: how crushed DRX would've been to see that face directed at him any other time. The memory was followed by that same distant, urgent cry: *No!* But it was still too tiny to bother with, especially when things were heating up and the resolution to this urge, the only way to feed this hunger, was so close.

Then Lobot caught sight of whoever it was that had been trailing DRX like a shadow, and his expression went from exasperated to shocked, then hardened quickly to enraged. Lobot advanced and DRX swung an arm forward, clobbering the liaison officer across the face, dropping him.

Kill.

But not this one, this was not DRX's target. He surged forward toward the door, toward Calrissian, toward the answer to the thundering demand within him for blood. And then stopped. Lobot had him by the ankle. He wasn't letting go. Pesky cyborg.

DRX was about to clobber him again (*No!* the tiny voice within screamed, *no!*) when a blast sounded and the room lit up as Lobot slumped forward, unconscious. The figure seemed enwrapped in some kind of blur, as if the atmosphere clouded around his dark robes. He lowered an old Imperial blaster and then handed it to DRX.

Kill.

The blaster was set to stun, but that would do. That would be a start. And then the door flew open and the impresario himself came barreling out, wearing only a towel but with a blaster in each hand. DRX didn't wait, firing once, hitting Calrissian in the shoulder, and again, the second shot blasting him backward against the wall. And then the whole world crackled to life as a red shard of light sizzled past, then another.

The Twi'lek: Kaasha Bateen. Also garbed in a towel, also armed, and in fact blasting away, teeth clenched, jaw set. The third shot flung toward DRX and found its mark, and the room spun as he tumbled backward and landed in a heap.

Kill, the voice raged, but it was a little quieter now, and the other voice, the deeper one, had grown, strengthened: *No!*

DRX looked up just in time to see the Twi'lek woman thrown back by a shot from the shadowy stranger, who then strode forward to the two crumpled bodies and let out a raspy, chilling cackle.

The *kill* voice was just a whisper now, and everything else in DRX screamed *No!* as another blaster shot echoed into the night.

PART ONE

CHANDRILA, NOW

". . . FOR PRINCESS LEIA ORGANA. Urgent message. Urgent message for Princess Leia Organa. Please respond. Urgent—"

"Hngh . . ." Han Solo woke with a tiny foot in his face and an irritating droid voice in his ear. "What?" The tiny foot was attached to the tiny body of Ben Solo, mercifully sleeping for what seemed like the first time in days. Han's eyes went wide. Would the boy wake?

"I will transfer the holo from Chancellor Mon Mothma immediately," Leia's protocol droid T-2LC droned.

"What? No!" Han sat up, still trying not to move Ben too much. He was shirtless, and his hair was almost certainly pointing in eight different directions. He probably had crust on his face. He didn't much want to talk to Mon Mothma under regular circumstances, let alone half naked and bedheaded.

"You replied, *What*, Master Solo," T-2LC replied. He was standing way too close. Droids had no sense of boundaries, especially protocol droids. "Therefore I—"

"Leia?" a voice said as the room lit up with the ghostly blue holoprojection.

Ben stirred, kicked Han once in the face.

"Oh," Mon Mothma said, squinting at the projection that was being transmitted to wherever she was. "Excuse me, General Solo."

"I'm not a general anymore," Han growled, still trying to keep his voice down.

Mon Mothma nodded. "I am aware." She already struck Han as a sort of spectral presence, all those flowy robes and that far-away look of hers. Being a see-through blue holoform only enhanced that. "It is my habit to refer to our veterans by their rank regardless of their status."

"Right," Han said.

"Is Leia around?"

"I could retrieve her for you," T-2LC suggested, turning just enough so the bright hologram Mon Mothma landed on Ben's sleeping face.

"Elsie!" Han snapped.

Ben's eyes sprang open to a shining blue form dancing around him. He burst into tears. Han shook his head; couldn't blame the kid, really—Han probably would've done the same thing if he'd suddenly woken to find himself enveloped in a Mon Mothma glow cloud. Which in a way he almost had, now that he thought about it. "Shh, come here, big guy." He reached his hands under his son's little arms and pulled him up so Ben was sobbing into Han's chest. Han felt that tiny heartbeat pitter-pattering away as Ben snorfled and sniffed.

"*Why didn't you just do that in the first place?*" Han whisper-yelled.

"I am sorry, sir. My programming indicates that when an urgent message is received I am to immediately alert the nearest member of the household, which in this case—"

"All right, can it, Elsie. Go find Leia."

"As you wish, sir."

"Just a moment, Elsie," Mon Mothma said. Han raised an eyebrow at the sternness in her voice. "General Solo, may I offer the admittedly unsolicited advice that you not be so brusque with your droids? They are, after all, committed to the service of all of our safety and comfo—"

"No," Han said.

"Excuse me?"

"You asked if you could offer unsolicited advice and I answered your question."

"I see."

"You're not going to come over to *my* house and tell *me* how to trea—"

"I am certainly not at your house, and I would further—"

"You know what I mean," Han snarled. Ben, whose sobs had begun simmering to a quiet moan, started bawling all over again. "Great! Thanks, Your Mothfulness. You've been a great help this morning."

Mon Mothma narrowed her eyes, exhaled sharply, and then motioned to T-2LC. "I bid you good day," she said, shaking her head as the droid wandered off, splattering the ghostly blue lights across the walls as she went.

"The nerve," Han grumbled, holding the still-crying Ben against his chest as he hoisted himself off the couch. "Ooh." A flash of pain simmered along his lower back. Old battle wounds. Or just oldness. Or both. Fantastic. The holoscreen across the room said it was 0430. He had a pile of boring meetings today, kicking off a week of planning and preparing for the inaugural meeting of the New Republic Pilots Commission, which Han had grudgingly accepted the leadership of—a mistake he was still trying to figure out how he'd been suckered into. Han hated planning. He also hated preparing. But what he really hated above everything else, besides maybe the Empire itself, was meetings. And now the Empire had been gone for more than two years, the remnants of their fleet blasted out of the sky over Jakku just as Ben was being born, in fact, and that cleared the way for meetings to take the number one slot on the Things Han Hates list.

And if there was one thing this fledgling republic loved, it was meetings.

Ben's sobbing had once again settled to a whimper and now became snores. Han laid him ever so gently on the couch and made his way toward the counter at the far end of the room. "Kriff," he whispered as the sharp edges of one of his son's cyrilform cambiblocks, and then another, dug into his socked foot. "Kriff kriff!" He glanced back at the couch, but Ben slept on.

"Caf," Han muttered to BX the kitchen droid, whose photoreceptors lit up in response. Mon Mothma's know-it-all voice rang through his mind: *They are, after all, committed to our safety and comfort.* "Please," he added grudgingly.

"Right away, Master Solo! It is my absolute pleasure to be of service."

BX-778, a brand-new class 3 culinary septoid droid, was supposedly an expert gourmet chef in more than fifteen thousand different styles of cuisine (although that remained to be seen). He was also way too enthusiastic about his job. Unlike the old WED septoid repair droids the Imperials used on their battlements, BX-778 had a rounded head planted among his seven arms. And since he was a household unit, Lando's creepy geniuses at Calrissian Enterprises, or perhaps Lando himself, had imbued BX-778 with a personality. Of sorts.

"Coagulating the finest Endorian caf beans," he chirped jauntily as one of his appendages swung open a floor hatch and another plunged into the crawl space below, appearing moments later with a scoop of the dark-brown beans. "Ah! Picked from the cliffs of the Campalan mountain range on the southeastern peninsula of the forest moon by well-compensated, humanely treated Ewok caf farmers!"

"Okay, okay, keep it down, scrap heap," Han said. "We're trying to keep this kid asleep for a minute."

"Ah!" BX-778 exclaimed.

Han rubbed his eyes and groaned.

"Apologies, Master Solo. Now lowering volume by twelve percent."

"Fantastic."

BX-778 poured the beans into a cylinder at the end of a third appendage. "Caf beans roasted at the gourmet artisanal factories of Hosnian Prime by the finest culinary master droids in the galaxy." He paused, directing those wide, yellow-lit eyes at Han.

"What?"

"*Except you, Beex,*" the droid said, shaking his head. "You're supposed to say, *The finest culinary master droids except you, Beex.*"

"Is there a mute button on you?" Han asked, but his voice was drowned out by the whir of the caf grinder. "Keep it down, I said!"

"In order to make caf, caf beans must be ground." Han was pretty sure he detected a sour note in the droid's voice. He opted to ignore it. "Put another way," the droid continued, "a culinary droid must grind the beans to make the caf, Master Solo."

The first hint of morning crept along the dark-purple sky over the towering spires and domes of Hanna City. From the bedroom, he heard the faint, urgent mutterings of Leia and Mon Mothma as they debated whatever new crisis had rocked the Senate. Han sighed. The endless series of meetings and paperwork of the day ahead jabbered through his mind like an angry ghost. How did Leia do it? His wife seemed to have been born for the tedium and drear of politics. Sure, she griped to Han late into the night about intricate Senate intrigues and intergalactic wrangling, but even when she was frustrated, the thrill of it seemed to somehow light her up—a world she understood completely and was intimately a part of.

Han, on the other hand, could barely make it through a whole paragraph of that mindless bureaucratic jargon. He tried to keep the thread, especially when it was Leia talking, but his mind inevitably spun toward thoughts of open space, the escalating tremble of a ship about to enter hyperspace, the thrill of flitting carefree from moon to moon. Everything had seemed so simple during those heady, breathless years of rebellion. It wasn't, of course—torture and death awaited any wrong move, and life in the grip of a seemingly unending war had ground them all down over time. But there was a mandate, a clear enemy to evade and destroy, a sense of mission, and with it all the reckless freedom of life in the underground.

Now . . . Han glanced at the small sleeping form of his son on the couch. The boy had seemed to light up the whole world when he'd first arrived: this simple, impossible sliver of hope amid so much death and destruction. But after all those years of war, Han was still braced for battle, and a new, fragile life meant a whole new sense of vulnerability. Leia had proven again and again she could fend for herself, even saving Han's life more than a couple of times, and Han had finally managed to stop worrying so much about her all the time. Now there was a small, squirmy extension of himself out in the world and he honestly had no idea what to do about it.

A burst of steam erupted from the other side of the counter. "One piping-hot and delicious mug of Endorian-harvested, Hosnian-roasted, and Chandrilan-brewed caf, Master Solo," BX-778 announced, now back to normal volume. "Get it? Because I brewed it here!" The droid placed the ceramic cup on the counter and threw all seven of his arms up, releasing a raucous peal of laughter. "On Chandrila!"

Across the room, Ben erupted into tears once again.

"Beex!" Han hollered. "I told you . . ." He sighed, rubbing his face, and headed back to the couch. What was the point? "I'm gonna bring you in for a personality makeover and a memory wipe."

"Oh dear," BX-778 warbled. "You seem testy, Master Solo."

"Han," Leia said, bursting into the room with her hands tangled in her long brown hair.

"Huh?"

"I need the room, love. Gotta use the holomaps, and the bedroom projector isn't big enough."

"Big enough? What are you—"

Leia shot him a look, the one that canceled out whatever he was about to say without a word, and Han held up both hands. "Say no more, Princess."

"Han," Leia warned.

The room glowed with blue light again. "If we triangulate the coordinates, we should be able to . . . oh!" Mon Mothma's flickering image entered a few seconds before T-2LC rolled through the door. "Excuse me once again, General Solo."

"Han," Leia said. "Put a shirt on, would you?"

"Caf for Senator Organa?" BX-778 chimed.

"Sure," Leia said, and then she slipped into a gentle coo, opening her arms to the still-crying toddler on the couch. "And what's wrong with my baby boy, hm?" She swept him up into her arms, groaning a little as she lifted him. "Ooh, he's getting heavy so fast. Come here, little man, hush." She rocked him back and forth, her braids dangling around him like a canopy, then shot a sharp glare at Han. "Did you feed him?"

Han raised his eyebrows. "Feed him? I . . . we were sleeping peacefully until the honorable chancellor here decided to—"

"Coagulating the finest Endorian caf beans," BX-778 announced.

"Oh, here we go," Han groaned.

Leia passed Ben to him as a map of the galaxy spun wild shadows and lights across the walls. "Take him in the bedroom, please? We'll talk about this later. There's something going on that Mon and I have to attend to."

Red and yellow lights flashed urgently at various points on the holomap, and Han recognized the converging blips of the New Republic fleet. "Are you mobilizing?"

"Han," Leia said. "Go."

"All right, all right!" He hoisted Ben onto his shoulder and headed for the bedroom.

"And put a shirt on, please!" Leia called over BX's babble about Ewok caf farmers.

PEACE.

Han took a deep breath. After all that fuss, he'd gone and left his caf in the front room. He sat on the bed, adjusting Ben in his arms. No way was he going back out there. Not even for caf. And anyway, the bed was so comfortable. Leia had been up late the night before going over some boring statistical analysis of crop production on Yavin 4 and Han had volunteered to keep Ben out of her hair, partially just to preempt any kind of, Force forbid, conversation about agriculture. He'd flipped on a holoshow, some cartoon they had now called *Moray and Faz*, and the next thing he knew it was half past four and the flickering chancellor was monmothmaing all over his living room.

He could probably catch a tiny snooze before he had to get ready, he thought, lying back. Little Ben looked up groggily, those dark eyes settling on Han, studying him. Han had no idea how a two-year-old could have such ancient eyes. It was as if Ben had been waiting around for a millennium to show up at just this moment in history.

Slowly, Ben Solo's eyes drifted closed as his chin settled on Han's shoulder.

Han shook his head, smiling. Here he was thinking about fates and destinies. He was starting to sound like Luke.

The thought simultaneously made him smile and unsettled him, and it was that muddle of feelings that drifted along with him as sleep crept up without warning once again, and dissolved the bedroom, the fussing on the other side of the wall, the chirps of morning birds outside, the half light of a new day, all into a pleasant haze . . .

. . . Right up until a frantic knocking shoved Han rudely back into the world of awake.

"What?" He slid Ben carefully off him and stood, heart pounding.

Bang bang bang!

The balcony. It was coming from the door to the balcony. Keeping out of sight of the tall windows, Han picked up Ben and laid him ever so gently on the carpeted floor, on the far side of the room from the knocking. Then he crept to the bedside table, slid open the drawer, and retrieved his blaster. Disengaged the safety. Made his way to the door.

Bang bang bang!

In the corner now, one hand on the doorknob, the other on the trigger, he glanced at Ben. Still asleep. Everything in Han wanted to just kick through the nearest window and let loose a barrage of blasterfire. But that wasn't the way, and if this was any threat at all, such recklessness would probably get himself and Ben killed.

Slowly, smoothly, he craned his neck to look at the small datascreen showing the balcony security feed.

All the tightened muscles in his body eased at the same time as he threw open the door, a huge smile breaking out across his face. There, in the purple haze of morning, stood Lando Calrissian, decked out as always in an impeccable dress shirt, half cape, shined boots, and a perfectly trimmed goatee.

"If it isn't . . ." Han started, but he let his voice trail off.

One thing that was different about Lando: that wide scoundrel grin was not stretching across his face. In fact, he looked downright pissed.

"What'sa matter, old buddy? And why are you—?"

Han didn't finish because now Lando was reaching back, winding up, fist tight, and then swinging forward with what looked like all his strength. And then, sure enough, fist met face and Han flew backward with a shocked grunt, thinking, as the world flushed to darkness: *I should've probably seen that coming.*

ABOUT THE TYPE

This book was set in Sabon, a typeface designed by the well-known German typographer Jan Tschichold (1902–74). Sabon's design is based upon the original letter forms of sixteenth-century French type designer Claude Garamond and was created specifically to be used for three sources: foundry type for hand composition, Linotype, and Monotype. Tschichold named his typeface for the famous Frankfurt typefounder Jacques Sabon (c. 1520–80).

A long time ago in a galaxy far, far away. . . .

STAR WARS™

Join up! Subscribe to our newsletter
at ReadStarWars.com or find us on social.

 @DelReyStarWars

 @DelReyStarWars

 StarWarsBooks